THE NAMELESS LAND

Also by Kate Elliott

Black Wolves

The Golden Key
(with Melanie Rawn and Jennifer Roberson)

The Labyrinth Gate

The Very Best of Kate Elliott
(collection)

Servant Mage

The Keeper's Six

The Court of Fives Trilogy

Court of Fives

Poisoned Blade

Buried Heart

The Spiritwalker Trilogy

Cold Magic

Cold Fire

Cold Steel

The Crossroads Trilogy

Spirit Gate

Shadow Gate

Traitors' Gate

The Crown of Stars Series

King's Dragon

Prince of Dogs

The Burning Stone

Child of Flame

The Gathering Storm

In the Ruins

Crown of Stars

The Novels of the Jaran

Jaran

An Earthly Crown

His Conquering Sword

The Law of Becoming

The Highroad Trilogy

A Passage of Stars

Revolution's Shore

The Price of Ransom

The Sun Chronicles

Unconquerable Sun

Furious Heaven

The Witch Roads

The Witch Roads

THE NAMELESS LAND

KATE ELLIOTT

TOR PUBLISHING GROUP
NEW YORK

This is a work of fiction. All of the characters, organizations, and events portrayed in this novel are either products of the author's imagination or are used fictitiously.

THE NAMELESS LAND

Copyright © 2025 by Katrina Elliott

All rights reserved.

A Tor Book
Published by Tom Doherty Associates / Tor Publishing Group
120 Broadway
New York, NY 10271

www.torpublishinggroup.com

Tor® is a registered trademark of Macmillan Publishing Group, LLC.

EU Representative: Macmillan Publishers Ireland Ltd, 1st Floor, The Liffey Trust Centre, 117–126 Sheriff Street Upper, Dublin 1, DO1 YC43

Library of Congress Cataloging-in-Publication Data

Names: Elliott, Kate, 1958– author
Title: The nameless land / Kate Elliott.
Description: First edition. | New York : Tor Publishing Group, 2025. | Series: The witch roads ; 2
Identifiers: LCCN 2025025418 | ISBN 9781250338648 (hardcover) | ISBN 9781250338655 (ebook)
Subjects: LCGFT: Fantasy fiction. | Novels. | Fiction.
Classification: LCC PS3555.L5917 N36 2025 | DDC 813/.54—dc23/eng/20250627
LC record available at https://lccn.loc.gov/2025025418

The publisher of this book does not authorize the use or reproduction of any part of this book in any manner for the purpose of training artificial intelligence technologies or systems. The publisher of this book expressly reserves this book from the Text and Data Mining exception in accordance with Article 4(3) of the European Union Digital Single Market Directive 2019/790.

Our books may be purchased in bulk for specialty retail/wholesale, literacy, corporate/premium, educational, and subscription box use. Please contact MacmillanSpecialMarkets@macmillan.com.

First Edition: 2025

Printed in the United States of America

10 9 8 7 6 5 4 3 2 1

The Witch Roads duology is the book that reignited my love of writing during a rough period when I wondered if I should just quit.

I therefore dedicate it to all who persevere even as it may seem easier to give up.

Never give up.

I hope that you, that we, that all of us, find the will and heart to keep going.

THE NAMELESS LAND

1

A Pattern, If One Can but Read It

In the summer of Year Fourteen of the Magnolia Emperor, I, Luviara, theurgist and investigator, completed my assigned inventory of all Heart Temples in the empire, including any that may have been left out of the census. The study covered the entirety of the empire and took sixteen years to complete.

In conclusion, I suggest that many of the Heart Temples predate the empire by hundreds of years. It is impossible to calculate exact ages because of the difficulty of dating reign lengths in the thousand-year Seven Golden Kingdoms era, and because of the paucity of evidence before the establishment of said era, when it seems there were widespread disruptions to the social order, a period which the poets indulgently refer to as "the Great Wars of the Sorcerer-Kings."

At the request of the palace archivists, I have included in my original report an *Official's Handbook* relating the customs, legalities, and historical anecdotes of the empire, appropriate to share with officials outside the temple who will benefit from its insights.

This addendum is meant only for the eyes of the Inner Chamber, who set me on this path.

As you know, my travels over the years have taken me to the Wandersea in the west, the Blasted Coast and the Storm Waters in the north, the Tranquil Sea and the impenetrable Stalking Forest to the south, as far along the eastern frontier as the Long Claws and the Dagger Spine, as well as a complete circumference of the borderlands surrounding the impassable Desolation. In all these places, I have explored major and minor heartland and provincial Heart Temples, as well as abandoned ruins, some of which are destroyed fortresses or collapsed dwellings, and some compounds which contain the remains of towers grouped in threes and occasionally referred to as "Spires."

Especially in the provinces and on the frontiers, I discovered Heart Temples that are mentioned in passing in the temple census as if they are of little interest but which are of unusual character and unknown age and provenance. Not a few are exceedingly difficult to reach and thus half forgotten. Some have preserved ancient scrolls seen nowhere else, and not yet chewed up into the palace's hungry maw. It is not clear when these most isolated Heart Temples were built, but they were certainly established long before the founding of the Tranquil Empire, as I have previously noted.

All this I dutifully recorded and sent to the Inner Chamber. After four months of waiting, and despite a respectful query, I have not yet received even the courtesy of an answer that acknowledges receipt of my extensive notes and findings after my many years of arduous journeying.

Thus, I repeat my preliminary conclusions here, in my winter report of Year Fourteen of the Magnolia Emperor.

That the Heart Temples and their worship predate the Tranquil Empire can no longer be disputed, that is, if the contrary was ever truly believed by anyone outside the palace. Certainly the local people of the intendancies understand the Heart Temples to be unimaginably ancient, the work of "old ones," or "guardians," or some other mysterious builders. Therefore, the claims that the empire built all the temples must be understood to be efforts by early palace archivists and historians wishing to embellish the accomplishments of the Lotus General and his heir, the Chrysanthemum Emperor. Whether they were ordered to make this claim, or managed to come up with it on their own, cannot, at this remove, be known one way or the other.

Yet the question of the Heart Temples' origins raises another related question, that of the curious mystery of the so-called witch roads, which protect against the Pall. To be clear, all "witch roads" are considered part of the network of imperial roads, but not all of the imperial roads repel the Pall. The official history of the empire states that the first emperors built all of the imperial roads, some of which have the protective quality mentioned above and others of which were built to facilitate the swift movement of armies and supplies.

But is that true? Why would witch roads be built before the rising of the Pall, an event that no one predicted? In addition, those of the imperial roads confirmed by work orders and manifests to have been constructed during the early years of the empire show no correlation to the oldest Heart Temples, even if new temples were built in association with these new roads.

Yet every Halt encloses a Heart Temple. This correlation suggests that the Halts and the Heart Temples were built at the same time and meant to be sited together. Some will object that certain Heart Temples lie far from the witch roads. The oldest and most remote of these, without exception, contain a pure-water spring, although not every Heart Temple has a pure-water spring. I have, as yet, found no explanation for why some temples have pure-water springs while others do not.

The only places known to always have a pure-water spring are the aforementioned Spires, whose three-tower construction and purpose remain a mystery. Their origins are shrouded by age and lack of evidence beyond the unusual statues arrayed at their entrances like guards. Most but not all of these statues depict animal-headed people with human- or aivur-shaped bodies. Pre-imperial poets fancifully called these statues "the Shorn" and claim they are noble warriors standing guard for eternity to make sure the evil sorcerer-kings of yore never return.

Witch roads often pass within a half day or less march to Spires, but never pass right up beside them, nor do the roads ever enclose Spires as Halts enclose Heart Temples.

I believe there is a pattern, if one can but read it.

I have requested of the Inner Chamber that I be allowed funding, travel permits, and full access to surveyor maps in order to continue my investigation into any possible relationship between Spires, Heart Temples, and witch roads, and what they may reveal about pre-imperial times and if their existence has any relationship to the dreaded Pall which now afflicts the empire.

Having been denied twice, I ask for a third time. It is foolish to believe we know all we need to know.

From the journal of Theurgist Luviara, working under the sworn seal of the Inner Chamber of the Heart Temple

2

Deadly Currents and Winds

Far Boundary Vigil stood on the southern shore of Far Boundary Pall, marking the northern limit of the Tranquil Empire and, people said, the end of the inhabitable world. At the top of the Vigil Tower, Elen and her nephew stood in a circular lookout chamber on the floor below the beacon that shone night and day.

Side by side, they stared north through one of the viewing windows. Like a vast sheet of low-lying fog, the Pall stretched north as far as the eye could see, and to the east and the west likewise, in the manner of a sea or a strait. That is, if that sea were a deadly mist that would kill on contact.

Kem sighed as he glanced back at the open door onto a stairwell. They were alone, for now. "I'd better go. I'm supposed to be caring for the horses."

"What?" Elen said with a smile. "You didn't get permission from Captain Simo to come up?"

He waggled his eyebrows, reminding her of all the escapades he and his great good friend Joef had gotten into as children. "I'm not supposed to be here but I had to sneak up and check on you. After everything you told me last night, I was worried about you. As for the prince . . ." He trailed off.

The haunt was gone. Her chest ached, missing him. Knowing his departure into the Pall was the only choice he could have made. And yet, in so short a time together, she had come to rely on seeing him every day, the easy grace of his presence near her.

Watching her, Kem frowned and was about to speak when a distant tangle of tense voices caught their attention and broke into Elem's pensive thoughts.

"Yes, the prince," she agreed drily. "It's better if he doesn't know you and I have spoken. Not yet, anyway. As unpleasant as he is, he's no fool. He'll guess I've told you everything. Go now, so His Exalted Highness doesn't find you here."

"Yes, that and the horses. Well, and figuring out what happened here at the Vigil. Why it's abandoned. Where the garrison has gone!" With this pronouncement, Kem took a step away, a lanky youth of seventeen discovering his place in the world with increasing confidence.

Abruptly he turned back and hugged her fiercely. "I was so scared for you."

"I love you, too, Kem," she said with a laugh even as his words set her heart at ease. After Ao's death two years ago and the haunt's departure just last night, she had been so afraid of losing him, too, feared him turning his back on her forever. Yet here he stood.

He snorted as he released her. "I guess we're stuck together for a while yet," he said with the wry grin that gave him a mischievous gleam. After a last glance at the silent Pall, he went to the door. He paused there to give her another frowningly concerned look, then hurried out of sight down the stairs.

She considered following him, but where could she go? She was in deep trouble, that much was certain. She and Kem were trapped by the circumstances that had landed them here at Far Boundary Vigil, at the edge of the empire. But Elen had survived bad situations before. Her instincts told her not to run, not yet. Ride this out a little longer. She had to protect Kem from the prince's wrath, that more than anything. But in addition, the mystery of the missing garrison and the unknown reason behind the prince's reckless dash from the heartland to this distant outpost was a puzzle she wanted to solve. As soon as it proved possible, it would still be better to walk away from any business that entangled her with the palace. She was no one, a mere provincial deputy courier, a minor official in the massive bureaucracy ruled over by the Magnolia Emperor. Chaff to be ground into dust and discarded by the machinery of the Tranquil Empire.

Yet, after all, chaff was not all she was.

Unfortunately, the prince knew it.

She crossed the chamber and looked down onto the courtyard in time to see Kem slip out of the lower doorway, race down the ramp and over the pavement, and disappear into the stables, apparently unseen by any of the others.

The murmur of voices from below ceased. Hastily she went back to the chair placed in the middle of the chamber. She sat exactly where the prince had left her when Captain Simo had come up to tell him Luviara wished to speak to him on a matter of great urgency.

Going forward, Elen and Kem's well-being depended on how

adeptly El handled Prince Gevulin. In her heart, the viper stirred, sensing trouble, or opportunity. She could kill the prince, and His Highness knew it. But if he died, then Kem would die, by the captain's hand. That was the hold the prince had over her. To protect Kem, she had to keep Gevulin alive.

The prince appeared in the doorway, pausing at the threshold to cast a keen gaze around the chamber as if expecting to find someone else lurking there.

Elen recalled the first time she had seen him when he and his entourage had arrived unannounced and unexpectedly at Orledder Halt. He was a handsome man, anyone would say so, with pleasingly symmetrical features, willow-leaf eyes, an attractive mouth, and a well-honed body. His long black hair was beautifully braided into multiple strands, the braids pulled back into a tail that dangled like a fly whisk hanging from the back of his head. Exquisite jewels beaded the braids with understated magnificence. His warden's tabard fit him with the perfection of excellent tailoring. Unlike the other wardens' unadorned tabards, its hardy indigo fabric was embroidered along collar and hem with tiny stylized eyes to represent his title as all-seeing eye, the prince-warden of the Imperial Order of Wardens.

Yet, despite his pleasing aspect, she wasn't drawn to him, not as she had been drawn to the haunt when the haunt had possessed the same body.

"Did you know about Luviara's complaint and saw fit not to warn me?" he asked in an arrogant tone. A rigid frown seemed to be his habitual expression, born of his scornful view of a world that had not yet rewarded him according to what his efforts, skill, and brilliance surely deserved in the hothouse of a palace where princes jostled relentlessly for status and rank.

"The worthy Luviara's complaint?" She kept her tone innocent, as she had trained herself over the years, the better to be overlooked as a person of no importance, nothing to see here, move on.

His frown tightened. "I've been watching you for days through the interloper's gaze. How you spoke one way to him and another to those you did not trust, not the way you came to trust him. You know exactly what I'm speaking about."

He shut the door and strode across the chamber to place himself in front of her. Given that she was seated and he was standing, armed with both a whip and a shrive-steel sword, his stance put her at a disadvantage. Just as he intended.

Yet the first thing she noticed now that he was standing so close was that his fine boots were dirty and scuffed from their long journey. She was surprised none of the wardens had cleaned them last night. Perhaps too much had happened. And it wasn't the duty of the wardens to care for the prince's person. Probably they hadn't even noticed. That was a task for the menial, Fulmo, and he hadn't arrived yet.

Still, she so hated to see good boots uncared for that she considered volunteering to clean and polish them herself—but rejected the thought immediately. To survive, she had to hold firmly to her status as a deputy courier. Even that modest rank gave her a tiny degree of autonomy and a clear list of duties to be performed within the grand imperial bureaucracy.

"Well?" he demanded. "What have you to say on the matter?"

It was stupid to goad him, but her instincts whispered that the moment she gave way, he would crush her.

"Your Highness, as I was not there for your conversation with the worthy Luviara, you will have to inform me of what took place."

He drew his whip from its loop on his belt. "This is some sort of game you play, is it not? Feigning ignorance when you know perfectly well. Luviara wishes to know why I did not tell her about the dead griffin scout we discovered outside Pisgia Moat. The very scout I had sent ahead to inform the intendant of Orledder Halt of my journey. Yet the scout never reached Orledder Halt. Someone murdered her and the beast together."

"A terrible thing, truly, to murder both scout and griffin. And for what?"

"To harm my mission. To harm *me* by fomenting trouble between me and the emperor. But you know all that. Why did the interloper instruct you to tell Kem and Ipis about the scout's death but, by omission, not to tell Luviara?"

"The interloper?"

"The one you call the haunt. The one who stole my body and walked in it while pretending to be me." His knuckles whitened as he gripped the whip more tightly. The memory scalded him: the indignity of his imprisonment inside his own body; his helplessness; the disgrace that he had been so easily trapped; the shame it caused him; the fear that others would find out and scorn him for his weakness. All this she could guess from his expression.

She moderated her tone, speaking as she would to someone in pain who wished to lash out at her even though she'd had nothing to do with their injury.

"Your Highness, I do not know. He did not confide his reasoning in me. If he had, you would have known, so your guess is as good as mine. Maybe better than mine. The passage spell that allowed him to take control of your body was meant to put you as if into a veil of sleep, yet it did not. You may know things I do not."

"When he walked in my body and spoke with my voice, I could not discern his thoughts. All I know is what I saw and heard."

"All I know is what he said to me, Your Highness. Perhaps he did not approve of theurgists and theurgy. I know that theurgy has something to do with control of elemental spirits, which are put to work on behalf of the empire. As a deputy courier, I rely on spirits who have been bound by theurgy and put to use to fight Spore. But I cannot sense spirits if they choose to remain hidden from me. All I can do is use vials of salt spirit to eradicate Spore, vials that are created by theurgists. He was able to sense that Luviara has spirits bound to her."

"That's true. He mentioned it to you, did he not? Perhaps he did not trust her since she made no mention to him of how many spirits she had at her disposal."

"Did she make no mention of this number to you, Your Highness?"

He shook his head impatiently. "Theurgists are not allowed to discuss their craft with people outside the order. Yet it seems the interloper had the means to discern the presence of spirits even though they are invisible to those who are not theurgists."

"Invisible even to you, Your Highness? You know a great deal about them."

"I know because I am prince-general of the wardens," he said with an impatient twitch of the whip. "Of course I know Luviara has spirits at her disposal, but not the details. How many she has can change at any given time, regardless, should she release some and bind new ones to her. That's common knowledge among wardens because all wardens benefit from theurgy. We do not wield theurgy ourselves."

"I see. Knowing is not at all the same as sensing the presence of spirits."

"How did he know? Why would the presence of bound spirits make him think her untrustworthy?"

"Actually, I think their presence made him hungry," Elen remarked, smiling as she recalled the haunt's more peculiar habits, how he had eaten alive a Spore-ridden mouse in order to ensure it did not infest any other living thing. "Maybe he smelled them as we do a fine platter of meat and turnips."

"You are no help," he remarked indignantly. "Although, remarkably, I believe you honestly do not know why he didn't trust her."

"My thanks, Your Highness."

He tapped the whip warningly against his leg. "Your impertinence is a disgrace."

He paused, but she sat primly with hands folded in her lap, saying nothing yet wishing he were still the haunt. But wishing got her nothing. She sighed.

His mouth pinched. He walked to the northern windows and considered the view. The openings were large enough that Elen, from the chair, could look out over the seemingly limitless Pall and the stub of a raised roadbed that ended about a hundred paces out from the tower, as if it were a pier set amid the poisonous fog.

Despite what was said in the palace archives and depicted on imperial maps, the Pall did not extend all the way to the cold northern ocean. The imperial road that seemed to terminate here was not the deliberate end of the road but rather a broken segment, shattered by an unknown force. Out of sight within the haze, yet not visible even from the upper floors of the tower, an intact segment of the road continued on through the Pall. It ran north to a nameless land, severed generations ago from the empire when the deadly mist rose in patches and lakes and seas across the land. She had hunted through histories and chronicles in the intendant's library and never found any mention of the nameless land's existence, as if it had been erased from the memory of the Tranquil Empire. Which meant no one knew what lay beyond the Pall except her, and the prince. The real question was whether he had only learned of the nameless land because he'd overheard her speak of it to the haunt, or if he'd already known. Yet how could he have known?

The prince turned away from the view and walked back to her.

"I am going to show you an item the interloper picked out of the ashes that were the remains of the individual who was burned at Pelis Manor. I wish to know if you recognize it."

"Why would I recognize it, Your Highness?"

"Because it comes from Farlandia."

"Farlandia?"

He gestured toward the north. "Do not play coy, Deputy Courier. I have heard all you have confessed."

He hadn't heard the story she'd told Kem. She smiled with polite agreement. "Your Highness, I mean I am not familiar with the name Farlandia. Is that the proper name of the land that lies north, beyond the Pall?"

"It's what I call it."

"Of course, Your Highness. A descriptive name, indeed." Gevulin didn't hear the soft sarcasm in her tone. The haunt would have replied with something witty or absurd or absurdly witty. How faded the world felt without him.

Watching her closely, the prince withdrew an item from a pocket in his sleeve and displayed it on his palm. It was a gold brooch in the stylized shape of a bear.

She flinched back from it. Caught herself. Breathe. *Breathe.*

"You recognize it."

It took her several swallows to recover her voice. "Yes. It is the badge worn by the personal staff of Lady Eleawona. Those closest to her, whom she trusted. That's why this one is made of gold."

"You were on her staff?"

She snorted. "Hardly. But I did grow up in her court. I was only a child then, and never an importantly placed person, Your Highness."

"Were you not? You are well-spoken now. Curious you speak with the accent of Ilvewind Province, not of the Farlandians."

"You've spoken to Farlandians?" The pieces were laid out. It was only a matter of fitting them together. "An envoy from a far land arrives at Far Boundary Vigil bearing a message for you. Captain Mekvo sends word of this envoy's arrival. So you hurry north to . . . meet? Interrogate? Kill this envoy? I haven't figured out whether you were expecting an envoy, or surprised by their arrival. But it seems to me that an envoy from a far land must seek an audience with the emperor, not with a prince. Is that why the situation threatened you? Why you had to get here quickly, before the emperor found out?"

He raised the whip. She braced herself, waiting for the welt of pain. But as the pause drew out, his expression flashed through a sequence of emotions: outrage, frustration, shrewd calculation, and at length he controlled his twitching arm and lowered the whip.

He said, "Your audacity and disrespect are unusual in a person of your humble status."

"It must have been a shock to find that Lord Genia had executed the envoy before you could get answers."

"Lord Genia is no one's fool, Deputy Courier, least of all mine. When the individual was brought before her and told her they were carrying a verbal message they could only deliver to Prince Gevulin, she understood that the arrival of an envoy from an unknown country who asked for me instead of the Magnolia Emperor would place me in a compromising situation. One that might cause the emperor to look unfavorably upon me."

"She killed the envoy to protect you from the emperor's anger?"

He looked at her blankly. "Of course she did. Too many people might have seen the envoy and passed the news on in a way that would reach the emperor's ears."

Elen gripped the chair, sickened and dizzied by the casual ruthlessness of his explanation. Living in Orledder Halt under the comparatively benign rule of the intendant had made her forget the harsh blade wielded by most of those who ruled.

"So the dead person wasn't really a Sea Wolf? The bone necklace was planted on them?"

"No, they were a Sea Wolf. That gave Lord Genia the excuse she needed to burn them. Convenient, really."

"Not for the dead person. But it isn't Lord Genia's actions that surprise me. It is your own, Your Exalted Highness."

His gaze flickered with an expression she suspected was that of a person determined to hide something that would get him into fatal trouble.

"Why would a Sea Wolf walk into the empire carrying Lady Eleawona's badge and your name if they did not think it would achieve something and gain them safe passage? Were you expecting an envoy from Farlandia?"

He gave her a sharp look and commenced a circuit of the chamber. When he did not answer, she guessed that, indeed, he had not been expecting an envoy and wasn't willing to admit the envoy's arrival had taken him by surprise.

If he had known nothing about a far land, then he'd not have been alarmed, only curious.

Instead, by his own admission, he knew the nameless land existed and the possibility of an envoy being sent to seek him was plausible. That alone was damning, and he knew it.

So why would Lady Eleawona have sent an envoy to an empire *she* had never heard of? To a prince whose name she could not possibly be familiar with?

Yet just because young El had not known of an empire south of the White Sea didn't mean the masters in the nameless land hadn't known. Before the Pall's rising, the main impediment to crossing would have been the two extremely wide and presumably deep watercourses, one of which might have been a strait. That would have been enough to limit contact between the barbarian north and the civilized empire, but it wouldn't have closed it off.

Which raised another question. Why did the surveyor maps in Orledder Halt's Map Hall show Far Boundary Pall and nothing beyond it, only a distant "here be the tempest-torn northern ocean"?

All the maps in Map Hall represented the empire *after* the rise of the Pall, as if the Pall had always been, even though it hadn't. The intendant had once said, "The emperors show only a strong face, never a weak one." Maybe they thought losing territory, even to a poisonous mist, was a sign of weakness. After all, the Pall was a foe they could not subdue, and thus their losses must be erased and hidden.

Yet surely the prince-warden would have access to maps concealed from intendants. The all-seeing eye *surely* would have the means to discover if such a place had once existed and might still exist if the Pall hadn't engulfed all of it. But how could Gevulin have traveled there and yet still be surprised to learn an envoy had come from the north?

Could the prince possibly have embarked from the Blasted Coast and sailed northwest across the tempest-torn ocean with its deadly currents and winds?

Which brought her back to her initial question: Why had he not expected and thus been surprised by the arrival of an envoy across Far Boundary Pall? What exactly was it about the envoy's arrival and possible mission that made it so important to make sure the emperor never found out?

3

The Shattered Wall

"Speak your thoughts," the prince commanded.

Elen knew better than to cower or cringe. "I have been puzzling over how and why Lady Eleawona would have sent an envoy to an empire she had never heard of, but the answer is obvious. She must have heard of it. And she must have some reason to believe the envoy she sent would have a proposal or information of interest to you, Your Exalted Highness. Although I cannot be sure how she would have known your name. I suppose the easiest thing to explain about the entire situation is why she would have sent one of her lifelong enemies as the envoy."

"Her lifelong enemies?"

"In the far land of my childhood, the Sea Wolves were ever and always at war with the Highmost and the lands of the humans, Your Highness."

He strolled closer, a predator sniffing a scent of interest. "Then how is it easier to explain?"

She held still, not retreating. "Because no human can cross without being taken by the Pall."

"Your sister did. Unless your deceased sister was an aivur able to pass as human."

"My sister was as human as your wardens, Your Highness. I carried her on my back the last part of the way, to keep her out of the Pall."

He halted in front of her, tall and imposing and implacable. "Are you a Sea Wolf?"

"I was a slave serving Lady Eleawona's court. I never even saw a Sea Wolf as a child. I know nothing of them except the stories I have heard. Have you met one?"

"I have." He preened a little, looking smug. "I have negotiated successfully with a Sea Wolf, killed a Sea Wolf, and fucked a Sea Wolf."

"Different ones, or the same one in that order?"

It came so fast: the whip cut hard across her cheek to raise a stinging welt that brought tears to her eyes but a fierce satisfaction to her heart at having gotten under his skin.

"Let that remind you to keep your mouth shut unless I have asked you a question. One word from me, and the boy is dead."

She kept her head high, as if the welt didn't throb as a pounding through her head. "Why you thought an envoy to be disposable I suppose I understand. But as Prince Warden, would you really kill a promising novice warden just to teach me a lesson?"

"A lesson you have not yet learned." He pressed the end of the whip against her chin and leaned into it, pushing her back against the chair with so much strength she thought the entire chair might tip over backward.

She fixed her expression to a mask even as her heart hammered. This knife's edge was a perilous balance. She feared for Kem, truly and deeply, and for herself, too, for that matter. Death was not an insignificant thing, and she loved the world and living in it. Her fear was not of Gevulin the man as much as it was of Gevulin the prince and the power he held. She wasn't sure if he was the kind of man, like Duenn, whose desire to hurt was inflamed when people cringed before him, or if he simply wasn't used to anyone contradicting him.

"Lose Kem, and you lose me," she said softly.

What he judged from her face she didn't know, but his eyes flickered with emotion as his hand tightened on the whip.

Footsteps sounded on the stairs. His voice muffled by the closed door, Simo called, "Your Highness, Jirvy has found the garrison."

The prince lowered the whip. "Enter!"

Elen sagged forward as the door opened. Simo's grim expression warned of bad news. The captain did not even look her way.

"They're dead?" the prince asked.

"Alas, yes, they are, Your Highness."

"Take me there." He tucked the badge back into his sleeve and the whip into his belt, then gestured to Elen to accompany them. "You'll stay with me at all times, Deputy Courier."

Simo's gaze flashed to the welt on her cheek, but he said nothing.

They descended. The map room where she'd glimpsed Xilsi and Ipis not long ago was empty. The courtyard was empty too. She could hear the restless horses in the stable. Kem stood at the stable door, eyes widening with alarm as he noticed the welt. She shook her head, warning him off. Pain pulsed through her cheek, but she knew how to breathe through pain. And this was merely physical pain, that would soon subside and heal. The haunt was gone, and still she breathed.

"Stay with the horses, Novice," called Simo.

His expression still dour, the captain led them out the gate and onto the street. They walked down the lane and past the compound's empty buildings.

Ipis stood by a loose shutter. The window let into one of the boarded-up barracks. She had a hand over her mouth and nose, and her eyes were wide and wild.

Simo climbed in through the window. The prince followed, then Elen. Inside was dim, but she could see a big, empty room, all its furniture long since hauled away. A breeze chased through from the next chamber. They passed a doorway into a barracks whose back wall was broken out as if something huge had smashed itself repeatedly against it.

Charred corpses lay in horrifying contortions. Most were clumped and jumbled together, as if they'd been trying to create a unified shield to fight an unassailable foe. One person had been caught against the far end, where they'd been trying to get out a window whose shutters were barred. The stench would have been worse, but some time had passed, and the cold kept down the rot. Most strangely, rats and other vermin hadn't been at the corpses. Elen knew from examining the bodies of people who had died in the hills that eyeballs and the soft viscera in the belly were the first to go.

Xilsi was kneeling beside a blackened body at the front of the wedge-like clump, using her short sword to drag an object out of the remains without touching any of it herself. Seeing the prince, she rose holding another sword in her gloved hand.

"Your Highness," she said gravely, "I must believe this is Captain Mekvo. This is his sword."

"How do you know it is his sword?" the prince asked.

"I gifted it to him. It was made to order. He applied for a special dispensation to train left-handed. Also, it's engraved."

The prince took the tarnished sword and used the blade to poke at the ghastly remains, counting the skulls. There were twenty: presumably the nineteen members of the Vigil garrison, as well as the missing South Flat Vigil warden. Holding the sword on guard, he walked to the shattered wall. Beyond the gaping splinters lay a large exercise yard for training and maneuvers. The dirt had been swept into erratic ridges and hollows.

"Sarpa," he said. "Their acid spit produces this burned effect on human flesh. It leaves behind a poisonous residue."

"That's what I suspected," said Xilsi. "But the Sarpa Corps belong to the emperor. Why would a sarpa rider attack wardens? I've never heard of bandits taming sarpa, though I suppose it's possible."

Gevulin surveyed the scene with a frown, wrinkling up his nose. He raised his voice. "Luviara! Have you heard any whisper of Prince Astaylin having a foot in the door of the Sarpa Corps?"

Elen had been so horribly riveted by the sight of the dead that she hadn't noticed a rustle in the shadows. Holding a lamp, the theurgist emerged from a room at the other end.

"Your Highness, I am not a purveyor of whispers from the palace. I am a traveler who records my observations of the landscape. That is why you retained me as your interlocutor, is it not? For my knowledge of the empire's frontiers and the places and peoples that lie athwart and beyond those frontiers."

Her tone was tart enough that the others glanced at her in surprise, all but Gevulin.

He said, "Simo, have you heard any gossip about rebellious discontent within the Sarpa Corps?"

"None, Your Highness. When I served in the east I only saw sarpa from a distance. The problem with their attack is that it burns indiscriminately. Still, the Blood Wolves can do little against a sarpa's thick hide and vicious temper. Their spider mounts are terrified of sarpa. To answer your question, I don't understand why a sarpa rider would attack imperial wardens."

"Xilsi?"

"All I know is that few from the Noble or August Manors join the corps due to the nature of the sarpa. Most of the corps' officer ranks are made up of people out of the provincial Manors. They're willing to gamble that serving notably in the corps will bring them enough glory and status to be worth the hardship and risk. Or at least a good death payout to their Manor, should they die in the course of duty."

"So to the question of why a sarpa was here we have no answer yet." He turned his attention to the sword. "This is a good blade."

"*Good?* It's an excellent blade!" Xilsi objected. "I commissioned it from the best bladesmith in the capital city."

In a droll voice, Jirvy said, "Mekky was the envy of the entire cohort, swanning around with that sword. It's a beautiful weapon."

"You never said you were envious of the sword," said Xilsi tartly.

His mouth twitched with a flash of charm that surprised Elen. "I had something better, didn't I?"

Xilsi gave a huff and turned her back on him. He stoically said nothing.

"That's my point," said the prince, as if he hadn't heard—or paid attention to—the exchange. "This sword was left behind. Like the griffin scout's personal belongings. That which was most valuable was not stolen by those who perpetrated this massacre."

"The griffin scout's message pouch was taken," said Simo, "and the dispatches gone when we recovered the pouch."

"I must suppose that was because whatever the dispatches contained was thought to pertain to my mission."

"Did they?" asked Luviara pugnaciously. "For I confess to you, Your Highness, that I still have received no answer as to why you withheld from me the death of the griffin and its scout."

The prince looked at Elen sharply, as if expecting her to have an answer, then back at the theurgist. "My meaning was mistaken. There are no secrets between you and me, are there, Luviara?"

The interlocutor's face settled into a benign expression. "I should hope not, Your Highness. You and I have traveled a great distance together. To the ends of the empire, and beyond."

And beyond.

A better picture of the situation was forming: Before Gevulin had been officially named as all-seeing eye, he had, by his own admission, traveled to the frontiers of the empire, an itinerary meant to acquaint him with the network of imperial roads he was soon to administer. He'd been accompanied by Simo, who had been promoted by the prince to the rank of captain. And by Luviara as well.

"If I may, Worthy Interlocutor," said Elen, deciding to see if she could soften the prince's antipathy toward herself by coming up with a plausible misunderstanding to placate Luviara. "His Exalted Highness merely did not want the matter spoken of once we returned to Pisgia Moat. That valuables weren't stolen suggested the griffin and its scout weren't killed by bandits. I saw a palace runner run ahead of us into the Moonrise Hills. Then the archon tried to kill us."

"She did not try to kill *us*, Deputy Courier," said Simo.

"I beg your pardon," said Elen. "We are but collateral damage. Someone is trying to kill His Exalted Highness. Why would a provincial upland archon have reason to assault a prince? It seems to me more likely that the archon is working with someone close to the palace."

"Exactly so." The prince handed the sword to Xilsi. "My meaning was mistaken. It was only at Pisgia Moat that we needed to keep silent to avoid alerting the archon that we had found the dead griffin and scout. Do you have any further questions on this matter?"

Luviara had no choice but to incline her head. "I am satisfied, Your Highness."

Was she? Elen could not tell.

The prince studied his wardens. "Has anyone found any letter or communication that could have originated with the envoy?"

Xilsi said, "Ipis and I found nothing in the map room. But . . ." She trailed off, looking thoughtful.

"Out with it!" snapped the prince.

Xilsi raised her eyebrows, as if surprised to be yelled at after so many days interacting with a more congenial fellow, or so the warden would surely think. Even so, Xilsi wasn't intimidated by the prince. Elen liked her for the way she blithely glided through life, even as annoying as she often was. Maybe it was the contrast that appealed.

"Mekky had a long-standing affair going with a married man. A high official, no less."

Jirvy gave a curt laugh. "I remember that. More like an ongoing wineshop drama."

"He would hide their love letters in a special hidden compartment in his calligraphy chest. He showed me how to get into it in case I needed to burn anything."

"Did you?" Elen asked.

Xilsi grinned. "A friend never tells."

The prince's hand tightened on the whip. "Did you find anything in the chest?"

"So far we have searched the Map Hall but not his sleeping chamber."

"Get to it, then!"

She hustled out, calling Ipis to go with her.

The prince walked a slow circuit of the space, looking for clues, but he found nothing that hadn't already been brought to light by Jirvy.

Simo said, "Your Highness, what about the bodies? They deserve a respectful funeral."

"Leave them as they are. I may need proof later that I have been maliciously targeted, and that a warden garrison was unlawfully attacked. When we return to Pelis Manor, I will task Lord Genia with sending a troop to make an official record of the incident. They can clean it up afterward. Luviara, there is something else on your mind, as I can see by the way you keep glancing toward that door in the back."

The interlocutor's frown told the story. "The Pelis Manor messenger, Your Highness. I found the body in the adjoining storeroom."

"Burned?"

"Throat slit. I searched the body but found no message, only their traveling gear and their Manor badge."

The prince gestured to Simo. The captain went into the dark chamber beyond. He reappeared, dragging a body by its armpits. The prince circled the corpse with the same expression he'd had when studying Elen seated in the chair. He drew his shrive-steel sword to probe here and there at the body, flipping cloth aside, folding back the gaping wound in the neck to display severed blood vessels and windpipe. The cut had been clean, down to the bone, wielded by an unusually strong arm. After he finished his thorough examination, he stepped back, wiped the blade's tip clean on the messenger's trousers, and sheathed the sword.

"So, a sarpa and its rider attack and depart. Who, then, killed this messenger?"

"Your Highness!" Kem's breathless shout came from outside. He appeared at the open door into the blasted barracks. His eyes widened as he took in the grisly scene, and he clapped a hand over his mouth as if he wanted to retch.

"Speak!"

Kem averted his eyes from the dead. His gaze caught on Elen's face before he gave a clumsy bow to the prince. "Your Highness, Warden Xilsi says to come at once. She's found something."

4

The Gold of Loyalty

They joined Xilsi and Ipis in the map chamber. Kem had followed them up and taken a place against a wall, pretending not to be there.

Ipis was methodically filing the scatter of maps and scrolls. Xilsi stood at one end of the biggest table, staring at two items placed on the cleared surface. One was a stout hallow-wood walking staff with a carved hand grip. The other was an ornate calligrapher's chest. She'd opened the chest to display a neat interior with ink stones, two shallow mixing basins, and an array of brushes and pencils. The backing of the lid's interior had been removed to reveal a hiding place for correspondence.

She handed the prince a papyrus note. "This was the only thing inside."

He scanned the writing. "This is a love letter. High Heavens! Execrable poetry! Does no one study the classics in the Manors?"

Xilsi's gaze flicked toward the ceiling as if seeking her lost patience. Dried tears streaked her cheek; she'd been crying for her lost friend. In a cold tone, she said, "He hid no envoy's message in the case. He received the gift of a walking staff after his injury. When I saw him last, before he left Warden Hall for this posting, he joked that now he could keep his love letters even closer to hand as he was limping around."

The top of the staff had been detached and set to one side. The staff was hollow, a perfect place to hide vials of salt spirits, or rolled-up documents.

"Is this what you're looking for, Your Highness?" Xilsi smoothed out a sheet of almost translucent vellum and weighted down its corners. It was both thin and tough enough to roll up into a tight tube that fit into the staff's hollow interior. A pattern of lines interspersed with blocks of writing marked the surface.

All stood in silence, studying the map.

"What is it?" Ipis asked finally. "The writing looks almost like imperial script, but what are those odd curlicues and hatchet spurs?

When I try to sound it out, it doesn't make sense, even though there are some words I recognize, like—"

She broke off as the prince raised a hand. "Were you asked to give your opinion, Warden Ipis?"

Her eyes widened. She exchanged a glance with Kem, who gave a warning shake of his head exactly as Elen had earlier given one to him. The wardens had all gotten used to the haunt's generosity of spirit and less formal demeanor.

Ipis cleared her throat and said, "Worthy Interlocutor, please convey my apologies to His Exalted Highness for speaking out of turn."

"I acknowledge the apology," the prince said before Luviara could repeat Ipis's words. He drew his whip and pointed in turn. "Ipis. Kem. Jirvy. You as well, Xilsi. Finish the search of the grounds for any sign of what may have happened. Collect supplies. Make ready for our return journey."

"Shall we collect the personal belongings of the deceased to return to their families, Your Highness?" Xilsi asked.

"Leave them for the local officials to sort out. Any such efforts must be left to what is perceived as a neutral entity."

Xilsi's jaw tensed. She replied in a tightly even tone. "Your Exalted Highness, I cannot recommend leaving the garrison's personal effects behind. We do not know why a sarpa attacked, much less who was in command of it. Sarpa and rider might return. Or some other party might pillage the Vigil between the time we leave and when Lord Genia sends a recovery expedition. Bandits might descend. Or poor villagers seeking food, as the deputy courier would remind us. Or whoever had the garrison murdered might come back to make sure they didn't miss anyone—"

"Do not tax me." He met her gaze with aggressive arrogance.

Xilsi did not lower her gaze. "As a courtesy to those who have lost their lives, I recommend we, at the very least, gather personal mementos that can be presented to the families of the fallen. They deserve that much after being posted out here at the back end of beyond."

"Go!" he snapped, but he did not tell her *not* to proceed.

She left the chamber with the others, Ipis and Kem with heads bent together, whispering, and Jirvy with his sword drawn, as if he expected to meet an enemy on the steps.

The prince placed himself at one end of the table, hands braced on the top, studying the vellum with a frown. Simo stood to his right, Luviara to his left, and Elen by the door.

The theurgist looked at Elen and then at the prince, seemed about to speak, but did not.

"What do you make of it?" the prince said. "By the pattern of the lines, I would say it is some kind of map. But not drawn in the manner of our surveyor maps. The writing is like to imperial script. Can you read it, Luviara?"

The theurgist studied the writing in silence, then went over to a cabinet and removed a writing case and a square of papyrus. Using a pencil rather than a brush, she began to write out the words in standard imperial script, inserting guesses for the unusual letters.

The prince and Simo discussed the other markings in low voices. In the unexpectedly relaxed quiet, Elen's mind wandered. Every time she glanced at the prince, a part of her was hooked by hope. Was that a flicker of humor in his eyes as he addressed a comment to Simo? Had the haunt returned?

No. The haunt was gone.

Made restless by this pointless dreaming, Elen prowled the room, opening cabinets and looking under writing desks. At length, propped against a cabinet, she found a waxed-leather tubular container embossed with the bear symbol of Lady Eleawona. It was empty but could easily have conveyed the rolled-up vellum. She brought it to the table.

"Perhaps this is how the map got here. You see the bear, here?"

Without looking up, the prince pressed the tip of the whip against her arm.

"Your Exalted Highness," she added.

He removed the whip and took the tube from her, turning it around to look at it from all angles before handing it to Simo. Then he turned back to her.

"Deputy Courier, what do you make of this map? Do you recognize it?"

She paced around the table, pausing to examine the map from various angles. "I do not, Your Exalted Highness. It doesn't seem to indicate landmarks, topographical features, or distances, the way imperial maps do. But I agree it could be a map. Are these parallel lines meant to be roads? Passages of some kind? They're strange because each goes through what looks like a wheel. This area in the middle has seven interlocking wheels, each with a line coming in from one place and going out to a different place. For example, here." She tapped an image that looked like a representation of a fortress with eight towers. "This reminds me of the Octagonal Palace in Arlewind Cross. That's the city where Xilsi spent her childhood, isn't it?"

No one answered her question, so she went on.

"A line goes from the eight-tower fortress into this central region, and from there to the upper left. See here, how the upper part of the route is dotted through this area marked with curls? Are those meant to be trees? Winds? Waves, like an ocean? Does the route cross the ocean? And look here!" She traced a blocky pattern at the top of the map. "Could this represent a piece of coastline? That crescent moon with a stick inside its curve could be a ship out on the water. But all these wheels in the middle of the map . . . I don't understand them."

Luviara set down her pencil. "Your Highness, I can read some of this, if I am correct about the letters. Most of the words are unknown to me, yet some seem related to Imperial. Here's 'emprar' which might be 'emperor.' This might be 'holy way,' as in 'path.'"

The prince said, "Deputy Courier, read it."

"Me?"

He slapped the whip on the tabletop.

Simo jumped, startled, then took a step back to give Elen room to come up to the table and examine the vellum's writing from a better angle. As she silently mouthed the letters Luviara had rendered in a more commonplace script, the rhythm and meaning began to fire in her mind. Snatches of conversation. The snap and clatter of the south-county speech as compared to Lord Thelan's slower north-county drawl. The language of her youth, different from Imperial but with enough links that she and Ao had been able to get along once they'd reached the empire. Masters and their most valued retainers often moved around courts, bringing varied dialects and accents. Atoners who survived were good at adapting, because if they didn't understand a command, then they would be punished, no matter the cause. An atoner was always at fault.

"Te veg ulbethot hal rad."

"I see. That pronunciation makes sense with these letters. But what does it mean?"

"To go upon the holy way."

The prince nodded, satisfied.

Luviara stared. "You can read this? What is it?"

"That is for His Exalted Highness to explain, I believe," said Elen tartly.

"Read it aloud, in Imperial," commanded the prince. "The secret of the envoy lies in whatever is written here."

She worked her way through the text, which was set up in three blocks and with additional captions set around the map, like labels explaining something.

"From this one, 'She Who the White-Haired God Has Anointed as Lady of the South, Heir to Her Anointed Mother and to the Highmost Among the Rulers of the Land, the Most Wise and Just Who Is Known as the Scourge of the Wave-Wolves . . . Sea Wolves . . . She Who Wields the Name Eleawona—'"

She broke off, choked. Her voice failed. Her mind went blank.

"Go on!" commanded the prince.

An atoner had to go on.

Hoarsely, she scraped out the words, though she had begun to sweat as if bathed in a furnace heat.

"'The Lady Eleawona sends her greetings to the First Lord who names himself Gevulin . . .' I think 'first lord' is meant to be 'prince.' She reminds him of the mutual friendship upon which they pledged their honor and their gold . . ."

"Gold?" said the prince.

"The gold of their loyalty. They pledged to come to the assistance of the other in the future should need arise and they have the means to aid the other one. 'Let Eleawona Most High remind Gevulin First Lord that so they did speak at that time on the Isle Tempest, under the light of the pearl moon which gathers the holy power of the white-haired god. There, they exchange oaths.'"

Strangely, neither Luviara nor Simo looked surprised by this startling assertion. How had Prince Gevulin met Lady Eleawona, when the nameless land was cut off from any part of the empire? Wasn't even acknowledged on any maps Elen had ever seen? On imperial maps the north consisted only of the Storm-Swept Ocean, ruled by the Sea Wolves, the marauding aivur in their ships.

"That's the first block," she said, and then to Simo, "Captain, is there anything to drink? My throat is parched."

"Go on," said the prince, pointing to the second block of text. He added, "No, Simo, do not leave."

Elen licked her dry lips with a dry tongue. Even so, nervous as she was, she gained confidence as the lilt and sound of her childhood language came rushing back in a flood she had never wished to experience or endure again.

"'The events of the last two years since our fated meeting would take too long to relate, so this brevity must suffice. My cousin Thelan has stolen the throne of the Highmost from our uncle. He intends to steal my throne of authority over the south from me, even as he pledged once, in honor and in the gold of loyalty, that he would never challenge my right as my mother's heir to rule the south. The local masters remain loyal to me, but they cannot stand against his army. They have advised me to agree to marry my cousin. This I will not do, although we were affianced as children, a betrothal to which I was not asked nor able to give my consent. Now I must ask of you that you come to my aid, as you promised you would in exchange for my agreement. Should you have forgotten, I promised to provide you with mineral resources from the eastern mines, ferried through the port of Isle Tempest and into your coffers and storehouses that you keep there. This I have done. I have kept my part.'"

Elen looked up. Her mouth opened, and almost the words popped out, *You keep storehouses and coffers outside the empire?*

Before she could speak, the prince raised his whip and pressed it to the welt on her cheek. The sting silenced her. Of course, this wasn't something he wished the emperor to discover. And he was no longer the haunt.

The other two followed the gesture without any change of expression. Everyone had seen the welt. Only Kem had reacted with surprise and dismay.

"You skirt the limit, Deputy Courier." Satisfied that he had made his point, he lowered the whip. "Read the third block of text."

Flushed, cheek still stinging, she turned to the last set of words. "'I would provide you . . . by means of my alliance with the Salt Spear Clan . . .' I think she means a Sea Wolf clan. Oh, I see. 'They with whom I have exchanged a blood oath of alliance, settlement lands for their clan in exchange for their support in the coming battle. Even with this, my forces are outnumbered. To this end, certain scouts of the Salt Spear Clan have brought to me in secret a map of . . .'" She smoothed her hand over the vellum. "'A map of . . .' I don't know this word. 'The desert out of which the lost . . . the emptied land out of which the lost ones depart . . . Along the course of these hidden passages, the armies of the empire may travel unseen into the mines of the eastern hills. By this means, they may set upon the army of the traitor and bastard, Thelan. Thus will the empire gain an ally in our rich kingdom. I, the Lady Eleawona, will stand as Highmost of the rulers under the eye of the white-haired god. To bring this about, I will offer, to my imperial ally, troops by which he may place himself . . .'"

She trailed off as the words finally made sense.

"Continue!"

"I think this is a map centered on the interior of the Desolation. A place no imperial surveyor has been able to explore because surveyors who enter those lands all die or disappear. But there is one thing all who have seen even the outer borderlands agree on. The land we now call the Desolation no longer looks like the land that was recorded on the old maps of the area from before the Pall rose. The old maps are wrong."

"What does that mean for me?" the prince asked.

"This region here, to the upper left, must be your Farlandia. It's an island with the Storm-Swept Ocean to the north and a Pall to the south. This, here, may indeed be the Octagonal Palace in Arlewind Cross, which lies a mere six days' journey from the capital city. If true, that suggests there is some kind of direct route between Farlandia and the heartland. I don't know how that could be, not unless it were . . ."

She looked up. They were waiting for her to go on, Gevulin looking eager and triumphant, Simo stern and determined, and Luviara as still as a windless day.

"The Lady Eleawona seems to be saying that her aivur allies have given her a map of passages through the Desolation. I don't know what sort of passages they are meant to be. Roads? Tunnels? Canals? Rivers? It's puzzling because it's not said what they are. Some of these passages would have to extend hundreds of leagues to cover such a distance, since at least one reaches deep into imperial territory. But, anyway, this message seems to propose that she will loan you seasoned aivur troops, who can attack directly into the heartland, and thus place you on the imperial throne. Then, once you are emperor, in exchange you will provide her with a loan of imperial troops to defeat her cousin's army and place her on Farlandia's throne."

5

The Element of Surprise

The prince went to the cabinets and began pulling out maps of the empire to spread out on the table. The first thing he did was link up a map that included Arlewind Cross with the corresponding eight-tower fortress featured on the vellum.

Elen now understood why a Sea Wolf would have claimed to be an envoy: because they had been. And why Lord Genia would have acted as she did in burning the messenger. The prince hadn't expected any contact at the Vigil. He'd had no idea a crossing at Far Boundary Pall was even possible. That's why he had hurried north. Rebellion against the emperor was a death sentence, so he had to make sure he wouldn't fall under suspicion. No wonder he'd thought it had been a malicious ruse, concocted by his rival Prince Astaylin as a means to ruin him.

But how had Lady Eleawona come to discover the White Sea could be crossed? How had she come to make an alliance with a clan of her people's most hated enemy?

"There's much here that does not link up," said the prince. "For example, if she has an armed force of aivur, why not use them to fight her cousin? Deputy Courier, do you know?"

"Your Highness, I do not know."

"Luviara?"

"It's been my observation that the Sea Wolf clans are not a united country like our empire, but rather many separate clans."

"Simo?"

The captain said, "Several times, in the east, the only thing that saved us from defeat was that the various factions within the Blood Wolves sometimes turned on each other for reasons we never understood. I can speculate. Perhaps this Salt Spear Clan is a small clan and lacks numbers and supplies to meet her cousin on the field. Perhaps some of their forces are tied up fighting elsewhere, or engaged in raiding, or protecting themselves against other Sea Wolf factions."

"How is such a limited troop meant to seize and hold the palace?" the prince mused.

Luviara said, "Your Highness, it may be these northerners, like Lady Eleawona, do not realize the extent of the empire or the size of the palace."

"That's likely," he agreed. "From what we saw on Isle Tempest, the Farlanders are a barbaric lot. Their weapons are antiquated, and their manners crude. I don't think they bathe. How can they understand the might and majesty of the Tranquil Empire from such a distance, and in such benighted circumstances?"

He considered the maps spread across the table.

"It would be up to me to take advantage of the element of surprise by putting certain of my sympathizers in place beforehand. Once we have control of the palace, then the palace councils and commanders and the Manors will defer to me."

"Why would they not defer to the emperor?" Elen asked.

The prince glanced at her contemptuously, his gaze dropping to her arm. Her hand twitched but she studiously did not rub her forearm.

He indicated the empty chamber. "Why do you think I sent the others out? They are wardens, but not my inner circle to be apprised of my most private thoughts. You should be clever enough to understand that, by that time, I would have declared myself as emperor."

"You believe the councils and Manors will support whoever is on the throne, regardless of how they got there?"

"Yes. Peace is better than war at the heart of the empire. Astaylin wastes her time by courting the provincial Manors in the hope of having their support, but they will never be influential inside the palace."

Luviara cleared her throat. "Yet, Your Highness, even if all this is so, and such a violent expedition succeeds, the councils and the Manors may still condemn you for murdering the emperor."

"As if it hasn't been done before! Anyway, they will have no reason to blame me if they do not suspect I am involved in the emperor's death."

Again, he glanced at Elen. She said nothing, although this time she did touch her arm reflexively. Simo frowned.

"Your Highness, I'm not sure I understand," Luviara said.

"It's simple enough. The best way to proceed will be to condemn the attack as a malicious surprise raid by vengeful aivur who are angry at the Magnolia Emperor for exiling their kinfolk. Aivur lived in the heartland peacefully enough before my sister came to the throne. All that they left behind, their considerable wealth and holdings, was confiscated by the imperial treasury. Some whispered that's why the emperor made the decree: to get her hands on aivur riches and estates. So, there's the motive. I would arrive just in time to save the imperial throne from the barbarians."

"There's no guarantee the raiders will be able to kill the emperor."

He ignored Luviara's comment as he tapped his whip against the table, expression thoughtful, more as if he were contemplating which supper dish to eat next, instead of treason.

"I could then have the aivur raiders executed. Although that would run the risk of alienating Lady Eleawona. Still, once I hold the throne, I no longer need her assistance, do I?"

"Surely honor would impel you to come to her aid, Your Highness," said Elen.

Simo and Luviara said nothing. Either they were shocked by the prince's bald declaration of his intent to rebel or, more likely, they had known all along. They had been traveling with him for several years, and apparently both had been with him when he had made, or received, the first overtures from the beleaguered Eleawona, beyond the shores of the Blasted Coast, on the aptly named Isle Tempest.

Lady Eleawona's situation, at least, was one Elen understood. Denied her birthright, Eleawona would do anything to get it back. If that meant other people died, so be it. Such was the world as the masters saw it.

Gevulin was no different. Here Elen stood, seen only as one of his "weapons." It wasn't even that she was trapped either way. It was the weight of the witch roads, in a manner of speaking. A deputy courier walked the paths of the empire as part of its network of control. Outside it, El was nothing but an outlaw to be burned. Inside it, she had found a way to live. Sometimes she asked herself if she had chosen the weak path of cooperation and collaboration instead of the angry defiance of outlawdom. Yet why throw yourself at a wall you could not topple? You would only break your own bones and bleed out on the uncaring ground. Survival was its own triumph. She meant to survive.

The prince straightened. His mouth tipped with a self-satisfied smile that made her nervous.

"To that end, Deputy Courier, *you* will go as my envoy to the north. You will deliver my reply to Lady Eleawona. I will await your return at Pelis Manor North. Worvua has grown into a reasonable-looking woman. She would be a good fit for an imperial consort, as well as tying Pelis Manor tightly to me."

"Not Xilsi?" Elen muttered, then regretted saying it.

Gevulin laughed derisively.

"Oh? Did you try and fail with her?" she said, too angry not to poke at what she hoped was a bruise.

"Deputy Courier, this is quite enough," snapped Simo.

Elen resolved to ask Xilsi, but she kept her mouth shut. For mysterious reasons, the prince did not seem offended.

Simo went on. "Your Highness, how is the deputy courier to reach Isle Tempest? It will take months of travel to reach one of the ports on the Blasted Coast and then to find a ship to the island. From there, she'll need to find another ship to take her to Farlandia."

"Luviara, roll up the other maps." The prince kept a hand on the precious vellum. "Simo, how do you think the aivur envoy and his map arrived at this Vigil?"

"You believe the aivur burned by Lord Genia really was an envoy from Farlandia?"

"I do."

Luviara said, "I beg your pardon, Your Highness, but I don't see how that is possible. This is the end of the road."

He strolled to the window that overlooked the north and its hazy mysteries. "But, you see, Luviara, it turns out that this is not the end of the road. The deputy courier knows how to cross the Pall, and so she will. Will you not, *El*."

On his lips, her childhood name was a threat, not a gift.

When he turned to look at her, she couldn't be sure whether he was more intrigued by the chance of her refusal, and the punishment he could then inflict, or the possibility of her submission.

She met his gaze, refusing to be cowed. A flicker of possibility sparked in her heart. What if, out on the Pall, she could find the haunt? "I will do as I am commanded, Your Exalted Highness."

The prince walked to a writing desk and set out paper, a ruler to line the paper, brushes, ink. He was a master of calligraphy, wasn't he? The note would be elegantly brushed, a thing of beauty to contemplate once it was finished. A work of art and a display of proficiency, as must all things be that are grown and polished within the palace walls. To be less than that was to prove your unworthiness for your place at the heart of imperial power.

He said, "Collect your gear. You'll depart as soon as I have composed my reply."

"Do you mean the deputy courier to go alone, Your Highness?" Luviara asked.

"Yes."

"Not even one warden in escort? It seems rash to send her without any protection."

"Did I ask your opinion on this, Luviara?" he said without looking.

"It's all right, Worthy Interlocutor," said Elen hastily. "I am grateful for your intercession and concern. But it isn't possible for anyone to accompany me."

"How can that be? If you can cross, then there must be a safe passageway through the Pall, although in all my travels I've never heard of any such thing." Luviara sounded offended that there might be something in the wide world that she, with all her experience and wisdom, had not heard of. "And besides that! I have my own means to avoid streams of Pall, should there be any in the way."

"If by that you mean the air spirit that raised you up out of the delving, it would depend on how powerful they are and how many you have left," said Elen. "I know nothing about that. Regardless, only the road is safe."

"This is the end of the road!" said the theurgist, again and more insistently this time. But then she paused, looked at the prince and the deputy courier in turn, and added, with a flash of intense curiosity, "Ah, I see I am mistaken."

Simo said, "There are a very few older maps that show what might be a continuation of a road beyond this Vigil. But the empire did not build them."

Luviara shook her head. "Did you know, Captain, that the few surviving chronicles from the last generation of the Seven Golden Kingdoms refer to a network of disused and damaged stone roads said to date to the wars of the sorcerer-kings? There is evidence, though it is hard to find, that the empire built only some of the imperial roads and otherwise repaired and restored an already existing network of roads. Do the wardens speak of this possibility? I have never been allowed into their inner hall. For that matter, the Heart Temple's governing council demanded I cease my investigations into the imperial road network and its associated temples and structures."

"I require silence to compose," said the prince.

The captain said, "Worthy Interlocutor, I will remain with His Exalted Highness. You could best be of service now by descending and telling Kem and Ipis to ready the carriage and horses for departure. We shall depart for the south as soon as the deputy courier is gone."

"Your Worthiness, I'll go down with you and fetch my things," said Elen.

"You will remain here, Deputy Courier," said the prince, again without looking up.

"Of course, Your Highness," said Luviara. "Let me just collect my writing things from the side table before I go."

6

WRITTEN IN THE MARGIN

So be it. If they cannot see the necessity, then I am forced to make my pleas where they will be heard, although I like it not. Yet even this may be turned to advantage.

Written in the margin in the journal of Luviara, theurgist working under the sworn seal of the Inner Chamber of the Heart Temple

7

Shadowy Whispers

While Luviara put her writing tools back in their box, Elen walked over to the north window and gazed out across the Pall.

Mostly, she dreaded what she would find on the other side. She would be vulnerable, and she could so easily be killed. But that had always been true, no matter where she was.

A part of her was curious. She wasn't the same El. She had skills, confidence, knowledge, and a strength that she had lacked then. Atoners El and Ao had been so ignorant that she couldn't even remember how little they'd known compared to how much their later experience had added texture and understanding to her memories. Their world had been so small. When each step was potentially fatal, a person had no choice but to keep their eyes on the ground and rarely risk a look at the stars. Hope for something different was out of reach. It was enough to stay alive one more day.

From a distance, it was easy to think of the Pall as motionless, but from this height, she could see the slow churn of currents in its depths, the way the wind caught and curled where the mist was thicker, more viscous, and where it spun around unseen whirlpools beneath. During the day, it was hard to make out the sparks that could be seen dancing in the Pall at night. She scanned for any sign of a moving shadow, a long sinuous shape, but if Sara'ala was still out there, he had departed from this shore hours ago. He, too, had a task laid upon him that he could not, and would not, shirk.

What if he was right about his task? What if the lost and defeated sorcerer-kings of deadly legend were rising again out of the shadows? Out of the past? Had the war he'd mentioned killed them or only contained them? How did that even work?

And if all this was so, did she have a duty to warn the intendant? Would he believe her? Would anyone believe her? The prince knew, but he would never admit to what had happened to him at the Spires, lest it make him seem weak. If it came to a contest of her word against a prince's, it would go ill for her.

Elen caught Luviara's eye and beckoned her over. Ever curious, the theurgist closed the writing box and walked over to the window.

Elen pitched her voice low. "Worthy Interlocutor, before I go, may I ask if you have ever heard stories of a great war that defeated the evil sorcerer-kings? Any stories or histories of how the wicked kings lie in some sort of bewitched state, waiting only for a chance to rise again?"

"A strangely random question on an arcane topic, Deputy Courier," said Luviara with a troubling smile. "As it happens, many years ago I was sent out by my order to inventory all the Heart Temples in the empire. They wished to see if there was any clue as to why Palls rose where they did and not in other places. If temples and their associated roads might be implicated somehow. Before I left, I spent months digging into the deepest and dustiest archives in the palace. I had always believed the long-lost sorcerer-kings were simply a literary device who appear in the works of the most overwrought dramatic poets or the more fanciful playwrights. Yet, in the oddest corners of the archives, I instead discovered oblique and fragmentary references to a great war in ancient times against wicked kings whose sorcery was draining the life from all that lay around them. The archivists dismiss these as villagers' tales. Superstitious nonsense. Folk drama. Like the belief that the imperial roads were mortared with the crushed bones of holy venerables and thus are able to repel the Pall by means of their lingering moral righteousness."

"Yes, I've heard that tale in Orledder Intendancy," said Elen.

"A shame I've not had the leisure to speak to you at length of the many local tales I am sure you hear on your regular circuit of the Moonrise Hills. As for your question, my curiosity was naturally piqued by these obscure and colorful references. Therefore I have continued to seek out similar stories or traces that might prove such wicked rulers actually reigned long ago. Perhaps the witch roads are proof. Perhaps the Spires and their odd statues present such a trace. But how can we be sure? And why do you ask about the sorcerer-kings?"

At the writing desk, the prince set down his brush, looked straight at Elen, and touched the whip, lying close at hand on the desk.

"I have not heard any such tales from locals, Your Worthiness. Only ghost stories to scare children into bed at night. But I am merely a deputy courier, not an archivist."

"Simo gave you an order, Luviara," added the prince. "Yet, here you still are."

She pressed hand to heart. "Your Highness."

As she went out, Elen almost called after her, to see if she would send Kem up. She couldn't bear to leave without saying goodbye to him. To depart without a final embrace would be so painful. Not more than she could bear, if she had to bear it, but not what she wished for when she was being ordered to walk alone into a perilous land.

"Simo," said the prince, "I require a message to be sent to Warden Hall, informing them of the death of this garrison."

"Yes, Your Highness."

"Do you think Senior Warden Haital serves Astaylin and not me?"

"I would not have said so, Your Highness. Haital has served loyally with the wardens for forty years and has never been seen to involve herself in the palace workings."

"How else could I have been kept in the dark about the blocked road?"

"I confess it is troubling, Your Highness."

"Haital has been in the thick of it for years. While you have been away from the palace for eight years, and you were never in line for a promotion to captain regardless. That's why I trust you."

Simo knelt. "You have done me honor, Your Highness."

"Yes, I have." The prince turned his attention back to the letter he was composing. "Tell Haital to assemble a new, larger garrison for this Vigil and send it north at once. Don't warn of the blocked road. Say nothing. We shall see what happens next. Do it now. Take the deputy courier with you."

"Your Highness?" This last request surprised Simo.

The prince smiled without looking up. "Yes. Make sure the deputy courier stands right beside you when you send the message."

The captain looked confused, but Elen understood. The prince was letting her know that he knew that touching the road would hurt her. He wanted it to. She did not protest, because the pain would be worth discovering the secret of how the wardens were able to send their speedy messages. The armies had griffin scouts and messenger pigeons, even sarpa, but she did not know how the wardens managed swifter communication than either of the other two, and neither did the intendant or any of his people. The prince did not care if she learned now, because he had the power to compel her service and retain her in his household.

But that was a problem for tomorrow.

"Deputy Courier," said Simo. "Come along."

They descended the stairs to the entry floor. Instead of exiting the tower via the ramp, Simo opened a door onto a narrow set of steps that descended one full level into the ground. The passage led to a landing and another door, which he opened with a key hung at his neck. The door opened into a dark tunnel that hummed as if struck by lightning. Elen's bones ached with it. The tunnel was a borehole struck into the road's base. Simo had to stoop. Her head grazed the ceiling. They were underneath the road's pavement, within its foundations. Farther in, only half distinguishable, a silvery glow pulsed in a steady rhythm, exactly like the beat of a heart.

Elen began to sweat, dampness on the back of her neck, a drop stinging in her eye.

"Are you ill?" Simo asked.

"Confined spaces make me nervous," she lied. Surely his errand would not last long. If she breathed slowly, accepted the pain, she could endure it.

He gave her a long look, as if he could hear the lie. "Follow behind me. Don't speak or make any sound or gesture."

She nodded, although it was so dim she wasn't sure he could see her.

He unhooked the key from the chain. In a low voice, he murmured words she could not understand, spoken in a singsong cadence like a children's rhyme. An eerie, wispy light began to limn his face. For an instant, she thought something—a face, a presence—was trying to push itself out of him.

He said, "To this, to that, be free, be bound. To Haital in Warden Hall, these words. Garrison found dead at Far Boundary Vigil. Send double as replacement. These words to Haital in Warden Hall. To that, to this, be bound, be free."

He placed the key in his mouth, on his tongue, and closed his lips. With a sizzling like boiling water, the air hissed. He entered the tunnel, and she followed. For once it was not just her feet that felt the prick of a thousand needles. It was her head, her face, her neck, her torso, her hands, her limbs like a swarm of unseen bees in a rage and she the target of their fury.

Count the paces, she told herself. *One two three four five.*

He stopped, so she stopped, panting in bursts through dry lips and teary eyes. Before them ran a glittering tube that was made not of a physical substance but of silvery light. It ran onward and back, like a tendon strung through the road, linking each Vigil with the others, as blood courses through a body, with the Warden Hall as its distant heart. What the silvery thread was made of, she could not know. That it was powerful, she could feel in the pain thrumming throughout her body, although she touched nothing but her boots to blessedly quiescent bedrock.

Simo knelt, his face lit by this mystery. He opened his mouth and removed the key. Once a stolid iron key, it now shone, light rippling around it. He held it up against the edge of the glow. A presence flashed; the outline of an aery spirit, a chortle of glee, a spin of energy that stirred Elen's hair. The presence vanished into the road of silver light. Headed heartward, for Warden Hall.

Simo stood. Elen retreated, nails dug into her palms, teeth biting her lower lip so she could not groan from the mounting agony of the road's magic. Stumbling, she knocked back into the steps and sat down hard, almost sobbing in relief.

He still had the key, now returned to dull iron. After hooking it back to its chain, he slipped it under his uniform and led her back up the steps.

She wiped her brow, hand slick with sweat, but the pain had gone, and she had survived. She even grinned as she caught her breath. The beauty of it, the revealed mystery, the flash of the spirit: all had been worth it.

"So, it's true," Simo said.

"What's true?"

"The road speaks the truth. You are the most human-seeming aivur I have ever encountered. No wonder the Magnolia Emperor exiled your kind from the empire, when more and more it got to be impossible to tell aivur from human."

"I'm not aivur," she said.

But what if she was? Might that explain the viper? The possibility had never occurred to her in all her years. Not once had anyone said such a thing to her as a child. People had whispered behind their hands about the red-gold color of Ao's stubble of hair as it started to grow out every month, right before it got shaved down again. But El had only ever been called lucky, or blessed, for her ability to scout out Spore.

In all her time in Woodfall Province and Orledder Intendancy, she had never seen an aivur, and why would she have? She only knew what poetry said of them: their dangerous beauty, their uncanny strength, their bitter savagery, how they shone under moonlight, how they ran more swiftly than beasts and loosed arrows with an accuracy unmatched by the best human archers. When actors pretended to be aivur in the plays put on by traveling troupes, they always wore furry vests or animal masks, or pinned tails or wings on their costumes. None of it matched what she knew of herself. She was just a girl who'd grown up into a woman. The viper was a mystery visited upon her by the High Heavens, as some babies were born with six fingers or the gift of luck-seeing. That didn't make them aivur.

She said, "You sent a message by an air spirit. Are you a theurgist?"

"I am not, nor would I wish to be. Carrying air spirits for messages is one of a warden captain's duties. I do not bind them, but they are bound to me by the same process as theurgists bind the salt spirits we release as needed to kill Spore."

"That's how you knew about the swalters up in the hills. The air spirit."

"You remember that." They were passing an open window, so she could see his amused smile.

"It seemed odd to me. Maybe I thought *you* were an aivur. Aren't the aivur said to have enhanced senses?"

"Aivur are dangerous because they are stronger than humans," he said. "They are most dangerous when they can walk among us without us knowing."

"Why do you fear the aivur?"

"Why do you not?"

"I thought they were all gone from the empire, forced outside our borders."

He halted at the door into the map chamber. "You have never served in the east, where we have been fighting the Blood Wolves for years. You have never traveled in the south, where Forest Wolves demand tribute from those who wish to pass through their territory. You have never set foot on the Blasted Coast, where only the Sea Wolves have the means to sail their ships to the scattered ports, where they sell their stolen cargos of fur, gold, and slaves."

"I've heard stories."

"Hearing stories is not the same as experiencing it."

"No, it isn't, is it?" She smiled wryly, then sniffed as a thread of smoke stung at her nose.

Simo said, "What's burning?"

They entered the chamber to find the prince feeding scraps of paper to a flame. The finished message he had written was folded and twice sealed, once with the prince's seal and once with the impression of Lady Eleawona's bear symbol, taken from the underside of the executed aivur's gold badge. He slid the message into a waxed envelope and handed it to Elen.

"Your Highness, may I ask a question?"

He raised his eyebrows. "I'm surprised you ask for permission, since people seem to have grown accustomed to speaking as they wish to me. Go on."

"Why did you send me down into the road with Captain Simo? Just now? I thought such knowledge was held secret by the wardens."

"So that you understand who you serve, Deputy Courier. I have the power to bind you into my service, just as I have the power to allow you to glimpse one of the secrets of the wardens that no outsider is allowed to learn. Do not mistake me for an intendant, or a Manor lord."

"No, indeed, Your Highness. I never would." Now that she had his attention, she went recklessly on. "Does Theurgist Luviara know about the use wardens make of air spirits to convey swift messages? Wouldn't theurgists have to capture such spirits for the wardens?"

"What is your point?"

"I understand Captain Simo's personal loyalty to you. I understand the other wardens' loyalty to the Imperial Order of Wardens. I understand Chief Menial Hemerlin's loyalty, and if he brought in the gagast, then perhaps Fulmo's as well. But I don't understand the theurgist's loyalty to you. What's in it for her?"

"Why should anything be in it for her? The emperor has shown herself to be weak-minded in the matter of her choice for crown prince. Minaylin hasn't the character or the discipline to rule after her, so another prince must rise to the test. The best candidate is me. That's all Luviara need know, especially since her greatest concern, like that of all in the Heart Temple, must be the health and prosperity of the empire."

"I see." Yet Elen could not shake the thought that there was something more to the haunt concealing the news of the griffin and scout's deaths from Luviara.

"You will cross the Pall, deliver the message to Lady Eleawona, wait for a reply, and return."

"If I am allowed to return."

"I have the boy."

"That's not what I meant, Your Highness."

"I know what you meant. It's a risk I'm willing to take. My success is assured if Lady Eleawona and I can cooperate. I will await you at Pelis Manor North. Simo, see her off." He rolled up the precious map, tightly enough that it could fit back into the walking staff, then looked up. "Simo? Did you not hear my command?"

Simo raised a hand to touch his own ear: *Listen.*

Footsteps clumped up the stairs. The viper hissed softly in Elen's heart. Not in a hostile manner. There was something stranger in its sibilance, more like the way the ears hum with the resonance of a bell.

Gevulin turned, grabbing his whip.

Fulmo appeared in the doorway.

Seeing Gevulin, Fulmo knelt—*as he had never knelt to the haunt.*

Had the gagast known all this time? Yet never alerted anyone? But she hadn't time to wonder. A reddish tone chased across the gagast's skin.

The prince cried, "Danger! Fulmo, you may rise."

Fulmo sprang to his feet and crossed to the southern overlook. Because the map room was a workplace, its windows were shielded by a glazed glass that let in light but not wind. The gagast opened one of the windows and gestured outside. The prince hurried over and looked out.

"Simo, my spyglass."

"It is downstairs, Your Highness. In the chamber where you recovered from your faint."

"Fetch it at once!"

As Simo went out, Kem slipped in and dropped Elen's pack at her feet. "Thought you might want this." He had the skill of anticipation, which he'd honed over years of dealing with his mother. "I added a few things I found in the barracks. Those poor folks can't use them now, but we can."

She met his eye and nodded, then pointed with her chin toward the door, eager to get him out of the prince's view. He hustled out.

The prince hadn't even noticed Kem's entrance. Gevulin was still gazing south, shading his eyes as he tried to perceive whatever it was that had alarmed Fulmo.

Elen got out her own spyglass and took it over to him. He grabbed it out of her hand, raised it to his eye, peered intently, then frowned in disgust.

"This is an inferior instrument. How does it adjust?"

"If I may, Your Highness."

He allowed her to take it. She raised it to her eye and targeted back down the long, straight road, adjusting the lens until the distance popped into view. The quiet landscape, the empty road . . . No, not empty. There was movement.

Charging north on the road, at speed and headed for the Vigil, came a force of at least two hundred riders mounted on bull elks.

8

NINE IS NOT ENOUGH TO FIGHT

"Duenn Manor," Elen said, handing the spyglass to the prince. "Unless Pelis Manor rides bull elks. And flies an antler banner."

He peered through the spyglass, waved Simo over and had him look.

"How can this be?" the prince demanded. "If the road is blocked, and it takes weeks more to go around by the Northwest Road?"

"It can't be Lord Duenn himself," Elen said, "but it could be his militia, since Duenn Manor lies in this same province—"

"Of course I know that! I meant how would they know I am here?"

"Messenger pigeon?" suggested Simo, still with the spyglass to his eye. "Or the sarpa rider?"

"Even so, it's a journey of weeks along ordinary roads and paths to get here from the home territory of Duenn Manor. They're far to the southwest."

Simo lowered the spyglass. "Your Highness, we cannot fight them."

"Why would we need to fight them? They cannot possibly think to assault a prince of the Third Estate! Let their leader be brought before me."

Elen and Simo exchanged a glance. For once she could see she and the captain were in complete agreement. The prince wasn't going to budge as long as he believed his rank protected him.

"Your Highness, I beg your pardon," Simo said, "but princes of the Third Estate have been killed before."

"By the emperor! How could a mere meritorious Manor lord possibly dare raise a hand to me?"

Simo said, "If they do have a sarpa at their disposal, as we suspect, then our bodies can as easily become charred corpses jumbled in with the others."

"But then the Sarpa Corps will be blamed. There would be an investigation."

"We'll still all be dead!" cried Elen, losing patience. "If anyone can even identify our corpses. It was just luck that Xilsi recognized

Captain Mekvo's sword. All anyone will know for sure is that you vanished on the road, no one the wiser. Eaten by Spore. Dragged off by the same bandits who burned the hallow-wood plantations. Fallen into a privy."

The prince was clearly still struggling with the idea that his exalted person might be assaulted by his social inferiors. "What business does Duenn Manor have with me, regardless?"

Elen's fear for Kem made her press on. "Your Highness, did you not insult Lord Duenn at Orledder Halt?"

"For supporting Prince Astaylin's intrigues and machinations! I had to put him in his place when he dared to speak to me!"

"Of course, Your Highness," said Simo in a soothing tone. "But the deputy courier is correct."

"How so?" The prince's anger buzzed like a charge in the air. He hadn't drawn his whip, but he might at any moment.

Elen broke in again, impatient with his unwillingness to grasp the danger. "The arrival of a troop of Duenn Manor soldiers may be a mere coincidence, perfectly harmless. Maybe they hope to escort you back to the heartland in exchange for your goodwill. Lord Duenn may have been impressed by the way you belittled him in front of so many people. He may wish to abase himself and prove his worth to you."

"Watch your tongue," muttered Simo.

"This is not the time to watch our tongues! I won't let anyone from Duenn Manor get close to Kem!"

"What has Kem to do with this?" Simo asked, then grimaced. "Ah, I recall it now. Lord Duenn was threatening to force the lad to rescind his previous Declaration, was he not? An unthinkable thing to do. I understand why Kem wanted to escape that situation. But he's a warden now. Out of Lord Duenn's reach, no matter what."

"Not if the prince is dead!" She turned back to the prince, too angry to speak with the cringing flattery princes expected. "Negotiate if you wish, Your Highness. But at least allow Kem to ride away or hide until we know what their intentions are."

"Enough!" snapped Simo.

But the prince set the spyglass again to his eye and, after a long look, lowered it. Through gritted teeth, he said to Elen, "You truly believe they mean to kill me."

"It looks like a war party to me," Elen said. "We are alone, exposed, and vulnerable. Lord Duenn has no reason to wish you well. And every reason to assist Prince Astaylin."

"There's nowhere to hide," said the captain, "but we could take the horses and split up."

"Run like a coward," muttered the prince. "I'd be laughed out of the palace. Never able to show my face again."

"They don't know we are here," said Elen. "They only think we must be. If we're not here, there's no reason for them to think we fled. Only that they missed us. Sometimes the best course of action is to not engage. This is one of those times, Your Highness. You know I'm correct. I gauge they'll arrive here in less than two hours. We need to move *now*."

"We need to choose our strategy first!" The prince drew his whip and ran its length through one cupped hand contemplatively. "Nine is not enough to fight. The necessity galls . . . and yet, here we are. Very well."

"Horses can't outrun elk," said Simo, shaking his head. "We would have to split up."

"No, I have a better idea," said the prince. "We'll conceal ourselves where they cannot find us."

"Beneath the tower, under the road?"

"No. We hide in the Pall."

"Your Highness, that's not possible."

"It's possible. The deputy courier crossed this very Pall at this very crossing point many years ago, did she not?" The prince fixed his gaze on her.

"She did, Your Highness," Elen replied with the obedience he expected.

Simo stared in disbelief. Fulmo's expression she could not read.

The prince tapped her on the shoulder with his whip. "What do you recommend, Deputy Courier?"

"Your Highness, if Fulmo can carry each person on his back and cross to the turtle-back rock, then you can conceal yourselves on its other side, out of view. It's likely the Duenn militia will search the Vigil, find only the dead, and leave."

"What if they don't leave?" asked Simo.

The prince considered, then took up the plan. "The deputy courier will take the horses as far south and east as she can and let them loose. The militia will follow that trail. Eventually they'll give up."

"If you take enough supplies, you can wait them out," said Elen.

"There's an isolated causeway beyond the turtle-back rock. It was once possible to reach it when the tides emptied the channel of Pall for an hour or more. Once across, you can camp on the causeway safely enough and return here once the Duenn militia departs."

The prince tucked the whip back into its loop. "Deputy Courier, you'll take your pack and go with the horses immediately."

Simo whistled. The door opened so quickly that it was obvious Kem had been standing there the entire time, listening.

Simo said, "Novice, go tell the others to saddle two of the horses, string up the rest, and gather gear and supplies."

"Yes, Captain." Kem glanced at Elen, and she waggled a hand to show that it was all right. He added, "What about the carriage, Captain?"

"No time. We will have to leave it."

"Novice!" To Elen's surprise, the prince spoke directly to Kem. "The tower facilities must have a supply of perfumed paper. Find it and bring it."

"Your Highness!" Kem bobbed a bow and hustled out.

Elen said, "I'll go now and meet you later on the turtle-back rock."

She slung on her pack as she ran down the steps after Kem. "Forget about the perfumed paper."

"What is 'perfumed paper'?" he called over his shoulder.

"Latrine paper."

"Perfumed?"

"I guess that's what princes are accustomed to. As for what we'll need—"

"Ipis and I already collected an extra square of oilcloth with stakes for shelter, a second tinder box, a spade, a hatchet, a couple of jars of lamp oil, and more rope and knives. Xilsi gathered up every shrive-steel blade she could find, and a cache of salt spirit vials. All for the journey back, I mean."

"That's a good haul."

"They know what they're doing. They're skilled wardens. I like them!"

They reached the courtyard.

She gave him a hard hug. "You know the rules."

"Don't get distracted or sloppy. No shortcuts. Stick to the routine. Stay calm. Aunt . . ." He rubbed at his eyes, sucking up tears. "Don't get caught."

"I haven't yet." She punched his shoulder. Then they hurried into the stables.

"What's got you looking like bees got in your shirt?" said Xilsi. She was bundling up a dozen shrive-steel blades.

Kem gave Xilsi and Ipis a quick and efficient rundown, no excess explanation.

"Fuck," muttered Ipis.

Xilsi said, "Let Jirvy go with you, Elen."

"He can't. I'm the only one who can do this part of it."

Ipis said, "I don't get it."

Kem was already hauling out saddles. "Ip, come on," he said, and the other warden hurried over. The two worked together smoothly, but Elen couldn't help but notice how it was Kem who took the lead.

Xilsi offered Elen a shrive-steel short sword and a little leather pouch. "Salt spirits. They have plenty here. You take care, El. I'm going to find Jirv."

"And Luviara," said Elen.

At the door, Xilsi paused with a snort of laughter. "That old coot! She won't let herself get left behind once she finds out there's a way to cross over the Pall. Or into the Pall. If we all die of Spore, my ghost is coming back to haunt you, I hope you know that."

"I'll count on it," said Elen.

The warden flipped her a rude hand gesture and went out.

As in a play, with exits and entrances, Fulmo arrived to accept a load of supplies.

"How soon will the militia get here?" Ipis asked nervously.

"I'm guessing about two hours," Elen said.

"Horses are ready," said Kem.

They led the string out past the corral and to the inner wall. At the gate, she mounted the lead horse, with the other seven on a string behind her.

"Kem, get moving!" she barked.

His anxious face settled into a determined grimace, and he saluted her with all the ironic bluster of a youth trembling on the cusp of adulthood, then ran back to the barracks. Jirvy and Xilsi rushed past with a wave of their arms, too like farewell.

Luviara appeared at the top of the ramp, beckoning toward Elen instead of sending her off. "Deputy Courier! A word, before you go!"

"No time!" shouted Elen, and she rode out.

9

Goats on the Rubble

She continued on through the outer gardens to the outer gate. From there, she headed east, cross-country. The land was burned black from the shore of the Pall for the regulation five hundred paces, and this boundary was further marked by a ditch that ran parallel to the Pall's edge. She kept to the landward side of the ditch. The vegetation was sparse: cold-weather grass and ground cover, and a few hardy shrubs. Every now and then a shallow stream flowed Pallward. The horses were eager to go.

She rode for a while, checking to make sure they left a trail of hoofprints and crushed grass, nothing that would be spotted immediately, but enough that a good tracker would find it once the war party's commander started searching more widely. Who was its commander?

Lord Duenn had many children by multiple wives and concubines. Duenn, like some provincials, held to archaic notions about the service he expected his children to provide to Duenn Manor. He expected his sons to prove their martial worthiness, and his daughters their fertility in marriages that would gain him useful alliances and grandchildren to be utilized, once they were old enough.

The unit she'd seen through the spyglass was a big troop, two hundred at least, and it might only be a vanguard. Not an army but, in provincial terms, a force to be reckoned with. In this case, a force large enough to be sure of killing a rival prince traveling with a small retinue, and then of disposing of the evidence. The prince's body could be pitched into the Pall and never found.

Never found, but for a shadow winding its way through the mist. No. This was not the time to think of the haunt. Don't get distracted.

She guided the horses inland, toward a line of juniper. The trees gave her cover as she rode, keeping an ear cocked for any sound of pursuit. A lazy wind was blowing from the northwest. After about an hour, she finally heard the shuddering blat she associated with Duenn Manor's ram's-horn trumpet.

At the next streamlet, she loosed two of the horses, slapped their flanks, and sent them on their way. They headed south, and she hoped they knew where they were going. Then again, horses usually did.

She rode a while longer before loosing two more. Rode on, loosed another two. A gust of wind shivered the branches of the juniper. She took it as a signal and rode back, Pallward, to the ditch. The remaining horses grew nervous, dancing sideways, reluctant to get any closer to the Pall. At the ditch, she halted, dismounted, and released them. They snorted, tossed their heads, and headed south at a run, away from the Pall.

After leaping the ditch, she picked her way across the scoured strip. The Imperial Order of Wardens took their humble scouring duty seriously. There would be watchposts farther on, garrisoned by sentinels, but this close to the Vigil, the warden menials had the responsibility to burn and salt. A few stubborn seedlings poked tiny stalks upward, out of the stony soil. She plucked them out of the dirt, although she hated to rip the life from them only because they had the ill luck to have gotten their start in forbidden ground. It reminded her of her years as an atoner. She didn't want to hold the knife of life and death. It gave her no pleasure, but in this case, it had to be done.

She sniffed at each scrap of plant, sensing nothing, but to be sure, she set her palm onto the ground. Pain burned through her flesh, and the viper emerged, tongue tasting the air. It wasn't interested in the uprooted plants, which meant they weren't infested by Spore. Instead, it slithered eagerly Pallward. It would come back to her, as it always had before.

As night settled over the land, Elen headed west, back toward the Vigil. She walked about a body's length from the shoreline of the Pall. The viper chased in and out of the mist alongside her, and she let it run, although she wasn't sure if it was feeding or exploring. About a league away, the Vigil tower's holystone walls gleamed like a glimmer of hope, like a promise of haven. Yet what hope or haven could it offer when such a place was overtaken by a rivalry between princes?

She scanned the pale mist. Sparks like fallen stars flashed here and there, but no shadow curled through the shallows. The haunt was gone. He had a duty. So did she, if by duty she meant she had to keep Kem alive. To keep Kem alive, she had to keep the prince alive.

Yet it wasn't only that. The emperor was a master preferable to the rule of Lady Eleawona and the masters of the nameless land mostly because the masters ruled through personal violence, intimately, while the emperor ruled from behind the screen of the palace, through bureaucracy. Laws backed by force were the architecture atop which the empire had built its power. Up in the hills, on ordinary lanes and behind unprotected walls, the imperial hand still fell, but it fell lightly because those places were of such little account that the imperial wardens didn't even carry maps of the outer intendancies, not as surveyors did. Thinking of surveyors made her recall the intendant's offer that she be allowed to train as a surveyor.

That was wishful thinking, given her current circumstance, so she set the thought aside. The prince was not going to release her now that he knew what a valuable weapon she could be in his hands.

The closer she got to the Vigil, the harder she listened. Had the prince escaped across to the turtle-back rock? Had the others—had *Kem*—escaped with him? *Don't get distracted.* Each step was the only step that mattered in this moment. Her footfalls were but an insignificant tread on the stony ground. The wind would blow away the marks of her passing soon enough. The haunt was gone. Ao was gone. But others she cared for still lived. Even striding alongside the eerie and deadly Pall, the world was still beautiful. The stars bright overhead, the half-moon risen with a serene beauty.

A song she hadn't thought about for years rose in her mind. A song the child atoners sang when they walked ahead of, or behind, the masters, as if a melody could be a protective talisman.

> *Old hand, old ghost, pray, stay away.*
> *Old hand, old ghost, you had your day.*
> *Once you wore a crown of light,*
> *On your brow it shone so bright,*
> *Fed by souls you burned that day.*
> *Old hand, old ghost, pray, stay away.*

Now, she wondered at the song. What had the haunt said about Flat Pall?

It tastes like ashes.

Elder Marillion had been correct about the Spires and haunts, hadn't he? That story about his grandfather's friend who had returned from a night at the Spires wearing the same face but with a stranger's eyes? Sometimes village stories and children's songs concealed truths that had been mostly forgotten. The passage of years and generations obliterated so many things. Even so close as she was to the nameless land of her early life, she recalled it only in snatches and bursts. Ao had remembered more. Too much more.

Ahead, lights bobbed and shifted along the palisade that surrounded the outer grounds of the Vigil. She walked forward without fear that they would see her. They wouldn't be looking at the edge of the Pall. No one would approach the shoreline this close at night, when Spore was most likely to rise. The viper whipped in and out of view. Twice, she saw it hook its fangs into a dandelion-wisp crawling out of the mist and toward her.

Even so, when she was close enough to the Vigil to hear human voices calling to each other as they searched the compound, she braced herself and made the decision she'd known was coming. Not since that last day of her and Ao's escape had she touched Pall, much less purposefully waded into its shallows. Maybe it was mere chance and Heaven-sent fortune she'd survived that time without being devoured by Spore. Maybe this time she would sprout two heads as her body was eaten away from inside in agonizing distortions and her voice torn into a whistle of agony.

The world didn't care about her fears, her loves, her hopes. She was just another seedling that might be plucked out of the earth to wither, or to grow, for a few days more. She had to find out where Kem was, and what had happened to the others.

She set her palm against the ground. The viper crawled back into her with a charge like lightning through her flesh. No point in hesitating. What would happen, would happen. The viper pulsed in her heart, as it had for so long. Its constancy gave her courage. She waded in.

As she forged outward, the mist did not get deeper, precisely. The surface of the Pall remained more or less level, so where the ground dipped, she descended, and where it rose, she ascended, the mist rising to her hips and then dropping to her calves. She felt a pressure against her not as heavy as water nor yet as light as air. Its scent bore the barest ashy residue.

Trailing a hand through the water, she said, "Sara'ala, if you are there, know I still think of you. That I will always remember you. Be well, my heart."

There was no answer except for the mist curling icily around her ankles as it tried to find purchase in her flesh. When it could not, it flowed around and past her, as if she were a stone in its current that annoyed it: *You don't belong here.* But it was just a whisper. It couldn't touch her.

She reached the outer edge of the Vigil, marked on its Pallward side by the holystone embankment. By creeping along the stones, she got all the way to the road's causeway where it thrust into the Pall. Through the dark of the night, she could see the "pier" of the causeway lit by lamps out to where the road ended, its stub demarked by a hallow-wood railing.

Two militiamen holding lanterns were pacing the causeway. She hung to the shadows, crouched low. Three people approached from the tower. From this angle, she couldn't see much in the gloom, only that one wore an officer's tabard and walked with a soldier's upright bearing. The second was tall and thick and powerfully built. The third, shorter and slighter, stood wrapped in a long cloak with a hood tugged low to obscure their face.

"Have you found anything?" The harsh, surly voice struck a blow to her heart. It was Lord Duenn!

How could he be here? It should have taken days to re-rig the rope bridge across Grinder's Cut. If there was another secret crossing, she'd have heard whispers of it, given the network of trust she'd cultivated over the years. Meanwhile, the imperial road north was still blocked. Wasn't it?

Then she remembered the goats on the rubble. She'd thought them local to Olludia Halt, but what if they weren't? What if a path through the avalanche, sufficient for goats, had been cleared? What if people could cross on foot on that same trail, and pick up mounts and carriages on the other side? Yet where had this large troop of mounted soldiers come from, then? The palace army didn't stable elks, who weren't suited to the warmer climate of the south. Lord Duenn hadn't had this many soldiers with him when he'd reached Orledder Halt, and Duenn Manor's territories were too far away for an army to have both been summoned and then have arrived here so quickly. Yet Pelis Manor had received an offer of a marriage alliance. And someone was vandalizing Pelis Manor's new hallow-wood plantations.

Yet here he was. At that moment, a thought slithered into her mind, a hunter's thought, cold and ruthless. What if she loosed the viper and killed him? Would that free Kem from the threat of being forcibly returned to Duenn Manor in the event of the prince's death?

One of the lantern bearers trotted up and bowed. "My lord, there's no sign of bloodshed on the causeway."

Duenn turned to the officer. "Might they be among the burned corpses?"

The slightly built and hooded figure stirred. A light, smooth voice emerged, so cultured that Elen tensed, for the diction had the same cadences as Gevulin's, only without the contemptuous arrogance. Instead, it was all silk and honey. Yet as the unseen person spoke, Elen's viper stirred as if to alert her to a more pressing danger than Lord Duenn.

"No, he was not with the garrison when the sarpa attacked. If Gevulin came here, as we know he intended to do, then he came afterward. The map room was much disturbed, troubled by hasty hands looking for what cannot be known. The Vigil captain's bed was recently slept in. Gevulin was here. The only question is, where did he go and how did we miss him?"

The two lantern-holding soldiers dropped to their knees and covered their faces. "Your Sublime Highness, we are at fault. We did not recognize you."

"Do not trouble me with this display. Arise. Do your duty."

Footsteps clapped in the shadows. A figure ran into view, dropping immediately to one knee. "Your Sublime Highness. My lord. The hounds have found a scent. Horses, more than one. They left the road, south of the palisade gate, and headed east."

Duenn's voice was a crow of triumph. "Excellent! We'll have them now! My elks can outpace horses."

"Leave a force to garrison the Vigil, in case Gevulin has laid a false trail," said the Sublime Highness. "Clean up the remains of the dead and throw them into the Pall. There must be no hint we have been here. No trace that a sarpa was ever here. Captain, keep searching. Maybe they're hiding, although that's not Gevulin's style."

"Yes, Your Sublime Highness." The officer bowed and, accompanied by the two lantern bearers, headed back to the tower.

The hooded prince stood a while longer, staring at the Pall. From here, at night, even the turtle-back rock wasn't visible, only the haze. The slow *shush-shoom* of the Pall's sluggish currents gave the cloudy night a melody, by turns calming and threatening.

At length, the Sublime Highness shook off this seeming trance. "Duenn, escort me back to the map room. There's something I'm missing, and I don't know what it is."

10

A Clout on the Head

She'd missed her chance to kill Lord Duenn. A single bite from the viper would suffice. That's how she'd killed the Duenn Manor captain who had assaulted Ao. But this time, her shock had frozen her. The viper's restlessness had distracted her.

Was Lord Duenn traveling with Prince Astaylin? Who else could the Sublime Highness be?

She had to warn the others. They'd need a new plan. More than anything, she didn't like the way they'd been cornered. Had Prince Astaylin, like a shepherd, been driving Gevulin to the corral where she wanted him confined for the slaughter? Could princes act so boldly against each other? Didn't they fear the emperor finding out and putting a stop to it? Elen simply did not understand the currents that ebbed and swelled in the palace, those waters of intrigue and the bloody winds of death. Life was precious, or it ought to be. People shouldn't be treated as fodder for the highborn's skirmishes, yet of course they were. The dead garrison were no different from atoners in that way. They'd died because they'd gotten in the way of someone else's poisonous plot.

Maybe Prince Gevulin had just been trying to defend himself all along. Maybe he wasn't so bad. Or maybe he was, and she just wanted to pretend she still saw glimpses of the haunt in him.

She swept a hand through the Pall, stirring the mist as the haunt had done at Flat Pall. Could he sense her, if she willed it hard enough? Beneath the icy touch of the Pall, ropy tendrils brushed against her, as fish tickle your toes in a stream, nosing against you to see if they can feed on you.

She snatched her hand out of the mist and made her way along the causeway to its broken end. From here, even after all these years, she knew the way across, felt as if the Pall recognized her. The weight of that passage—when she thought she had left Ao forever and that she would die never knowing if Ao lived—had baked itself into her heart, into her bones, into her soul. You did not leave the ones you loved, not unless you had no other choice. These fragile ties wove the world together, for if they were not honored, then what was left?

When Ao had taken the captured child from her hip that day, and pushed him toward his outlaw father, El had protested, but she'd not reached out to grab back the boy. He deserved better than an atoner's life, even if an outlaw's life ended in just as cruel a death. All of life ended in death. At least with his father, he'd walk into death of his own will, by his own decision.

A whistle pierced the night—once, twice, thrice—its shrill piping a blade grinding into her bones. She'd never heard any sound so physically painful. The viper went taut until the after-tones of the long blasts faded.

It was time to go. She mustn't linger, caught in the looping maze of memory.

She moved carefully through the dark, testing each unseen step on the stony ground, over the rubble of the collapsed bridge. The haze was strong. Clouds covered the stars. Although the Vigil tower shone, its light was a beacon, not a spear. Duenn's people wouldn't see her.

She sensed the steep slope of the turtle-back rock before she saw it. Clambering out, she loosed the viper and sat in stillness as it inspected her to make sure no Spore escaped her body. But there was no passenger Spore. She climbed to the top of the rock, calling softly to warn the others. No answer came.

No one waited on the other side of the rock. All that greeted her was a wide channel of Pall seething with a glimmer of currents like a tide coming in. It was too dark, too hazy, too far to see the next section of the causeway. She didn't dare call out, lest someone at the Vigil hear.

She bent her head, praying they'd simply gone on. Not lost to the Pall, not that. If the "tide" had gone out, the others might have crossed in haste. Maybe to then repent in leisure, realizing they were trapped on the severed causeway, but the tides would recede, as tides did. And they had Fulmo with them.

Could Fulmo be an agent of Astaylin? Had he led Lord Duenn and his noble companion to the Vigil? No, she didn't believe it. For one thing, it was Hemerlin who had brought Fulmo into Gevulin's service. Strangely, after all this time, she found she trusted Hemerlin to have done his best by the prince he served. Seen from a distance, the old man's ill temper might be taken more as protectiveness of his prince than jealousy of his status as chief menial. Gevulin's movements were easy enough to trace from his stops upon the road.

She set out across the next gap. She had to believe Kem was waiting for her on the causeway. She even had it in her heart that she wanted to make sure Xilsi, Ipis, and Jirvy were alive and well, that Simo and Luviara had survived. Even the prince, if only because, at moments, when she glanced at him, she could not help but see the memory of the haunt's rascal smile. Even if that was only what she wished to see, not what was truly there.

It was a long slog, mist curling and swirling around her knees, her thighs, her calves, up and down, and once all the way to her waist, as cold as the grip of snow. But she pushed on because she always pushed on. One step, and the next, and the next.

A jingle of sound whispered from up ahead.

They were alive! Heart pounding, steps quickening, she hurried to reach the jumble of stone that was all that remained of the wingwall and abutment of this end of the bridge. It was steeper than she remembered. Her hands were so stiff with cold that she struggled to get a grip, but she climbed, teeth chattering. Her right hand grabbed the edge of the roadway. She heaved herself up.

A broad hand caught her under the arm and yanked her up with such strength that, for an instant, she lost all contact with the earth—and then was slammed down onto her back, wind knocked out of her as her pack jammed sideways into her ribs. A flood of pain coursed up through her backside, where it touched the surface of the road. Only her clothing separated her from the stinging pavement. Her head buzzed, and her teeth hurt.

A lantern swayed into view above her head. A voice spoke words she did not know, in a language she did not recognize.

A face loomed over her. A sharp face to match the sharp words. A humanlike face of steely beauty, ears with tufted points, spiky, steel-gray hair, although its color was not from old age, if the smoothness of their complexion was anything to go by. An axe was strapped across the person's back. But it was their yellow eyes that really stunned her.

A Sea Wolf. What else could this stranger be?

Their keen gaze sharpened with a sudden distrust, as if they'd seen something bad. The flat of a blade pressed against her chest, pinning her down. With the hilt of a knife, they pushed her braid away from the curve of her neck. Seeing the wavy scar that curled up behind her ear, the Sea Wolf recoiled with a hiss followed by a gesture like a warding against evil.

The light overhead snapped out, as if it hadn't been flame but something stranger, an essence of light controlled by one who had the power to summon a fire spirit.

Dragged upward by people she now couldn't see because of the abrupt darkness, she was roughly hauled away from the edge of the roadway, and her arms were yanked behind her back. They had horses. The jingle she'd heard was a harness.

"Where are the others?" she asked. "Can I at least sit up properly?"

A clout on the head answered her.

A buzz of conversation, again in an unknown language, swirled around her as she was rolled over, her wrists and ankles tied, and then heaved up and over a saddle. She could barely discern her attackers because of the awkward way she'd been bundled on her stomach. From this upside-down position, she saw no boots on the ground. Everyone around seemed to have mounted. How could there be horses here?

The group began moving. The pressure of the saddle against her gut, and the increasing dizziness created by her head bobbing and swaying below her heart, made it impossible for her to do more than barely hold on to consciousness as the mounted riders raced north on the causeway. North, toward the nameless land.

11

Rising to Meet Her

After an agonizing ride that dragged on and on and on, they finally halted. Elen was too dazed to struggle as they slung her off the horse and into the bed of a wagon. A wagon! Its presence made no sense, but she was too muddled to grapple with what it might mean.

Instead, she slid into a half-conscious doze, then into a hard sleep.

After an unknown time, she woke. The wagon was still moving. She had no idea whether it had ever stopped, or how long she'd been out. Her bound hands tingled behind her back. Her shoulders ached. At least her feet weren't numb, only tied together loosely to make sure she couldn't run. Yet where would she run? Into the Pall? Aivur could follow her. For now, she had a hope of finding out what had happened to Kem and the others.

She lay atop empty sacks that smelled of barley and oats, of all things. The wagon rolled along at a decent clip, accompanied by thumps like the beating of a drum and a robust voice speaking singsong words that rose and fell with the rhythm of a work tune. How had the Sea Wolves gotten a wagon and horses onto the causeway? Why was the ride so smooth? The sound was all wrong for iron wheels on uneven stone.

She lurched over onto her side and struggled up to sit. The cloudy night made it difficult to see, but she guessed it was getting close to dawn.

A lantern swung from a post set into the driver's bench. Farther ahead, another runner carried a lantern to light the way. It was easy to see over the heads of the people braced in the harness.

People! Not horses or oxen or mouflon, but twelve people in a harness pulled the wagon. They pressed forward, jogging in unison. Were these human slaves? Thank the High Heavens she and Ao hadn't turned north!

Two people sat side by side on the driver's bench. The passenger was silent, while the driver was singing. In a strong voice, the driver repeated melodic words, like a refrain, and left an empty space into which the people braced in the harness could shout a reply in jolly voices, if a bit strained of breath.

The shared chant with its laughter, coming from the people in the harness, wasn't even the most shocking thing. The wagon was running along a surface made of planks. It looked as if the entire roadway had been covered with planks, half set aside for travelers and the other half for a column of wagon after wagon at rest along the route. This was apparently an encampment strung along one side of the causeway. Canvas awnings protected the beds of the wagons from rain or snow. At intervals, horses were tied up along the lines. The wooden planks separated the wagons, horses, and people from direct contact with the road.

Now and again, Elen glimpsed faces illuminated by lantern light. Many seemed as human as her own, whatever that meant. Others, like the steely soldier who had dragged her up onto the causeway, had human-enough faces, but were favored with an inhuman quality of sleek beauty or glittering menace that made them look utterly different from humankind. A prominent nose gave one the look of an alert eagle. Thin nose and lips and pointed ears gave another the sharp-faced intelligence of a rat, although they might have passed unremarked in the crowded common room of a busy inn. Probably to do shady business in a back room with smugglers, she thought, and then was ashamed of herself. She knew better than to judge folk based on first impressions and old prejudices.

In slow stages, light limned the eastern horizon, shading the hazy Pall to a pink-yellow undertone. The passenger seated on the driver's bench opened the lantern's glass door and, with bare fingers, pinched the flame dead.

Shouting erupted ahead of them. Whoops burst from the people in the harness. Ahead, people gathered in two columns, one on either side of the open lane. As the wagon approached, they all began clapping to the same rhythm as the unison pound of feet. Some of the waiting people set out at a jog. One by one, they shouted a word, were answered by someone pulling the harness, then ducked in, at speed, as the person who had been pulling ducked out. Switching places while in motion! Like it was a game.

It was so terrifying that Elen found herself holding her breath, awaiting disaster with each dash and duck.

There it came!

As one ducked in, the one ducking out missed their footing and stumbled. They fell right in front of the wagon—which kept moving! A roar of cheers and jeers drowned out any screams. The wagon didn't falter. Elen braced for a sickening thud, but there was nothing. As the wagon rolled on, the fallen aivur emerged from beneath the wagon, tucked up into a ball. The wheels had missed him. He got to one knee, rubbing a shoulder. As the scene receded, the wagon charging on, Elen watched as the people around him laughed and mocked him. And he was laughing too!

She panted, as if she was the one who had been hauling the wagon all night. As if she had fallen and barely missed being slammed by the inexorable turn of events.

The sun was rising. The deadly mist stirred with unseen currents. There was no sign of land in either direction because of the obscuring haze.

A body thumped down beside her. The passenger had dropped over the driver's bench to sit on the sacks, regarding Elen. She had a lean, attractive face, her dark complexion enhanced with a silvery shimmer, as if subtly dusted with glitter powder. Her stare was direct and unforgiving, but it was her eyes that really gave Elen pause. They had no white, just a curve of brown so dark that the black pupil was barely visible in contrast.

She spoke in what Elen thought was the same language the other Sea Wolf had used. Her voice was like distant thunder, low, dark, and with the promise of a coming storm.

"I don't understand your words," said Elen. "My hands are going numb. I'm no threat to you. Might you untie me?"

"No threat? To be sure, that is a lie. You are *osge*. What did you do with the deputy courier meant to be following behind the others?"

Elen puffed out a relieved breath at the mention of the "others." They might or might not be safe, but this aivur knew of them. She patted her own chest. "I am the deputy courier."

"Ne, ne, it cannot be, for if you were, then they would have warned me you are osge."

"I don't know what osge means." She thought back through the encounter. "Are you talking about my scar? It's just a scar." She tilted her head sideways, her braid slipping down her back, to display the side of her neck.

The Sea Wolf hissed, exactly as the other one had, and made the same warding gesture. "Not even the highborn warned us."

"The highborn? The prince?"

"It is impolite to say nothing, at the least, and a breach of alliance, at the worst, to not mention it."

"I don't think my companions know the word either. Nor is the scar anything unusual to them." Elen paused. The aivur said nothing, just watched her with those uncanny eyes, so she went on, "Are the others . . . alive?"

"They were alive when I spoke with them and sent them onward."

"Spoke with them? Are you—" She broke off. Was this company of aivur the Salt Spear Clan, and thus Lady Eleawona's allies? Yet on the chance they weren't, this was not the time or place to give away Prince Gevulin's desperate alliance. She dredged down through her conversations with Luviara, searching for any secondhand knowledge she could wield.

"Am I what?" asked the aivur with an amused lift of her mouth.

"Are you a bequeather? The interlocutor, we would say."

"A bequeather is not an interlocutor, but, yes, I am that one among my clan."

"I am called Elen. Is there a name I may call you?"

"You may call me Captain Raven."

The bequeather touched two fingers to her own forehead, then leaped gracefully off the back of the wagon, landing lightly. A soldier whose hair stuck up in a spiky rooster's crest brought her a saddled horse. She swung on and headed north at a gallop.

Onward the wagon went, all day. Four times Elen asked for something to drink, and four times was ignored. At intervals, the haulers swapped out for a fresh set of harness-pullers with the same reckless ritual. The danger itself seemed to be the point. Even the driver swapped out, but the wagon never stopped.

Elen finally could not hold her need to pee, and although she asked for a pause, or a basin, no one answered. She could move her hands just enough to winkle down amid the sacks and pull her trousers partway down, but the whole enterprise was so awkward that some of the urine trickled onto her on own skin and leaked into her clothing. Afterward, the new driver sniffed but mercifully made no comment.

She kicked the sack she'd peed on into a corner of the wagon. She could always pee there again if need be, although as she got dehydrated, she'd have worse things to worry about than urinating on herself. On top of which, she had no way of getting more information from her captors or even trying to strike up a conversation to connect with them. If they were captors. Allies. Enemies? Not friendly, at the very least.

And what was osge? Simo had a scar by his eye, small and unexceptional, not as unusual as the finger-length wavy line of the one on her neck, but everyone had scars, even if most of theirs weren't immediately visible. And where were the others, anyway?

The narrow encampment stretched on and on, stacks of chests and sacks and other bundles of supplies, strings of restless goats, dogs who yapped in excitement as the wagon passed. Children in clusters, babes in arms, toddlers, smalls, and lanky adolescents who reminded her of Kem. Well, if Kem were aivur. Did aivur travel with their families, all together as one?

These bystanders hooted and hollered at the people hauling the wagon and always raised a song to sing them past, stamping and clapping to the rhythm of the twelve pairs of feet running in unison. In its way, it was glorious and heartening. But when the bystanders caught sight of her, their expressions changed, and silence crushed the hearty spirit of their greeting, leaving a hush in her wake.

Definitely, she and Ao had been fortunate when they'd been forced to turn south. She did not feel welcome here. And while she was hungry, she knew how to deal with hunger. It was the thirst that was most debilitating. Thankfully, for a while there came a light rain. She turned her head skyward with mouth open to at least wet her palate. Praise the High Heavens for small gifts.

Twilight came. Lanterns were lit. Night fell, and they rolled on. Elen slept, rocked by the unceasing rhythm. It was better to rest and conserve her energy.

She roused when the wagon stopped.

"Aunt Elen! Are you all right? Why are you tied up?"

She blearily opened her eyes. By the light, she guessed it was dawn. The long journey and lack of drink and food had exhausted her, and her hands had gone entirely numb. But that was Kem's anxious face above her, and his hand shaking her shoulder.

She croaked a relieved sound.

"This is no kind of hospitality from people the prince claims are our allies!" Kem's mouth pinched with anger before he turned away, calling, "Ip, she's here. Can you give me a hand?"

"What you doing here? Where others?" Elen choked out, tongue too thick to form proper sentences.

Kem rolled her onto her side, used his knife to cut the rope that bound her, and helped her sit up. Her shoulders screamed as she shifted them forward. Her hands had no feeling at all.

"You look awful," said Ipis as she hurried into view.

She and Kem helped Elen off the back of the wagon. Her legs worked all right. Kem began massaging her arms, and soon enough, or perhaps too soon, sensation returned in a rush of pins and needles all stabbing at once. They helped her hobble a few steps across the roadbed, whose sting through her booted feet barely registered through the planks.

Ipis sniffed and muttered, "Did they not even let you pee properly? What savages!"

"I don't know if they understood me when I asked to stop and pee. I had to go in the wagon, while it was moving."

"Are you joking?" Ipis looked genuinely puzzled. "We were with the prince. Of course they understood, and halted to let him do his business."

"You'll be glad to hear I found the perfumed paper before we left the Vigil," remarked Kem with a waggle of his brows.

Elen snorted, as close to a laugh as she could manage with all the other sensations flooding her body.

"You can't joke about His Exalted Highness!" protested Ipis.

"Watch me," said Kem with the cocky belligerence that sometimes spat out of him and got him into trouble. He'd never had to learn how to stay small and unnoticed. "Here we are."

"Here" was a sturdy coach. Horses waited in their harness, ready to go, but where were they going? Kem and Ipis helped her inside onto a padded bench. Kem slung her unopened pack at her feet.

Shutters had been slid aside to allow them to look out. The last group of wagon haulers were clambering out of the yoke, accepting cups from their waiting fellows, everyone talking and laughing. A few gestured toward Elen and whispered together with frowning glances. Elen rubbed her forehead, dizzy, disoriented; probably the lack of food.

"Have some bread." Ipis unfolded a length of cloth to reveal flat rounds. "They gifted us this. Oat bread, so nothing fit for the table, but it will fill your stomach."

"She can't eat yet." Kem unstoppered Elen's flask, which she'd not been able to reach while tied up. "Just a few sips first," he ordered fussily.

She sipped obediently at the flask. She'd already drank most of its blend of apple juice and a steeped tisane of white-star flowers during her flight with the horses from the Vigil, but there was enough left to soften her dry mouth and ease her cramping stomach.

The unseen driver gave a whistle and a command. The carriage moved forward.

Kem said, "Do you want me to dig out your spare clothing so you can change out of those stained trousers?"

Elen considered, then shook her head. "If you two can endure the smell, I'd rather wait until I can wash myself. If I change now, I'll end up with two smelly pairs and no clean spare."

She sighed and sank back, able to relax as she shut her eyes. Hooves clipped in a stately rhythm. Wheels creaked on wood.

Kem elbowed her and said, "Look! Look! Wouldn't this be the first crossing you spoke of?"

The first crossing? She leaned out the window. The haze on either side was lightening as the sun rose behind an unbroken canopy of clouds. Ahead, the road broke off: the northern end of the severed causeway. What had taken her and Ao so many days to trudge, the wagon had accomplished in two nights and a day. But it wasn't the end of the causeway and its collapsed pillars and remains of an ancient bridge that caught her attention. That made her mouth drop open.

The aivur had built a rigid bridge of wood and rope across the gap, anchoring it on the old piers. This astounding construction ran above the surface of the Pall, in stages, across the riverbed. Braided channels created streams, both water and Pall. The bridge overarched them all.

The coach moved at a stately pace, its driver understandably cautious. It reminded her of the rope bridge she and the others had pulled into place over Grinder's Cut, only this temporary bridge was far more stable and able to support the weight of a coach-and-four. If the Sea Wolves could wade into the Pall without dying, then they could have built, stage by stage, a long, elevated bridge to link the nameless land to the causeway . . . a causeway that ran south to the Tranquil Empire.

Ipis stared out the other window, onto the Pall. She murmured, "Do you think they're intending to invade the empire? We don't have forts or garrisons to stop them, not along Far Boundary Pall."

"Invade? No. Raid, maybe," said Kem. "This isn't an army. More like refugees, don't you think? Children and old people too. No one sends children into battle."

"Ipis shot him a superior look. "The Sea Wolves are savages. They start training to fight when they're five."

"That's not what Joef says."

"Yes, and provincial Joef knows everything!" Her sarcasm dripped like hot oil sizzling.

"He even went to the heartland once," said Kem, "so I don't know why you don't like him when you've never even met him."

"Can I have a bit of bread?" said Elen. She was hungry, but she also wanted to end their quibbling. Later, when she felt better, she might try to talk to Kem about Ipis's apparent jealousy of Joef, and why the otherwise nice young warden might feel that way. Or maybe she'd keep her mouth closed and let Kem sort it out himself.

Kem handed her a chunk of bread. "Not too much at first. Your eyes are baggy and dark. Mama said that was a sure sign of dehydration."

"Where are the others?"

"They went across already. His Exalted Highness assigned Ipis and me to wait for you."

"Across?" The word sent a chill into her heart. "Where are we going?"

"Wherever the prince went," said Ipis. "Or so we hope. This all seems like a terrible idea, but I guess we had no choice. What happened at the Vigil? How did you get across the Pall? I thought we were leaving you behind, but here you are, not dead of Spore."

Elen rubbed her face wearily. The prince could explain! She wasn't going to.

"Let her be." Kem's gaze was cautious and kind. "Listen, Ip, I know things look bad, and maybe we'll all die, which Joef would say would make a great tragic poem—or maybe a comic one. But I, for one, want to see this 'Farlandia' that lies on the other side. Isn't that why you became a warden? To see the world?"

Ipis muttered, "I did it to get as far from home as I could."

"That bad, huh?" he asked with a commiserating smile.

She shrugged, embarrassed, then lifted her chin as if on a dare. "People are nicer to me in the wardens, that's all. Captain Simo's been keeping an eye on me. He says I remind him of him when he was a novice, which is pretty flattering, given he's risen so high. And I miss Qari. He's a good one, always watching out for the novices.

Jirvy's amazing. Best archer anyone has ever seen. He's always willing to help correct your technique, not in a mean way but in a way meant to help you improve. I want to be him someday. Well, except for the love life. And Xilsi's funny. The biggest snob you will ever meet, but I'll tell you something, Kem, she won't leave a warden behind. That's how she got mixed up in this expedition, because of her friend Mekvo. Anyway, I've said too much."

He bumped shoulders with her. "No, you've said just the right amount. I don't mean to talk about Joef so much. It's just he's like a brother to me. We grew up together. Did everything together. So I miss him."

"Oh," Ipis said, then softly, enviously, "A *brother*."

The juice and bread, like rain on parched ground, was starting to seep strength back into Elen's limbs. Her hands still burned, but the pain was beginning to lessen. She and Kem were together. The prince hadn't left her behind.

Then, for the first time, she saw the dark hills of the nameless land in the distance, the long-buried past rising to meet her. She took in a breath, let it out slowly, bracing herself. There was no turning back now.

12

Written in Cipher

Your subject, Luviara, most humbly and with the greatest devotion for the distinction shown to one who is the least of the emperor's theurgists, sends reverential salutations and a reply unworthy of the emperor's magnificence and benevolence.

It is true, as you have heard rumor of, that the Inner Chamber of the Heart Temple has censored certain entries of my compiled tome, *The Official's Handbook of the Empire*. The Inner Chamber determined that some information was either too volatile or too speculative to be included in a handbook that would be widely distributed among imperial officials, and which might even be read by people outside the sworn seal of officialdom.

With humility and respect, I venture to argue that it is my observation that more knowledge is better knowledge. Knowledge allows those who need to make decisions to filter through and compare more evidence, rather than less. However, the Inner Chamber does not agree. Yet, if we do not examine with a clear gaze the past that lies behind us and the world that spreads around us, then how are we to recognize the dangers and possibilities that lie athwart our path or that arise in the hazy distance that represent potential outcomes?

It has become clear that the Inner Chamber, in coordination with the Primary Council of Archivists, has long cooperated to suppress, conceal, remove, and even destroy an unknown number of documents, chronicles, manifests, poems, and artifacts said to belong to the legendary era that came before the rise of the Seven Golden Kingdoms, which some poets call the Era of the Wicked Sorcerer-Kings.

Most especially, the Inner Chamber and the Primary Council have, in concert, suppressed all public discussion of magic, of which the empire recognizes two forms: theurgy and sorcery.

As is proper, the knowledge of theurgy has, since the establishment of the Tranquil Empire, been restricted to those who dedicate their lives to the Heart Temple and to the service of Your Most Majestic and Benevolent Highness.

Of sorcery, none will speak except to say it is a wicked practice that must never arise again in the world. To this assertion, I can currently give no answer except my usual concern that sorcery, like Spore, can only be rooted out if trained officials, like wardens and couriers and surveyors, know how to recognize and thus destroy it when found.

Yet that is not the whole of my concern. If magic is woven into the world, or if the world is woven of magic, then we humans are not the only peoples in the world who may manipulate unseen lines of intangible power. It has been my great good fortune to have observed and even spoken with some individuals from among the noble peoples who walk the world alongside us. They, too, have their traditions and practices that interact with the weave of the world, even if one such as I can only have glimpsed a tiny corner of the vast tapestry of their lives.

For example, the aivur are said to resemble humans, although with features made more acute by a magic that allows them to share the attributes of beasts. Thus, one aivur might hunt with the remarkable hearing of an owl, while another might be able to dive deeply like an otter into the bitterly cold northern sea without dying of the cold as a human would.

The swalters, meanwhile, live in small clans ruled over by a clan mother, of whom it is said can communicate with her clan members by means of a witchcraft that allows all swalters in a clan to know where each of the others are at all times, and also to be aware of the movement of other creatures, even if out of their sight, even at night, with their third eye.

As the palace well knows, the gagast are immune to all known poisons and venoms. Additionally, they have the facility of armoring themselves against physical attacks, including all common weaponry, although they pay a price for this magical effort. Some in the palace even claim individual gagast can live for what would be generations of human lives, but this remains hearsay. Nor have I ever had the chance to enter territory where gagast live in their own communities, whatever those may look like.

Of dragons, less is known. Sightings are rare and most often reported from the borderlands of the empire. Some insist that even these sightings are fabrications. It is said in some poetical accounts that dragons were in ancient days the most adept at wicked sorcery, being the only creatures able to regenerate themselves faster than their practice of sorcery could drain their life force. But as I have not to my knowledge met nor spoken with a dragon, this magical supposition must, for now, be considered only a poetical fancy.

As for the fregir, they are mentioned in a few ancient chronicles of which only fragments survive, and none are known to walk the world in these days. Still, I wonder, for what if fregir do walk in the world only we do not know it because we cannot see them, or if we do see them, we see them only as they wish to be seen, that is, as ordinary creatures like humans or beasts or in some other form.

However, the Inner Chamber does not wish to encourage speculation. Thus, I have been required to set aside many inquiries and exploratory commentaries written over the course of my journeys. In truth, I still know very little compared to what there is to know and what I might discover, should I only be granted the opportunity to continue my investigations.

I offer these thoughts to Your Most Majestic and Benevolent Highness in the hope of gaining your approval for the task I wish to undertake, and for which the Inner Chamber has denied me funds and permission. All that I discover in the course of my wanderings is to the benefit of the Tranquil Empire and in service to your most glorious and gracious rule.

> Written in cipher in a draft in the journal of Luviara, theurgist and investigator, working under the sworn seal of the Inner Chamber of the Heart Temple

13

A Stony Land

The carriage descended from the bridge and back onto the last long stub of the causeway, the one that connected to the nameless land. On they went, inexorably onward. Elen shivered. Was it colder here? Or was it dread? Dread that Eleawona would recognize her and demand El become an atoner again, to punish her and Ao for escaping.

Kem took hold of her hand, squeezing it.

She did not want to return, had never wanted to, and yet here she came. She was no longer El, the powerless child, yet even that child had wielded a measure of power, if by power one meant life and death over others. Men and horses were dead because of her, eaten alive and warped to the bone in the most torturous way possible. The weight of the deaths rested in her, because deeds could not be erased from a life. But she'd tell the child she'd been to do the same again. So what did that make her?

A murderer. A fugitive.

Would Lady Eleawona demand El be punished for the deaths of Lord Thelan's soldiers? Would Prince Gevulin allow it? At least Kem would be safe, as long as Lady Eleawona never knew that Ao was his mother, lest she, like Lord Duenn, claim ownership of the youth.

They emerged out of the Pall and into a stony land. The barren ground was dusted with snow and littered with rocks. Here and there rose heaps of bones like the old bone pile she'd scouted by Lancer's Ridge, so long ago it felt as if it had been years. Were these the remains of the scouting party that had pursued her and Ao, only to meet their own deaths? Or were these newer dead?

Ipis pointed toward a line of spindly trees ahead. "What is that?"

They were not trees, but posts staked parallel to the shoreline of the Pall. From each hung a corpse—or what was left of a corpse—some twisted and blackened as if executed by fire, some withered and gray as if frozen to death and left strung up until summer rotted them through, bones and leavings scattered onto the ground to be picked apart by birds and beasts alike.

Past the fence of death rose two parallel hedges of yew. She knew them like memorable acquaintances, met once and never forgotten. Yew hedges outlived those who planted them. She and Ao had run in terror past this place, but there lay no trace of their passage. The two girls had vanished from the nameless land like smoke in the wind.

Past the yew hedge lay blackthorn, an orchard of hazelnut and walnut, harvested fields whitened by a layer of crusty snow. A rabbit scampered away into cover, startled by their approach. Buildings ahead: the road fort, and the houses and huts clustered as close to the road as they were allowed. Was the little village larger now? Were more huts and sheds huddled along the base of the road's embankment?

Yet the village looked a ramshackle affair. Not even the poorest hamlet in the empire would have tolerated so many broken-down buildings, badly patched with mismatched half-rotted-out wood planks and sagging sod roofs. A handful of folk, out in the frozen lanes and gardens, looked up at the carriage. Their clothing might once have had color from the many plants available for dye, but mostly they looked dirt-stained, as if there wasn't enough water for washing nor leisure for the task. Not like the empire, with its public baths and community fountains and wells and springs.

"Everything is so dirty," said Ipis. "And it stinks!"

Kem glanced apprehensively at Elen. Ipis noticed, and hastily added, "Oh, I don't mean you, Elen!"

Even the fortlet atop the road had an unpleasant odor about it when their carriage rumbled into its tiny courtyard so the horses could be changed out. The space was cramped and crude. Refuse lay tumbled against the walls, as if no one could be bothered to sweep it up.

"Is the prince here?" Elen asked, unable to imagine him in this setting.

Ipis and Kem jumped out with the anxious legs of people who really needed to pee. She got down with trepidation, not that anyone here ought to recognize her after so many years. The soldiers looked so thin, as if they never had enough to eat. The retainers who scurried to change out the horses were thinner yet, as emaciated as the holy beggars in the empire, who ate only what was placed in their offering bowls, their ritual of devotion to the grace and generosity of the High Heavens. In the empire, such severity was a choice made by holy beggars, a sign of holiness that everyone praised but few emulated. As the temple song went, "These shall starve, so the rest may eat," which had never made sense to Elen, except perhaps as a different way of being an atoner.

Ipis fixed an imperious, Manor-born gaze on the tallest of the soldiers, mistaking height for importance, for the man wore a boot-man's stripe on his sleeve, while the shorter, stockier sergeant wore a wooden bear badge.

"We need a latrine," Ipis said.

They looked at Ipis uncomprehendingly.

The sergeant spoke to the boot-man in words that woke old memories in Elen's head. "That's some kind of bird chatter. Can't get over how tall and meaty they are. A bit funny-looking, too. The eyes. The tar-hair. You think they have clan blood, eh?"

"Nah, they's human, not Wolves. Got master's blood, I'm thinking, with that dark hair and those sharp-leaf eyes. Who else can wear such fancy garb. Look at that cloth. It shines, though it be dark."

"Can't be masters. Where's their soldiers? Where's retainers to wait on them? Where's their atoners? Don't make any sense to come if they've no army, that's what I'm thinking. I don't get it."

Atoners. The word fell like a stone into Elen's belly. She shifted nervously.

"I really have to pee, too," muttered Ipis, mistaking Elen's body language. "These people can't even speak correctly."

Elen almost addressed the men, but prudence stayed her. Better to let them think no one in the prince's entourage could understand the northern speech. She wanted to be a stranger here, even if she wasn't.

The boot-man nodded toward Kem. "Yet, look at that one's hair. Got the west-county shine."

"Shut up, you. That's dangerous talk. You should know it, too, since your mother was one of them serving Lord Arwona, back in that day."

"Yah, yah, you're right. We all knew what he got up to during that time, and his wife never forgave him for cheating her when she was the higher born. Misery life, he had after that. No doubt happy when he finally croaked it. Though her young ladyship wept for him, her blessed father as he was."

"She was the only one who mourned him."

Kem and Ipis hadn't understood a single word of the exchange. Ipis tried again, speaking loudly and with exaggerated slowness. "We. Need. A. Latrine."

"They don't speak the language," said Kem. "Here."

He gave a friendly grin and mimed squatting, waving his hand at his backside as if to waft away a stink. The soldiers chortled, amused by the theater. So, indeed, they were taken aside into a stone corridor that stank of damp. Frost crunched under their feet because it was that cold. There was no heating. In a wood-planked roofed balcony that stuck out from the fortlet's wall, they were left to squat over a gap above the road's embankment, urine and feces dropping into a smeared, frozen heap atop whatever had been left before. In the summer, the stench would have been unbearable. Yet Elen didn't remember a stench. Maybe she'd never noticed it.

"No vinegar? No sponges?" Ipis asked. "How do we . . . ?"

"This is disgusting," said Kem. "No wonder—" He broke off, looking at Elen.

"Yes," she agreed. "Let's hope the prince has found better accommodations. He won't want his retinue to smell, I'm sure of it."

Ipis got out her flask and poured the last of her water over their outstretched hands. "I can't bear it otherwise, thinking about it."

They headed back to the courtyard. By now, the stained patches on Elen's underclothes and trousers had gotten stiff, if not quite dry because it took so long to dry in such cold weather, so the disgusting conditions made little difference to her. Good boots and a warm cloak made up for a lot of mild discomfort.

"I wonder how much farther to reach the prince?" Ipis asked as they came into the courtyard where a new team of horses had been harnessed.

The soldiers had retreated to the gate with their fellows. A tall figure stood by the carriage, waiting for them. The person turned as they came up.

It was the bequeather.

14

THE BEQUEATHER

Captain Raven was outfitted in a tight leather vest and an armored skirt made of leather strips fitted with metal studs. A sheathed sword hung from her belt. A bow quiver leaned against a carriage wheel. Her well-cut arms were bare, skin gleaming with the silvery shimmer Elen had noticed before. Below the armored skirt, she wore not soldiering boots but summer military sandals that laced up to the knee around muscular calves. If the cold bothered her, she didn't show it. She was beautiful as a well-made sword is beautiful: because it can do what it is forged to do.

She had one hand propped on a hip in a position either impatient or amused. The gauzy sunlight, muted by clouds, made a spiky crown of her short-cropped hair, but the strangest thing about her was a tracery like a faint, silver halo, or aura, limning her figure, like a cape made of intangible wings. Nothing that could be touched, but part of her.

Luviara had said the aivur were not human, even though some might be mistaken for human. Captain Simo called them monsters and said they carried inside themselves the attributes of beasts, which gave them enhanced senses, strength, and speed. Seen up close, the bequeather seemed to Elen both stranger and perhaps more ordinary than expected.

The bequeather said, tartly, "Come along, come along, enough rude staring, osge. At least you southerners seem to understand cleanliness. To be sure, I have observed that most of the humans in this land can barely feed themselves and aren't allowed to do better than walk at the edge of starvation. You would think they would kill those who feast while letting the rest starve, but instead the hungry crawl along after them on their empty bellies. Very odd, to be sure."

She climbed into the carriage with her gear.

They got in. Kem sat boldly beside the bequeather, while Ipis and Elen sat on the facing bench. The driver whistled to the horses, and they headed north on the holy road.

"Not far to South Ring," said the bequeather, eyeing each of them in turn. "Are you two not disturbed by the presence of the osge?"

"What is an osge, Your Worthiness?" Kem asked, taking a respectful tone. Ipis still looked suspicious, as if she wasn't sure she was willing to have a conversation with a barbarian, especially one who her revered Captain Simo considered a monster.

"One who carries poison. Deadly to all and any."

"She means my scar," said Elen impatiently, touching her neck.

"That thing?" Kem asked, baffled. "Why?"

"The scar is the brand that marks the poison inside," said the bequeather.

The brand that marks the poison inside. Had someone deliberately cut her, so long ago that she didn't even recall the incident? Was it the act of the mysterious figure who had shown tiny child El her reflection, and thus the egg that rested inside her, in a pure-water pool? That would explain the reaction of the aivur, and the scar could even have been how the haunt had been able to identify her on their first meeting, although his heightened senses, or the magic of the Spires, might truly have allowed him to have felt the presence of the viper if it meant she was a vessel no Shorn could enter.

"Oh, I see," Kem said, grasping the connection and formulating a reply while Elen was still too tongue-tied to speak. "No. She's not osge to us, you see. But I can understand that you might not know if she is osge to you."

"You're a clever one," said the bequeather.

"My thanks. Do you have a name? I'm Kem. This is Ipis."

"Are you always so free with your names?"

"With our use names, we are as free as mice amid the wheat," he replied with a charming smile.

Ipis bit down on a grin because it was a line from a terrible old play about aivur and secret names, and how a farm boy had outwitted an aivur prince but had also frolicked bare-assed in the hay with him, nothing about how itchy it surely would have gotten, which for sure meant the author of the play had never spent any time frolicking naked in actual hay. Although Elen wasn't sure aivur even had princes the way the empire did.

"I believe the Worthy Bequeather goes by Captain Raven, for she and I met before, in a rather less comfortable wagon," said Elen, feeling that she had been politely silent for long enough. Osge, indeed! "I have a question, Captain. Why are Sea Wolves camped on a causeway in the middle of the Pall? And not just a few, but what looks like an entire community?"

"I'm intrigued by your expectation of an answer to such a question," replied the captain coldly.

"I had to try," said Elen, although she couldn't help but think of how the haunt would have infused the same sequence of words with a warm wealth of rascally insinuation.

"So it seems," agreed the bequeather without the least flicker of amusement. Perhaps she'd been born bereft of humor. "I will bequeath you answers, but only those I so choose."

"You are commanded by no one who can compel you to speak?" Elen asked.

"What a strange way of doing things these human folk have, as I have often remarked. If you have no further questions, I would prefer silence."

"I have a question," Kem said. "Where are we? The locals can't call this Farlandia, because it's not far for them."

"If you do not know, then it is not my place to inform you."

Ipis said, "All our maps show the Northwest Road ends at Far Boundary Vigil. So who built this road, then? It's exactly like an imperial road."

"Surely you jest with such an ignorant question." The bequeather looked Ipis up and down with scorn.

Ipis flushed, cheeks darkening.

In a clipped tone, the bequeather went on, as if she felt obliged to correct Ipis. "Every child knows that the sorcerers of ancient days wove the road with wicked sorcery. That's why it stings us, we who were their mortal enemies and who alone fought to defeat them, even at such great cost to ourselves. But you folk are destitute when it comes to your hoard of the elder past. Even your interlocutor has only scraps in her knowledge basket. Yet that, at least, is more than I can say for those who rule in this destitute land. They believe their white-haired god built everything for their convenience. Imagine living amid such squalor and yet having such a high opinion of yourself."

"I'm sorry I asked," Ipis muttered with ill grace, not that Elen blamed her. Kem tapped the young warden's knee in sympathy. He looked ready to ask another question just to get the attention off his comrade's embarrassment.

Elen hadn't wanted to broach the subject in front of Ipis but she didn't know if she'd ever get this chance again. "Captain, what do you know of the Shorn?"

The captain's attention sharpened like a bowstring drawn taut before its arrow was loosed. "There is a question I did not expect. You have surprised me, osge."

"I would prefer if you call me Elen, as that is my use name, and not some vaguely threatening insult. But call me whatever you wish, Captain, if you'll just answer my question."

"Then so I shall, osge. The Shorn wait to be called, as our ancestors taught us. But this you must also know, since you speak of them."

"If one of them were called, then do you know what would happen next? Do you know of something called a passage spell?"

The captain leaned forward as if spotting a rich trove or a splendid feast. "I have never met a human who has spoken of this matter. To be sure, I still have not. It is clear to me you have something else on your mind. What is it you really wish to know, *Elen*?" She spoke the name with a bite like scorn.

Captain Raven didn't intimidate her! "If one of the Shorn had awoken, and now resided in the White Sea, as the people here call it, is there a way to call them, to reach them?"

"There is. This history I will bequeath you because you have intrigued me. That makes it a fair exchange. I have only once in my life encountered one of the Shorn. That was many years ago, by the measure of the sun. They told me they had walked far afield, in search of other strongholds that shelter their Shorn brethren. They told me that many of the strongholds had fallen into ruin, that the spell-cases embracing their brethren had been shattered by careless or malicious hands, or sometimes simply by an accident of storm or the weathering of implacable time. I never saw this individual again, to discover what became of their quest. I have long wished to speak with another of the Shorn. They are so old, and their duty so burdensome and yet necessary, beyond all things, should the worst happen."

"What is the worst?" Kem asked.

The captain met his eye and stared for so long that he flushed to the roots of his hair. "You are so young," she said, not as a criticism but as an observation. "It is odd, for you have the same hue of hair."

"The same hair as what?" Ipis asked. "Your hair is an odd color, Kem. I've never seen its like in the heartland. Up on the Blasted Coast you'd sometimes see foreign sailors with something like, only not so shiny as yours is. Theirs was more washed-out, like worn silk that's been scrubbed too many times."

As a girl, Elen had walked through life knowing only what was in front of her feet and within reach of her hands. She'd had nothing to compare her life to. No means to measure it, to draw conclusions or see where chains linked up to create a path of one thought to the next. So she'd never given much thought to Kem's hair being similar in color to his mother's, who had come from the north. When she was a child, Ao's hair had been shaved short every month. It had only grown out once they'd escaped. Only after they'd reached the empire had they realized what an unusual color it was.

But that was a question for another time. This chance might not come again.

She broke in. "Captain, can a bequeather call one of the Shorn out of the White Sea, and perhaps ask of that Shorn a question, or give them a message?"

"A bequeather could do so, but would need a true name to call. Thus we find ourselves at an impasse, do we not?"

"We might not, Captain, had you the ability to return to the White Sea with me. Or if without me, then to bring an answer back to me."

"A cryptic proposition. But at the moment, as you will have observed, we are being conveyed to South Ring, as I have been tasked. This prince named Gevulin seems particularly concerned that *you* not be lost, which, after some consideration, has brought me to see that he knows you are osge and what it means. So, I take leave to warn you that I would not trust him."

"How dare you show such disrespect to His Exalted Highness!" cried Ipis.

"Dare? What have your customs to do with me? He holds no authority over me or mine. Our alliance is not with him. Now, if you will, I require rest. This conversation has become tiresome."

She closed her eyes, and Elen had to admit to herself that she missed the enthralling glow of the bequeather's lambent eyes. The captain was no sea *wolf*, not with those wings. A gilded raven more like, to go by her name. Intelligent and clever. Not human and not animal, but another kind of being woven out of familiar thread into an entirely different weave of cloth. How could people so varied in form and abilities as humans, aivur, gagast, swalters, the mysterious fregir, and even the lofty dragons come to exist? And what was she, if she was not quite human but not any of the others either?

Did magic weave the world and the creatures into being, or did the world weave magic?

Human theurgists bound and released elemental spirits; that was the magic they wielded.

Sorcery, it seemed, fed off darker currents. If sorcery was related to Spore, then that perhaps meant sorcerers could draw on or transform the life force they drained from living creatures, something like the passage spell she had teasingly described to Kem. Only, draining life from another living being was no jest. If true, then no wonder sorcery was condemned as wicked and evil.

As for aivur, if it were true their ordinary attributes were amplified by a magical enhancement that gave them extraordinary powers, at least compared to humans, then it was no wonder the Magnolia Emperor looked upon them with suspicion. It was no wonder that, upon taking the throne, she had exiled all aivur from the heartland. An emperor might reasonably fear that, with time, the aivur would come to believe they could overwhelm and conquer the empire, ruled as it was by mere humans.

Was that what Prince Gevulin hoped for in allying with Lady Eleawona? To use her alliance with the aivur against his own people?

The more Elen thought about the bridge the aivur had built, the more it troubled her. Humans were trapped by the Pall, but aivur weren't. They could pour across the last breach and into Woodfall Province at any time, and if things went poorly for them, they could as easily retreat out of reach of the imperial armies. For that matter, what about the communities of aivur who lived along the borderlands of the Desolation? Were they innocent villagers, or were they hiding something?

Kem shifted on the bench. Ipis shook her head as if warning him not to disturb the bequeather. To be fair, even though the captain might actually have been asleep, Elen felt as if the woman could cut off all three of their heads without even opening her eyes.

She leaned on the open window's rim and watched the countryside pass. The road was lined by stubbled fields, by rows of orchards, by frost-crackled ditches, and by a steady string of houses that ran as an elongated village parallel to the road. These residences were separated from the embankment by a packed dirt lane that would churn to mud come the spring rains.

She didn't recall the landscape looking this threadbare, but probably she hadn't understood it back when she and Ao had walked as atoners in Lady Eleawona's entourage, all of them children. Most of their travels had been along ordinary lanes as the noble girl made her itinerant way from one royal villa to the next, from the holy road to the bitter lakes and back again to the safety of South Ring for the worst months of bleak winter. Only the masters were allowed to walk on the holy road, safe from Spore. Atoners walked alongside on the dirt lane. She'd never seen the land, or the approach to South Ring, from the height of the holy road.

The people out and about in the countryside and villages reminded Elen of ghosts, wispy, pale, fragile-looking as they chopped wood and hauled water. A gang of children stacked rocks, their bare hands red with the cold. A rag-cloaked tinker plodded along the dirt lane, leading a donkey that looked better fed than he was. Farther along, a stone-walled forge pulsed heat into the cold day. Artisans' work sheds had been built in an oval around the forge to catch heat for their winter work, although they would be sweltering in the summer.

None of this she remembered. Seeing it fresh gave her a traveler's vista. It was a drab and impoverished place, although the landscape itself had a stark beauty. Beyond the inhabited strip rose woodland, rocky hilltops, and the cloudy sky. As the carriage rolled past, people glanced up to mark its passage, but no one sang a hymn or bowed as folk in the empire would do, showing respect to an imperial official or excitement at the arrival of merchants, who might bring a troupe of players or a table of interesting goods to bargain over. They seemed too exhausted to care. More likely, they knew a fine carriage brought nothing for the likes of them.

Ipis snorted in her sleep. Kem gave Elen a searching look as he handed her a flask and a piece of flat bread wrapped around salty goat's cheese. She took a swallow of spicy wine, savored the bread and cheese, and gave him a reassuring nod. He sighed, turning his attention to the window. Questions creased his brow, but he seemed determined not to disturb the bequeather, who sat with closed eyes, as still as if she had become spell-cased like one of the Shorn.

The Shorn, whom the bequeather had heard of—and claimed she knew how to call.

15

South Ring

For the rest of the day they traveled in silence, halting twice to get fresh horses. Each time they were offered bitter ale and dry turnip bread. Elen was grateful for both, although Ipis's shock at this humble fare was its own form of entertainment.

"More like slops for pigs," Ipis muttered.

The bequeather shot her a look that made Elen think of beaks tearing into raw flesh. Beautiful the bequeather might be, but beauty was a complicated thing and might as easily signal danger as welcome.

Ipis flushed. She ate without further complaint.

Later in the day Elen spotted two slender spires and a stub of a tower, clustered together and barely visible above a distant tree line. She stiffened, squinting. Memory sharpened. Was that Parlay Hill Hall, whose slender stone towers were the tallest in the south, or so the retainers said, taller even than the lady's mother's four-story tower in South Ring? Lady Eleawona's court had stopped at Parlay Hill Hall once a year on the usual circuit, but no one ever went up the towers because some master's child had once died there, falling down the stairs, and everyone said it was an evil ghost that had pushed him.

How differently she saw it now. Surely it was a set of damaged Spires, one broken, the other two more or less intact. Yet she recalled seeing no statues at the entrance to the tower enclosure. Yet what if there were statues there, and she'd never realized that's what they were? Her hands twitched. She wanted to go, to see if the place was what she thought it must be. If somehow its existence might link her to *him*. If he might step out of the shadows, say her name, and smile.

But she hadn't the authority to stop the carriage. And a dreamy wish was not a plan.

At last they came into sight of their destination. The setting sun cast a pallid light across the fluttering white ribbons and gold banner atop the tower that marked South Ring, the seat of the ruler of the south. Lady Eleawona's mother had marked her personal court with the badge of the marten, but the marten banner was gone, meaning the woman was dead. In its place flew the badge of Eleawona's bear.

Elen pressed a hand against her chest, expecting to feel the wooden badge, but of course the badge was long gone now, thrown into the Pall all those years ago at Ao's urging. Left to her own devices, maybe El would have held on to it in case the wood or the sharp point of its pin might be of future use, but Ao had insisted the badges be tossed away, a clean cut for a new start in a new land.

The carriage slowed as they reached a ramp that led from elevated roadway down into the crowded town. In her youth Elen had simply accepted the holy road and its entrance ramps; they were just another part of the world she walked. Now she was hit by the shock of recognition: South Ring was a Halt, built with the same layout and protections as every Halt in the empire. Not that anyone here called South Ring a Halt. They did not know the term.

The carriage rattled down into the town. She expected them to turn aside into the imperial quarter immediately, but everything looked different from the imperial Halts she'd grown used to. Instead of spacious gates and interior courtyards, wooden buildings were crammed cheek by jowl to either side. Open gates let onto narrow courtyards where washing hung to dry and iron cauldrons were set over open fires. Dogs barked. Wood smoke hazed the air, stinging her eyes. Ipis sneezed. Kem coughed.

The carriage remained on the main avenue, rolling toward the central plaza. Or what should have been the central plaza, which was always a community gathering place in every imperial Halt as well as the site of centralized water distribution for all the residents.

Instead, a stone wall blocked the avenue. Iron-bound gates were swung open by guards as they approached. The carriage trundled beneath a stone arch and over a crude little bridge. The bridge spanned a narrow stone canal hacked out of the ground and filled with flowing water. The heavy *thump thump thump* of a water wheel drew her gaze: an old aqueduct had been redirected through the water wheel to create a canal of flowing water around the edge of what had once been a spacious central plaza and which was now the seat of the ruling master.

Here rose the winter palace of the lady. Beyond a ring of fences and further walls lay a kitchen compound. An entire complex of precious granaries and storehouses, royal workshops, barracks, and stables ran east and west along the crosswise avenue. Stone alleys or courtyards created space between buildings as a precaution against fire and Spore. Covered walkways, elevated above the ground, offered a protected way for the masters to move outdoors within the complex during the months when rain, sleet, and snow troubled the land.

The masters had built their winter palace in the place they considered safest—at the center of the Ring—and had demolished the community gathering place in order to do so.

Directly ahead stood the heavy stone building that was the lady's great hall, fronted by a wooden portico that served as an entry porch. Soldiers wearing bronze bear badges on their fur caps stood on guard, spears in hand, to make sure no vehicle came too close. The hall's great doors were open, with retainers on duty. A solitary figure, heavily caped and hooded against the cold, waited off to one side of the wide porch.

As soon as the carriage halted, grooms took charge of the horses, and retainers came running to open the coach's door. The bequeather hopped down with an aggressive speed that drove the retainers to step back. Seeing her, the soldiers gripped their spears a little harder, although they did not give ground.

"Come, come," Captain Raven called back over her shoulder to the other occupants.

"Eager to get rid of us?" Elen asked as she emerged.

The captain gave her a cutting look. "On the contrary. I am keen to speak more of the Shorn. But I perceive we will have neither leisure nor privacy to do so. Here arrives your comrade."

As Ipis and Kem emerged with their packs, the solitary figure at the door tipped back her hood to reveal herself as Xilsi. She hustled over.

"Oh, thank the High Heavens. I was getting worried, but you're all here and safe. Even you!" She slapped Elen on the shoulder, then sniffed. "Did you pee yourself?"

Elen grinned, so relieved to see Xilsi that she almost laughed. "They tied me up and threw me in the back of a wagon. I did my best with hands tied."

"How rude! We'll get you sorted out. The prince won't stand for it, for one thing. For the other, he and the woman lady, or whatever they call princely folk here, seem to be thick as thieves already. I think she's mostly taken with his good looks, given the sad state of these maggot-skinned northerners." She took in the bequeather with an unexpectedly long look. The captain met her gaze with chilly reserve, so Xilsi offered a curt nod of acknowledgment and turned back to the others. "Kem, why is everyone staring at you?"

"Are they?" He looked around in confusion. It seemed everyone in eyeshot was suddenly staring self-consciously at the ground.

The bequeather stirred, as if about to answer Xilsi's query, but the aivur was only gathering her gear. Without any further word or even a polite goodbye, she strode toward the hall. Soldiers and retainers alike scrambled to get out of her way.

The House of the High Hall was the main building of the winter palace of the ruler of the south, once the Lady of the Marten and now her daughter, the Lady of the Bear. The blocky stone building had two stories, with a four-story tower attached at the opposite end. To young El and Ao, the winter palace and, in particular, its main hall had seemed the most monumental and stupendous construction ever raised upon a lowly world. Seeing it now, the building looked substantially less impressive than the intendant's Residence in Orledder Halt, which possessed all the architectural elaboration and airy confection of every official imperial residence in the empire, without which those who lived inside would be known to arise from a low estate indeed.

The hall had four entrances: the covered portico for the masters which connected to the walkways, as well as a side entry for retainers and supplies, and a back entrance through which soldiers and officials might enter and leave about their duties, neither of which were visible from here. Only atoners used the fourth entrance, a hatch in the wall next to one of the chimneys, easily missed if you didn't know where to look. It led into a warren of narrow passages and crawlspaces, few of which were large enough for a grown man of any bulk. Elen had never actually set foot in any of the winter palace's rooms or chambers. She had only seen them through grilles.

The bequeather vanished around the building, evidently headed for the officials' entrance.

Elen looked around with the greatest interest as Xilsi led her, Ipis, and Kem to the great doors, which were meant only for the masters. She'd never gone through these doors.

The captain in charge of the guard cleared his throat as a prelude to barking an order to halt. A haughty glare from Xilsi shut him down.

The four of them climbed the two steps to the front portico and swept through into an entry hall. The high chamber was dimly lit by the greasy light of tallow lanterns, nothing like the clean oil that brightened imperial spaces. Retainers wearing the gold bear of the lady's personal attendants hustled up with expressions of shock at seeing such people where they were not meant to be. A prim-mouthed chatelaine gestured decisively toward a door into a lower passage.

Xilsi marched right past her and started up the wide stairs reserved only for the feet of the masters. When the woman reached out to stop her, fastening a firm grip on her arm, Xilsi grabbed her wrist and twisted. The chatelaine released her with a cry of pain.

The warden was splendid in her anger. "You will refrain from touching one such as I, Xilsi Bakassar, child of Bakas House, granddaughter of she who was the perfumed and most resplendent beauty of the Flower Court, her name not to be uttered by the undeserving. Do I make myself clear?"

The woman flinched away, shaking loose as she backed off. She might not have understood the words, but she understood the tone. Then her gaze caught on Elen's face, and she did a double take, puzzled, curious. In the northern speech, she said, "Do I know you?"

Elen pretended she did not understand.

Xilsi said quickly, "Don't give them the idea they can order us around, or they'll think they can chew on us until we're nothing but cracked bones."

Unimpeded, they climbed the stairs. But now, after what Xilsi had said, Elen noticed how every gaze fixed on Kem with a shocked expression, which was then quickly hidden by an averting of the eyes. Whatever it meant, she feared it was nothing good.

The stairs ended at a barricaded balcony overlooking the entry hall, a good place from which to shoot at invaders. A single corridor ran down the center, with rooms opening off to either side. The air was warmer up here than in the hall below, heat rising, which made the higher story a more comfortable winter habitation.

Xilsi ignored the comments of the waiting soldiers and retainers and strode down the corridor with the intent look of someone who has already scouted out her territory and therefore knows where she is going.

"The prince was given use of a guest suite adjoining that of the lady," Xilsi remarked as the others hustled after her. "We're all sleeping in there, which will make it difficult for Her Ladyship to sneak into his bed, if she's a mind to do so."

"Do you think she's got a mind to do so?" Elen asked. "Seems a bit rash, so soon."

"As I said, I think she's taken by his handsome face. But there's something else going on, and I haven't figured out what it is yet. Rash, maybe. Desperate, perhaps. Lonely, could be. But this isn't a good place. We're all in danger here. Keep your eyes sharp and your ears open."

"Understood," said Ipis with the brisk obedience of a well-trained warden.

"Uh, yeah," said Kem uneasily. It was clear he had noticed that people were looking at him askance, and he didn't like it. He self-consciously ran a hand down the front of his jacket as if to make sure his chest binding was still in place.

Xilsi went on. "Elen, you should change right away and get your soiled garments washed and dried. Though I haven't much faith in the possibility of decent laundry service here."

"Have you not? The *masters'* courts have the best of everything," said Elen.

"What's *master*?"

She'd forgotten Xilsi and the others didn't know the northern words, even if some of those words sounded very like imperial speech. "I mean only that the highborn always have the best. Surely, since their lady prince must require clean clothing, they can manage the same for His Highness. Or even me."

"I'm not so sure. The lady is a bit pungent if you get close to her, but more as if she's layered on too much strong perfume. The soldiers and servants reek. And that's with my nose already stuffed up from the stink of mildew, and all the herbs they bundle in corners to try to cover it all up." She halted at a closed door. "Here we are. Let me tell you, the prince wasn't amused to see this."

She indicated the symbol of a handsome ram carved into the door. It had magnificent curling horns and a virile stance.

"A fair enough resemblance," said Elen.

Xilsi laughed as she set a hand to the latch and opened the door. "Someday you'll get executed for insolence, but not soon, I fervently pray."

The suite's outer chamber had two thickly glazed and rather small windows. A briskly burning fire in a manteled fireplace kept the room warm, if a little smoky. The space was furnished with couches so its resident could take a leisurely afternoon to entertain companions, should they wish. A recently patched and rather faded tapestry hung from one wall. The wardens' gear was lined up neatly beneath the bottom edge of the tapestry's scene of men hunting deer through a wooded landscape while foxes and wolves looked on from the forest shadows.

Ipis stared about the room in appalled astonishment, then hurried to follow Xilsi and Kem into the inner chamber. Elen brought up the rear.

The inner chamber also had windows and a fireplace, but it was a smaller and more private room, fitted with a large four-poster bed whose curtains were tied back. Jirvy was sprawled asleep on a blanket on the floor. He startled awake as the door creaked open, and he hastily sat up, grabbing for his sword. His gaze took them in: Xilsi, Kem, Ipis, Elen. With a sigh of relief, he set down his weapon.

"You can go back to sleep," said Xilsi.

A retainer stood nervously in the corner, watching all this. The man's gaze took them in, and he visibly startled when he saw Kem. What was going on? She caught Kem's eye and gave him what she hoped was a reassuring nod.

"You can change behind that screen," said Xilsi to Elen.

Once behind the screen, Elen stripped down, leaving on her rumpled official's tabard as a concealing coverlet. The tabard, at least, hadn't gotten in the way. There was a basin and a pitcher of water for washing, even a linen towel, so she took the liberty of washing her face and hands, and then her thighs and privates, smiling all the while at the thought of the prince's indignation were he to discover what she'd done with linen meant for his exalted self.

Her spare clothing was rolled up at the bottom of her pack: drawstring underpants, wool trousers, and a shift. Xilsi took away the soiled clothing.

As Elen finished dressing, Xilsi addressed the retainer. "I know you don't understand me, so I will use gestures. Smell these garments. Yes! Now, you see, they need to be cleaned. You understand? But you see, the trousers are leather so not dunked in water, or boiled, as you will for the linen. Rather wiped clean and aired out. Good? Yes. Very good."

"I'm ready," said Elen, stepping back into view. "Kem, Ipis, you can wash back there."

"That's for the prince, isn't it?" asked Ipis.

"How will he ever know if none of us tell him?"

Ipis looked shocked. Xilsi snorted. Jirvy was already asleep again. Kem glanced a question at Elen. She nodded, and he went behind the screen to wash. Ipis hesitated, then followed.

"It stinks here." Xilsi wrinkled up her nose.

"It's worse in the summer . . . Must be worse in the summer, I mean. Or maybe better, since it's easier to do laundry in the summer in streams and rivers."

"I feel certain it is appalling both winter and summer. As the poet sang, 'Don't uncover that pot!'" Xilsi tapped a foot, waiting impatiently for the youths to clean up. "Are you done yet, you two?"

Elen studied the posts on the bed, which were carved with vines. She'd seen this bed before. She looked at the ceiling and, in the corner, found the grille onto the atoner's passage.

A strange sensation, like dizziness, rushed through her, leaving her blinking and unsteady. Was that blot of darkness behind the grille a person, watching? Was it Ao? No, of course not Ao. But another child, as she and Ao had once been. It's what they would have done, seeing foreigners or any manner of stranger come to the court. Both she and Ao had been curious. And anyway, atoners saw all kinds of things. Since they had no power, it didn't matter what secrets they learned.

For so long, she'd deliberately kept her memories closed away. Now, like the broken shards of a pot, they began to fit back together to form a remembered shape of the life she and Ao had lived as young children.

This was the bedroom where young Lord Thelan, sent to live with his aunt, had dwelled for his first winter with the court. That had come before he had been sent off to make the spring, summer, and fall circuit of the south county with his betrothed, Lady Eleawona. He had paced here, too restless to sleep. She'd watched through the grille, unseen and unheard, as he'd mouthed words she couldn't quite hear and gestured with his hands as though speaking to an audience. His gestures mimicked those the Lady of the Marten had used when she made proclamations from the High Seat. It looked as if he was practicing to be ruler, to make proclamations himself someday. But he was a bastard, and thus not eligible to rule except as consort to his legitimately born lady cousin, who, in the fullness of time, would inherit the rule of the south county from her mother. Even young atoner El, who knew nothing about the world beyond Lady Eleawona's traveling court, understood that Thelan had been sent south to marry his cousin in order to get him out of the way of his legitimate half brothers as they grew up in the Highmost's court in the north.

At that time, Lord Thelan had been an adolescent. Although most of the masters, especially the male-folk, began taking their sexual pleasures early, he'd never once, that winter, brought a person to this bed. Not that she'd seen, anyway, and she'd watched him too much for her own good. Poor young El. He'd spoken kindly to her three times. That had been enough to knock her over into admiring him and thinking him different from the other masters, somehow.

Once, when he and the other masters had gone off one morning to the worship of the white-haired god at the temple, two of his retainers had sneaked into his room and had sex on the floor. They'd giggled softly and whispered sweetly all the while. El had watched in complete astonishment. The sex she'd spied on up until that day had been dutiful, or bored, or reluctant, or unpleasant and mean. This coupling had infused her youthful flesh with a sense of longing and desire, an idea there could be something wonderful in the mingling of bodies. This was an astonishing secret that no one had ever let on within her hearing. It had made it possible for her, many years later, at Orledder Halt, to assay her first sexual experience with another person, to discover this form of intimacy could indeed be delightful when each person came to the act of their own desire and at their own choosing.

Looking around the chamber now, the sequence of events in her and Ao's last year as atoners began to fit together. Thelan had arrived at South Ring the winter before the summer when she and Ao had escaped, a time when both girls were closing in on adulthood and all the sensations and desires and troubles it would bring, Ao especially. Now, Elen looked up at the grille as a visitor in the hall of the Lady of the Bear. If an atoner stared back at her, she could not tell. She was on the other side now, the part of the world who did not see atoners because the atoners were there to die for them.

Xilsi bumped shoulders with her in a companionable style, jarring her out of her jagged thoughts. The warden spoke in a low voice so the others wouldn't overhear.

"How did your scheme go? Did you draw off the pursuers? How did you get through the Pall, anyway? What haven't you been telling me? Why did His Exalted Highness know you could get back to us? You should be dead. And you're not a gagast. So your ability to get through the Pall only makes sense if you're aivur . . ." She scratched her head. "No, you're missing that shine they have, so it's not that. What is it?"

Elen had to answer something without answering anything, so she took mock offense. "I'm missing that *shine*? Whatever can you mean? I feel quite drab now."

Xilsi chuckled. "That's not what I meant—" She broke off as Ipis and Kem emerged from behind the screen.

Ipis looked refreshed and eager, gaze fastening brightly on Xilsi. "Now what?"

Xilsi sighed, clearly annoyed at being interrupted, but Elen was glad. Avoidance was generally a bad strategy because it only pushed the problem off into an unknown future, but all too often in her life it had been the only strategy she had.

Xilsi said, "Now we go down the hall to the ladyship's parlor, where she and the prince are having a parlay." She fixed the young ones with a stately stare. "Remember that you are imperial wardens, officials of the Tranquil Empire. Do not let anyone here show you disrespect. They are barbarians, and it mustn't be allowed."

"What about the Sea Wolf?" asked Ipis. "Captain Raven, I mean."

"That bequeather is the only pie-not-sausage person I've ever felt a hankering after," said Xilsi, sounding like she meant it.

Ipis gave her a startled look. "That wasn't what I asked."

Xilsi went on as if she hadn't heard. "You could have tossed me over with a feather when she spoke to us with that icepick of a voice, right after Fulmo got us across the Pall to the big rock. Those Sea Wolves scare the fucks right out of me."

"Really?" Elen countered. "I mean, I'm happy with sausage, and pie, or however you want to bake it, but that cold chilly aspect puts me off. I'm more into sly wit, honey words, and warm groping, when I can get it."

"Really, must we?" Kem groused.

"You do yours, and I'll do mine," said Xilsi with a grin, although the grin soured to a frown as she glanced at the sleeping Jirvy.

On this note, they left the suite and walked down to the end of the corridor. Xilsi did not wait for the guards to allow her in. She brushed past them with a sniff of disdain, opened the door, and entered without announcing herself.

This corner room graciously boasted four glazed windows, expensive carpets, a writing desk, a shelf where codices and scrolls were neatly arranged in cubbyholes, and a set of handsome couches. Four velvet-gowned women, wearing golden bear badges, stood in patient attendance.

The bequeather had already arrived. She stood beside a window, magnificently aloof, with her arms crossed, as if the proceedings were too insignificant to attract her interest.

Simo stood against a wall. It seemed odd to Elen that he was carrying a sword in such close proximity to Her Ladyship while her guards stood outside the chamber's closed door. If the lady's woman attendants were armed, then they were hiding their knives.

Luviara stood behind the couch upon which Gevulin sat, the interlocutor positioned to interpret when needed. Gevulin's posture was rigid. He was also freshly shaved and as well turned out as a prince could be, under the circumstances. In other words, he'd made an effort to appear at his best.

On the couch opposite him, leaning forward as if yearning toward the heat of his attractive presence—or perhaps the promise of the alliance he brought—sat Lady Eleawona. Elen knew her at once by the blue kirtle she wore, embroidered with bears cavorting. As a girl, Her Ladyship had always worn blue, her preferred color, and her garments were always decorated with dancing bears. She was about the same age as Elen and Xilsi, no longer a youthful adult, but not into middle age either.

But it wasn't her elaborate kirtle or the gold diadem she wore that arrested Elen's eyes, that caused Kem to gasp behind her.

Eleawona's braided hair was so rich a red-gold that the late-afternoon sunlight through the windows gilded it with a peculiar majesty. Kem's hair wasn't so bright, not as bright as his mother's had been, diluted as his was by his Duenn paternal bloodline.

Yet not even that was what stopped Elen's heart and made the prince turn to see who was causing the interruption. Lady Eleawona looked up with an intelligent, anxious gaze, as if not sure what awaited her from these newcomers.

Eleawona could have been Ao's real sister, the Ao who had lived to become an adult, whose hair, after their escape, had grown out into the extraordinary splendor that had so horribly attracted Lord Duenn's eye. The two women looked that much alike.

16

The Lady and the Prince

Kem staggered. Ipis grabbed him under the arm to hold him upright.

The movement caught Eleawona's eye. At first, she studied the boy with great concentration. She spoke Imperial with careful diction, as if she had practiced diligently so as to make no errors. "Cousin Gevulin, these are the remainder of your court?"

If her use of the appellation "cousin" annoyed him, he was wise enough not to show it, outnumbered as he was in these unfortunate circumstances. "They are."

"So few, when one wished in vain for so many," Eleawona murmured in the language of El's youth, with a flash of wry disappointment that made Elen want to like her. Eleawona went on in Imperial. "I knew not the empire has among them living descendants of the west-county people. My father, His Grace the Lord Arwona, was a son of the west-county ruling clan. Because of that honor, he came to marry my mother. The west-county people are known for sunset hair, as it is called. Like my own. It fades in intensity when people breed outside the lineage. What is your name, young one?"

A chill rushed through Elen. Yet, no, she had to calm herself. Kem's name betrayed nothing.

Kem had gotten the expression of a cornered mouse, quivering, wishing to bolt. "I'm called Kem, Your Highness."

"It surprises me to see a person from the empire bearing a trace of our noble line. Has your lineage told you anything of your sunset hair?"

"I never heard a word of it before now, Your Highness," he said in a choked voice. Softly, he murmured to Ipis, "It's my *hair* they've been looking at. Not me."

"Told you," she whispered.

Gevulin cocked an eye at Elen and remarked, "My youngest novice warden is even more valuable than I had imagined, and I had rated him highly before this."

Elen pressed a hand to her heart in the show of obedience he so clearly desired. "Your Highness. You find me as surprised as you."

"Do I?" he remarked skeptically.

Luviara gave Kem a considering look before addressing the lady. "Your Ladyship, are you saying that Duenn Manor may have some old link to Farlandia's ruling clans? Perhaps dating from before the Pall?"

Eleawona had been sitting with an embroidery circle in her lap, neat stitches outlining a half-finished pair of dancing bears. Now she clenched the loose ends of fabric in her hands as she cast a gaze toward the wall. Two portraits hung side by side, a woman and a man. "I do not know this 'Duenn Manor.' But as for the other, these are, as you see them, my blessed parents."

Elen had only vague memories of Eleawona's parents, always ever so far from a small atoner, but she recognized the then-middle-aged lady ruler of the south county by the black-eyed marten fur draped across her shoulders as a stole. Her hair was partly covered by an embroidered scarf, in the manner of married women, the cloth held in place by a gold diadem; it was the same diadem Eleawona now wore. The bits of her hair that were revealed showed it to be a dark chestnut brown streaked with silver. The portrait of the man depicted him in his youth, a good-looking man pleased to sit for a portrait, with his long red-gold hair unbraided so its beauty might be admired.

Eleawona had her father's looks more than her mother's, and she wore no married woman's scarf, although she had been betrothed to her cousin since the age of thirteen. Twenty years was a long time to forgo a planned wedding, especially among the nobly born, to whom marriage was about advantage and alliance, not love or partnership.

With a grimace as of regret, the lady turned back to the prince.

"It may be such a connection is possible. My father often told stories of his grandfather's brother. He sailed away with his court to seek a safer land after the White Death rose. What you call the Pall. No one knew what happened to them after that. Some must have come ashore safely, to leave such a child as this on your far shore."

"This is an unexpected revelation," agreed Gevulin in the most pleasant tone Elen had ever heard the prince use. She was sure it boded ill. "But first," he added, "I will retire to my rooms to take a report from my deputy courier."

Eleawona looked at Kem, then Ipis, then Xilsi, and finally paused at Elen.

Brows furrowing, the lady said, "This 'deputy courier' looks in some fashion familiar to my eyes. But that cannot be. Unless she was among your retinue when you and I met on Isle Tempest. How long ago that seems now!"

Gevulin stretched an arm along the back of the couch, relaxing, as if it amused him to know secrets his lady ally did not. He seemed like that kind of person. "Almost three years, by imperial reckoning. I do not mind saying that you surprised me, Lady."

"Did I?" Her cheeks flushed a delicate pink. Did she admire the prince? Did his handsome, elegant appearance attract her? Or was it only the promise of imperial power, brought to her defense, that tickled her interest? Why not both?

"It was your intelligence and your notable command of my language. But let me not flatter you, lest you believe I am merely a poet in the wineshop, hoping for my cup to be filled."

Xilsi's gaze flicked ceiling-ward, and Elen made the mistake of catching her eye, and knew they were thinking the same thing: This was exactly Prince Gevulin's situation. He needed the wine.

"As I said, before we proceed to discuss our situation, I desire to speak in private with my deputy courier."

"Cousin Gevulin, what secrets can you have from me, when I have risked as much as you? Perhaps more. For you come with less than promised, not even an army, just these few companions. Pray, show me I can trust you. I would not wish to wonder if the promises we exchanged on Isle Tempest were false coin. I sense you need me as much as I need you, although you are a prince of a mighty empire, and I am but a ruler of the small patch of ground my blessed mother held on to for me."

Gevulin rose abruptly, perhaps in anger. The prince was more of a mystery to Elen than the haunt had ever been. Eleawona remained seated, which would have been an unforgivable insult in the empire but was a daring statement here. They were equals because they were both desperate. He knew it and so did she, and she was letting him know.

He took a restless turn around the room, every eye watching him except for Eleawona's. She loosed a needle and set back to her embroidery as if she had all the time in the world to wait.

The gambit worked. He returned and sat. "Cousin, if I may call you so."

She inclined her head graciously. "You may, and I pray you will."

"I regret the death of your envoy. I traveled north as quickly as I could to discover why an envoy claiming to be your representative had appeared at the Vigil. At that time, I did not know Far Boundary Pall could be crossed. I thought the envoy was part of a scheme by my sister, Prince Astaylin, to discredit me. I had to reach the envoy before news of their presence reached the emperor. That was managed, but at the cost of the envoy's life."

Eleawona raised a beckoning hand. "Captain Raven?"

The bequeather stepped forward. "The envoy was a bequeather. There is a blood price to be paid for their death."

The prince said, "How can there be a price when the envoy did their duty, as commanded? Those who serve the empire understand they offer both their life and their death to the emperor."

The bequeather blinked twice, her expression both inquisitive and judgmental. "We of the Salt Spear Clan are not servants of the empire. We expect payment. In this case, restitution."

In the palace, only the emperor could demand restitution from a prince. The bequeather's statement must have struck Gevulin as absurd, even insulting.

Lady Eleawona had the skill to see him grow angry and the deftness to swiftly intervene. "Cousin, let you not be alarmed. The Sea Wolves have their own customs and manners, apart from ours. But they have proven loyal allies to me in the past few years. I would have been overrun by the usurper—my bastard cousin, Lord Thelan—had it not been for their support. In exchange, I promised the Salt Spear Clan settlement lands in the east county. But . . ."

She stuck the needle back into the fabric, took a few moments to recover her poise, then went on.

"Thelan and I were betrothed in our youth. His father and my mother were brother and sister and decided on it between them. My uncle, Thelan's father, ruled as Highmost in the north county, and my mother in the south county as lady ruler of her own lands. It took all their combined efforts to hold off the raids of the Sea Wolves. Now, both reside in the arms of the white-haired god. Thelan has stolen the throne from his father's legitimate heirs, his own uncle and brothers! He has named himself Highmost. Of the four quarters, the north, west, and east counties bow to him. I am the last holdout. My people are loyal to my mother's memory and thus to me, her sole heir. Thelan demands I marry him. I refuse. My refusal is all well in principle and in honor, but I cannot defeat his army in battle, should he attack."

"Yes, I recall all you told me when we met on Isle Tempest. I said I would be willing to assist you to remain ruler, in exchange for access to your mines."

"I have kept my part of the bargain. I gave the Salt Spear Clan permission to settle in the east county in exchange for their promise to come to my aid should Thelan attack me. I put my people in charge of the east county mines. But Thelan's army marched in and took over the territory. He wanted the mines. He drove the Salt Spear Clan out of the land. They came back to me."

Gevulin said, "Why did the clan approach you in the first place?"

The bequeather said, "We left our homeland because of disputes among our clans."

"Which are?" asked the prince.

"Your Ladyship?" The bequeather gestured to show she would abide by Lady Eleawona's decision: to answer or to remain silent.

The prince looked at Lady Eleawona. For the first time, as he arched an eyebrow, Elen thought she saw a trace of levity in him, although perhaps it was just sarcastic gloating. "Let us not have secrets among us, if we are to be allies," he said, echoing her previous words.

"You may answer with my blessing, Captain Raven," said Her Ladyship with a faint smile, as if amused that the prince's arrow had struck home.

The bequeather's icy seriousness never wavered. "The White Death and its poisonous Spore may not afflict my people, but it afflicts animals and plants. These we need to survive, as much as you do. There is no longer enough land for all the clans to remain in the homeland without starving. That is why some set sail."

"Ah." Gevulin nodded. "Is fighting over land rights why the Pall resulted in a surge of aivur raids some years after its rising? I refer to the raiding that has afflicted the empire's northern and western coasts and its eastern border?"

"I would suppose it is a part of the reason," Captain Raven replied coolly. "As for our current encampment on the causeway, we still hope to settle in the east county lands Lady Eleawona promises to us. For now, the causeway offers a temporary refuge for us, and a defense force held in reserve for her, should she need it."

He gestured agreement. "It seems all our backs are to the wall."

Eleawona nodded. "Now that the rest of your party has rejoined you, let us adjourn to the map room and make plans."

Gevulin glanced at Elen, his expression a promise that he and she would speak later. Then he smiled with worthy grace. "As the poet sang, better to move now than be caught unready later, although I admit that was a song describing a different sort of endeavor."

Xilsi stifled a laugh.

Eleawona smiled politely, too tense to notice Xilsi's amusement. After a effortful pause, as if reluctant to let go of something that gave her comfort, she loosened her grip on the embroidery circle and set it aside on the couch. An attendant darted forward to take it away to a side table.

"Accompany me, cousin. Marvilia, bring refreshments."

The lady and the prince rose. An attendant opened the door. Simo and Luviara followed.

Elen whispered to Xilsi, "Where's Fulmo?"

"Kitchen." Xilsi caught Ipis and Kem. "You two, go back to the suite and sleep. You'll be on night duty with Jirvy. Kem, wrap a scarf over your hair and keep it on at all times."

"Women and girls wear scarves," muttered Kem rebelliously.

"Like Jirvy does when he's on the trail, do you mean?"

"That's not a scarf, it's a kerchief. And it makes him look badass."

"Yes, it does. He wears it because it's the tradition in Wellwroth Province—where he comes from—for hunters to wear scarves. You can call it a kerchief if it makes you feel better. However, you might want to pay attention to the fact that he calls it a scarf and doesn't care. Anyway, ask him to help you. I didn't like the attention your hair was getting before, and I like it even less now. Our situation is complicated enough. We need to calm that down. Got it?"

He hunched his shoulders, obeying under protest. "Yes."

"Good. Come on, Elen. I've been waiting to see their map room."

17

Four Quarters Province

They processed out the door with the leisurely tread common to masters, who need not hasten. At the end of the corridor a gate opened onto a fortified bridge. This bridge spanned the windy gap between the winter palace's upper story and the second story of the four-story tower.

South Ring's tower was said to be as old as the holy road. Young El had never doubted this tale, although Ao had once asked why, then, the stonework looked different, a question to which neither girl had an answer.

Now, though, looking over its square efficiency and the excellence of its stonework, she thought it bore a resemblance to the military construction common in the empire during its early phase of expansion, before the rise of the Pall. How like little Ao to notice such a detail.

The hall and the adjoining tower were far enough apart that a person could not quite leap between them, but close enough that long, sturdy beams had been laid across the gap, between an opening in the hall and another in the tower, to provide a foundation for an enclosed bridge. Its peaked roof sheltered the masters when they crossed, and its walls and planks were made of precious yew, since yew wood was known to repel Spore.

Elen had never been inside the tower because only the Lady of the Marten's atoners were allowed inside, a privilege that could, in the future, belong to Eleawona's atoners, should they outlive her lady mother, which no one expected them to do. All Elen knew, then as now, was that its four stories rose high enough for its flat roof to offer a good view over the countryside. Therefore, the tower was a crucial guard station.

As she entered at the back of the procession, she examined the square chamber with the greatest curiosity. It was floored with yew. Not even the main hall had such a valuable floor; there wasn't enough yew wood to spare.

Besides the luxuriousness of yew planking, the square chamber had the look of a utilitarian military installation. Arrow slits pierced the walls, making it dim even in daytime. Casks of ale, sacks of grain, and sealed oil amphora were stockpiled in neat rows. Racks of weapons stood crammed in between the provisions. Maybe the tower had always been used in this way, or perhaps Eleawona was preparing for a siege.

A wooden staircase took their group in single file up to the next floor. This chamber looked very like the one below, filled with chests and casks and sacks, as well as many bushels of arrows. Still, arrows ran out as they were shot outward. A tower could shield you for a time, but it would also kill you in the end, if you could not leave. Wasn't this the truth of so many promised protections in life?

They ascended to the tower's top floor. Instead of defensive arrow slits, this room had a window on each wall. The layout reminded Elen of Vigil towers. These viewing windows were fitted with paned glass to protect against winter storms.

The prince and his wardens took a tour of each window, Elen trailing after them. To her surprise, the lintels above each window had imperial letters carved into them, marking the directions for north, south, east, and west. Casks were set up around the perimeter, but otherwise no provisions were stored here. Instead, its furnishings reminded her of the sentinels' command hall at Orledder Halt, where strategies were laid, tactics devised, and next week's training regimen decided on. Elen had sat through some of those meetings with the intendant and his captains.

Two shelves, fitted with cubbyholes, stood in the middle of the tower next to an oak table that was scored with age. Unlike the other furniture in the winter palace, the shelves looked exactly like the cubbyhole shelves found in map rooms in the empire. They too wore a patina of great age.

The table at the center of the room also looked as if it had come from another land. Its legs were carved to resemble bamboo, an odd plant to find represented in the north where it didn't grow. Each elegant leg was branded with the stalk-and-leaf reign symbol of the Bamboo Emperor, who had died about one hundred and sixty years ago. She examined the tabletop. A larger version of the Bamboo Emperor's reign symbol was incised on a leather inset, rather faded and thus easy to miss at first glance.

Lady Eleawona unlocked a cupboard in one of the shelves and removed two leather tubes. She withdrew a map from each and rolled them out side by side on the table, anchoring their corners with small figurines in the shape of sarpa and griffins.

Luviara picked up one of the figurines to examine it. "Where did these come from? They are beautifully carved. This was a style popular during the early empire."

"They are so old as to be from my grandparents' grandparents' grandparents' day, or so my mother told me. They are toys for children. That is why I have them."

The prince made a sound as if about to scornfully correct her, but then he paused, his right eyelid twitching at some internal dispute, and cleared his throat, after which he spoke in a softer tone. "Cousin, these are not children's toys. They are pieces for a game we call Many Weapons. Sarpa and griffins are two of the weapons. Swords, spears, archers, cavalry, and siege engineers are the others. Where are the rest of the pieces?"

She shook her head. "These are the only ones I have. Just these eight."

Luviara peered at the underside of one of the tiny griffins and exclaimed in delight. "Look here! This is the maker's mark of a well-known manufactory in the capital city. This set might have belonged to the provincial governor's residence. It must explain why the ruling lineage, your mother's line, I mean, has darker hair than most here."

"How do you mean, Interlocutor?" asked Lady Eleawona.

Luviara set down the piece. She sighed. Frowned.

The prince said, "Go on, Luviara. I'm curious to hear what you seem hesitant to say."

"Four Quarters Province was the last province conquered by the Bamboo Emperor. It was lost to the empire after the Pall rose. It was assumed the northern province had been engulfed by Pall. The Hibiscus Emperor had the imperial archives scrubbed of any and all accounts of a province he no longer ruled. He felt the memory of such losses of territory diminished the prestige of his reign. Be that as it may, and I apologize for any insult to your glorious lineage, Your Exalted Highness, but during the investigations I carried out in my youth, I uncovered evidence that there existed a northern land, one spoken of by the Sea Wolves, that must be what remains of Four Quarters Province."

Gevulin looked annoyed. "I'd rather have known of the existence of this land before you told me of it on the day we met four years ago. But go on. What are you saying about the ruling lineage here, in this south county?"

"Lady Eleawona must be in part descended from whoever the imperial governor and high imperial officials were, whoever was dwelling here when it was a imperial province. They'd have been cut off from the empire by the Pall. Lady Eleawona, your mother has something of the noble appearance of a prince of the Fifth or Sixth Estate. Some generations removed, of course."

"But not my father?" Eleawona asked.

"You spoke of a 'west county' ruling line. From all you have said, I would speculate that when the empire's armies arrived, at the time of the Bamboo Emperor, your father's lineage was the ruling line. Perhaps you have records, Your Ladyship. I would gladly see them."

"All old records were removed to Last Tower at North Hold during my grandfather's reign. Out of my reach."

"Ah," said Luviara. "Some will always seek to veil our eyes when all we wish is to see the truth clearly."

Was the comment directed at Prince Gevulin? If so, he appeared not to notice. After all, he didn't need to listen closely to other people, or at least, not to those beneath him.

"North Hold is the name of your Highmost's seat of power, as I recall," he said to Eleawona. "What is Last Tower?"

"Do you not know? Have you not the same in your empire? It is the last tower on the holy road. Beyond it lies the northern ocean."

Was Last Tower the long-lost terminal Vigil of this broken witch road? Elen looked at Gevulin, wondering if he'd had the same thought.

He frowned, considering. "Cousin, it would assist our situation if you used these maps to better describe this land and its administration to me."

"Of course." Eleawona unhooked a silver pointer, dangling from the table's edge by a chain, and used it to indicate the map on the right. "This is south county's oldest map, a map of the Four Lands." The yellowed vellum and patched rips did indeed suggest great age.

Using the pointer so her skin did not touch the fragile vellum, she traced a doubled line that ran through the center of the map. "These doubled lines mark the holy road. This is South Ring." The pointer's tip came to rest on a stylized oval set athwart the doubled line, then moved down to an area with nothing marked on it at all. "This blank area to the south is the White Sea."

"Far Boundary Pall," Gevulin said.

She went on. "As you can see here, and here, the west county and east county have an ocean shoreline, and thus several ports of call. The south county does not. We have only the White Sea." The map's outline did not look as clean and accurate as imperial maps. Rather than a surveyor's precise measurements and lines, it had the clumsy feel of a rough hand drawing by eye or guesswork. "But let me return to the holy road. As you see, the holy road runs south to north through the center of the Four Lands. We call the holy road 'the spine of the white-haired god,' the spear and strength of the god's power. Yew wood has the power to repel Spore, but the holy road alone withers the deadly mist and its poisonous Spores."

"So does salt water," said Gevulin. "Fresh water, less so. Unless it is pure-water."

"As I've just explained, we have no access to salt water here in the south county, so we cannot rely on it. I have not heard of 'pure-water.'"

"I see," said the prince.

She paused. When he did not explain, she went on, moving the pointer toward the top of the map. "Last Tower marks the end of the road in the north. The city of North Hold grew up next to it. One time only, as a small child, I was taken there to witness my uncle's anointing as Highmost. There is no tower as tall as Last Tower, a full eight stories."

"Like a Vigil," remarked Luviara.

"Is it an actual Vigil tower?" Gevulin asked Eleawona.

"I do not know this word 'vigil.' Last Tower has always stood at the end of the holy road. Thus it is the seat of power of the Highmost."

"What is this other map?" asked the prince. "It looks like a new copy of the old map. Yet lines and contours are drawn in the blank area, in what should be the Pall. What you call the White Sea."

"Yes. Before, we knew only that the White Sea is deadly. That we cannot walk there without dying. Thus, it was a blank to us. Now I have allies from among those who can. They send scouts from their clan into the White Sea. After the scouts return, they stand inside a ring of fire while the Spore is chased off them and burned. Afterward, they are safe to return among us. They report on what they have seen to my mapmaker and me. This is the accounting we make, our mapping of their reports."

Elen took a step closer to the table. Her movement caught Lady Eleawona's eye once again. An attendant seemed ready to charge forward to shove Elen back, but Her Ladyship glanced at the prince first. When he beckoned Elen forward, Eleawona gave a quick shake of the head to her attendant, who settled back. Elen came right up to the table. She now had a clear view of the two maps.

Here lay a rendering of the nameless land where she'd walked as a child. In those days, she and Ao had never once seen a map, never known their world as anything except the dusty path before and behind their dirty feet, and the miserable pens in which they slept and ate what scraps of food were thrown to atoners. Nothing of these memories infused either map. The lives of atoners were invisible to mapmakers—and not just atoners' lives. A map's lines and angles and markings meant many things, of course, but they related nothing of the living or the dead, of pain or joy, cruelty or kindness.

The prince considered these same lines and angles as if they were a battle he needed to win. The increasingly desperate nature of the situation seemed to be bringing out a different side to him. The intendant had once told Elen that to truly master the palace arts, a person had to devote themselves tirelessly to practice, study, and contemplation. Had to never quail even when their limbs grew tired and their mind exhausted by the weary round of discipline. No one who faltered could survive the palace's vicious knives. He himself, he'd intimated, had spent a year in the palace and had escaped the bitter arena willingly, by taking a humiliating assignment to the provinces.

Arrogant though the prince might be, he was quick to adapt to the calamitous nature of his dire circumstances. As the ground shifted under him, he sought to balance himself without falling. He would not give up. No wonder his sister Astaylin saw him as a rival to her power in the Third Estate. Curiously, Elen reflected now, no one had ever ventured an opinion on what his young nephew, the crown prince, might think of him. No one really spoke of the crown prince at all.

"It's an interesting venture to map that which lies beneath the Pall," remarked the prince as he bent low to squint at the faintest lines drawn on the new map. "What is it you hope to gain from this study of the drowned lands? Yet I have one answer already, do I not? You have used this knowledge together with the ability of the aivur to walk within the Pall without dying. You have seen there is land lying beyond the end of the road. You have built the bridge by which we crossed the last gap in the road, the gap closest to the Four Lands. But the gaps to the south are wider and deeper, in their way. They will be harder to bridge by a crude wood-and-rope structure. Even so, what benefit does it gain you to build bridges onto a land you dare not enter? How does hiding a clan of Sea Wolves on the causeway help you, when it seems they are not strong enough in numbers to defeat your rival?"

She folded her hands calmly before her. "I shall be happy to relate my thoughts on this matter. Before I do this, let me ask. Did you not say you needed to receive a report from your courier? Let her speak before us all, as you agreed. Together, we can hear what news comes from beyond the White Sea. From your empire."

He straightened up, frowning at this demand, but he swallowed his irritation. Perhaps he had decided to change his tactics. Perhaps he realized she'd cornered him with his own words. "Deputy Courier, your report."

The prince, the lady, the interlocutor, and the bequeather all looked at Elen with a degree of attention that might have disconcerted another, but Elen had gone through too much to be intimidated by their regard. Also, she was intrigued. How would her news about Lord Duenn and the hooded figure addressed as Sublime Highness fall among them? How would they respond? What *were* their plans, now that they had their backs to the wall? The haunt would have smiled in his mischievous way, enjoying the show. Well, she would give them a show, in his honor.

She lifted her chin. Best to start with the worst. "Your Exalted Highness. After your departure, a large company of Duenn Manor soldiers arrived at Far Boundary Vigil."

"Yes, as expected. Go on."

"I released the horses well away from the Vigil. Then, as planned, I returned. From hiding, I was able to overhear some of their plans. One cohort was sent to search the countryside for the missing horses. It's thought you rode away overland, headed back to the heartland."

"Good," Simo muttered with an approving nod. "The plan worked to draw their attention elsewhere."

"The other company was ordered to set up a temporary garrison at the Vigil. Ostensibly until a new garrison of wardens arrives to take charge of the Vigil. In my opinion it was more of a territorial power play. Lord Duenn himself was with the company."

"How can that be?" asked the prince. "He was stuck on the other side of the avalanche. You must have been mistaken."

"I am not mistaken. He was there. How it can be, I do not know. The most likely explanation is that the engineers had cleared a path stable enough for goats to cross the rubble. If they managed that, then people on foot may have followed after the goats. I don't know. I do have a question, if I may, Your Highness."

"Go on."

"Who is addressed as Your Sublime Highness?"

Gevulin's expression grew tight. His lips pinched together. "Explain."

"I observed a cloaked and hooded figure standing alongside Lord Duenn. Their face and garments were obscured. I can tell you nothing more than that the others addressed them with that honorific. They were in charge. They were looking for you."

"That can't be," he muttered. More sharply, he added, "How many were in Duenn's company? Can the Salt Spear Clan defeat them, were their fighters to cross the gap in force and attack Far Boundary Vigil?"

The bequeather took a step forward but halted when Lady Eleawona raised a hand.

Eleawona said, "You wish to use the Salt Spear Clan to attack imperial soldiers in imperial territory?"

"Is that not what they are on the road for? As a prelude to an assault on the empire?"

She exchanged a look with the bequeather before setting a hand on the unrolled map. "Cousin, the Salt Spear Clan is *hiding* on the causeway, amid the White Sea. Thelan's forces burned their ships. Even had they another place to go, which they do not, they can't get there now."

"Besides that," the bequeather remarked drily, "it is the law of the Four Lands that any and all of my people—aivur, as you call us—who are captured on Four Lands soil will be burned to death."

Gevulin stared at Captain Raven, then said, "I thought the clan was on the causeway in order to defend South Ring, should your enemy attack."

"Did I not already say that they are not numerous enough to defeat Thelan's army, should he invade? It is why I called for your aid. Our situation is desperate!" Eleawona indicated the White Sea and the hidden causeway. "For now, I am keeping my allies protected by concealing them from Thelan's spies while we figure out what to do next."

"But I thought . . ." He shook his head.

"Why did you think I would attack your empire, which is far larger than my modest militia can possibly handle?"

"Is that not the point of the map and its written message, the one you sent with your envoy? That you have collected allies who can raid into the empire via these mysterious passageways that lead through the Desolation? That, with their help, I can make a lightning strike into the palace to establish myself on the throne? After which, with the forces I would then command, I can aid you in return. Was that not your plan?"

Eleawona withdrew a step, as if the prince had begun speaking in a disturbing gibberish. "What map are you speaking of? I sent no map with the envoy."

18

The Crossed Lances

Gevulin snapped his fingers. Simo handed him the map tube. The prince removed the vellum and unrolled it atop the other maps, moving the sarpa and griffin pieces to hold down its own curling corners.

"We found this map in the possession of the Far Boundary Vigil captain. The captain had been killed by sarpa acid but had hidden the map before his untimely death. You sent it with the envoy."

Eleawona swayed as if in shock. An attendant hurried forward with a stool. Her Ladyship sat, a hand pressed to her chest. "I sent no map."

Gevulin stared at her. "Here is your message written upon it!"

She rose to examine the map and the message written in squares across its contours. After a long silence, she took an edge of the vellum between her fingers and rubbed it, as if reading answers from its texture.

"This is ill-omened," she murmured in the language of the north. "I like it not."

"Speak in a language I can understand!" Gevulin demanded, slipping back into his hectoring ways.

She switched to Imperial. "I would never send a written document to you. A document might fall into Thelan's hands, a risk too great to take. That is why I sent as envoy a bequeather, like Captain Raven. The envoy carried a message for you, memorized, not written down. Bequeathers do not carry written messages. They carry them on their tongues. If they die, the message dies with them."

"Unless they are tortured and reveal all," said Gevulin.

Captain Raven spoke as softly as a knife slipped between the ribs. "Do not insult us. We speak only when we choose to, and never when coerced."

Gevulin considered the bequeather and, at length, gave the aivur a nod of acknowledgment, the closest he would come to an apology. "It is true, Lord Genia discovered nothing from the envoy. But if you did not send the map, cousin, then who did? And why?"

"To implicate you, Your Highness," said Simo. "That seems obvious, if what Her Ladyship says is true." He inclined his head toward Eleawona to indicate that he was not accusing her of lying.

"Yes, that is clear. That leaves the question of how Astaylin could have managed this. I suppose she has her own sources of information and various tricks up her sleeves. Including suborning Captain Mekvo, it seems."

Xilsi walked up to the table, inserting herself into the conversation. Until now, she'd remained quietly in the back. "I refuse to believe Mekky was party to any betrayal of the wardens. He lived for the order. He cared nothing for the palace, only for the safety of the roads and the empire."

"Do you have a better idea, given the evidence?" Gevulin asked a bit snidely.

"I have a better question," Xilsi retorted. "Who could have known Vigil Captain Mekvo's staff concealed a hiding place?"

"You knew the staff was hollow," said Gevulin.

"So I did. But I came with you, Your Highness, so I arrived at the Vigil at the same time as you did. Ipis was with me the entire time. I had no opportunity to hide the map and then rediscover it."

Xilsi's tone was so tart that Elen expected the prince to reprimand the warden, so Elen quickly dove in. "Which suggests that the plot was carried out before we arrived, likely in concert with the sarpa attack, and by someone who suspected Prince Gevulin would discover the map. How did Captain Mekvo acquire the staff?"

"Oh," said Xilsi, as if she'd forgotten to ask herself that even more obvious question. Then, with the query answered in her mind, her aspect altered to one of sudden, intense apprehension. "*Oh.*"

A silence descended as everyone stared at her, hearing trouble in her tone.

Gevulin placed a hand on his gold-plated knife hilt. Simo shouldered up to stand at his prince's back. Luviara took a step away to give the others room at the table. The bequeather clenched her hands as if hearing an evil truth in Xilsi's voice.

To be fair, Elen feared the answer too. Xilsi had just realized something that had genuinely shocked her, and she was a Bakassar scion who knew the palace so well that nothing should shock her. Eleawona kept her hand pressed to her chest, while her attendants clustered close in the manner of selfless retainers hoping to take a sword in the heart as long as it saved the one they served. In their way, they were atoners too, were they not? Elen pitied them. They would never escape.

A horn's resonant blare rose from the rooftop above. Even after so many years Elen recognized the sentry call's three blasts, *warh warh warrhh,* a pause, and again three blasts, a pause, and again three blasts.

A trapdoor clapped open, a ladder unfolded from above, and a guardsman climbed down.

"Your Ladyship!" he cried, startled to find her there. "Urgent news!"

"What is it?"

"An armed force approaching. Several hundred mounted soldiers, perhaps more."

"Our troops, I pray?"

"I'm not sure, Your Ladyship. They're too far away."

"Let me see with my own eyes," she cried, all else forgotten.

She clambered up the ladder, flipping the front of her kirtle out of the way of her feet.

The prince looked at Xilsi. "We shall return to that topic. For now, guard the map."

He followed Lady Eleawona up the ladder, with Simo at his heels. Elen dashed after and went up too.

Unlike all the other buildings within the Ring, which had steep, peaked roofs, the tower's roof was flat and surrounded by battlements to create a viewing platform, a splendid sentry post. The view in all directions was astounding, as well as tactically useful.

"A cavalry company, approaching in haste," said Lady Eleawona as she joined the guardsman at the battlement, Gevulin beside her.

The prince gestured. "Simo, my spyglass."

The captain dug the instrument out and handed it over. Gevulin set the spyglass to his eye as Lady Eleawona watched in puzzlement.

"What is that object?" she asked.

With a show of courtesy that surprised Elen, the prince handed the lady the spyglass and patiently helped her adjust it. Her gasp when the distant figures leaped into closer view made Elen smile. Strange to think the masters of the Four Lands had fewer modern tools at their disposal than did a mere deputy courier. As she watched Gevulin's strained politesse she thought: *That is the gist of it, the measure of the empire's strength and the prince's weakness.*

The prince said curtly, "Are we in danger?"

The lady's shoulders dropped with relief. She lowered the spyglass. "We are not. They fly my personal bear banner. I embroider each banner myself, and send one out with each of my companies. It is a sign of my trust in them. The regimental flag bears the crossed lances of Captain Dinec's Second Cavalry. He was meant to return a month ago, after he went out on an extended patrol of the Menel Hills. He is come at last." At Gevulin's querying look, she added, "We patrol on force in the Menel Hills, to hold our honor against the pressures of the usurper. This *spyglass* is a miraculous instrument, for me to see all that at such a remove."

"Then it shall be yours, cousin," he said magnanimously. "You have seen something that has given you heart."

"I have! Let me go down to greet Captain Dinec, as he deserves."

Had her cheeks flushed at the mention of this mysterious captain's name? Did unmarried ladyships take lovers, or was it just the cold wind bringing color to her cheeks?

Or perhaps she was responding to Gevulin's gift and what she thought his generosity might imply about the future of their relationship. Elen could not tell, and she was already going down the ladder.

As Eleawona descended, Gevulin said to Simo, "We will give her Ipis's spyglass, not mine."

"Yes, Your Highness. I'll see to it."

The prince then climbed down, followed by Simo.

Elen lingered above. As children, she and Ao had never had the chance to see so far, like birds on the wing. Their eyes had always been on the ground, from which danger sprouted, or lifted, at most, to the surrounding trees and plants, the wandering beasts and the perilous humans who might harm her and Ao. From this height, the gentle rise and fall of the ground had a pleasing aspect. Here and there, a dusting of snow had settled. There was so much forest, mostly hardy oak. She also spied trees with medicinal properties. Ao had taught her to collect aspen's bark, beech mast, and birch leaves. The inner bark of northern pine could be ground up to make bread.

The main stretches of settlements and fields ran north and south, parallel to the holy road. Lanes cut stripes through the countryside to the east and west, toward the villas and estates and farms that fed the court. She could even see the tower tops of Parlay Hill Hall, to the southeast, sticking up above the forest canopy. By the shape of the intact ones and the position of the broken one she remained sure these were a set of Spires. Maybe she could convince the prince to investigate them, and bring her along. If she walked among broken Spires at moon-bright, could she speak to the haunt?

No, it was wistful thinking on her part. The haunt had departed into Far Boundary Pall. If Spires connected to any Pall, then the haunt would have escaped Three Spires long ago. She would not find him at Parlay Hill Hall, if the old ruins truly were the remains of a Spires compound.

She had to accept she would never see him again. She had to cherish the time they'd had and let go of the story she'd begun to weave, in her own heart, about the two of them. Spinning a flowery tale out of air didn't make it come true. Fortune had brought them together for a brief span. Duty and honor had torn them apart. She couldn't regret meeting him, though his loss hurt. Life was still better for the touch of his lips to her palm, for the memory of his laugh and his sardonic asides.

Elen's gaze returned to the distant company approaching South Ring. Her spyglass was in her pack, which she'd left stowed in the ram suite, so there was nothing she could learn about the riders without waiting in the chill a lot longer, which she was not inclined to do. Beyond one curious glance at her, the guardsman on watch kept his eyes on the road. Feet scraped on the ladder. A new guardsman clambered up, gave her a suspicious look, then hurried to join his fellow.

In the northern speech he said to the other man, "Peculiar doings, I'm telling you. I think Her Ladyship has gone sweet on that outlander. But it's not like he brought an army with him, just a ragtag patrol and that hulking monster in the kitchen."

It was a relief to hear confirmation that Fulmo was alive.

The new guardsman went on. "Hard to see how the monster can cook, with such meaty hands, eh?"

"Hsst. That's one of the foreigners, there."

"Eh, they can't understand us. Funny to think I've gotten used to the Sea Wolves stalking around. Captain Icicle, some call the bequeather. Cold as a raven's heart. Do you think Wolves ever smile?"

"Only when they're killing people or savoring their flesh."

They chortled companionably. Elen decided her hands were cold enough, even with gloves on, and she climbed down into the map room. The others were all gone, except Xilsi, who was carefully rolling up the fragile vellum map of the Desolation. She glanced over as Elen thumped onto the floor.

"They were in such a hurry even Simo neglected this. Whatever its origin, it's still evidence of whatever is going on."

"What do you think is going on?" Elen asked, chafing her hands together.

Xilsi had a way of frowning that meant she was thinking through troubling connections, and she clearly was a person who had spent many years not getting tangled up in palace intrigue. She slid the rolled-up vellum into the waxed tube and slung it over her shoulder. "We'd better go. I don't like to leave His Exalted Highness roaming around unattended. To my utter surprise, I believe he rather likes Her Ladyship. That makes me nervous."

As Xilsi strode toward the door, Elen said, "Who gave Mekvo the staff, by the way? You never said. And for that matter, who is addressed as Your Sublime Highness?"

Xilsi paused. When she looked over a shoulder at Elen, her expression held a weight that made her youthful features look as if she had aged half a lifetime between one breath and the next.

"It's the same answer to both your questions. The crown prince. His Sublime Highness, Prince Minaylin."

19

THE PETRIFIED HEART OF A DRAGON

They caught up with the others because Lady Eleawona had taken a turn into her chambers. Rather than remain in the corridor like a lackey, Gevulin had retired into the ram suite. Simo stood at the suite's door to warn the prince when it was time to come out. It was a delicate dance. The prince could not insult Eleawona by making her wait for him because he hadn't the power to force her to comply, yet neither could he be seen to be kept waiting by her.

Eleawona emerged wearing a magnificent bearskin cape worthy of a ruler. Simo's warning knock brought Gevulin out to smoothly intercept her. It was well timed.

As the door into the ram suite closed, a hand from inside caught it, and Kem peeked out. A drab kerchief—one of Jirvy's—was tied with cunning knots to conceal his hair. The style gave the lad a daringly raffish look that caused one or two of Eleawona's younger attendants to give him an admiring glance. Had it been Jirvy's bold flouting of heartland conventions that had first drawn novice Xilsi's attention to a young man so far below her in Manor status? Or had his unerring aim pierced her haughty armor? It was pleasant to know she could ask Xilsi and not be rebuffed. Probably she would soon hear the entire story, at length.

But this was no time for levity. Elen waved at Kem to shut the door. Just before he did so, Xilsi handed him the tube with its mysterious map. He took it and retreated into the suite.

Trouble was brewing in a worse way even than conflict between two princes of the Third Estate. What had Crown Prince Minaylin to do with this debacle of a mission? Elen struggled to accept that the hooded figure she'd seen and overheard at Far Boundary Vigil had really been the crown prince. Ipis had claimed the mysterious and disliked Minaylin was so protected by his mother, the Magnolia Emperor, that he was not allowed to ever leave the palace grounds and its adjoining parkland except for seasonal tours in her company to the spring-and-autumn palace. How could he have learned about his uncle Gevulin's doings with the wardens when he was not himself in the wardens? How had Lord Duenn become acquainted with the crown prince, and not just acquainted, but deep in his confidence? Hadn't Duenn Manor marched with Prince Astaylin at some festival? How did that fit in?

No wonder Xilsi had wanted out of the hothouse that was palace intrigue. What an ugly nightmare this was.

As Elen fell in at the end of the processional line, she noticed Luviara was missing. She signaled Xilsi to stay where she was and eased up until she was walking to the left of Simo, two ranks behind the lady and the prince.

"Captain, where is the interlocutor?"

"Luviara went ahead with the bequeather. We are meant to greet the regiment and thank them for their gallant service and tireless patrol of the border. They really go in for payment in this place, don't you think?"

"What do you mean?"

"We serve because it is our duty and honor to serve. An honorable official of the empire does not need to be praised and patted like we are dogs. It's demeaning." He gave her a sharp look. "Don't you agree, Deputy Courier?"

"I always hope not to be treated like a dog," she agreed. "Unless the table scraps are particularly tasty that evening."

He gave a chuff of amusement. Simo was prickly, but she liked that he was honest about who he was. Or who she hoped he was. What if he was a spy the crown prince had inserted into the wardens? Simo had been elevated to become Prince Gevulin's personal captain even though—as Xilsi had said—a man of his modest meritorious Manor affiliation wouldn't otherwise have expected to attain such a superior rank. But that didn't make sense either. As a warden, Simo's status was secure as personal captain to the all-seeing eye. Besides the prince, only the chief warden could gainsay Simo's orders. And only a prince could become the all-seeing eye. So what had the crown prince to promise a man like Simo, who had never shown himself to be in any way duplicitous, not from what Elen had seen? Yet she knew nothing about Simo's years fighting in the east. War could corrupt a man, so the poets said.

Even so, she couldn't see it. She sensed no touch of poison in him, no lurking spore of venal corruption.

She dropped back beside Xilsi. Could the Bakas Manor scion be in league with the crown prince? As quickly as the thought rose, she dismissed it. Xilsi had many flaws, but ambition wasn't among them. There was nothing the crown prince could offer Xilsi that Xilsi hadn't already refused. And Bakas Manor was too powerful to be blackmailed. So, not Xilsi.

Fulmo? That seemed unlikely, unless Hemerlin was the spy and Fulmo his agent. Yet Hemerlin was so status conscious with his whip and his crabby complaining that she couldn't see it being him. If the chief menial on the prince's staff loved anyone, he loved the prince he'd raised from childhood. No, not Hemerlin.

Jirvy? He, too, had a modest background and might crave riches or status for his meritorious Manor. After all, he'd married to accommodate his family, and then lied to his long-time lover Xilsi about his marriage and the children it had produced. So, he was capable of lying.

What of Ipis? Elen knew almost nothing about Ipis except that she seemed not to have a lot of friends or close family, and this expedition was her first long-distance outing as a warden.

As for Luviara, she had by her own admission traveled a great deal, and for the last few years in Gevulin's company. But she belonged to the Heart Temple, not to the palace.

The lady and the prince descended the wide staircase side by side. They looked quite handsome together. Eleawona's bearskin cape rippled with power. Gevulin walked with the confidence of a man who has always crushed flowers underfoot and never had to sweep up the ruined petals. They crossed the silent entryway to the throne hall's closed doors. These iron-banded doors rose twice the height of a man. The wood panels were carved with figures of animals: martens, bears, deer, wolves, aurochs, onagers, tapirs, foxes, antelopes, horses, lions, and the fearsome, twin-jawed sea-jackal of legend.

There was a separate back entrance, a passage that led to the rear of the throne hall's dais. As a child, she had crept up and down it as part of her atoner's patrol. The secret corridor allowed a ruler to appear as if by magic on the throne; messengers could also race an urgent message to the ruler while the ruler was holding court, without having to display their presence before the gathered assembly. It made a ruler seem all-knowing to have answers immediately to hand.

As a matter of course, the Lady of the Marten had always preferred to enter the throne hall through the main doors, which she had always had thrown open with a fanfare of trumpets to allow her to process with stately authority past her waiting court. Who she acknowledged and who she ignored measured people's place on the complex ladder of the masters' hierarchy. The masters had rungs of status, too, which placed all of them above retainers while ranking value among themselves. Even atoners scraped for their own tiny slivers of status, short-lived though they might be. Everyone clawed their way up or slid their way down. They copied what they saw from those in power. No one knew any other way to live.

The bequeather and Luviara had indeed arrived at the doors before them, as befitted interlocutors. Elen cut a glance at Captain Raven, who was standing silent and expressionless. Did aivur live the same way, always clawing? Yet from the bequeather's words, Elen wondered if perhaps they did not. Or not in a way humans could easily recognize.

Guards straightened to attention as Her Ladyship approached the doors. Attendants grasped the heavy iron rings and tugged the doors open. Hinges groaned. Gevulin winced. Nothing in the Orledder Halt Residence groaned, nor in any imperial compound. Everything was swept, cleaned, oiled, and inspected regularly.

Everyone waited for the lady and the prince to enter, then fell in behind the nobles but ahead of Simo, Xilsi, the attendants, and Elen, who kept pace at the rear.

Being on the ground floor, the throne hall had no windows lower down, only horizontal slits running just below the ceiling. It was a defensive building, built to outlast a military attack. The high windows meant the hall was relatively dim even in the daytime, and especially in winter.

Lady Eleawona said to an attendant, "See to the lamps—"

She broke off. A lamp already burned at the far end of the hall, up on the dais. This lit lamp hung from a tripod set beside the famous south-county throne, which was carved from an ebony wood–like substance said to be the petrified heart of a dragon.

A dragon. Elen's breathing quickened, thinking of *him*.

But it wasn't the lamp or the throne itself that caught Eleawona's eye. That made her halt dead.

"What means this?" she hissed. In an altered tone, low and harsh, Her Ladyship said to the prince, "Cousin, your weapons."

The doors clanged shut behind them. Soldiers filed into place, cutting off the exit.

A man sat on the throne, so relaxed he was slumped, chin resting on his hand.

"Nay, my beloved, do not leave so soon," he said in the northern speech. Then he switched to the same imperial diction Eleawona used to speak to Gevulin. His was more fluid and easy, as though he had practiced with more diligence and employed a better tutor. "Bring forward your imperial guest. I am keen to meet the man with whom you have been plotting my downfall."

Gevulin said, "Who is this upstart who dares to sit upon your throne?"

"Thelan!" Eleawona cried, gone rigid. "My cousin. The usurper."

20

A Calculated Insult

"You may address me as Highmost," said the man on the throne, his amused tone underlaid with a steel-bladed spine.

Even as a youth Lord Thelan had been striking, a good-looking boy with the darker hair, brown eyes, and olive skin tone characteristic of the ruling lineage. Only now did Elen understand these features as signaling descent from an imperial governor who'd been cut off from the Tranquil Empire in the south by the rise of the Pall, all those generations ago.

After the cataclysm, this small group of ruling officials would have had to walk a delicate balance so as not to be cast out or murdered. Some had clearly managed to marry the right people at the right time and had left what they could to their descendants. Who Thelan's mother actually was, Elen did not know. No one had ever spoken of it, except to call him a bastard. Now she wondered if his father had strayed farther afield, maybe bedded a foreign courtesan or an imperial adventurer bold enough to set sail from the Blasted Coast in search of fortune in the storm-swept northern isles.

The silence in the hall became oppressive. Eleawona stood as if struck dumb. Gevulin kept a hand on his sword hilt but made no foolish moves. He, Simo, and Xilsi scanned the hall's dim corners and high ceiling beams, searching for ambushers and an escape route.

"No greeting, my beloved Eleawona?" Thelan asked. He did not rise. It was a calculated insult. Although he wasn't smiling, he oozed smug jubilance.

"Where is Captain Dinec and his company?" Eleawona asked. "I saw their flag."

"Ah, yes." He nodded. "Well, here I am now. You have offended me, beloved. Insulted me by refusing all my most humble overtures. We were so close when we were young. What happened?"

"You can answer that for yourself, since you mock me with this scene."

"I have wished for nothing but that you receive the honor that you deserve."

"It has long been clear to me that the honor you believe I deserve is to be your prisoner, your subordinate, your retainer."

He clucked his tongue, shaking his head sadly. "You have always misjudged me."

"Have I? I think not. You remain vulnerable. I have my own far-ranging plans."

"Do you?" How he managed to sound so sincere and concerned while twisting the knife was impressive. He made a sweeping gesture with his arm, indicating the hall in which Eleawona stood alone, but for Gevulin, Simo, Xilsi, the bequeather and the interlocutor, Elen, and Eleawona's four personal attendants. By Elen's count, Thelan had twenty-two of his own soldiers ready to spring. "Then by all means, show me your power."

If Eleawona was frightened, her stance and expression did not show it. Her cool composure drew the eye toward her face, but Elen saw how her left hand twitched, closing.

"I surmise you are out ahead of your army, Thelan. You liked playing that game when we were young. Your lightning dashes make you vulnerable. My supporters dwell in great numbers in South Ring. All the south county are loyal to me, as my mother's heir."

Thelan had lazy eyes, flickering as if he could scarcely stay awake, so bored was he of this byplay. "You are too slow, my beloved. Always a step behind. I fear you have not learned the most essential lesson."

He paused.

Eleawona did not bite. Neither did Gevulin, who leaned to whisper something in Simo's ear and cast a signaling glance back toward Luviara. *Ah,* thought Elen, *he means the theurgist to release an air spirit to blow a wind of confusion through the hall.* That would throw the cat among the pigeons and give them a chance to escape, or even to bind and capture the overconfident Thelan.

"No? You haven't learned the most essential lesson?" Thelan smiled. It was the same smile the adolescent Thelan had turned upon young El, asking the atoner how she spotted Spore so cannily and exclaiming when she'd said she "sniffed it out, my lord," as if it were the wittiest and wisest answer ever heard. "Then you must allow me to demonstrate. Captain Raven?"

He beckoned with a hand.

The bequeather walked forward to halt at the base of the dais steps. "Highmost," she said. "The council of the Salt Spear Clan formally accepts your offer."

"Offer!" Eleawona sputtered. "What does this mean, Captain?"

The bequeather said, "I merely deliver the council's decision."

"What does it mean?" Thelan quipped lightly. "It means I promise the Salt Spear Clan a settlement and territory in the east county."

"I promised them that!"

"But you couldn't give it to them." He arched a coy eyebrow. "I can."

Eleawona's mouth worked as if she was trying to speak but had been stripped of language. Finally, in a choked voice, she said, "But you have only ever fought the Sea Wolves. I'm the one who offered them an alliance."

"So you did, which is what gave me the idea. You see, beloved, the lesson of battle is that you never know when you have to change up your line of march. It's true the Sea Wolves have long been our enemy and a dire threat. No offense intended, Captain," he added with a nod.

Captain Raven said, "No offense is taken."

Thelan returned his attention to his cousin. "My father and your mother joined forces to fight nobly against them. They drove out the most troublesome of the invaders and corralled others within the west county. You and I could have continued this fine tradition, were you not so stubborn. But that's neither here nor there, is it? Not anymore."

He paused again, allowing Eleawona room to reply.

Gevulin whispered something in Her Ladyship's ear. She replied in a similar whisper, stiffened with new resolve.

Thelan went on with the glib assurance of a man who has trapped his foe in unbreakable chains. "With the throne of the Highmost in my hands and control of the Four Lands in my grasp, I now turn my attention to making this blessed kingdom a safer place for my people to live and prosper. Is that not what the white-haired god desires from us, his chosen and anointed rulers? There shall be peace in the Four Lands for the first time in many generations. We shall no longer fight among ourselves. Neither shall our shores be raided by outsiders, for rather the outsiders will become like to us, a godly and peaceable people. May we all praise the white-haired god, whose lightning scalds the path of the wicked and brightens the road of the righteous." He raised both hands as to the heavens.

Without looking around, Gevulin said, "Luviara, now is the time to end this dire performance. Any actor in the empire would be ashamed."

Thelan settled back as if enjoying himself.

"Luviara?" Gevulin turned to glare at his interlocutor.

The theurgist released no spirit to trouble the air and bind the usurper. Her bland expression made Elen abruptly watchful. This boded ill.

Luviara placed a hand on her heart and offered Prince Gevulin a respectful bow. "Your Exalted Highness, I regret to inform you that is no longer possible."

"You've used up all your air spirits? You are meant to keep me apprised when that happens."

"Strange that, days ago, you asked me how many I had bound, as if you could sense them, and yet now you don't know if I have any bound at all. But the mystery of your uncharacteristic behavior can no longer be my concern. Your traitorous rebellion is over, Your Highness."

Xilsi muttered, "Over? By the High Heavens, what soured wine is this set on my table?"

Simo said, "Luviara, what do you mean by this disloyal speech toward an exalted prince of the Third Estate?"

"Disloyal? I serve the empire and thus the Magnolia Emperor. I certainly do not serve the treasonous ambition of a prince who thinks too well of himself."

Her cool proclamation dropped like a blast of ice, freezing everyone in their tracks.

So angry was the prince at her refusal that he turned his back on Thelan to confront the theurgist with the whole force of his fury. "Did Astaylin put you up to this? What did she offer you? I'll triple it."

"Your Exalted Highness, I do not serve Prince Astaylin. Nor has she been under my surveillance. There are others appointed to that task."

"Surveilling *Astaylin*?" Xilsi rubbed her eyes and muttered, "Oh fuck, this is bad."

Simo looked as if he'd been hit by an anvil.

Gevulin fumed. He had questions but was too proud to ask.

Elen had no such qualms. For her, it wasn't personal. It was survival. "Worthy Interlocutor, are you saying you have always been the emperor's spy? All the time you traveled with His Exalted Highness around the empire so he might get to know the roads his wardens would patrol and guard?"

"It was the bargain I made with the emperor," Luviara said mildly. "To bring in absolute proof of treasonous intent. His Exalted Highness's actions at Far Boundary Vigil and onward have left no doubt. The letter he wrote condemns him in his own writing. This letter is in my possession, together with a missive detailing Lord Thelan's support of my endeavors on the emperor's behalf."

The prince's posture remained that of an enraged man, but a slow tidal change shifted across his face as the reality sank in.

Elen took advantage of everyone else's shock to speak again, trying to draw out more information. "Worthy Luviara, I always thought the Heart Temple's venerables opposed the Lotus Clan when it conquered the Seven Golden Kingdoms. When the Lotus General proclaimed the beginning of a new and tranquil empire. So it surprises me to hear you speak of a bargain with the emperor, rather than your loyalty to the Heart Temple. Surely you, like all theurgists and healers, pledged an oath to devote your life to one of holy service."

"The temple turned their back on me. The emperor listened when the Inner Chamber would not. It's true, we of the temple make an oath to nourish the hearts and minds and bodies of the emperor's subjects with our prayers and our healers. But we also guard against the grievances of those whose malicious ambitions would disturb the empire's tranquility. For as it happens, the most munificent Magnolia Emperor has had her eye on her younger brother Gevulin for a long time." She bowed to Gevulin. "Your Exalted Highness, your rebellion is over. I pray you, accept your defeat in the name of those who serve you, so they do not receive punishment merely for showing loyalty to their prince-warden."

For the first time, Gevulin looked at Elen. In his furious gaze she saw the command she had feared. For all his discipline, in the end anger and pride governed him, as she'd guessed from the start.

But the viper could only kill one person at a time. It had to move across that floor, vulnerable all the while, a small white snake easy to crush or cut to pieces. It was a foolish gamble with a low chance of success. On top of that, she didn't know what would happen to her if the viper was killed, and she wasn't about to find out on the prince's behalf, not when he was outnumbered. Luviara's death wouldn't change anything about their circumstances. Gevulin was just lashing out in the manner of a small child thwarted of a coveted item.

Unfortunately, Gevulin's attention brought Thelan's alert gaze to settle on Elen for the first time. The lord shot to attention, standing up. His soldiers leaped forward to press around him, in case he descended the dais, but he merely pointed at her.

"Bring her forward. Yes, that one at the back."

21

The Nose-Smart Girl

Elen did not wait for the soldiers to close in around her. She walked past the others. Xilsi signaled some sort of message with a lift of her eyebrows, but what she meant, Elen could not guess.

As she passed, Gevulin caught her eye and touched his forearm in a brusque, silent command as he reoriented himself to the shifting movement. The new opportunities.

Yes, she now had a chance to kill Thelan. Maybe Thelan's death would even be worth it. Cut off the head, and the monster dies. To take care of the soldiers, Gevulin had his sword, as did Simo and Xilsi. They were badly outnumbered, but the death of Thelan would leave Eleawona as the sole master in command.

However, Thelan was a cautious man. His soldiers halted her a good ten steps from the throne. Its oily substance gleamed as if charred remains had been polished with blood and tears. Did dragons have burnt, evil hearts? Thinking of the haunt, she could not accept it. Surely their hearts must be as fierce and as golden as their fabled beauty described in old poems: *More splendid than the sun, they rise from the sea at dawn. My heart breaks, knowing I shall never again see these bright wings fill the sky. Nor you, my love, gone into evening's twilight and never to return.*

"An unusual color of eyes you have, that greenish cast," said Thelan. "I've only ever seen one person who had them, and that was about twenty years ago. She'd have been twelve or thirteen then, I suppose, so you're the right age now. You look like enough that you could be her. There's one other way to tell for sure."

He rose and descended the several steps to the main floor. He took a spear from one of his followers, halted just out of Elen's reach, and lifted the spear. With a threatening feather-touch of its point, he tapped the side of her neck, the old wavy scar. She tensed, but he merely lowered the spear and set its haft on the ground.

"I'll be cursed for an atoner," Thelan muttered to the puzzlement of all listening. "It's the nose-smart girl, all grown up and with her hair grown out, I swear it. El, isn't it? Named after my cousin, so I was told, when you were a nameless orphan placed in her court as an atoner."

He paused, inviting her to answer. When she said nothing, except to clench her hands, he went on.

"So you and that sad bastard escaped, did you? Everyone thought you'd been eaten up by the White Sea along with an entire squad of my best soldiers. And their fine horses too. I was so angry." A flicker of intense emotion shuddered through his smiling expression like a glimpse into a concealed pit of venom. She braced herself for something terrible, but the lord controlled himself and went on in a tone so jovial that it flayed. "What happened to the sad bastard, that girl who was always with you? Did dearest Eleawona even ask after her own sister?"

Her own sister.

Ao? Eleawona's bastard sister? Could it be true?

"How dare you!" Eleawona cried, when she had managed with such composure up to now. Only with this revelation did she lose her carefully bridled temper.

He mocked her with a lifted eyebrow. "Truly, it was the measure of your mother that she took her revenge on your father's infidelity by punishing his innocent by-blow in his stead. She had so many other options. She could have refused his bed. Sent him back to the west county in disgrace. Yet she chose to visit her fury upon the most helpless of those involved, the one who was entirely innocent."

"That is enough, Thelan!"

"Oh, no, no, no, it is not nearly enough. I have long wished to unburden myself on this score."

Of course it could be true. Elen knew it in her bones. The hair being shaved every month, to conceal its color. And yet at the same time, the extra food the two girls would sometimes get, although maybe the extra food was only for Ao, who simply shared it with El as if it were for both of them. The way the soldiers had ogled Ao as she neared womanhood. It was almost too horrifying to contemplate.

Thelan went on in an almost giddy tone. "When I realized what was going on with that atoner—Ao, wasn't that her name?—I was genuinely shocked. Growing up as I did in my grandfather's and then father's court, I was spat on and despised by those who thought themselves above me. Little could shock me, or so I believed. But your mother was the cruelest person I have ever met."

Ao was Eleawona's half sister.

"My mother wasn't cruel! She was kind and beloved by all!"

"Of course she was," he retorted sarcastically. "That's why she punished your father by taking the bastard child he'd got on one of his retainers, shaving the child's head, and sending her to you to become one of your atoners. The story goes that your father genuinely cared for the mother and child and had hidden them away. That it was him going to visit them that caused them to be discovered. He wasn't clever enough to keep them safe. Your mother wanted him to know, every single day, that his beloved bastard child would soon die an agonizing death. That it was his fault, and there was nothing he could do about it. Think of it! Slow torture, really."

"She's dead, Ao is dead," cried Elen, cutting in, disgusted by this appalling speech. She was glad Kem wasn't here to hear it. What sickening people, even Eleawona, pleasant enough if you looked only at the surface of her but oblivious to all except the power she clung to. "She lived many years free of your rotten chains. An accident claimed her life while she was aiding people who needed her help. Her good life was no thanks to the likes of any of you."

"Aha! The nose-smart girl's tongue burns as a sharp blade. You always had that obstinate look in your eye. But what interested me most about you, the reason I remember you, is how you were able to detect Spore so accurately."

"I can smell the stink of corruption."

Gevulin would have whipped her, had the comment been directed at him.

Eleawona swore an oath in the northern dialect, looking offended.

Luviara snapped, "Deputy Courier, that is enough!"

But Thelan only laughed. "This one will become captain of my atoners!"

"I will not. I am an official of the Tranquil Empire and thus serve the Magnolia Emperor." Elen wasn't going to be bullied by the likes of him. "Worthy Interlocutor, surely you do not intend for the emperor's authority to be challenged? Her officials stripped from her service at the demand of a foreign barbarian?"

Thelan raised an eyebrow, feigning surprise, but Elen had an unpleasant feeling he was enjoying himself. "Yet are you therefore not such a barbarian also, atoner?"

"I am a deputy courier. The empire welcomes all who pledge their service, regardless of their origins. My 'curious eyes' are not so unusual there, for people live as imperial citizens who come from all over the many provinces."

"Except the Sea Wolves," Thelan pointed out. "For I have it on good authority—that of your interlocutor, I should say—that on the very day the Magnolia Emperor—how fragrant these titles are!—ascended to the High Throne of the empire, she took it upon herself to rescind her respected ancestor's decree. The one that proclaimed the right of Wolves—aivur, as they call themselves—to live at peace within the empire. Instead, the Magnolia Emperor banished all aivur from the empire upon pain of death by burning. Why would she do so if she did not fear their power? That's what I must suppose. Emperors may speak of gods and stars and honor, but really, does anyone believe in those things? What lies beyond the heavens, I don't know. In this world, power is honor. Is it not, El?"

She hated hearing her childhood name on his lips. He was a dangerous man because he knew himself and what he wanted, and he didn't pretend otherwise.

But so did Gevulin.

The prince took action at last: a step away from Eleawona. "Cousin," he said, addressing Thelan, "you have been misled by my interlocutor. I can offer you an alliance that will benefit us both."

Thelan returned to the throne and sank back on its cushion with a smile. "Can you, so? Bring a stool for my cousin. Let him sit next to me while we parlay. And Captain," he addressed one of his soldiers, "see that the gracious Lady Eleawona is taken to the stables and confined in the prison carriage. Her attendants may pack a few things to make her journey comfortable. The rest of her belongings can be sent on after. The carriage will depart at dawn. I rely on you to bring her safely to the strong room in Last Tower, where she'll be held until our wedding day. Your reward for completing this task will match its importance to me."

"Your Majesty, I will not fail you." The captain bowed.

"You dare not! You cannot!" expostulated Eleawona.

But, of course, Thelan both dared and could. The lady had either to struggle in a demeaning fashion or to walk away with her head held high and the hope there would be an opportunity later.

"My loyal soldiers will not let this stand!" she cast over her shoulder like a final arrow.

Thelan mimed catching her anger out of the air and kissing it.

The captain and his squad escorted her out. As the door closed behind her, an attendant set a stool down beside Thelan. Still armed, Gevulin moved cautiously forward and seated himself. It was a bit demeaning for a prince of the Third Estate to sit on a stool, even if its cushion was pleasingly embroidered with a pair of martens twined around each other in an unbroken circle like love everlasting. But he was out of options. He had been driven north by an unseen hand with a skill Elen admired, now that she had the hindsight to do so. The crown prince, possibly in concert with his mother, had led Gevulin on by playing off his suspicions of Prince Astaylin. Gevulin had never seen it coming.

"Refreshment," said Thelan to an attendant. "I have worked up a thirst with all this talking. Now, cousin. What is it you wish to say?"

The prince was clearly marching at speed, trying to cook up any nourishment from the dregs he found himself mired in. He hadn't given up. Adversity made him stubborn, or perhaps this was the measure of a man who had such a splendid list of accomplishments that Elen was coming to believe he really had mastered them all and wasn't just preening about them.

"I have long understood that my older sister, the Magnolia Emperor, fears the aivur. The Blood Wolves have disrupted the eastern borderlands with their raids. Some say they intend to invade our heartland. The northern and western coasts are vulnerable to attacks by the Sea Wolves. The empire lost all its ports along the Blasted Coast when the Pall rose, which is also when we lost contact with your Four Lands."

"Go on," said Thelan with a magnanimous nod. If he was worried about Gevulin's knife and sword, he showed no sign of it. But he was the one with multiple soldiers surrounding him, all of them keenly attentive, likely the sort of exceedingly competent but lesser-born men who would cast their lot with a bastard who could give them the rewards they could never expect to receive from his legitimate half brothers. Simo and Xilsi were too far away to protect the prince from a stab to the back, and Jirvy, Ipis, and Kem were probably locked into the ram suite by now. Surely Luviara wouldn't just let them all be slaughtered. That truly would insult the emperor's authority.

Only Fulmo was still free, as long as no one in Lady Eleawona's household told Thelan's people there was a gagast in the kitchen. If he even knew what a gagast was.

Gevulin went on. Elen rather admired how tendentious he could be even in this moment of defeat, but perhaps it only meant he still couldn't believe he'd been outmaneuvered.

"When the Pall rose during the reign of the ill-fated Azalea Emperor, its poisonous fog blanketed the entirety of the imperial province known as Wheathome Province for its productive grain fields."

"With such a name, I'd never have guessed," remarked Thelan, mouth twitching.

"Yes, its fields fed the imperial palace and its surrounding heartland," replied Gevulin. Elen wasn't sure if Thelan's sarcasm had flown over the prince's head or if he was adept at deflecting it with pedantry. "The loss of Wheathome Province left many hungry, while others scrambled to plow new fields elsewhere. Furthermore, the southernmost extent of the Wheathome Pall came within a mere four days' ride of the imperial city. Naturally, people feared it might grow, although it never did. But my point is, during the reign of the Mulberry Emperor, the Wheathome Pall vanished over the course of a few short years, drained away, if you will."

Thelan leaned forward with sudden interest. "I did not know that was possible on such a scale."

Taking advantage of Thelan's attention being focused on the prince, and not on her, Elen began a slow slide step by slow, slow step back toward Xilsi.

"I must suppose no one did, since none had prior experience with the Pall. Regardless, what emerged when the Pall vanished was a mysterious region which we in the empire call the Desolation. At first, this land was stripped bare of vegetation and animals alike. These have slowly returned, often in strange and deadly forms never before seen. As well, its paths are shifting and treacherous. Even the imperial road that ran through the province became warped by means no theurgist or scholar understands, turning it into a sort of unthreadable maze, or so we are told. It is impossible to know for sure. Many surveyors and unofficial explorers have died attempting to map its trackless and perilous wilderness. Eventually its borders were closed. No one now goes in or out."

Gevulin paused, ostensibly to clear this throat, but Elen thought he was fishing, to see if Thelan would say something, reveal what he knew or what Luviara might have told him. But Thelan had no need to inform others how clever he was; his success spoke for itself. He said nothing, so the prince gave a slight cough and went on.

"It was only after the Desolation emerged that the empire was able to reach the Blasted Coast and rebuild the lost or abandoned imperial ports on that shore. Even so, the northern ocean is a tempest-wracked sea, treacherous in every season."

"It's true, only the Sea Wolves dare venture upon it, whether to raid or to trade," agreed Thelan companionably. "It's said some among the aivur can wield a magic that allows their ships to survive the wild winds, the dangerous currents, the heaving waves, and the sudden storms. Or maybe they just have ships built for hard seas, and the skill to sail them."

"Thus my point," said Gevulin. "My sister, the Magnolia Emperor, fears the aivur because they possess a magic we humans lack. She's not been able to put an end to the raids in the east by the Blood Wolves. She dares not venture any ocean expeditions except in the pacific southern waters of the Tranquil Sea, which have long been the locus of imperial trade and wealth. But, in partnership with the aivur, you and I can remove my sister from the imperial throne."

"To what end? Ah. My thanks, Omvir." This to the retainer who brought a covered pot and two empty glasses shaped from a twinkling green glass. "I'll pour."

Elen had gotten about twenty slow sliding steps back, about halfway to Xilsi, but she paused, curious. What would Gevulin do without Fulmo to test for poison?

Thelan poured one glass, took a swallow as a taster would, and presented it to the prince before pouring a second glass of the red wine for himself. He then raised his glass, and therefore Gevulin had to offer the same courtesy. They drank together, and set down the glasses together.

"To what end, cousin?" Thelan asked again. Elen recommenced sliding away. No one looked her way, all eyes on the two noblemen. "If I may repeat myself. Why would the aivur assist us in this unequal endeavor? The empire is large. Four Lands is small and weak."

"The aivur will assist us if I agree to rescind the imperial decree that mandates their expulsion. If I pledge to allow their clans to settle within the empire again. In our heartland cities, into their old neighborhoods. It can only be to our mutual benefit. As for you, cousin, the imperial treasury is vast. You may choose, as you please, such funds as you need to build a larger army or . . . to build a stronger land. You said you wish your people to live in peace and prosperity. In the empire, we have many precautions and measures in place to protect ourselves from Spore. Couriers. Surveyors. Maps. Various kinds of moats. Salt spirits. Hallow-wood. The list is extensive." Notably, the prince did not mention shrive-steel swords. "All this knowledge could be yours as well, and the manpower to create and maintain it. The empire does not use *children* to scout out Spore. We use skilled adults, who have trained for years under the parasol of imperial security. That is how we live with the Pall and with Spore. We fight it. We manage it. We don't cower from it, building hovels along an ancient roadway that is your only sure protection. I would share these secrets with you."

"Go on. How is this overthrow to be accomplished? The imperial palace is a long way away, is it not?"

Elen couldn't tell if Thelan was playing with the prince. Was he offering Gevulin more rope to hang himself, or was the new Highmost tempted by this promise of riches? As for Gevulin, gathering his thoughts, was he ambitious enough to betray that there existed a newly discovered back-door road via the Pall into the empire, as long as he believed the betrayal would help him gain what he thought he deserved? He did not look toward Luviara, who waited beside Captain Raven. Both interlocutor and bequeather were as silent as thieves, although Elen did not get the sense the two had known each other prior to this meeting. They appeared more like cautious travelers forced to cooperate because they needed to share the same hazardous path for a time. Did Thelan even know the Salt Spear Clan was encamped on the road, within the confines of Far Boundary Pall? Would it serve Gevulin to tell him?

Elen took another pair of slow, slow steps, closer to Xilsi.

Gevulin clenched a hand, making a decision. But Thelan was watching the prince's face, not his hands, and the prince's expression did not by the least flicker betray emotion.

"I have in my possession a map. The map marks a secure path through the hidden wilderness of the Desolation and straight into the heartland. A strike force traveling at speed along back roads could reach the palace before the emperor, or anyone in the empire, could be warned it is coming. Once she and her son are dead, I will become emperor."

Thelan's eyes widened. "Fascinating. The interlocutor made no mention of such a precious artifact as a map."

Yet his tone betrayed amusement. Elen felt it as a shiv of warning. She took yet another slow step away, almost to Simo, and only he noticed, giving her a tiny, encouraging nod. The captain's expression was grave.

"Nor would she make such a mention," said Gevulin tartly. "Her goal is to discredit me and remove me from power, not to dethrone the Magnolia Emperor, whom she serves. Nor can she pass on any of this conversation to the emperor, as long as you *don't let her leave*. Were you and I to act quickly, with the aid of the Sea Wolves, the emperor will have no warning."

"I see. What of this Prince Astaylin? Astaylin is not here, but I am."

"He who raises the fruit to his lips is the one who can savor its sweetness."

"A poetic saying, to be sure. We say, he who has the stronger arm can take his pick of the fruit." Thelan took another sip of the wine, as if mulling its flavor—or the flavor of conspiracy and ambition, Elen supposed. "But I know nothing of the truth of this Desolation you speak of. Nor of any *map*."

"How could you? Lady Eleawona arranged for the map to be delivered to me with the connivance of the Salt Spear Clan. It was the clan who shared it with her."

It was a clever falsehood, if Gevulin was astutely trying to sow doubt in Thelan's mind, to make him wonder if the alliance the Salt Spear Clan had offered Thelan was merely a smokescreen for later treachery against him? A desperate toss of the dice, but it might work.

Thelan's mouth curled up with mockery. He seemed suspiciously sure of himself. "It's all very well to speak of a valuable map, but I see no map in your hand."

The prince glanced at Xilsi, whose stoic expression did not alter, although she blinked twice. "Ah. The map must have been left in the map room in the tower."

"How careless. Omvir, send someone to retrieve it, for I confess to the greatest curiosity. Interlocutor Luviara, might you enlighten us?"

She bowed. "Highmost, there is no map. Lady Eleawona already told us so."

"Eleawona was lying to throw you off the scent, for she already suspected you," said Gevulin smoothly. It was another bald-faced lie, but he pulled it off. "The fact remains that I possess a map. Can you claim otherwise, Luviara?"

"The map was meant as a lure. As a test."

Gevulin stiffened. Luviara had taken him by surprise. "A test?" he demanded, finally losing his cool.

Thelan smiled. It seemed clear to Elen that he had already known. She slid one more silent step closer to Xilsi. Almost there! Yet disaster loomed, a scent as telltale in its cloying sweetness as the rose-oil scent of Spore.

The interlocutor cleared her throat, folded her hands at her belly, and took in a fortifying breath like a soldier about to plunge into battle. Her tone was smooth, but the tightness of her gripping fingers upon each other betrayed an inner turmoil.

"The Magnolia Emperor, in her compassionate wisdom, utterly refused to believe her dear younger brother Gevulin would attack the very heart of the empire, its peaceful fabric, its tranquil waters. His Sublime Highness suggested this scheme to his mother."

"His Sublime Highness?" Gevulin shook his head.

"If you were innocent, Prince Minaylin proposed, then you would bring the map to the emperor once you had it. If you harbored wicked thoughts, then you would go into the Desolation and seek out these mysterious passages. There, you would either die, as so many surveyors have before you, or her imperial enforcers would be waiting to arrest you."

"Clumsy little Min-lo?" Gevulin could not disguise his bafflement and disbelief.

"Yes. Not only did His Sublime Highness Minaylin concoct the scheme, but he drew the map himself."

22

THE NEXT STAGE OF THE CAMPAIGN

Gevulin stared at the interlocutor, stunned and unable to speak. Xilsi pressed her hand to her forehead as if in pain, while Simo stood with rigid composure, mouth strained.

Luviara looked not one whit ashamed or discomposed. It wasn't as if the scheme amused her, but more that it had fallen out as she had predicted. She was ready to get on to the next stage of the campaign: the calamitous fall of His Exalted Highness Gevulin, Prince of the Third Estate.

She said, "Once we reached Far Boundary Vigil, nothing went as planned. It's true I did not know about the causeway."

"Causeway?" Thelan sat straight, tense as a held sword. "What mean you by that? The holy road is broken. It goes only a short distance into the White Sea and ends in a ragged embankment. I've seen the broken edge of it myself, twenty years ago, when I was but a lad of fourteen and pursued two rogue atoners who'd murdered my loyal soldiers."

Elen set her jaw, waiting for him to call her back to the throne and to reveal to the wardens that she had been one of those atoners. But he didn't need to look at her to know his arrow would hit her.

Instead, Luviara was the one who looked surprised. "Did the bequeather not tell you, Lord Thelan?"

"What is there to be told?"

"That the Pall can be crossed on this causeway, as long as your party has the assistance of the aivur over the broken gaps."

"I'll be burned by the white-haired god," Thelan muttered, rubbing an ear. He shot an accusing look toward the bequeather. Captain Raven remained impassive.

"How did you think we arrived here in the south of your land?" Luviara went on. "We came from the south, over the causeway."

"From the south, through the Pall, over a broken holy road, with the aid of my new allies, the Salt Spear Clan." Thelan took a sip of wine as if to settle jangled nerves. He set down the glass. "I had wondered where the Salt Spear Clan was hiding. Now I know. It's a good thing I was mopping up the last resistance of Captain Dinec's regiment nearby when your air spirit whispered a warning in my ear."

"Your air spirit!" cried Gevulin, his taut silence shattered. "You sent an air spirit to warn him! And now you reveal to him that there is a means to cross into the empire? Is this how you show your loyalty to the emperor? You have betrayed us!"

All this time, Simo had been standing straight and sure, a proud warden captain. At this disclosure, the shock of Luviara's treachery finally felled him. With a gasping groan from deep in his chest he went down on one knee, head bent.

Elen took two more slow steps backward and, at last, eased in beside Xilsi. The warden surreptitiously nudged her with an elbow to acknowledge her presence. They did not look at each other. Elen was surprised to realize that, among the prince's party, and not counting Kem, it was Xilsi she had come to trust. Xilsi had spurned the palace, ambition, even a strutting life of glorious notoriety as the subject of wineshop poems. In her gut, Elen was sure Xilsi had nothing to do with the secret map, with any of it. She'd come to check on her good friend Mekky, whom she cared about. That was all.

And it wasn't just Xilsi. Jirvy and Ipis were innocent of scheming, Elen was sure of that, too. They'd done their duty as wardens. Fulmo as well, whatever his position was in the prince's retinue. Even Simo, who had hitched his wagon to Gevulin's ambition either because he wanted to or because he hadn't had a choice, didn't deserve this disaster as a reward for his years of loyal service to the empire.

They'd have to find a way out. Them. Kem. Herself. Luviara could go hang. Elen wasn't going to lie down and give up. She'd gotten out of worse, and she'd get them out with her, one way or another.

Into the silence, Thelan said derisively, "Yet what of this precious map, Cousin Gevulin?"

Gevulin's mouth pinched angrily. "I didn't—"

He broke off as Simo caught the prince's eye and gave a slight warning shake of the head.

The prince grimaced before saying, prudently, "I didn't have anything to add. You heard the interlocutor."

"So the map is indeed a clever fake? You lied straight to my face with no intention of following through with an alliance? The empire is nothing but a snarling pack of backbiting jackals?"

Gevulin lunged off the stool, hand on his sword hilt as he drew.

Thelan flung up a hand. Gevulin was immediately buried beneath a pile of soldiers, overwhelmed by sheer weight and numbers. Simo bolted up to his feet.

Xilsi whispered urgently, "Simo! Don't do it!"

Elen added, "Not now, Captain. Bide your time."

Simo muttered an oath and, before he could be piled on, raised both hands.

More soldiers had entered while the highborn were talking. With her eyes fully adjusted to the dimness, Elen could see some had come directly from battle with bloodstained tabards, linen-wrapped wounds on an arm here and a leg there, although nothing serious, with dirt-grimed helmets tucked beneath doughty arms. She shuddered, remembering Thelan's sergeant on that long-ago day that both she and Thelan recalled so clearly, although for different reasons. Life or death was a game to Thelan and his soldiers, pieces put in play on a game board Thelan meant to control.

"Enough! I'm bored of this entertainment." He clapped his hands mockingly, then stood. "Interlocutor, I think it best to proceed with the agreement we have already made. You will travel on the holy road to North Port."

"I can travel south more quickly, back across the Pall, Highmost."

A disquieting expression flickered in his eyes. He was not a man to cross, not unless you knew the blow you were about to strike would kill him instantly. He didn't want Luviara to go back across the Pall. He no longer trusted her—if he'd ever trusted her.

"Yes, of course. But not yet. Have you forgotten the shipload of engineers and surveyors and equipment you arranged for as part of our agreement? They reached Isle Tempest some months back. They've been waiting for your arrival. With your seal to release them, they will enter the Four Lands and my court and begin their work to fortify my realm from the scourge of Spore."

Xilsi exchanged a startled glance with Elen. How long had this conspiracy against Gevulin been hatching?

Thelan had the look of a well-fed predator pleased with its kill. "Why, it is the very offer Prince Gevulin made, already arranged through your auspices and direct from the emperor. How tidy!"

Luviara's frown came and went as she adjusted to his riposte. "I had not realized the officials were already at Isle Tempest. Of course, I shall journey north at once, as you and I agreed."

"Very good. I shall send you with an escort. The journey will be swift and agreeable. The holy road is entirely under my control now."

"Your generosity is a blessed honor, Highmost. The prince is yours, as agreed. You may take his captain as well. Simo is implicated in His Highness's treasonous plans. But by my own observation, the other wardens and the deputy courier are innocent of any plot against the empire. They merely did their duty, in ignorance. Let them return with me to the empire."

"You may have the other wardens, but not the atoner. The deputy courier, I mean. She is mine, Interlocutor. I will not negotiate on this."

"The deputy courier? Why?" Luviara asked sharply.

"Ah, yes, our exchange may have been elliptical, to be sure. She and I have unfinished business, as she knows perfectly well. I wonder at her effrontery in returning here. But maybe she was just doing her duty, as she did not do, as a child."

Xilsi's fingers brushed Elen's arm in warning, but Elen was churning her thoughts through this morass and wasn't sure what to say or how to proceed. Could she trust the untrustworthy Luviara to at least get the other wardens—to get Kem—safe into the empire? Could Luviara protect them from execution? That alone would be worth it to see them go with her.

"Very well, Highmost." Luviara knew when to retreat. After all, what was a single provincial deputy courier to the emperor when compared to the advantages this alliance would bring her, including the downfall of her ambitious brother? "We shall depart as soon as you have carriages ready."

"I'll have them made ready immediately. After all this, it occurs to me there's no reason to wait for dawn. We have oil enough to light your way on the holy road. You shall accompany my beloved Eleawona all the way to Last Tower. Although you'll ride in a separate carriage. Collect your wardens and go, with my blessing."

Xilsi stepped forward. "Thelan. That is your name, is it not?"

The bald lack of use of a title brought every soldier's head around to glare hate at her presumption.

Thelan descended the dais and walked right up to Xilsi, looking her up and down. Not in a lustful way, precisely, but as though he'd just figured out there was something about her that ought to interest him.

"Who are you?"

"With the demotion of Simo, I am now the senior warden present and thus stand before you as the highest-ranking official here in the service of the emperor."

"Higher than the interlocutor?"

"Yes. Both by rank and by birth."

"I see," he said appreciatively. "Go on. I'm listening. For this day has been filled with so many remarkable surprises."

She ignored this aside. "We wardens serve in the Imperial Order of Wardens. His Exalted Highness Prince Gevulin is the all-seeing eye, the prince-warden of our order. You might say highmost captain or general. We serve at his command. After him, we serve at the command of the chief warden, who is not here. After that, we serve according to the command of the senior warden present."

"What did you say your name was again?"

"I did not say. Nor am I accustomed to needing to do so. My rank is senior warden. Let me assure you that the interlocutor does not have the authority to determine a warden's movements or to depose the all-seeing eye just on her say-so. Until we receive a direct confirmation from the palace, we stay with His Highness."

"The interlocutor may not have the authority, but I have the weapons to force you to do as I wish you to do."

"At a time like this, when you hold all the pieces on the board, force is an admission of weakness."

"Ah. I see you understand power." He rubbed his chin as he considered. "Very well. You may join your prince in the pits, if that is your wish."

"What do you mean to do with the prince?" Luviara asked, although it seemed, to Elen, a little late for that question.

Thelan gave an airy wave of his hand. The heap of soldiers, still in a pile on the floor, slowly pulled back to leave the prince facedown, trussed up like the chosen lamb before a festival day.

"I haven't quite decided. Tie him to a post and use him for archery practice?"

The prince spat an oath, struggling against his bonds, but it was useless. The Highmost's men knew what they were about with prisoners. They had a lot of practice chasing down outlaws and binding them to be burned later.

Thelan smiled as he went on. "As we say in the northlands court, he has the look of the lost regime. That's the branch of our ancestors who came generations ago from the south; that is, from your empire. I have a half sister who might wish to marry him for his looks. It would give her cachet to have an imperial prince as her husband, even a disgraced one. Even better, he'd have no power within my court nor relatives clamoring for privileges and positions. Or perhaps

I will tie him to a horse . . . and send him racing into the Pall." These last words were spoken with the same glib mockery as the others, but as he said this he shifted to address Elen. The look in his eyes was hard. "What would you think of that, El? Is that a fitting punishment?"

With that look he made it clear he intended to have his revenge on her for leading his troop to their deaths. They had both been young adolescents at the time, and twenty years felt like a long time to her, but he would never let go of his grievances until he had won a clear and implacable victory. Thus, Eleawona. Thus, the nose-smart girl.

In a way, she pitied Eleawona for becoming Thelan's prisoner, but Her Ladyship had looked the other way for the entirety of her life as she proclaimed the sentence of life or death over those beneath her. She lived atop the master's tower, far beyond El and her own bastard sister, Ao. So let Eleawona walk her own road now. Ao was dead, and El was no longer her atoner.

But Elen needed an opening.

Before she could speak, Luviara broke in, looking alarmed.

"Highmost, I must object to the senior warden's request to remain here." The theurgist's demand struck Elen as an odd misstep from a woman who had, before this, shown such skill in keeping her true game hidden.

"I've already decided," said Thelan. "You may go."

"May" meant "will."

A captain and his squad converged on Luviara and escorted her to the doors.

"Good riddance," shouted Xilsi at the interlocutor's back.

Luviara turned to call back. "You might consider that just as you are loyal to the wardens, so am I loyal to the empire. We are not different."

"Make whatever excuse you wish. I did not act to gain the confidence of people only so I could betray them."

"Enough!" cried Thelan. "Write recriminating letters to each other. This is giving me a headache. Go! *Go!*"

Luviara was marched out. The doors closed with a solid thunk. Elen felt torn between anger at the betrayal and a strange grief that the woman whose company she had enjoyed so much wasn't the person she'd thought she was. But there wasn't time to poke through these feelings. It was all moving much too fast, like spring floods when the snow melts.

In the northern speech, Thelan said to a soldier, "Take the prince and his captain to the pits. The senior warden will be confined with her comrades in the ram suite."

Gevulin was lifted and carried out through the back of the hall. A door-shaped segment of wall slid open to reveal the secret passage beyond; no longer so secret, Elen supposed. Simo exchanged a sharp glance with Xilsi before following his prince into the darkness.

When they were gone, Thelan said to his people, "I need food. I'm sure my supply captain has commandeered a feast fit for us all."

One of the soldiers standing guard came forward to kneel before him. Thelan seemed to have no servants or attendants as Eleawona did, only military surrounding him.

"Highmost, you have traveled far, at speed, and that after fighting all night. May I recommend that you rest? The orderlies will have prepared a secure chamber by now."

"Yes, yes, in a bit. Food first. A man cannot live on air and triumph alone." He addressed Xilsi in Imperial. "You may accompany me, Senior Warden. As for you, atoner, you are assigned to my household."

Elen caught Xilsi's alarmed, angry gaze and shook her head firmly to say: *We will talk later.*

Thelan climbed the dais steps, headed for the back passage. By the throne, he paused, finally realizing that the bequeather was still standing quietly to one side, as any good diplomat would, gathering information while drawing no notice to themselves.

"Is there anything you forgot to tell me, Captain Raven? Perhaps the location of your hidden campsite? I had assumed it was somewhere in the hills, close to the shore of the White Sea, where we humans fear to tread. But upon reflection, I, too, would hide my forces on the causeway within the Pall, were I able to and needed an unseen staging point for an attack."

The captain offered a nod in calm acknowledgment. "You will understand that our camp shelters our entire clan, not just a military force. Our council first, above all things, seeks to protect our children and our elders. Therefore, we have withheld our location from you and your messengers until the arrival of the trust-guests you and the council agreed upon."

"Ah, I see. The hostages we agreed to exchange. I understand your caution completely. It's in my interest that your clan and I remain at peace, especially given all these new revelations. The empire, reachable by this unexpected route! Quite astonishing! But, a matter for another day. I had to race ahead of my own royal cavalcade in order to fight the stalwart Captain Dinec and his regiment. The hostages should arrive in a few days."

Captain Raven's bland expression of chilly boredom did not alter. "With respect, Highmost, my people will remain where we are in the safety of the White Sea until the trust-guests enter our keeping and we hold them as surety of your good intentions."

"I would do the same, were I you!" he said jovially. Elen honestly could not tell if he was annoyed at being thwarted or if he respected their prudence. Maybe both. People could be complicated like that. "Just as well, now that I consider the speed and the timing. My troops will need a few days to empty the settlements you've been promised, since we didn't have control of South Ring until today. It will all work out just as your wise council and I have decreed. You will gain a foothold in these lands with the safety of the White Sea at your back."

Elen said, "They're not going to the east county. You're settling them here in the south county?"

His gaze on her was unsettling, but she held herself still. "You always were a mouthy one, even as a child. That's why you were so intriguing. Mostly it was your nose for Spore, of course. Your impertinent talk. Your face has an unusual shape, round like the moon. And those curious eyes, gold-green. Have people not remarked on it?"

"In the empire? I am not the only moon-faced, green-eyed person, no. And the scar, I suppose," she replied.

"The scar?" His gaze flicked to her neck as he scoffed. "Scars are a trifle. Anyone may have a scar, though few so distinctive as yours. As if someone carved it there deliberately."

Osge, she thought, thinking of what Captain Raven had said upon meeting her. Who had given her the scar? She doubted she would ever know.

"But to answer your impertinent question, yes, the Salt Spear Clan will stay here in the south. It's a wise arrangement. It allows them to stay out of the way of the other clans, some of whom have proved hostile toward them. Meanwhile, I can disperse a substantial portion of the south-county population to the other counties of the Four Lands and thus break the hold my cousin has on their loyalty. The key to success, you see, is that everyone should get something."

"Lady Eleawona got nothing," said Elen.

"She got to live."

"What about the villagers you're moving? They're losing everything."

"Not at all! They'll be placed in new settlements built on imperial lines, with all these promised protections against Spore. If everything I'm told is true, they'll have better lives than what they suffer now, living beyond the protection of the holy road, on forested lanes where deadly Spore and lawless outlaws may attack at any moment. But you know all about that. Don't you, El?"

He cocked an eye at her. There was vengeance in the flare of his gaze.

She did not look away as she said, "What about these hostages you are offering up to the Salt Spear Clan? Are they anyone you actually care about?"

His gaze narrowed, but unlike Gevulin, he wasn't one to lash out. He'd lived with disrespect his entire childhood and had learned how to absorb it silently—until he had the means to strike back with the decisive blow.

"It's now become clear that, should I be so foolish as to renege on my agreement with the Salt Spear Clan and attack them, they can retreat into the White Sea and henceforth harass my borders. Regardless, I will not renege, because the arrangement benefits us all. Captain Raven, if there's nothing else, you may go, with my blessing. I pray you, carry with you my oath-deep greetings to your wise council members. Better times lie ahead for us all."

"So it shall be," said the bequeather.

"Bring these two," said Thelan to his guards, indicating Elen and Xilsi. He went into the dark passage behind the throne without a backward look.

As Captain Raven walked toward the main doors, Elen saw her opening. She stumbled on purpose, as if exhausted or heartsick, and staggered sideways. The movement brought her closer to the bequeather's path. Going down on one knee, Elen flung out a hand, pretending to catch herself, but, really, extending it far enough that the bequeather broke stride in surprise. She paused, within earshot.

In a low voice, Elen said, "Captain, I trade you his name, so you may call him and he will come to you. Sara'ala, of the Shorn. In return, tell Sara'ala I sent you and where I am."

23

An Elaborate Display of Knots

Two soldiers grabbed Elen roughly by the arms. "Up! Up! Come along!"

They hauled her toward the passage, their grasps tight, but she did not struggle, knowing they would have to release her once inside. Two more guards approached Xilsi, who set one hand on her sword hilt and the other on her knife hilt as if daring the barbarians to touch a Bakassar heir. The men did not physically engage with her. In a show of impressive discipline, or perhaps a consciousness that she wore the status of a master, they called over more guards to create a ring around her, keeping their distance but at the same time making it clear they did not intend to allow her to escape. Xilsi assessed the situation and caught Elen's eye just as Elen was propelled over the threshold into the darkness.

Once inside, the guards did have to release her. The passage was too narrow to allow two people to walk side by side. One walked before her and one behind. The weight of their presence felt strange to her, she who had so long ago padded up and down this very corridor, alone or with Ao, or with the littler ones, Nep, Nap, and Nup, who she and Ao had taken under their wings, or any one of the others whose names had faded as into a distant, hazy smear.

The passage's dusty, musty smell hit hard, like she had breathed it just yesterday. She blinked back a surge of memories: the floor worn smooth beneath the tread of countless atoners; her threadbare tunic catching on a nail and ripping; her and Ao huddling together for warmth, one particularly bitter-cold winter night when they'd been stationed on watch over the empty hall, their feet wrapped in rags because they weren't allowed winter boots inside the palace, lest the noise of their footsteps disturb the masters.

There had never been light, not in those days. Atoners did not need light. They learned the intricacies of the passageways and crawlspaces quickly enough, mapped by the touch of hands and hips. An atoner who did not quickly learn to anticipate where edges would bump you and splinters catch in your skin did not last long, taken by infection or simply giving up hope.

Today, someone had set a lantern on a ledge, its sullen light accompanied by a swirl of greasy smoke. Elen expected she could still find her way through the unlit passages; that was one advantage in her favor, as she considered her options. Behind her, Xilsi sneezed. And Xilsi, Jirvy, Ipis, and Kem would be together. That was another.

At an intersection, the passage split into three. The soldiers prodded Elen up a steep staircase so narrow that her shoulders brushed the walls on either side. The soldiers had to turn sideways and go up awkwardly, step by step, muttering under their breaths. Halfway up, they passed an alcove tucked alongside the blessedly warm bricks of an interior chimney. A small figure was wedged within the tight confines of the alcove, waiting for them to pass.

Almost, she said Ao's name, thinking it was her sister. But of course it wasn't. It was some other atoner, face obscured by darkness, crouched in this space to catch warmth on cold nights. So she and Ao had done, trading off who got to squeeze into the alcove, for even as small as they had been in those days, the space only fit one child's skinny body. This child had no Ao to keep her company through the lonely night. Instead, they crouched alone in the dark, watching the intruders pass by.

An ache rose in Elen's heart. She had survived because of Ao. Alone, she would have withered and died. She had had the strength to live because she and Ao had had each other. Who was this solitary child? From whence had the child been torn? What loss endured? What lonely hours awaiting the terror of Spore, the rising of misty threads as if out of nothing except the antipathy of the universe toward the helpless?

The thoughts stung at her like the red-hot punctures of a wasp. She hated that she must walk past, as unseeing as the soldiers, who did not consider atoners to be fully human.

So she sang, in a whisper, one of the songs she could never forget, woven as deeply into her bones as the thread of life itself. *"Old hand, old ghost, pray, stay away. Old hand, old ghost, you had your day."*

The child stirred, no doubt wondering how this adult knew the secret atoner songs. A light, high voice joined hers, barely more audible. *"Once you wore a crown of light, on your brow it shone so bright."*

"Shut up!" snapped a guard. "Creeps me out, it does. Better if their tongues were cut out."

"Fed by souls you burned that day," Elen murmured defiantly, under her breath.

What did it mean, this ancient caution kept alive in a nonsense children's song? Who had worn a crown of brightly burning light? Who had fed on the souls they burned?

Behind her, the atoner whispered a word, but she couldn't quite hear it, and she couldn't turn back to ask. That was the worst thing of all: she had become one of those who left atoners behind in the darkness. Her hands felt clammy, and her chest tight, as if she might never catch a full breath again.

They reached the top of the stairs. A door creaked open on rusty hinges into the outer chamber of the suite where Lady Eleawona's mother, the Lady of the Martens, had lived for as long as Elen had ever known. Eleawona had apparently not taken over these rooms upon her mother's death. The light and clamor here eased the grip on Elen's heart, if only to make way for a swell of anger.

Thelan's soldiers had been here already, shoving furniture aside in the most disrespectful way. They'd carried in tables and shoved them together so thirty might be seated. Men—all of his attendants were soldiers and all of his soldiers were men, unlike in the empire—waited in line to wash their faces and hands from a basin set on a side table. With better light, Elen could now see they wore tabards bearing a green tree that matched the brooch Thelan wore.

The Highmost was already seated at one end of the table. He did not rise, which would have been too great an honor, but he gestured magnanimously toward Xilsi. He had taken her measure and judged her to be someone who might be worth something to him.

In a jovial tone he proclaimed, "Let the senior warden be seated at my left. The atoner will stand behind me."

"She'll sit, or I won't sit," said Xilsi, immune to his display of charm.

"You'd rather *starve*?" His curiosity did not seem feigned. Of all the folk in the Four Lands, masters alone need never go hungry, except in the most dire circumstances. It was the chief mark of their high status.

Xilsi gave him a scornful look. "I've been a warden since I was seventeen, so fifteen years now. Part of our training is enduring lack of water, lack of food, lack of sleep, and weary marches. I have traveled a long distance with this deputy courier, who, like me, is an official of the empire. How you treat one of us is how you treat all of us."

Xilsi's tone got under his skin, maybe because it hadn't occurred to him that an obviously highborn master would champion a lowborn atoner as her equal, even if only in status as an imperial official.

But mostly, Elen guessed, because the soldiers gathered to share his meal were officers and thus also masters. Even after all his victories, the bastard-born Thelan could not risk losing face in front of them.

His hand tightened on his cup. "Then you shall starve, Warden. And your comrades as well."

The door opened just then, as if it were part of a play, timed for best effect. Soldiers shepherded in the other three wardens. Elen tensed with such a gut-seizing moment of terror that she pressed an arm to her belly. If Thelan guessed that Kem was Ao's child, their situation would become a worse disaster than it already was.

Ipis walked in the lead with wide eyes and a stiff-legged stance. After Ipis came Jirvy, an indigo kerchief bound around his hair with such an elaborate display of knots that every eye fell on him and his confident swagger. Even Thelan dealt only the most cursory of glances at Kem, who walked with a careful slump and with his hair completely concealed by a faded green-yellow kerchief knotted in only three places. His hair might have come from his mother, but his features had more of Woodfall Province and the Duenn bloodline in them, so he looked more akin to Simo, Xilsi, Ipis, and even Gevulin than did Elen, or southern-born Jirvy, for that matter.

"Do menfolk in the empire wear women's scarves?" scoffed one of the officers, in the northern speech.

"Why are these two men wearing women's scarves?" Thelan asked in Imperial.

Jirvy and Xilsi exchanged a glance that contained a thousand words in an instant. They knew each other that well.

Jirvy gave the lord a scathing look, as if the man had challenged him to an archery duel. "Among the folk I hail from, only a man who has killed another man in *honorable* battle is allowed to wear a warrior's kerchief. So, I wouldn't know if any of you lot would be eligible."

The room broke into an uproar. Apparently, some of the officers had studied the imperial language alongside their lord. One overeager fellow lunged for Jirvy, who sidestepped with the grace of a light-footed fighter.

"Stop!" Thelan did not rise from his chair, but his temper had a sharper edge than before, his iron control wearing thin. "Put them in the pit with their prince."

Elen shook her head at Xilsi. *Don't resist.* She caught Kem's gaze briefly, so as not to alert anyone, and gave a tiny dip of her chin and a flick of her eyes toward Xilsi, a message he was to follow Xilsi's lead.

As a warden, he would have had to anyway. It was time for Kem to understand that their paths, from this time onward, must diverge.

As the wardens were taken out, she moved to go with them, planning to bring up the rear so she could scan their route for any options for a daring escape.

Thelan snapped, "No! Not you!"

Soldiers shut the door behind the others, trapping her inside.

She had to stand behind Thelan's chair while he and his officers ate a feast of fresh-slaughtered roasted fowl, smoked mutton, honeyed beef, pickled vegetables, cream-cooked barley with black currants, bread hot from the ovens, all so mouth-watering that she was flung back to the days when she and Ao would stand in the atoner's pen and feast on the smells of all the food they would never taste.

As the men ate, they discussed the campaign. Elen kept her expression impassive, pretending not to understand the flow of words. At first, some of the phrases fell strangely on her ears because it had been so long since she had heard Four Lands speech, or made no sense because it was north-county cant, but soon enough the rhythm caught up to her.

Battles against Sea Wolves in the north county. The final capitulation of the east county. Thelan's half brother, fled to the west county, who had died untimely or been poisoned; no one was quite sure, not even Thelan, or so he claimed. The careful encroachment, stage by stage, into the stubborn south. The final push that had ended with the battle against Captain Dinec's regiment. The air spirit's message from the imperial theurgist, much discussed among the officers, who wanted to know how the Four Lands could gain theurgists for themselves. So far, Thelan let them know, the empire was not willing to part with the secret of theurgy. He filled them in on the causeway and its possible link through the White Sea and into the long-lost empire, but the officers remained skeptical. A few argued that the foreigners were mocking him with this unbelievable tale, to which Thelan calmly replied that they would soon discover the truth of it once they had pacified the area around South Ring and could ride along the holy road to the White Sea.

Elen hadn't been this hungry for many years, yet she found it remarkably easy to fall back into the old method she and Ao had used to get through days of hard hunger: describing in their mind's eye every stone and leaf of their favorite villa, called Nesting Glade, a quiet place hedged by yew, where Lady Eleawona liked to spend an entire month in late summer, just after harvest. Spore had never broken out there, but the food reserves were too small to sustain the court for more than one month, and Elen was never sure how the locals survived once the court stripped the storehouses and departed for the next villa.

It took her some effort to get back on that path: the eleven stepping stones over Silver Stream, Starling Meadow where the horses grazed, the recently mown west pasture where haystacks dried in the sun, the clean, bright pool behind Nettle Rock where the atoners were allowed to swim, the only time all year they really got clean.

Bitter memories, because it was a bitter time, except for Ao's presence, and now Ao was dead. But the recollections held her away from the gnaw of hunger as the men ate and ate and ate, and washed it down with mead and wine. Even so, Thelan was careful about how much he allowed his officers to drink. They had won, but they were still in territory not fully under his rule, and thus they needed to keep their heads about them.

Listening in allowed her to recognize Thelan's strategic intelligence.

Settling the Salt Spear Clan here in the south was a smart move.

Even smarter was not letting Luviara return the way she had come. The crown prince didn't know the Pall could be crossed. The Magnolia Emperor didn't know. That made emperor and heir vulnerable. If they thought the only path to Four Lands was across the tempest-wracked ocean, they wouldn't be looking north to Far Boundary Pall.

All else aside, she had to wonder about the crown prince, that shadowy, hooded figure with the soft voice. The map of the Desolation he'd had Luviara plant for Gevulin to find was a finely honed weapon, a brilliantly unexpected stab in the dark—and it had worked. "Clumsy little Min-lo" did not seem so clumsy when viewed from this end of the scheme. It seemed Gevulin had thought too well of himself and not well enough of his younger rival.

"Any scraps for the atoner?" Thelan asked, his words breaking into her thoughts.

A plate was passed around to collect bones and leavings. Thelan himself offered it to Elen with that half-hostile and half-amused flicker of his eyes, waiting to see if she'd refuse out of pride. She took it and ate the scraps, even licked the bones with relish while the officers roared with laughter. They thought their scorn would hurt her, but what did she care? She got fed. Food was strength. She would need all her strength.

The man called Omvir seemed to lap at Thelan's heels. As the orderly tasked to take care of all his lordship's needs, he was the sort of retainer who had tied his fortune to personal service to a master, rising and falling with the one he served. Not unlike Hemerlin.

"Highmost, a bed has been made ready for you."

"Yes, yes, I suppose so." He looked at Elen, rubbed his chin, and said, "Put her in the pits. One by herself. Don't mix her in with the others. Just until I wake up."

One of the officers—he had the darker reddish-brown hair that spoke of diluted westlands ancestry—spoke with a bit of drunken bravado. "That one imperial is a good-looking woman, if you can get past her bitch-faced arrogance. I'd have her crawling, haha."

Thelan sighed audibly, long and drawn out. Every officer tensed. The one who'd spoken went white with fear. The Highmost's gaze made a sweep of the table. It got so quiet that Elen could hear the clop of horses' hooves pulling a wheeled vehicle outside.

"If you wish to indulge yourself, then you may ask for reassignment to the regular army. Those who ride in my personal staff, with my shock troops, are those who understand that victory happens through discipline and patience. We take advantage of the weaknesses of our enemy. We don't make a present of our weaknesses to them. People can be used as weapons as easily as swords and spears can, if they are properly wielded. The imperial officials will not be molested in any way. No prisoner is to come in or out of the pits without my direct order. Am I understood?"

They each tapped fist to chest.

Thelan rose. They all rose.

He went to the door that led into the Lady of the Marten's sleeping chamber, where young El had once watched as the great lady required her reluctant husband to pleasure her in the bed without giving him any release in his turn. It had seemed mean to her at the time, but she hadn't understood why. Now she did.

At the door, Thelan turned to look right at her, as if he were about to command that she be brought to him, to that very bed. Elen couldn't hide her revulsion. His smile was hard and cruel. He'd seen what he needed to see: a glimpse into where she might be vulnerable.

All he said was, "Wake me only if there is urgent news."

24

Written in Cipher, a Draft of a Letter

Your subject, Luviara, reverently submits this report in the Copper Month of the Eighteenth Year of Your Benevolent Majesty's tranquil reign.

All is in readiness.

The map is a peculiar thing, which His Sublime Highness claims to have discovered in an obscure corner of the South Library. If I may not be deemed discourteous for the reminder, the South Library pavilion was sealed off by your order, upon the death of the blessed Lily Emperor and his departure to the halcyon gardens of the High Heavens. Therefore, I have no information on how its rooms were accessed, nor would I be so presumptuous as to inquire of His Sublime Highness for any further information than what he has already shared. Nor would I wish to impose upon His Sublime Personage even an hour more of my presence in His Sublime company.

I will note, however, that when examined carefully by holding a light behind the vellum, it is possible to discern that in one corner of the vellum an inked mark was imperfectly scraped off. This is a jagged line, resembling a stylized lightning bolt. This mark may indicate the identity of the maker or holder of the map, if it were to be investigated.

Out of respect for your wishes, and in recognition of your wisdom and far-seeing eye, I will state this much: The Sublime Highness's scheme is convoluted and may fail. Its utility lies in the determination of Prince Gevulin to accomplish more than others are capable of, as he has earlier proven through his own efforts, in a manner that has alarmed and disturbed Your Benevolent Majesty's heart.

Beyond this, I have done my part by copying phrases and modeling diction on documents and letters carried off from Isle Tempest. His Sublime Highness suggested I need only write gibberish, for none in the empire have seen nor can read the pigeon-scratch scrawlings of the Farlandians, and thus no one will be able to do more than guess at its contents. However, as the playwrights say, the illusion must be complete for the audience to believe. Thus, I have written what seems to me a stately letter that, should it by some chance be translated, shall reinforce the deception.

I am deeply grateful to Your Benevolent Majesty for charging me with this somber responsibility on behalf of the empire. Once the intended result is achieved, I will await my funds and travel permits so I may continue my research, as you, Benevolent Majesty, have so graciously and generously agreed to, after our private meeting in the Larkspur Pavilion. Until then, etc.

From the journal of Theurgist Luviara, working under the sworn seal of the private secretariat of the Most Benevolent Majesty, the Magnolia Emperor, by her secret instructions

25

Five Pits

In the empire, every Halt was built to the same plan, with four quarters and intersecting cross streets inside every protective enclosure created at points where the witch road split apart and remerged.

South Ring's layout still followed the basic architecture of the Halt it had once been, a hundred and thirty years ago. Elen was led under guard along the east–west crosswise avenue, still intact. The residences of the lesser masters lined the avenue, each steep-roofed residence separated from the next by an alley and a low fence—but never a gate, as if the lady feared revolt from within and made it impossible for any master to use their family home as a fortification. Only the high hall and its tower could be closed up against an attack from without.

When they reached the east ramp, the guards took Elen off to one side onto an enclosed area tucked up against the elevated roadway and ringed by a stone wall and a yew hedge. When they entered through a reinforced gate, she realized that, ironically, the prison was situated in the same place in South Ring as the couriers' cottages in Orledder Halt. It was almost like coming home.

The prison ground was entirely paved in stone. By its neat lines and good workmanship, the original pavement had probably been laid down by the first builders, whoever they were. The space was so clean that it was obviously kept painstakingly swept by retainers on the hunt for any seedling weed trying to sprout through cracks in the cobblestones.

The long stone prison blockhouse had a chimney at one end to warm the guardroom. This area was called "the pits" because the main holding pens were well-like pits dug deep into the ground, lined with stone, and whitewashed so as to offer no fingerholds for prisoners who might try to climb out. The only way in or out was by ladder, which had to be lowered down from above.

The pits were open to the sky, each one covered by a big iron grille fastened to the ground with an iron stake and ring. Wooden planks could be laid across the grille if needed, in case of rain or snow. Or if the master in charge decided to execute the prisoners by burning them to death while they were trapped in the pit and chose to be merciful by letting them asphyxiate more quickly due to smoke inhalation instead.

Soldiers wearing the tree badge of Thelan's forces paced a circuit around the five pits. From the first two pits, faces stared up at her, shivering attendants, huddled together, all wearing clothing embroidered with cavorting bears. The third pit was empty, smeared with recent ash and debris. Elen shuddered. Eleawona must have ordered someone to be burned, not so many days ago.

In the fourth pit, six familiar faces looked up as she leaned to see, and then was yanked back for her trouble.

"Not in there. In the other one," said the guard. "By the Highmost's order."

A rough but creditable imitation of a rock pigeon's croon floated up from the pit, Kem signaling that he'd seen her.

The fifth pit was the smallest. Not so small that a person might attempt to climb out by pressing feet to one side and shoulders to the other, but not much larger. This one had a small shelter built over it: four posts and a roof, but no walls. Still, the roof gave this pit a trifle better protection from the elements. Perhaps Thelan meant her to be grateful for his consideration.

A lever and pulley were used to raise the heavy grille. After the grille was anchored by a chain to an iron ring, the guards shoved a wooden ladder down into the hole.

"You're even to get fed hot porridge and wrap yourself up tidy in a blanket," he said in the northern speech, then laughed with his fellows, for they assumed she could not understand. He added to the others, "They are sending over that martinet, Captain Mudpants, for that he can understand the southern speech. Haha! He'll have to spend the night in the cold, whilst we toast warmly in the barracks until dawn watch."

They all found the appellation "Mudpants" hilarious and began arguing over how exactly the infamous incident had taken place. Elen climbed down before they got the idea to grab her pack from her. What amazed her most about all of this was that their captors had never taken her gear from her or the others; not their weapons, nothing. Was this part of the deal with Luviara? Some delicate scheme Elen did not understand? A way for Thelan to show he did not fear them? Or maybe he feared to be seen as weak if he tried to handle shrive-steel, which only wardens could wield because of some manner of theurgical magic that bound a metal spirit to the warden, or the blade, or both. But no, there was no reason for Thelan to know about shrive-steel and its properties at all. Surely Luviara didn't intend to reveal even that secret to him as part of their deal!

None of this would matter, however, if the bequeather wasn't as curious about the Shorn as she'd professed herself to be. The best news so far was that Elen and the wardens weren't dead. Not yet. Elen was also grateful—strange to say!—that Thelan had stymied Luviara's attempt to return to the empire across Flat Boundary Pall. He didn't want the emperor and the crown prince to know how accessible Four Lands could become, lest they get ideas about the feasibility of taking back their long-lost province.

Would he attack the empire? Maybe. But he'd need time to consolidate his power base, fortify his country, and build a bigger army. Even then, it was difficult to imagine how a minor regional king could invade an empire. Perhaps he hoped to persuade the aivur to his side, but why would their clans place themselves under his rule? Salt Spear Clan was too small on its own, and the other Sea Wolf clans weren't his allies. Not yet, anyway. But what if he offered them territory in the empire, a permanent place to settle, as Gevulin had suggested? What then?

The instant she touched the ground at the bottom of the pit, the ladder was pulled up and a rolled-up blanket dropped down to smack onto the dirt beside her. The lid-like grille clapped back into place with a thunk.

The pit was deep enough that it was a smidgeon warmer down here than up on the surface, with no wind to cut a chill into a person's flesh. She looked up to make sure no one was looking down, then pulled off her glove, uncovered her sleeve, and let the viper emerge. It patrolled the space, found no Spore, and returned into her arm.

There was no bucket, nothing sanitary at all. She sniffed around to find the worst of the urine-and-feces smell. Fortunately, the stink was concentrated in one corner. The opposite corner was slightly elevated, while the center of the pit was damp, as if rainwater collected there.

She crouched at the elevated corner and went through her pack, piece by piece, to make sure everything was still there and ready to go. Amazingly, her other set of clothing was neatly rolled up at the top, damp but not wet, and smelling of vinegar instead of urine. She grinned. That was a blessing, indeed!

She folded up the blanket to sit on. First, she combed out and tightly rebraided the long, messy curls of her hair, grateful to have this chance to tidy it up before it got hopelessly snarled. Then she cleaned her boots. Her thoughts were scattered, buzzing like disturbed bees, and the familiar routine calmed her. After this, she sat cross-legged and recited the Courier's Code and the long preamble to the oath every official memorized when they entered the empire's service. Now and again, she heard conversation from the other pit, and once a bitter laugh.

Much later, the man who must have been Captain Mudpants appeared, a pallid face on high, set against the gray clouds and dimming light. He wasn't interested in her or the others; he was just checking to make sure they were all there. At his order, a guard lowered down a covered pot of startlingly warm porridge, and a spoon, too. When they pulled the pot back up, they demanded she send up the spoon with it or they'd come down themselves to take it. It was easy enough to obey. She had a spoon and knife of her own in her pack, which they'd never taken the time to search.

It got darker and even colder. She wrapped herself in the new blanket and her long wool traveling cloak that doubled as a blanket. Warm enough to think, she tried to calculate how long it had taken them to travel from the edge of the White Sea to South Ring, there and back again. Would the bequeather call the haunt? Was there magic involved, or was it an old ritual long forgotten in the empire? Would his name on the bequeather's lips reach him at all? Elen had no way of knowing how far away he might be by now, or where he intended to go, or where he even could go. Even then, if he heard his name, would he come to the bequeather's call? And if so, then what?

Then what?

Captain Mudpants made another round before he told his sergeant that he was going into the guardhouse for the night, instead of freezing his balls off out here. Guards stomped around for a while. Elen heard the clap of flint being struck and the hiss of a lantern as it was lit. Doors shut. All was still.

Xilsi's voice lifted, not too loud. "Are you there, Deputy Courier?"

"I am. How are you all?"

"Cold, but we can huddle together for warmth, so that's something. Is anyone in there with you?"

Only the viper, but Elen wasn't about to say that.

"No, but they gave me a blanket."

"I guess he doesn't want you to freeze," said Xilsi.

The prince said, "You have a weapon, Deputy Courier."

"Which I can only use once, Your Highness."

"What weapon is that?" said Xilsi, tone sharpening.

Kem said, "Her wit. She doesn't have much, so she has to be careful not to use it all up in one go."

"How would you know?" Ipis asked.

"I'm just making a joke to pass the time," said Kem, realizing he'd said too much and the wrong thing at the wrong time. It was remarkable that, except for the prince, the others still didn't know she and Kem were aunt and nephew. Yet why would they? The whole story stood too far outside of what Manor-born scions likely knew of the world. There was no reason any of it would occur to them.

Still, Xilsi and Jirvy, and maybe even Ipis, would eventually start putting together some part of the pieces, so she needed to get out in front of them. It was always best to tell part of a truth and let it stand for the whole truth.

Elen said, "His Exalted Highness has caught me out. There's something I haven't told you all. I thought I had left it behind."

"What's that?" asked Xilsi. "I knew there was something."

"I was born here, in this land."

"Ah, so that's it." Xilsi, again. "It explains how you knew about the crossing. Not your looks, though, since you don't look like the folk hereabouts. But if you weren't born in the empire, then how did you end up in the empire as a deputy courier?"

"My sister and I fled the Four Lands when I was about twelve or thirteen. I was what they call an atoner in the court of Lady Eleawona. That's why Lord Thelan remembers me. My looks are unusual here, it's true. He also recalled the scar on my neck."

Jirvy said, "I'll be a cursed uncle. I was sure you must be some seedling descendant of Iroon traders, the ones out of Ice Falls Province. They travel all across the empire by sea and land, leaving sprouts here and there."

"Or the child or grandchild of a Monrul soldier garrisoned far from their home province," said Xilsi. "Not at all out of place in the empire. But a strange cast of feature in this grim place."

Simo said nothing.

The prince remained silent, which Elen hoped meant he was

smart enough to understand that he had to keep the viper secret. Kem certainly was.

Yet Jirvy and Xilsi's speculation offered Elen a good opening. "To be honest, I have no memory of those who begat me. That's likely why I ended up as an atoner, as orphans often do here."

"What is an atoner?" Ipis asked.

"Atoners are the children the highborn here use to walk before and behind their traveling parties. So Spore will fasten in them first and warn the masters."

Ipis said, "Children! That's horrific."

Jirvy said, "Why wouldn't you want your most skilled people hunting Spore?"

Xilsi said, "That explains a lot about this filthy land."

Footsteps clumped over. A guard shouted down, "Shut up, you lot, or I'll give you something to natter about!"

The words were in the northern speech, but the message was clear.

Bundled up in the blankets, Elen settled herself against the wall. The cold didn't bother her much. The viper liked cold, and it had always seemed to her that the colder it got, the more vibrant the viper felt, gathering strength to use up later as if cold to the viper were like sleep to a person.

A faint *chwao chwao* call floated in the air, the cry of the marsh owl local to Orledder Halt. It was Kem, signaling that he and the others were all right for now.

Elen slept lightly, dozing on and off, attuned to changes in the air. By the third time she woke, the light had altered. Morning had come at last. She whistled the simple three-note call of the black-cap to alert Kem, and he—or possibly one of the wardens—answered in kind.

Not long after, horns blasted, followed by the sound of running feet and a man calling, "Captain! You're wanted at once."

After a pause, the guardhouse door opened. In a bleary voice, Captain Mudpants said irritably, "What's going on?"

"The Highmost is assembling the troops. Captain Dinec—"

"We encircled his remnant."

"He broke out, Captain. That's what they're saying."

"By the piss of the white-haired god, I thought that fox went quiet too easily. Still, Dinec's badly outnumbered now. We'll have a fine hunt of it."

For four hours—Elen checked her courier's watch—a clatter of activity rang in the air. A great many horses were ridden out, followed somewhat after by wagons. Then, the town grew uneasily quiet.

Guards still peered down at intervals. Food was lowered eventually, more hot porridge, this time flavored with an herb she recognized—fairwater dill—which Fulmo carried because it was a favorite of the prince's and not grown in the northern provinces. She supposed the presence of this herb was meant as a signal to the prince that Fulmo was cooking, and tasting, for him. Hidden in plain sight. Kitchen workers for a large household or residence always seemed to be scrambling to keep up. Perhaps the winter palace's kitchen staff had welcomed the extra help. Yet given the usual suspicion with which people in the Four Lands tended to treat outsiders, it was odd the kitchen folk had so easily taken Fulmo in and were allowing him to cook. A gagast, at that! But if people here didn't know that gagast even existed, then Fulmo might simply seem an overly large and oafish retainer who couldn't speak and who froze up with fear at night, and thus would be judged as slow and stupid—but still a useful pair of working hands.

Most likely, Eleawona had arranged Fulmo's kitchen privileges as a courtesy toward Gevulin. He would have reached South Ring a day or so ahead of Elen's belated arrival. He wouldn't trust Eleawona's cooks and, even if he'd been offensive about it, Eleawona would want to placate him as a sign that she wished their alliance to flourish.

By now, everyone in the winter palace must have known that Lady Eleawona had been hauled away to the north and the prince shoved into the pits. Maybe allowing Fulmo to cook for the foreigners was their way of displaying loyalty to their lady, of letting Gevulin know they had not forgotten that he and Eleawona had shared a measure of trust between them. For herself, Elen felt better knowing Fulmo was not in custody, and that he knew exactly where they were. That was a start.

She whistled a deliberately merry tune as she paced herself through stretches and training movements, since she had enough room at the bottom of the pit—three paces square—to turn around.

In the other pit, Xilsi said, deliberately loud, "How can she be so sunny in these dire straits?"

The prince said, "Deputy Courier, have you a plan?"

"Be patient, Your Highness," Elen replied. "If Captain Dinec defeats Lord Thelan's army, then I expect we will be freed."

"And if he does not? You should have struck while you had the chance."

"Then we'd all be dead."

"I think not," said the prince. "You would be dead, but the lady would have seized the opportunity to retake control. You are not as loyal an official as you are meant to be, Deputy Courier. You should have sacrificed yourself. Now we are trapped and helpless. Soon to be executed, I presume."

Elen smiled, aware no one could see her. "Actually, I heard Lord Thelan discuss marrying you off to one of his half sisters."

"Do not be absurd!"

Silence followed this expostulation.

Yet in a while, Gevulin spoke in an altered tone, the cunning locution of a prince who knows how to work the bureaucratic compounds and bustling corridors of a palace. "Still, there's a foothold to be grasped there. He did not allow Luviara to return south by the crossing we made. He doesn't want the empire to know how close we really are to this pathetic land, though it is all the world to him. I daresay he may have the theurgist killed on the road to keep the knowledge away from the palace."

"More likely imprisoned until she reveals the secrets of theurgy," Elen said. "Maybe she sent an air spirit to the palace already."

"Unbound air spirits can't—or won't—cross a Pall," the prince said, sounding annoyed that she didn't know what was obvious to him with his princely education. "As well, a theurgist's control is limited by distance. The binding begins to fray as it stretches. Which means Luviara did not send the spirit to Thelan until after we crossed the Pall. I suspect she only did so once she confirmed Thelan might be close enough. Besides that, air spirits can only convey extremely simple messages. Why do you think the emperor relies on griffin scouts and sarpa riders? Spirits have intelligence, of a kind, but you can no more expect an air spirit to convey complex instructions or ciphers than you can expect a Manor's genius to comprehend a ship or a gallop."

His easy talk of theurgical secrets surprised her. Maybe their desperate situation had loosened his tongue. Nevertheless, she was always grateful to have more knowledge to stash away for times of need. Knowledge kept you alive.

So, Luviara could indeed not have wafted the party across any gap of Pall, regardless of the strength of the spirits she still held. The revelation made Elen think about the message Simo had sent via the road. Was that type of communication possible only because the air spirit was sealed—trapped—inside the magical bones of the road, and could only get out by delivering its message?

Gevulin was still going on, as princes did. "I need only play this game with skill and attention. I wasn't intending to make my move on the imperial throne this soon. I don't have enough allies in place yet. A delay does not hurt my longer-term plans. The barbarian wants something, or he'd already have killed us. I need only figure out what it is he wants—"

"Shut it! Shut it, you cursed jabberers!" Liquid splashed from above—into the other pit, not on Elen.

Ipis yelped. "Oh, foul!"

"Shut it! Or I'll toss down the whole bucket of piss on your heads. I might do it just for the fun of hearing you squeal more!"

"What were they saying?" asked another guard.

"How do I know? I'm not one of the masters, am I? Nor you, are you? Get out of my way, my feet will freeze off if I don't keep walking. I hate this duty. I hate the south county. Pissing whiners, all of them, nasty and proud."

Still, the guards patrolled all day with commendable vigilance, even as they groused to each other. Maybe they were nervous about being fenced into a town populated by Eleawona's partisans. Maybe they were worried in case Captain Dinec, with his fox-wise ways, had won whatever battle had erupted elsewhere and was already swinging around to take back South Ring and slaughter all Thelan's troops left to garrison the winter palace. Maybe they genuinely respected and admired Thelan.

A late-afternoon meal of porridge was lowered, this one flavored with dried cloudberries.

Incredible. Too bad they'd used up the drugged cloudberry brew on the smugglers. She'd have laughed at Fulmo's wit but contented herself with a spark of hope, relishing the berries' sweet tartness. They could get out of this.

As twilight settled, she set free the viper to see how far it could climb. Had the pit walls been built out of mortared brick, it could have crawled all the way to the top, but the whitewash laid atop the vertical walls hacked out of the ground didn't give its body quite enough purchase.

The viper dropped from the wall, and she caught it on her head and in her hands. Kneeling, she let it slither down her arms and then around the floor of the pit as she paced restlessly alongside.

Would the bequeather call the haunt? Would he answer? What did Elen expect from this gambit, anyway? That the Salt Spear Clan would raid South Ring because one of the legendary Shorn asked for their help to free the woman he loved? What could she possibly hope for?

Long ago, as a very small child, before she became an atoner, she had drifted alone, afloat and afraid in a wide salt sea. It was one of only two memories she still had from before becoming an atoner, before Ao.

That day, no one had called for her or come for her. She'd gotten to shore by the grace of the High Heavens but mostly because she'd refused to stop paddling to keep her head above water.

You had to rescue yourself. It was a lesson that had served her and Ao well over the years. The haunt was gone about his own duty. She had to accept that.

In the distance, she heard the gate into the prison yard open and close. She crouched to let the viper burn back into her arm. Brisk footfalls sounded as someone approached the first of the pits, followed by silence. A few more footsteps, and again silence.

Then, from the pit nearest hers, where the prince and the wardens were being held captive, the sound of a sly, delighted laugh. She knew that laugh, even if the voice was no longer the prince's cultured baritone but a softly thunderous alto.

"What an unexpected well of sorrows is this! Here I find not water that gives us life, but a cuddle of unfortunate fish caught in a most unpleasant quandary. Yet I count only six."

"Are you not Captain Raven, the bequeather of Salt Spear Clan?" demanded the prince. "You must get us out of here at once. I will make it worth your while, offer your clan a better alliance—"

"Yes, yes, that's all very well, but *where is the deputy courier?*"

"I'm here," she said hoarsely, barely able to speak because suddenly she couldn't breathe.

He had come for her.

26

Be but Patient

The night beyond the grille lightened as a lit lantern approached. Between one moment and the next, the lantern was held out over her pit. The flame burned modestly enough that she needed only a few blinks to adjust her vision. The person holding the lantern, staring down at her, was indeed the bequeather. In body, at least. The loose-limbed way the normally rigidly imposing aivur woman carried herself told Elen otherwise.

"Are you going to stand down there in that stink of urine all night?" the haunt asked. "If it pleases you, I suppose you could. No accounting for tastes."

"It does not please me. But unlike the theurgist, I can't call an air spirit to lift myself out. There should be a ladder."

"Ah. I shall investigate this benighted domicile. The smell is frightful."

The haunt and his lantern retreated. She heard a bit of muttering, the grille dragged aside, a curse as if he'd stubbed his toe, and then the ladder came slamming down into the pit. She had to jump aside so it didn't crash into her head. Unscathed, she grasped the rungs and climbed, pack on her back, careful not to scramble in haste lest she slip and hurt herself, careful, so careful because her breathing was all out of rhythm.

From the other pit, the prince commanded, "Release us at once! What are you doing over there?"

"Was he always this annoying?" the haunt remarked, swinging the lantern farther out over the pit to give her better light. His tone was light, yet with an undercurrent that sounded a lot like worry, so she concentrated on the rungs.

"Far more so than you suspect. Your passage spell's veil did not work on him, so he knows the whole."

Of course he laughed. "There's a wrinkle I did not expect. And here you are."

As she reached the top, the haunt grasped her arm. He hauled her up and over the rim with such strength that she stumbled forward into the bequeather's body. It was like hitting a wall. A warm, attractive, beloved wall of strength and stability. He steadied her at once, arm tightening around her, pulling her close. The bequeather was taller than Elen, taller than the prince, lean and muscular and beautiful in the way glorious raptors are beautiful. Elen's hands pressed against his shoulders, the length of her torso held hard against the bequeather's body. Elen lifted her gaze to a gleaming stare that searched hers. But it wasn't the chilly hauteur of the aivur captain that met her eyes. It was heat like embers about to burst back into flame. He parted his lips, inhaling as he took in her presence. They were so close, chin to chin, nose to nose, as if to share their very breath.

"You came for me," she whispered.

He gave a little puff of a sound, as if offended. "Of course I did."

She rose up on her toes because, after all this, she had to kiss him at last, let all the rest go hang for one precious moment. He sighed and bent his head toward her . . . but before their lips could touch, he stiffened and said, in a fraught whisper, "No, not yet. I was given permission for one kiss. I will not waste it when we must be hasty. Dear one, be but patient. Can you?"

"What is going on up there?" hissed Xilsi. "Can we get out of here *now*?"

One kiss. The words struck through her like lightning. But Xilsi was right. This was not the time. She shook off the veil of distraction—of desire and hope and joy—that threatened to engulf her head to toe.

"Of course," she said, more harshly than she intended as she struggled to get her heart to cease its unruly gallop, all of her gone hot even in the cold night air.

Take action, that was the key. She stepped back, grabbed the ladder and, with his aid, hauled it up. They carried it over to the next pit.

In a whisper, she called down, "Beware. Watch your heads."

They had to hold the ladder awkwardly high before lowering it until the legs thumped into the ground below.

"Let me go first, Your Highness," said Simo. The ladder trembled as he started up.

Elen said, "If there are other ladders, we need to get the other prisoners out."

"Why?" asked the haunt. "I thought they were the enemy. Do they all love you now, too, dear one?"

She laughed, unreasonably pleased by his use of this ridiculous endearment. "I doubt that, but they serve Lady Eleawona and therefore not Lord Thelan and his invading soldiers. Throw the pigeons among the cats, especially when there are more pigeons than cats."

Simo emerged and immediately drew his sword. He turned a defensive circle, searching the darkness. "Where are the guards?"

"I ate them," said the haunt.

Elen snorted, then frowned and said, "Surely not."

"Not to my taste, I assure you."

Simo held his sword to guard against the person he knew as the bequeather. "So, it's true! Just as we said in the east. Aivur crave human flesh."

"Of course it's not true," snapped Elen.

"How would you know?" Simo countered. "You never saw what I saw."

"Yes, I never did," she agreed irritably. "Captain, find another ladder." She looked around, then at the haunt. "Where *are* the gate guards?"

"They're dead." The haunt waved the lantern toward the open gate, where two blots darker than shadows lay on the ground, visible from this distance only if you thought to look for them. He swung back to give Simo a narrow-eyed stare. His eyes had an eerie glow in the darkness that made the captain take a step away. "But not eaten, I assure you. It was a jest, Captain, meant to lighten the dire mood. But I suppose you see only darkness ahead since you hitched your pony to the wrong princely carriage, and now you're stuck with a traitor's brand upon your back."

Simo was so shocked by this reply that he gaped instead of answering in anger.

In the silence, Jirvy emerged from the pit and whispered down, "Next up."

The door into the guardhouse clicked and opened, visible because of the lit lantern set on an iron tripod beside the door. Jirvy immediately went down onto one knee to string his bow in a practiced movement. A guardsman came out, staring toward their lantern and shouting, "What's all this noise? Can't a man sleep in peace—"

He grunted and collapsed to the ground with an arrow planted deep in his chest.

"How many in the guardhouse?" Simo asked.

"I don't know," said Elen.

"I smell the souls of thirty-three," said the haunt. "But many may be prisoners, for they stink of fear and neglect."

"To arms," said Simo.

A second guard emerged, stumbling over the body of the first. Jirvy's arrow took him in the fold between neck and shoulder, and he spun with a gurgling oath and fell back. The door scraped shut, cruelly leaving the first guard outside, where he moaned and writhed, for he wasn't dead. Jirvy nocked another arrow.

Simo said, "Don't waste an arrow on him unless he starts crawling toward us. It's impossible for us to get inside. We'll bolt as soon as we're all out of the pit."

"Leaving our backs vulnerable?" Jirvy asked.

The haunt set down the lantern and ran into the darkness, toward the doorless end of the prison blockhouse.

"What's she doing?" Simo asked.

"I don't know, but you'd better make ready," Elen said.

The prince swung himself out of the pit. Without a word, he drew his sword and settled back-to-back with Simo, as comfortable a fit as if they'd fought together before. As if they trusted each other.

"A shutter is opening," said Jirvy. "Get the light away from us. Draw their aim."

Elen grabbed the lantern and ran toward the other pits. An arrow skittered at her heels. A voice yelped as Jirvy's reply struck flesh. An argument broke out inside the guardhouse as the shutter slammed shut again. Someone inside clanged pots together, but the sound remained muffled by the thick walls.

Xilsi dragged herself over the rim of the pit.

Simo said, "Xilsi, guard the gate. We need to get out that way."

Xilsi jumped to her feet and raced away, running low. Elen swung the lantern over the rim of the next pit. Pale and frightened faces stared up at her, bodies crammed in like unfortunate fish being made ready to salt in a barrel, just as the haunt had observed. Voices rose in a clamor from below. "Who are you? Was that Her Ladyship's bequeather? Help us up! Please, get us out! We pray you, by the mercy of the white-haired god."

The point had come where she needed information more than anyone's belief that she couldn't understand the Four Lands speech. Words spilled out like rusted hinges opening creakily. Her accent sounded off to her own ears, but the words were recognizable. "Is there another ladder? Where is it?"

A man in soldier's garb was jostled. He said, "We hang them from the eaves to the left of the door."

Just as he said, there was another ladder, hanging from the eaves of the building where the armed enemy were making their plans. She loped over to the next pit and swung the lantern out again. If anything, more people were crammed in this pit, most wearing the garb of Lady Eleawona's personal household attendants, gold brooches still on their kirtles and tunics as if left for looting once they were dead. Many were injured. One had a horrific broken arm, bone showing white against bloodied, twisted flesh. Another had blood smeared all over their hair, and they slumped unresponsively against a companion. Probably Thelan's troops had just shoved them into the pit, let them fall and be broken.

"Please. Help us! We pray you, by the mercy of the white-haired god."

How strange to hear them speaking to her as if she were the same as them rather than a despised atoner. But, of course, they didn't know. Only Thelan had recognized her. Not even Eleawona had, because she'd never looked closely enough at her atoners. Maybe Thelan, a bastard as he was, had had to be far more observant, since he could take nothing for granted. Or maybe it was just his nature.

And unlike Thelan, Elen did not feel herself yoked to the past.

"I'll do what I can," she said to those below.

She set the lantern down by the pit and ran back to the other wardens. As dark as it was, her eyes had adapted to the hazy aura offered by the two lanterns and, anyway, she'd always had the ability to sense the nearness of other living creatures, not quite sight but enough to avoid that which she could not necessarily see. A lithe figure clambered onto the roof of the blockhouse. The bequeather! No, it was the haunt. He lifted himself to the top of the smoking chimney and pitched over into the hole, dropping inside straight down toward the burning hearth within.

Kem had just gotten off the ladder, and he startled when Elen grabbed his arm. "Kem! Once Ipis is up, we'll get the ladder over to get those people out."

Simo said, "Do no such thing, Novice. We're leaving at once."

"We need to find the kitchens and Fulmo," said the prince. "But why has the bequeather returned? Has she rethought my offer?"

"Alert," said Jirvy, tensing as he made ready to loose another arrow.

A crescendo of shouting rose from inside the prison blockhouse.

The door burst open. Guards piled out, shrieking as smoke boiled around them, darker than the night and so hot that waves of heat washed over Elen and the others even at some forty paces away. Jirvy took down the first two guards in quick succession, then a third as the rest scrambled to flee. Simo and the prince raced forward to attack, taking advantage of the soldiers' confusion.

Ipis clambered up at last, panting. Elen grabbed the ladder and started hauling it up before the young warden was even firmly on the ground. But it was too heavy for her alone.

"Kem. Help me. One pit is all we need. Then they can help each other."

Swords clashed with a ringing clamor, accompanied by shouts that surely woke the entire quarter. Ipis strung her bow, going down on one knee beside Jirvy. Elen and Kem ran with the ladder dragged all unwieldy between them. It took them two tries to get it raised to the correct angle. Even then, they hit the sides of the pit several times before the ladder's base hit the bottom. Below, people cried out as the ladder struck them.

Elen turned to look back, but the skirmish at the blockhouse had ended as abruptly as it had begun. Six guards lay on the ground, unmoving. The haunt limped out of the prison house, brushing his hands together as if meticulously dusting off a layer of unwanted soot. Then he swung a ring of keys around his fingers in such an insouciant manner it made Elen want to laugh despite everything, although she did not laugh; not aloud, anyway, yet her heart lightened and she smiled.

He said, "I unlocked the cells. What shall I do with these charmingly useful if roughhewn implements?"

"You're limping, and no wonder; the way you threw yourself down the chimney I can't believe you didn't break an ankle."

"I daresay I might have," he said through gritted teeth as he tested his weight on his right foot. "But no matter. It will pass soon."

"Pass soon?" Then she realized that the "soot" he'd been dusting from his hands was skin flaking and peeling. He was ruddy and blistering where the fire had touched his hands and face, although the bequeather's tough leather garments seemed mostly unharmed. "You're burnt!"

"So I am, for this body does not love fire as it ought to do," he said lightly, even as his mouth twitched with a grimace that looked suspiciously like a wince of pain, "but I assure you, dear one, it will heal soon enough."

Gevulin cast a suspicious glance toward the person he knew as Captain Raven. But before he could ask any questions, Xilsi's shrill warning whistle sounded from the gate: *Hostiles incoming.*

27

The Kitchen Compound

"Form up," Simo barked to the other wardens. "Your Highness, I recommend we make for the ramp and get out of town immediately."

"Where are the kitchens?" asked the prince. "We must go there first."

"I smell trouble," said the haunt, shifting to put his weight solely on the unbroken ankle. No one but Elen seemed to notice. "Must we go all the way back to the palace? If we do, trouble will certainly find us out. We can go up and over the road using that very conveniently located ramp, and therefore be quickly gone from this benighted and foul-smelling place with its miasma of misery and dread."

The prince did not raise his voice, but his words were clipped and sure. "We find Fulmo before we go."

Simo cleared his throat. "Your Highness, to return to the palace is to place ourselves in greater danger."

"I cannot leave him behind with no means to track me!"

"Of course, Your Highness."

The haunt cast a questioning glance toward Elen, asking whether he ought to protest. She shook her head in reply. Of course it was hazardous to go back to the palace compound. But it seemed far worse to abandon Fulmo alone, in enemy territory, with no means to know where they'd gone. Even if the gagast was, to a degree, invulnerable, what would happen to him? If Thelan had him pushed into one of the pits and then planked it over, would Fulmo starve because he was unable to absorb starlight? Whatever the prince's reasons, she respected him for the decision. And she was curious to discover by what means the prince would make it possible for Fulmo to track him. It was an absolute fool's errand, and yet, here they were, headed back into the enemy's strongest-held position, which lay at the farthest remove from any escape ramp out of South Ring.

Surveying them, Gevulin's upper lip curled. He added with smug superiority, "Has it occurred to none of you that without Fulmo's aid, we cannot cross back across Far Boundary Pall?"

The haunt raised a hand with a lazy wave that drew the prince's attention away from the scolded wardens. "An unassailable argument, under the circumstances. Since it must be so, then I know how to get to the kitchen from here. I sought out the gagast there, not knowing where your prison pits were located. He was star-touched and thus uncommunicative, but the kitchen staff were eager to inform me exactly where you were being held. They assigned a little lad to show me the way. I suspect the child remains in hiding outside, waiting for you to come out. They seem to believe you can do something to help their kidnapped lady. Can you?"

"No, I cannot," said the prince coldly. "Her fate is on her head now. This expedition has proven disastrous. Min-lo has outmaneuvered me. I underestimated him, to my cost. But with Luviara still in Thelan's hands, for now, the emperor has no proof, only suspicion. We will find Fulmo, get out of South Ring, and by one means or another, return in secrecy to the empire. Once there, I will figure out a way to make sure Luviara never reaches the palace. The emperor and the crown prince will wonder, but they will never know what happened here. Without definitive proof, they cannot act openly against me. Now, I am forewarned and thus forearmed against further covert plots against me."

His warning gaze made it clear there would be no more discussion. Eleawona was, like a broken weapon, to be summarily discarded.

Prisoners staggered out of the smoky billows boiling out of the blockhouse. As more pushed into the prison yard, they clotted in a mass around the entry as they tried to figure out what to do and where to go.

The first of Eleawona's soldiers heaved himself out of a pit, calling, "Grab that other ladder, you fools. Bring it over here! Move! We have to get everyone up. We're going to hunt down that bastard's stinking troops and slaughter them like the pigs they are."

The man looked over at the prince. "Whsst! You! Who are you lot? The foreigners?"

"Move," said Simo to the wardens.

They settled their packs and gripped their weapons as they ran for the gate.

Elen grasped the haunt's wrist. "Are you all right? Can you even run?"

He bent a warm gaze on her. "Pain is easiest to bear when one knows it is fleeting. However sharp these injuries hurt now, it is nothing to how it felt when I had to leave you. For these will heal swiftly enough, but there at the Vigil, I did not know if I would ever see you again."

"Sara'ala," she murmured, too choked to say more.

He smiled. "My name upon your sweet lips is all the balm I need."

A brisk whistle alerted them that Xilsi was waiting impatiently by the open gate. They ran over, and Elen had to keep her mouth shut because his gait was staggered and uneven, each touch of the broken ankle clearly an agony, but he bore each step as he bore the burnt skin, with his eyes a little shuttered and his jaw clenched, but not a sound of complaint.

Fortunately, none of the others had been hurt in the skirmish, although Ipis had bruised a knee coming up the ladder and favored that leg as they ran to the gate.

Eleawona's soldier shouted after them, but no one pursued. Whoever had taken charge was wise enough not to waste their time on foreigners. Thelan was their enemy, not random strangers.

At the gate, Xilsi pointed down a lane. "I saw someone moving."

The haunt sniffed at the air, nodded as he recognized something he was seeking, and whistled three notes. A small figure slipped out of the shadows.

"Our guide approaches." The haunt limped forward to greet the boy with hands extended and flat as if to show he was unarmed. It wasn't a gesture Elen recognized from her childhood, but the boy touched his own open, flat palms to the haunt's palms as if closing a circle of trust or alliance.

"Are you burnt?" the child whispered, as if he'd seen burns before; maybe, as a kitchen worker, he had.

"Only a trifle."

Reassured, the boy looked past the haunt to stare with wide eyes at the prince and the wardens, as if they looked far stranger to his eyes than did an aivur.

He whispered, in the northern speech, "You got 'em out, Captain."

"So I did. Take us back to the kitchens, I pray you. We must go at speed and keep out of sight. My thanks for your service and skill, child."

The child's pale face flashed with startled wonder. No one ever thanked retainers. "Yes'n, Captain." He addressed the others with a submissive bob of his head, as if apologizing for speaking. "We got to go 'round, not by the masters' road. Stay out of sight."

"Do they delegate children for all the dangerous jobs?" Jirvy muttered in disgust.

No one answered. The noise of tramping boots grew in volume from along the avenue. The child led them hurriedly aside, into a narrow alley where they halted. There they sheltered, unseen, as a file of soldiers ran past them and toward the prison yard. Trash had been dumped into the alley and, fortunately, the cold held down the stink, although unseen objects squished beneath Elen's tread with a faint crackle. Ipis flinched at something that touched her but made no sound. All of them knew better.

When the soldiers were out of sight, the child led them back out to the avenue. Almost immediately, he directed their party onto a lane that wound a back way through the masters' houses and outbuildings, a path by which retainers delivered goods and hurried on errands, out of sight of the masters. Their group didn't run. Running was too loud. For this journey, they needed stealth. The haunt was still limping, but he kept up. The darkness hid the condition of his hands and face from the others.

From behind, in the direction of the prison yard, shouts rang out into the cold night air. It wasn't clear if the cries came as a prelude to more fighting or from the joyous reunion of Eleawona's partisans. Briefly, Elen wondered at Eleawona, what little she had ever truly seen of her, now, as then. What sort of person had the quietly dignified girl of long ago become? What did she want? Was she merciful or cruel, or did a lady think in such terms at all, for as a master she need only rule all that the white-haired god had given her to rule, according to the law of the Four Lands.

Not my law any longer, Elen thought with a fierce swell of anger, of triumph. *Ao and I escaped.*

How she hated this place and the way it crushed those who lived here, the way it fed itself on the blood of the smallest and weakest. Yet was the empire any better? She had to believe so, even if that belief was an illusion. Or an excuse for her role in the imperial bureaucracy. The empire called itself "tranquil" because it claimed to shepherd and shield all its people. Yet princes and high officials in the empire had the power to whip and to kill, and to use imperial law to justify their actions. Perhaps, as a minor official, she had trained herself to not look too closely so as to avoid seeing what she didn't want to see.

Well. For now, they had to get out of here. This was not the time to dwell on things outside this night and this escape.

Beside her, the haunt brushed a hand against her arm. "Are you well?" he whispered. "You are not hurt? Or harmed?"

Her heart swelled with an almost obliterating spike of pure joy. He had come for her.

"Never better," she murmured, bumping an elbow softly against his arm, feeling more than seeing the answering flash of a smile in his exhale. "But what of your injuries?"

"Healing, according to the nature of my essence," he said so lightly that she realized he was unconcerned by a broken ankle and blistering burns, willing to bear the pain because he knew it would be temporary. "I am content because we are together."

Then so was she content, even in the midst of peril.

They hurried on, strung out in single file: the child and Simo at the front, the haunt and Elen next, then the prince, Kem, Xilsi, and Ipis, with Jirvy bringing up the rear. They'd fallen into a line of march with the discipline of well-trained people, and they walked as quickly as they could, given the darkness.

Once, Jirvy whispered from the back, "Captain Raven, are you limping? Did you take an injury?"

"Just a twisted ankle, nothing to signify," replied the haunt cheerfully.

"Hush, I hear something," said the boy. He shuttered the lantern he held, its frail light vanishing as they all stood stock-still against a wall, waiting in silence. A clatter of footfalls passed on the next street, fading away to silence. After a short wait, the boy opened the shutter enough for a thin gleam, and hurried on.

Night gave them an advantage as they reached the outer ring-wall of the palace compound. The boy had left the latch off a small pedestrian gate, and here they slipped through, one by one, and crossed a little bridge over another section of the encircling canal.

The noise from the east had faded, while fresh sounds of confusion and clamor rose from ahead: distant shouts, a clatter, a silence, then yet more shouting. They moved through a section of crowded storehouses. The child knew every cramped alley, every alcove suitable for hiding. Three times, they crowded into a concealed nook when they heard running feet coming too close. Yet no one disturbed the closed doors of the storehouses. A more consequential struggle than petty thievery was afoot.

Back in the direction of the prison a clamorous hammering rang out, followed by a scream, which cut off as if swallowed by an anticipatory tension. A murmuration of many angry voices growled in the distance. The stamp of booted feet moving in unison. People were moving, but who? And where?

"This way," the boy said, tugging on Simo's arm.

They cut through a courtyard crudely paved in brick over a foundation of what looked like old planting troughs and garden beds, now nothing but rock and bare soil. Maybe this courtyard had been a garden once, but inside South Ring nothing could be allowed to grow. Fields and gardens and orchards were planted outside the Ring only. Let others live at risk, and let retainers cart the harvest to the winter palace once it was safely cut and dead and thus no longer viable for Spore.

A garden gate opened onto a forecourt facing the main gate and an inner wall that fenced off the kitchen compound. To the left rose the shadowy bulk of the high hall and, beyond it, a view of the barracks where torches ominously flashed in and out of view. To the right, a pair of nervous guards, both wearing the badge of the lady's dancing bears, stood within the hazy aura of a lantern hung above the closed gate.

"Here you are, Barrow!" the shorter one exclaimed as the lad trotted up.

In the light, Elen got a better look at the boy. He was small, perhaps ten or eleven, but he had a healthy-looking face, pale, with the clear eyes of a person who was not struggling with a disease that would soon kill them. He was dressed in a retainer's thick wool tunic, neatly darned at the elbows, and a pair of worn but well-kept boots, a mark of a certain distinction. In her childhood as an atoner, Elen had never worn anything so fine, although any master would have scorned such garb as rags.

"Be this him, the foreign lord?" the taller guard asked, taking the lantern out of the boy's hand and raising it to peer at Simo's face. "They don't look rightly like people nor like aivur, do they?" he added with a puzzled frown, adding, "Begging your pardon, Captain Raven, no offense meant," when he saw the haunt.

"No offense taken, but there be trouble behind us, so you must be wary and be ready," said the haunt, in the accent of the north.

"We shall throw them bastards out," proclaimed the tall guard.

The short one opened the gate for their party to hurry through.

Well past midnight as it was, the kitchen complex lay in hushed darkness: the big cookhouse as well as a scullery annex, food storage, the royal granary, and a set of covered cisterns linked to the aqueduct. Open space kept the necessary cooking fires separate from vulnerable wood structures. Heat swelled off beehive-shaped ovens where fresh bread would be baked at dawn. The roasting hearths were banked, awaiting the morning's rush of preparation for the midday feast. Elen couldn't make out much, and all of it appeared strange and rather magical to her eyes. She and Ao had only patrolled the kitchen grounds once or twice when young. All she remembered from that time was how astonished both of them were by the overwhelming presence of so much food and so many varied and appetizing smells.

But the nose-smart girl, just one of the general band of atoners in those early days, had soon after been folded irrevocably into Eleawona's personal court, thanks to her uncanny skills. Only now did she understand why Ao had been held so close to the lady, who had been her half sister all along.

By the cookhouse, Fulmo's distinctive silhouette stood statuelike, blocky head bent back so his face was turned up toward the sky. Scraps of clouds blew wisps across stars that flashed in and out of sight.

There were a surprising number of people awake and huddled around the seeping warmth of the ovens and hearths. They turned anxiously as the wardens entered but were too obedient to approach. The prince was a master, after all. As one, they knelt with bowed heads.

Ignoring them, the prince strode across the kitchen yard to approach Fulmo. He slid a decorative bead off one of his braids. This tiny object he pressed between the gagast's lightly closed lips. When Fulmo woke at dawn, Elen supposed, the bead would somehow guide him to wherever the prince was.

The prince turned to glower at the staff. "Where can we get horses?"

One man crept forward on his knees. His brass brooch marked him as the highest rank of retainer and therefore the person in charge.

"Your Highness, the bastard's soldiers be in control of the barracks and high hall. They leave us alone because we feed them. We cannot fend them off with our cooking knives."

The haunt translated.

Simo added, "We have weapons enough. We need horses and a path out of here. Where are the stables? Can we sneak in and steal horses while there is confusion and fighting elsewhere?"

Once the words were translated, the boy looked doubtful. "Stables stand past the high hall, north of the barracks. Mayhap, if we stick to the shadows, we can run there and not be seen."

A bell tolled once, twice, three times with the call to arms. The alarm rang through the night. Its deep tones cut right down through to Elen's bones, a sound so harsh and long forgotten yet so familiar and urgent that she froze in stunned fury. Hadn't she left this all behind?

A martial horn blared from the direction of the high hall, or the barracks beyond, a swelling noise of people gathering, the rumble of feet, raised voices, the shaking of shields and the pound of spears against the ground in a threatening rhythm. From farther away, a clamor of fighting rose as the serious clashes began, so distant that it might have been a play being enacted for the entertainment of the locals. So hard to fathom that this night was real. That blood would flow. Was flowing.

A hand touched her arm. Kem, coming up beside her, whispered, "Are you all right?"

Elen blinked away the paralysis that had seized her. She breathed again.

"We need to get out of here before they realize we've escaped the pits," she said, but her words came out in a whisper. No one but Kem heard her.

The head of the kitchen staff gave another bow. "If ye go back out through the main gate and through the storehouses, then turn for the north ramp through the retainer tenements, that be your best path out, I reckon, Your Highness," he urged. "If you can but come free and save our beloved lady—"

A tramping of boots interrupted the man's heartfelt plea, which the prince could not understand and would have had no intention of fulfilling regardless. A hazy light flared as torches approached along the lane. The gate opened. The two guards scurried inside and slammed it shut behind them.

"The bastard's soldiers are coming here!" they cried. "Let us block the gate. Haul over any object to bar it!"

The gate had no inner lock or bar. Retainers could not bar their workplaces or living quarters against the soldiers who served the masters. The kitchen yard was not a fortifiable position. Yet retainers ran to the gate and, alongside the two guards, pressed their bodies against the wood while others dragged benches and tables over to create a makeshift barrier.

"Are we trapped, or is there another route out of this compound?" Gevulin cast his gaze around the enclosed yard. His voice didn't break or grow shrill with panic. He remained poised and alert. "Is there a way over the wall?"

"Open up! Open up!" A pounding shuddered the gates.

The head of the kitchen rubbed his face with frantic worry, then addressed the haunt. "I have an idea. The bastard's troops cleared out the high hall, for the most part. My servers did see with their own eyes, when they took food in, that few bide there now. Our cistern gate opens onto the masters' walkway, that one by which we take provender to the high hall. Mayhap if you can get along that walkway, then turn to go past the tower. There's a culvert through the wall, that part of the canal that does connect to the waterwheel."

After the haunt had translated, the prince exchanged a glance with Simo. To the haunt, he said, "Tell these menials their loyalty is commendable. Let them know the gagast will awaken at dawn. He can make his own way to me now that he has the bead. Simo!"

Without a backward glance, the wardens raced to the cisterns. Elen lagged behind to watch as the pounding at the gate increased in intensity. The head of the kitchen called out, "What brings ye to this clamor? We are trying to sleep!"

Then, the haunt was beside her, chivvying her forward. "Hurry. If you're caught here, they'll kill you. And I can't have that!"

"What about the kitchen staff?"

"Ah, well, dear one. That is the conundrum, is it not? It hurts to leave people behind, in danger, yet here we are, and we must do it or the harm that will come to them will be even worse, will it not? Better they be whipped for refusing to open the gates when commanded to, when they can plead they were merely afraid, than executed for harboring fugitives."

The truth of his words bit like a wolf at her belly. The other wardens had already disappeared behind the raised cisterns. A wooden ramp led up to a well-oiled door that let onto the covered walkway by which kitchen help carried platters of food, in bulk and at speed, to the hungry masters, come rain or shine. The servers' door stood ajar, Kem waiting anxiously in the gap. Meanwhile, the shouted discussion continued at the kitchen gate.

"Come on!" Kem whispered, gesturing urgently. He gave a curious glance at the haunt's reddened, blistering face. "Were you injured in the fighting at the blockhouse, Captain? Are you limping, too? Is a wound on your chest?"

"Nothing to signify, and I will thank you for forgetting you ever saw anything," the haunt said briskly, and when Elen again hesitated to leave the kitchen staff, he added, "The soldiers won't know we were ever here. They'll search, and find no one."

It hurt to go, but they had to go, and she desperately wanted to go, to get out of this place she and Ao had never wanted to set foot in ever again. The wardens huddled on the other side of the door, arguing in low voices. The raised walkway cut straight across an open space between the kitchen compound and the high hall. No one was on the walkway, at least not that they could see, but even if they crouched as they ran, their figures would be spotted by the sentries and soldiers now racing about the open area.

"We can't get out this way," said the prince in a low voice.

From behind, a crash splintered the kitchen gates.

"We can't go back," said Simo.

"We'll go under," said Elen. "We'll crawl under the walkway to the hall. By then, fortune may favor us, and the soldiers will disperse into the town. If we stick by the building, night will cover our run to the culvert."

Wardens had the discipline not to hesitate or dispute when only one course of action remained. They were trapped on every other side, so they had to go forward. One by one, they jumped to the ground. Fortunately, the walkway was low enough that they could crawl on hands and knees beneath it, but not so high they would be spotted in the darkness. The boy went first, followed by Simo and Xilsi, the prince, Kem, and Ipis, with Jirvy, Elen, and the haunt bringing up the rear. Packs had to be pushed ahead of them, weapons dragged in their bow cases and scabbards.

As they made their way forward, there was no way of knowing what was happening in the kitchen, though it made Elen heartsick to think of it. She heard more shouting. A crescendo of crashing and smashing subsided, followed by an exchange of heightened voices. But no screams. The wardens had left no evidence of their passage. No reason for anyone to think they had been in the kitchens at all. If the white-haired god had any mercy upon those who worshiped him, he would spare the kitchen staff. Yet she doubted Thelan's people knew the meaning of mercy. Nor Eleawona either, in the end. Had the young lady known who Ao was the whole time? And done nothing to stop it? Or had she known and done what she could do to protect her half sister, as little as it was?

So many questions in life could never be answered. People crawled forward with equal parts hope and dread. Oftentimes, the best you could hope for was a good pair of sturdy gloves to protect your vulnerable hands. And good boots. Definitely, good boots.

The pavement beneath the walkway was not particularly grimy. It had to be swept and cleaned like every other place in the winter palace, the retainers alert for any sign of Spore.

"Hsst!" She bumped into Jirvy, who reached back to tug on her shoulder in a gesture that meant *Go forward*.

She crawled past him. The party had reached the wall, and the walkway ended at the wall. Above them was the side entrance for retainers. The entry door opened, and people piled out, footsteps pounding like a hailstorm along the walkway as they raced toward the kitchen. To the left, a troop of soldiers—Thelan's—marched into view on the plaza, assembling at the front of the hall, their ranks lit by blazing torches. About half were leading saddled mounts. Thelan had taken troops with him in pursuit of Captain Dinec, but clearly, he had not taken Eleawona's partisans for granted. He had more people left in South Ring than anyone had guessed. Or perhaps he had been preparing for this day by inserting his own loyalists into Eleawona's court for months or years, who now revealed their loyalty.

They were truly trapped. No way forward. No way back.

The boy bravely stifled a sob. The wardens waited in a silence so heavy that Elen could almost hear their minds working through the problem, seeking a solution. Jirvy shifted, deftly tucking an arrow along his bowstring in case he needed to let loose the moment they were spotted, as they would inevitably be spotted, now or come dawn.

A cold, hard, unpleasant idea rose in Elen's mind. Even the viper in her heart shuddered as she touched the thought and flinched from it. The haunt touched her boot, hand settling lightly around the curve of her ankle in the most reassuring way. She determinedly pulled the unpleasant thought closer. This was no time to be squeamish.

She said softly, "If we're quick, and lucky, we can get to the one place where we can hide, and they won't look for us."

"There's nowhere to go," whispered the boy.

Simo whispered, "What happens if we surrender?"

The prince said, "We don't surrender. Deputy Courier, if you know of such a place, then lead us there now."

The walkway quieted as the soldiers reached the kitchen and went inside by the cistern door. Someone was calling orders to the troops in front of the hall: which squads were to go where, a description of a skirmish by the prison and a tangle of melees to the south, and which soldiers were to sweep the surrounding area and search for the escapees. All too soon, the place would be swarming, and then it would be too late.

"Follow me," Elen said as she clamped down on her doubts. This was the only option left to them.

"Where are we going?" Gevulin whispered.

She swallowed a sick, poisonous dismay. "Into the atoner passages."

28

Old Hand, Old Ghost

A surge of bile soured her throat. A desperate flutter of panic hammered in her heart. She and Ao, crowded into a passage, trapped, hungry, cold, with nothing but days and months and years of the same in their future, right up until Spore devoured them as they screamed.

Sensing something amiss, the haunt again gently squeezed her ankle, bringing her back to herself.

No. She had escaped. Going back in as an armed adult with the wardens around her and Kem and the haunt beside her was different from being a captive child with only her equally small and vulnerable sister to cling to.

She scrambled out from under the walkway, on the side away from the main entrance, bent low as she raced along the wall toward the tower end, toward the great block of a hearth and chimney built halfway along the eastern side of the high hall.

The hatch she remembered from twenty years ago was too dark to see in the gloom, but her body recalled its placement exactly. She reached too high, angling her hand like the child she had been, then groped downward, found the recessed latch—and clicked it open. The atoners' hatch was about half the height and width of an ordinary door. The biggest risk now was that they would be forced to leave someone or something behind, because she had no idea if the men's broader shoulders would fit, or if their packs would get stuck. Atoners carried nothing because they possessed nothing, not even their lives, since even those belonged to the masters.

At her heels, the boy yanked on Elen's coat. "I can't," he said frantically. "If I go in, they will make an atoner of me."

"Not if they don't know you were here." She grabbed him roughly by the collar and ruthlessly shoved him up and into the opening. He was smart enough not to yelp, though she felt him jerk as he stumbled when she shoved his backside. Whimpering, he vanished into the implacable darkness. She clambered in after him, her body forcing his to move forward.

Walls rose to either side, caging her. The rancid musk of the air scraped at her lungs, dry and dusty. A breath of warmth leaked through from the chimney and hearth. By the hatch lingered the smell of dried-up urine, left by a desperate child who couldn't hold it in any longer. Atoners were not meant to defecate or urinate anywhere inside the high hall, lest the masters smell the least taint of their waste.

Ahead, the boy yelped in startled fear. Too much noise would carry to the retainers and masters inside the hall. That's why atoners only spoke in whispers, if they spoke at all, lest they be whipped.

With her pack slung against her chest, Elen squeezed forward, shoulders brushing the passage walls, until she bumped into his back. His way was blocked.

A thin figure stood in the passage, their presence smelled more than seen, like dried-up marsh waters, a rank scent of damp, old and weak rather than fresh and strong.

A hand pressed on her back. Xilsi whispered, "Keep moving. We can't all fit in yet." A pause, then: "What's that stink?"

"Ye cannot come in." The thin figure spoke with the light, high voice of a child who has not yet reached the age of maturity, and who may never reach that age, a voice made scratchy by a lung illness that had never healed and might never heal.

Elen said in the northern speech, "Old hand, old ghost, let me and these who I shepherd to safety, let us in, for the sake of the atoners who came before and those who will come after. We must hide, or else we will be captured."

"You're her," said the atoner. "The one I saw with the lady's cousin, Lord Thelan, he who steals that which belongs to the lady. You be the nose-smart girl we sing of. El and her sister, Ao. So, you two did get away. They said you must have gone away to the Island of Feasting. I didn't believe it. I reckoned you died like the masters said you did, eaten by the White Sea."

If the ground had fallen out from under her and she plunged back into the prisoner's pit, Elen would not have been more surprised. *Sing of?* Her voice failed her. Her mind went blank.

Xilsi said urgently, "What's she's saying? Who is that? Elen!"

"Yes!" Elen rasped out, still fumbling for the northern tongue that had once been all she'd known. "Yes, I am she. The nose-smart girl."

"And your sister, Ao."

"She died three years ago. The lad with us is her son." Elen glanced back but could not distinguish Kem in the shadows. "Ao and I escaped on the road through the White Sea, to a peaceful land in the south. We did not die. We lived."

Simo's sharp whisper hissed forward from the hatch. "Soldiers coming back. Hurry, so we can all get inside and move out of range of their spears if they open the hatch."

Not understanding a word of Simo's command, the atoner did not budge but said, in a hoarse murmur, "You lived! Ah! Both of you lived!"

"I can't go any farther," sniveled the kitchen boy. "I don't want to be an atoner."

Elen pressed a hand between his shoulder blades. She spoke in her sunniest, and thus most merciless, voice. "It's already too late for you, Barrow. You are already inside. If they catch you, they will kill you for a traitor, or they'll make you an atoner. Your only chance is to get through here with us, help us get out of South Ring, and hide until it's safe to come out. No one need ever know you were in here."

A spasm of fear ran through Barrow's body. But he couldn't move, because he, indeed, had nowhere to go.

"Old ghost," said the atoner, addressing Elen, "pray tell me, where is it you are bound?"

"Out of South Ring. We need to reach the culvert behind the tower without being seen."

"So it will be. I take you to the first turning."

The atoner moved away swiftly, at ease in the darkness. The boy followed with a jerky, stumbling step, sniveling as he tried to restrain his tears. Elen set a hand on his shoulder once again, humming softly as she and Ao used to do together, holding hands, when terror swelled up inside like surging floodwaters. The soft melodies had calmed them, then, and it calmed Elen now thinking of Ao and how they carried each other, here, in this dark place. In all the dark places where they had walked together in those childhood years.

After so long, Elen had forgotten how low and narrow the atoners' passages were. In her adult body, it was so much worse. She had to stay bent over to avoid hitting her head. The walls pressed in on either side as if to crush both your lungs and your spirit. Even had she not been able to see the atoner ahead, she could have followed the smell left behind. It wasn't nasty like a latrine, but it was distinctive. A bit like the bottom of the cabbage barrel if it were soaked in sour brine.

Xilsi pressed up against Elen's backside. "I swear I am going to start screaming," she muttered with a brittle edge to her tone. "It's too tight. I'm going to get stuck."

"You're going to be fine. Keep a hand on my back."

Xilsi gulped down a sob. Her hand gripped against Elen's coat as if she were clinging to a branch on a churning river to keep from drowning. No one else spoke, but Elen heard the labored breathing of the wardens and an occasional pained grunt. How was Kem doing? Yet hadn't he and Joef crawled into the depths of the attic more than once? Tight spaces wouldn't scare him. Mostly, she was terrified that Simo, or the prince, would get stuck. As if in response to her agitation, a whispery whistle came from the haunt, signaling to her that he was safe and bringing up the rear. Should any soldiers try to pursue them inside, they would have to contend with the same magic Sara'ala had used atop the cliff at Grinder's Cut.

They reached the first turning. The atoner slipped aside to squeeze into a tiny alcove and, once there, she coughed rackingly.

Recovering, the child whispered, "I let you pass and to go on your own way. Do not take the ram path, for your big people will not fit in those crawls."

While she rested, hands on knees, crammed in between the smothering walls, Elen rifled through her memory. Had she forgotten the paths by which the passages snaked through the building like a snake's constricting belly that dissolves its prey? Strange echoes and throbbing rumbles filtered through, although mostly the sounds seemed to be coming from outside. The escapees had had no chance to get into the high hall, so why search for them there? They still had a chance to get out. But they could not afford any mistakes if they wanted to reach the culvert and get out by the aqueduct before Thelan's soldiers thought to search in such an unlikely place.

She said to the atoner, "Can you take us to the culvert?"

"Pfft! An easy path. Can you not divine the way on your own, old ghost?" retorted the atoner.

"I might miss a turning. It would be faster and safer if you led us."

"All right. I take you."

The child emerged from the alcove and padded into the right-hand passage.

Moving Barrow behind her, Elen hastened after the atoner, although she could not see their guide and could barely hear her soft footfalls, but she trusted that the floor would be smooth, with no bumps or breaks to trip up their feet. Atoners had to know their spaces intimately in order to creep through the walls with never a sound, so they brushed and smoothed the path as well as they could, over and over. No one else concerned themselves over the well-being of those whose main purpose in life was to die so that others would live.

The passage seemed endless as they shuffled forward, their line moving slowly because some had to walk sideways and their weapons and gear made them clumsy and awkward. The back of Elen's head bumped the ceiling as she tried to ease her aching back from being constantly bent over. Her entire existence had once again become a dark tunnel beyond which lay the muffled noises of a brighter world, glimpsed only through grilles and peepholes. Behind her, Xilsi's ragged breathing intensified. The weight of the darkness pressed in all around. Sweat and fear permeated the closed passageway like a hand choking them.

Then, someone farted.

Kem stifled a laugh. Ipis hissed, "It wasn't me." Xilsi snickered.

That suddenly, the mood lightened. The path proved easy enough once Elen remembered where to turn, where to ascend a ladder-like stair and where to descend, working a twisting and hidden way to the far end of the palace. Her feet still knew the way, and the atoner led them unerringly.

Elen whispered to the atoner's back, as she had always conversed with Ao to make the time pass inside the endless days and nights of winter darkness, and amid the constant dragging apprehension of summer's burgeoning life. "How is it you know me?"

"We remember your story among us. You are the only ones who got away from the masters before you were eaten by the White Sea."

"How can you know our story? You weren't born yet."

"The story is told among us, I just said so. The ones who were there when it happened. Their names were Nep, Nap, and Nup."

Elen caught in a trembling breath, hit with a rush of grief and pain at the sound of those names. She couldn't recall their faces, only Ao coaxing the trio along with soft words and gentle hands. The three new atoners couldn't have been more than six or eight years old, so scared, so hungry, so small. So resigned to their fates.

The atoner spoke on. "They passed on what you taught them to the atoners who came after them. Those ones taught me and my sister."

"You have a sister!"

"We all choose a sister when we are sent to the pens. Is that not what you taught? A sister helps you survive."

A sister helps you survive. Had she or Ao spoken those words to Nep, Nap, and Nup? Maybe. Probably. Without meaning to, and only because it was true.

"What may I call you? You know my name."

"The masters give us names. We do not use them with each other. We keep private names with our sisters."

The child did not offer a name, so Elen did not ask again.

They reached the dead end of the passage. The atoner pressed her face against the metal lattice of a spy grille. It was too dark to see into the chamber beyond. First, she listened. Then, she inhaled, sniffing several times. Finally, she squeezed back so Elen could come forward. A line of dots, readable by touch, had been pecked into the soft metal of the grille by generations of atoners, each pattern of dots a crude form of secret code that described what sort of room lay beyond.

Elen ran her finger down the dots and blanks even though she knew where they had to be. This grille overlooked the royal bathing chamber. Long ago, Elen and Ao had watched as the Lady of the Martens, or her young daughter Eleawona, were bathed by attendants, washed and dried, although never at the same time, each in her own royal state. Eleawona's mother had demanded silence while she pontificated about the cares of being a ruler. Eleawona had liked her people to chatter around her. Little Ao and El had listened, soaking up these glimpses of a world they couldn't enter.

It was too dark to see any furnishings, but the scent of lavender soap and a taste on the air of lingering dregs of water, not fully drained, suggested someone had bathed here earlier in the day. No one was here now.

The atoner nudged past her and deftly unhooked the grille to create an opening. "The hatch into the trough. Past the tower to the culvert."

Elen hadn't thought much past hiding in the passages inside the high hall. Waiting out the conflagration. Sneaking out later to the culvert, somehow. She had forgotten that the royal wash water was poured out via a hatch in the floor and into a trough dedicated to this purpose. The trough was covered by a wooden roof so no people or animals could imbibe the water that had touched the holy and sanctified person of a royal master. Instead, the trough cut past the tower to empty into the outflowing side of the culvert, where it mixed with mundane water and was diluted.

The atoner whispered, "The outflow goes to water the lady garden beyond the Ring. I saw the garden one time. So many flowers. Skybright, they call one flower. It is the color of my sister's eyes."

"The lady garden." A surge of excitement made Elen tremble. She remembered where the lady garden was, on the east side of the river, close to one of the paths that ran parallel to the holy road.

Now she knew exactly how they could escape.

She whispered excitedly back to the others, "We will pass through a bathing chamber, down a hatch, along a covered trough to a culvert, and via that culvert cross under the palace wall. From there, we can take our bearings. See if we can determine where the fighting is. If we are fortunate, we can follow the canal all the way out of the Ring. Or take another route. Your Highness?"

"That seems feasible," Gevulin said in a low voice.

Simo said, "If I light a lantern to get us through the bathing chamber, will the flame be seen?"

Elen said to the atoner, "Before, there was only this grille and the door. Is it still this way? No windows? No other grille?"

"That is so," said the atoner in her raspy voice.

"Captain, we can risk a light to get through the chamber, but not once we move outside."

"Understood." Simo struck flint.

Sparks caught on tinder, and tinder caught the sturdy wick of a travel lantern.

Elen kept her gaze on the chamber beyond as the fragile glow illuminated its corners, the door, the wooden tub, the stone-lined rinse pool. The hatch that led into the trough was set into the floor, its iron handle chained shut.

Behind her, Simo sucked in a shocked breath, Jirvy swore quietly under his breath, and Xilsi gasped out, "By the High Heavens, bless us." Barrow whimpered.

Elen turned her head. The passage was crammed full of everyone's bodies like sardines salted and set aside for winter, their faces smeared within the darkness as if they were occluded moons in the night sky. All but the haunt, who was too far back to be in view, or maybe he had wrapped himself in his shadowy wings.

Kem had pressed a hand over his mouth, his aghast gaze flashing to Elen and then back to the only other person still there who wasn't reacting.

The atoner had a startling and almost grotesque figure, like sticks lashed together and haphazardly draped in rags, for the child was skeletally thin except for an implausibly swollen belly. The skin of the atoner's shorn head was rash-raw and scaly, both ears scabrous, one eye puffy and pink-tinged. Sores split parched lips alongside flecks of frothy blood. She held one hand clutched to her chest, the hand curled up in a claw from an old, untreated injury.

Had lightning struck Elen from out of the hard, hot sky, she might have felt so: blistered, speechless, burned. How could anyone look so and yet be alive? How could anyone still be alive in such a state of neglect and starvation?

Is that how she and Ao had existed for all those years and never known to think it strange or terrible?

The wardens gaped at the atoner in undisguised horror, or maybe it was pity, and what if pity was worse, when pity meant nothing except that they were going to move on and leave the atoner behind? Yet the child did not look away in shame, did not fear their disgust and dismay. The stare she threw back at them was fierce.

The atoner's rags were neatly tied in elaborate bows where strips held them together. Her foot-wraps were braided cunningly by clever hands that had clearly taken pride in their work. A colorful necklace of chipped beads and broken buttons had been strung together with twisted scraps of wire. A triangular scrap of hammered bronze hung at the center of a pale forehead, fastened to a circlet woven out of reeds, a proud diadem that glinted in the lantern light. No one but other atoners would ever see her beauty.

"Go," said the prince from behind his wardens, unmoved by the sight of the atoner. Such suffering existed far beneath his exalted realm, an unsightly mess to be swept out of sight as he walked the magnificent corridors and spacious chambers and perfectly manicured courtyards of the Tranquil Empire's majestic palace and parkland.

"Go," repeated Simo with the crack of a captain's command.

Elen obeyed because she had been trained to obey as a deputy courier. Because she could not bear to stand there for one moment longer. She set her pack on the floor, then paused, slipped its ties, and dug down for a cloth-wrapped vial of walnut oil she kept for cooking on the road. This vial she pressed into the atoner's rough hands. Then she closed her pack, slid through the gap, and dropped to the floor below.

After her, Xilsi handed through Elen's pack, then her own pack, then wiggled through herself, panting with relief, "By the High Heavens, I can move again. But what a frightful vision. How can anyone live that way?"

"Do you suppose that child *wants* to live that way?" Elen snapped. "Keep moving!"

Down the others came, one by one, their gear, their weapons, even the bundle of shrive-steel swords, for who would leave behind such a precious hoard? Barrow descended, too, his eyes grimly shut, shaking, Ipis moving the boy as if he were a big, stiff doll.

After so much time in darkness, the frail lamplight was more than enough to see what mattered in the chamber. Jirvy and Xilsi unchained and unhooked the hatch and opened it. Simo went down first, then the prince, Ipis directing the boy, Xilsi after them. Kem hesitated, wanting to say something to Elen, but she had nothing to say and he knew her well enough to see the grim silence in her expression.

Then only three were left, not counting the atoner, who remained in the passage above.

Jirvy said, "What a disgrace these rulers are, to trap a child so. I've never seen anything so shocking. I'm sorry we can't bring the poor sprout with us." He met Elen's eyes with regret. "But we can't. Even if we wanted to."

She could not speak.

The haunt said to Jirvy, "Go. I will bring up the rear with the deputy courier."

Jirvy's gaze flickered between the haunt and where Elen stood frozen beneath the open grille, staring into the darkness at the shadowy figure that had once been her and was no longer her. The haunt said something more to Jirvy, but it fell on Elen's ears as a meaningless buzz of words. Jirvy dropped into the trough, gone away.

The haunt said softly, coaxingly, patiently, "Dear one, you must come."

She had not taken her gaze from the grille's opening. "Come with us. You can come with us."

"What do you mean?" The atoner's whisper was hoarse, as with emotion, but probably it was the illness tangled in fragile lungs.

"Come with us. We are going to the White Sea, past the Island of Feasting, to the land I told you of. The land where my sister and I went. It's a fine land, with enough to eat every day and a place to sleep and bathe, and the good boots you always wished for. You will be safe there."

"Ah! A holy place. But I cannot go."

"You can. You can come with us now."

"No. I cannot leave without my sister."

For an instant, it was as if it was Ao's shadow, Ao's ghost, standing there, looking out at her. "Your sister?"

Beside her, the haunt sighed but said nothing.

"We all take a sister when we come to the pens, whether we are boy or girl, it doesn't matter, we become sister to the other. He took me as his sister as I took him as mine," the atoner repeated, as if realizing Elen was too slow to understand what had already been explained.

Elen shook her head angrily. She could not leave without the child. It was unbearable.

"Then fetch him, this sister," she demanded. "Be quick!"

"He winters at Pine Grove Hall, by order of the lady. We meet again at the turning of the spring. All summer and autumn, we two of us walk the paths together between the lady's villas. I cannot leave without him. Would you?"

Elen thought her heart would stop for it hurt so much. She had lost Ao. But not then. Not that day, long ago.

"No," she said hoarsely. "No, I would never have left without her."

The figure in the shadows shifted. The grille clicked into place, returning the atoner to the darkness.

The haunt took Elen's hand. "Dear one," he said, that was all.

She knew she had to go.

She had to leave the child behind.

29

Uncle Crackface

The trough was shallow and just wide enough to crawl along. A thin crackle of ice slid beneath her hands and knees. Hand, foot, hand, foot, one after the next. That much she could manage.

By the time she reached the culvert's opening, Simo and the prince had killed the two sentries left on the nightly guard. She'd heard nothing, no altercation, or maybe she hadn't been listening to anything except the shame and anger that pounded in her heart. Even the viper stayed wrapped up tight, as if it knew better than to jostle her brittle control.

Kem shoved forward, stepping over a corpse to grab her arm and then embrace her, hard. He didn't say anything. His cheeks were moist. Had he been crying? She had no tears. Not even for the proud and self-possessed child who had shut herself back in the atoners' passage and watched them go.

"Deputy Courier," hissed the prince. "Where to, now?"

She had to move.

The palace's encircling canal met at the culvert, a low tunnel beneath the palace compound's outer wall. A wooden barrier separated the channels, one flowing in and one out, with one side higher than the other. She didn't remember if it had been like this twenty years ago, nor did it matter. A stone ledge gave them space enough to shimmy beneath the wall without having to get into the water.

On the other side rose the wooden scaffolding of the waterwheel's house and, looming over it, the old aqueduct's heavy shadow. They hid, catching their breath, crammed in on a lower platform alongside the *thunk thunk thunk* of the waterwheel as it redirected a constant stream of water through the canal. Stairs led to a second platform above. People were stamping around on the platform beside the big mechanism, speaking to each other, although it was impossible to make out distinct words above the noise of the waterwheel. Whoever they were, they had a lantern whose aura spread just far enough that Elen could see Simo's gesture, drawing a finger as if across his own throat as he looked a question at Gevulin.

"No," she said softly. "It's retainers at their work. Let them be. They're no threat to us."

"They can call an alarm," muttered Simo.

"Hush," said the prince.

They listened to get their bearings. From afar, the sound of fighting hammered on and off in a spreading tumult of clashes within South Ring. Huddled beside the noisy waterwheel, it was impossible to know who was fighting where, much less who was winning. Down here, they couldn't really see anything.

Above, the lantern was abruptly doused. The retainers fell silent but stayed up top. She guessed they were hunkering down, frightened and worried. Eventually, Thelan's soldiers would search through this area, but she guessed no one really thought the prince would trap himself by running back into where he had been captured. Not unless one of the kitchen staff confessed. But if one spoke up, the rest would be executed by Thelan's people. It might be a good risk for a person who could be assured of reward from Lord Thelan and who cared nothing about the people they had worked alongside for years, as long as they were assured the bastard would win the struggle for control of South Ring. But no one could know the outcome of tonight's desperate battle. Not yet.

Suddenly, Barrow whispered, "There's a walkway atop the aqueduct. People walk it back and forth every day to rake out debris."

Elen translated for the others.

"Where does it go?" murmured the prince.

The boy said sullenly, "I don't know."

"Captain Raven?"

"I defer to those more knowledgeable than I," said the haunt smoothly.

"Deputy Courier?"

"We get out of the walls, beyond the road, first," said Elen, "and then decide. They'll search here soon. We can't stay."

The waterwheel's steady thunking covered their stumbles as they slipped away from the wheel's housing and made their way to one of the aqueduct's massive stone pillars. The boy led them up a ladder fastened onto one side. They were exposed, but there was no light nearby, and the night was cloudy enough that no damning moon would reveal them. At the top of the aqueduct, they tipped over the edge to a sturdy stone walkway that ran alongside the burbling flow of constant water brought in from a nearby river in the hills.

The masters kept it repaired, but they hadn't built it. They said the white-haired god raised it for their use, but it was clearly of imperial design and engineering: good, strong, solid, and meant to last for generations.

They headed north along the aqueduct, moving fast, hoping no one looked up. From here, they had a view across the densely packed buildings of South Ring. Torches had massed at the western and eastern ramps, and the clamor of skirmishes rose out of the south quarters. In the north, the tidy district where the lesser masters bided over the winter remained deathly quiet. People were either hiding, or they were already out on the streets.

Elen followed along, numb. The weight of the past had settled on her shoulders. Hadn't she shed herself of this burden years ago? Hadn't the silence she and Ao shared put it into the grave?

She had been lying to herself if she thought she could leave it behind. The past would always live bound within her flesh and her bones. She was both who she was now and who she had once been.

Behind her, the haunt said, in a very gentle tone, "If you do not allow that child the trust that she can make her own decisions, from a place of intimate knowledge of her own circumstances and her own desires, then you are not respecting her. She deserves our respect, don't you think?"

She couldn't reply. Her heart was still too full.

He added, even more softly, "Surely we have all, in our time, made choices we regretted later, and choices we were proud to have made. Sometimes they are the same choice, seen from a different perspective on the road. I know well of what I speak. It speaks well of you that you made the offer, especially knowing the prince would not allow it."

"I wouldn't have let His Highness turn the child away," Elen muttered sourly.

"Of course you would not have, dear one."

She stumped along in anger and despair. "But the child is there, and we are here, so it comes out the same, does it not?"

"Do not drag her after you, El, not even in your thoughts. She had the choice, and she chose. That is not a tragedy. It speaks well of her and her loyalty and love for the one she walks with. I for one am glad for her sister, should they be reunited, as we must hope they will be. None of us can ever know what the future will put in our path, can we? You. Me."

She rubbed furiously at her dry eyes. Tears might be easier, but tears availed nothing. He was right, but she could not bear to say so out loud. Nor did he push her to reply.

After a moment, she asked, "What of your injuries?"

"They hurt less and less as they heal, and my kind are fast healers, lest we lose our glorious shine," he said with a tender humor she was sure was meant to soothe her aching heart.

They walked the length of the aqueduct without incident. Increasing numbers of armed people headed to the palace forecourt, but she couldn't be sure whose partisans they were. Shouts broke out as a group of soldiers fought their way from the main gate to join their fellows. Arrows spat across the night. To the east, some reckless fools threw burning torches into buildings. Seen from afar, the battle might have been a theatrical production played out on the streets below, as the annual festival of lights sprawled its dances and historical skits and festival cakes and flirtatious promenades across all four quarters of Orledder Halt on a midwinter night. Thus was the darkest night made bright and filled with good cheer.

But not here. Not now. That child and her sister had their own story, however it would end. Elen was merely the old ghost in their tale, encountered once and never to be seen again.

"Here," whispered Barrow, startling her out of her thoughts. "The holy road lies below us now."

How many times had she drilled into Kem the courier's rules: *Don't get distracted or sloppy.* To survive, and to ensure the party survived, she had to pay attention.

The only ladder down was the one they'd climbed up by the waterwheel. But where the aqueduct crossed above the elevated roadbed, midway between the north and east ramps, the drop to the roadbed was only about her body's length.

Elen turned to the prince. "We should leave the boy here, atop the aqueduct. He can make his way back to the kitchen when it is safe."

"Captain, what do you think?" the prince asked Simo. "It would be safer to kill him. But that would dishonor his loyal service."

Simo patted the boy on the head in the manner of a man who might have a child or two of his own about this age, and Elen realized she had never asked, nor had the captain shared such a detail. "Let him go, Your Highness. He did well. And the deputy courier assures us he has reason not to betray us lest he betray himself and his people."

Elen shooed Barrow off quickly, before the prince could change his mind. "Be careful. The masters will never know you were ever gone. But don't even tell your mother what you did tonight."

He hurried off, as well he ought.

Working in pairs, the wardens lowered their people down to the road, one by one, after which each person scrambled down the steep embankment. As the others descended, Elen scanned the land beyond the road, what she could see of it as the cloud cover began to pull apart to reveal clouds and a waxing quarter moon: a strip of bare ground beyond the embankment, and on its outward side the lane by which folk traveled. The humble homes and busy workshops belonging to the retainers who were allowed to live this close to the holy road, which meant they had the lady's sanction to run up onto its protection should Spore sprout nearby. The line of the village ran north and south as far as she could see. It was bounded at its outer limit by a high hedge, past which lay gardens, fields, orchards, and pastures.

Should they go north, after the lady? Or south, toward the White Sea and the empire? Or was there a third option? Speed mattered more than anything. They had to outpace and avoid the pursuit that would inevitably come, unless the lord and the lady fought themselves to a standstill. But they couldn't count on that outcome. Elen had to assume the worst: that Thelan would win.

A nudge to her ribs brought her attention back to the aqueduct.

Jirvy whispered, "You next. I'll stay up here with Captain Raven."

She had an instinct Jirvy was doing his best to protect her from the potentially lethal presence of an unpredictable aivur. Almost, she protested, but the haunt gave her a nod. An argument would just slow them down. She let the two lower her down, dropped, landed with a sting like bees swarming straight up her legs. A quick jump got her off the holy road's pavement and onto the blessedly quiescent stone of the upper embankment, where she crouched, waiting but ready to move.

Sentry lanterns burned at the distant ramps, beacons for masters and retainers: *Here you will be safe.* The northern quadrant within the Ring remained quiet, for now. The fighting in the central and southern districts had turned into a soup of noise, bubbling, sloshing, slurping, sticks and stones and shouts and screams, but no center to it, a wash of movement tugging back and forth. Most of the village buildings outside the road lay dark, shutters tightly closed, but skeins of movement spun half-seen, all the way south, by the east ramp, too far to make out anything except lantern light like fireflies rising and falling. Voices arguing. A surge of shadows like people grappling with hard decisions in a crowd. Fear lay like a haze on the night air.

Would the atoner meet up again with her sister? Would they seek the Island of Feasting and the fine land, now that they knew it could be reached? Or would they stay on the paths they knew? But the haunt had spoken truly: It was not Elen's choice to make for them.

Jirvy thumped down and scuttled past her to climb down to the others. Last of all, the haunt hung over the side of the aqueduct by his hands and landed deftly and lightly on his feet in a swirl of smoky wings. He didn't even wince at the impact.

"You heal fast," she remarked.

His slyest smile peeped out. "It's one of my best tricks."

Together they descended to where the wardens awaited them at the bottom of the embankment, all their gear in order. She respected their discipline. Arrogant the prince surely was, and mired in an ambitious and power-hungry world of intrigue that she hoped never to get any closer to than this, but he'd done the work to be a worthy all-seeing eye for the wardens who were required to obey him.

"How shall we make our way?" asked Simo. "Captain Raven, have you any recommendation?"

"Best if you inquire of the deputy courier," said the haunt. "For myself, I must return to the south, back to the Pall."

"We cannot trust either side," said the prince. "It would be foolhardy to go north. So, let us return south as well. We can make good speed on the road."

"The road is the first place they'll look, Your Highness," said Elen. "We're on foot. They'll have horses."

"What do you recommend?" asked the prince.

"Did you really come from here originally?" Ipis asked her.

Xilsi murmured, "Out of the Heavens' latrine, we might say. Sorry, Elen."

Kem reached out to squeeze Elen's hand.

"I'm all right," she said to Kem, then to the prince, "We need to get past the houses and the first hedge, then through the fields to the second hedge. From there, we'll walk south to Uncle Crackface."

"Uncle Crackface?" asked Simo.

"You'll see."

A horn blared from the direction of the north ramp, a fair distance and probably nothing to do with them specifically, but why take the chance that they weren't about to be overrun?

"Be ready to fight, but don't engage unless we have no choice. Let people think we are panicked retainers running away. Captain, light your lantern."

She took a final scan of the empty dirt, the quiet lane, and the shuttered houses. Someone inside might see them, or their lantern could easily be spotted from afar, but they had to take the chance.

Sparks spun skyward. Flame caught and burned. The captain swiveled the lantern's shield halfway round to create a directed line of light; less than a full glow, but enough to illuminate the ground. Elen led them at a measured but swift stride across the gravel strip and over the rutted lane that ran parallel to the holy road. The village had grown larger from the ramshackle collection of buildings she recalled. It was now three lanes deep, crossed by alleys, and down each alley lay a mess of churned mud blessedly frozen to make a hard surface. They dashed across each lane, hoping not to be seen. Some distance away, outside a blacksmith's glowing workshop, a crowd of people had gathered and were shouting at each other as they argued about what to do. The ruckus gave the wardens cover to cross another lane without being spotted.

Past the last line of huts, they reached a ditch whose murky waters were patchy with ice. This they leaped across, helping each other scramble up the far slope. Here they were met by the first of the Ring's yew hedges.

"Keep your steel and nose open for Spore," Simo said to his wardens.

Elen poked with her walking staff until she found a spot they could push through the hedge with a minimal amount of disturbance. After they were all through, complaining in mutters about scratched faces and needles stuck in their hair, she directed them to cross a patchwork garden, all husks and autumn-dry weeds, and wait beneath the canopy of a huge, gnarled yew tree.

Setting the lantern on the ground, she pushed and pulled the branches of the hedge, doing what she could to conceal evidence of their passage. Anything to delay pursuit.

The haunt stuck with her, holding branches and asking, "What else can I do, dear one?"

"That you are here is all that matters."

His hand on her shoulder was the answer he gave.

From the shelter of the tree, Simo called softly but impatiently, "Are you done?"

The haunt whistled the three-tone warden signal that signified, *Wait for a moment more.*

In a tight voice, Ipis said, "My shrive-steel is tingling."

The wardens all began scraping the points of their shrive-steel swords in circles against the frozen soil, feeling for the presence of Spore. Elen backed away from the hedge. She grasped the haunt's wrist, taking comfort from his presence. He inched his bare hand down to grasp her gloved one, even dared twining his fingers through hers, more than he had allowed himself in the prince's body.

"Don't distract me," she said, "but don't let go."

Exhaling, she emptied her lungs, then inhaled, seeking the rose-oil scent.

"Over here," murmured Ipis, who had carved her way into the stubble of a harvested field, about twenty paces east from the tree.

Elen released the haunt's hand and hurried over, not smelling anything until she came up beside Ipis. The young warden stood with her sword's point resting on the ground. Only here did a faint aroma tease Elen's nose. She knelt, fumbling to get her kit out of her pack.

"I'll get it." Ipis drew a vial of salt spirits from an inside pocket of her coat. With a deft twist, she dug her blade's point into the ground. A sharp whine buzzed in the night air as a pale cap was revealed in the soil.

Spore. At its earliest stage, before its first tendrils probed lifeward.

Ipis bit the seal off the top of the vial and, in a single motion, knelt and poured the salt spirit into the hole, then leaned into the shrive-steel with an angry grunt as the Spore hissed and sizzled and died.

"Fuck you, you poisonous shit," Ipis declared triumphantly.

Elen rose. "That was well done. I didn't smell it until I was right on it. I'd have passed right by."

"Shh. Let me listen."

They stood in silence for a while more. Elen inhaled slowly. The cold was as bracing as its promise of death. Beyond the hedge and the village, a glow intensified from inside South Ring. A bigger fire had caught hold, accompanied by an even more frantic pitch of shouting and screaming.

"Ipis?"

The young warden shook herself. "Nothing else."

"You're extraordinarily sensitive."

"I'm a trained warden," Ipis shot back, but she grinned.

They hurried back to the yew tree. An alarm bell began to ring. In the distance, out of the north, a military horn call cried *ta-ta ta-ta ta-ra*.

"Who is that?" said Simo.

"I don't know, and we shouldn't stick around to find out," said Elen. "Whatever happens, it will take the victor time to figure out we're missing and start a search for us. But we're where we need to be. This is Uncle Crackface."

"Uncle Crackface?" asked Kem. "Who is Uncle Crackface?"

She rested a hand on the tree's peeling bark. "This venerable yew tree. The old ones all have names. A path runs east from here. At Wellwing Stream, we'll head south and get up onto a path that runs along Parlay Ridge. The masters won't look there, not right away."

"Why not?" Simo asked.

"Because it leads to the towers of Parlay Hill Hall. They're known to be haunted and are thus avoided except in early spring, when there's a good early crop of nettles, split leaf, and fat baby."

"Those are weeds," said Kem.

"Not for the hungry whose winter stores have run out. That's where we're going to go next. Keep your shrive-steel drawn. Ipis, walk up with me."

"She's the best Spore-hunter I've ever trained," said Simo. "She has an uncanny gift for it."

"I'm impressed!" said Kem in the friendly tone he used with Joef.

Ipis shrugged uneasily, shoulders hitched up as if she couldn't decide whether to be flattered or embarrassed. "Sure, but half my cohort called me goat-eyes because of it. Said only aivur can feel out Spore like that. I'm as human as anyone!"

Everyone looked at the person they thought was Captain Raven. The haunt leaned casually against the tree as he listened to their discussion. The bequeather had always sat straight, stood straight, walked straight. In her brief acquaintance with Captain Raven, Elen had certainly never seen the woman lounge with such nonchalance, as if the tree were an old friend to get drunk with.

"Why did you come back, Captain Raven?" asked the prince.

"After all that has transpired, I am puzzled and even incredulous to see you reappear."

"So much of life is a puzzlement of incredulity, is it not? Yet I believe it is prudent for us to steal away now, while we can still do so. Get a jump on the many factions eager to devour us in their hunger for power. You excepted, of course," he added, indicating the prince in the most offhand manner. "Well. Perhaps."

The prince said, "You aren't the bequeather, are you?"

Lantern light played a dance of shadow and light across the bequeather's usually austere face. There were a few red patches of skin still, some scratches from the hedge, but the blisters from the burns he'd taken at the blockhouse were simply gone.

The haunt smiled with lazy charm. "I see you have learned something despite yourself."

The prince drew his whip, quivering with fury and pride. "You fucking monster. I'll show you what it means to insult and demean a prince of the Third Estate."

Elen took a step forward, thinking to get between them.

The haunt raised a languid hand to halt her. His smile sharpened with the threat of a dragon's teeth. "I wouldn't," he said easily, gaze steady on the prince, "and you know why."

The prince stood rigid with anger, expression frozen. His lips moved, although no sound emerged. To everyone's shock, he sheathed the whip.

Lowering his hand, the haunt spoke in the most casual voice imaginable. "El, shall we go?"

Everyone shifted from staring at the haunt to staring at her.

She raised the lantern. "Follow me."

30

Always by the Emperor's Design

After the rise of the Pall, it was always prudent to stay inside at night, especially for those who lived outside the protection of road, moat, or hedge. Yet, walking with these wardens, Elen felt the danger but not the stark fear that had stalked alongside her and Ao all those years ago, two girls so young and ignorant and alone but for each other. Now, she couldn't have asked for better companions for such a journey. Each warden possessed a unique trait or skill that, taken together, made them stronger as a whole than as their parts.

She led the way with Ipis right behind her. It was uncanny how much the landscape flung her back into a past she had never wanted to revisit. The trees. The smells. The silence of a land so sparsely inhabited this far away from the protection of the road. The memory of the atoner she had left behind. The atoner she had once been.

But Ipis wasn't Ao. The young warden had a firm hand on her steel and the stride of a person who knows what they are doing and is ready to face the unexpected. Something about the darkness gave Ipis an uncanny look, as if her acute senses were owed to a sixth sense she'd been born with, as if an invisible presence eddied around her. Not like the viper, but something else. That uncanny presence did not bother Elen, but she could understand why it might have made the novices of Ipis's cohort uneasy, especially if they were a hidebound lot who had never trod anything but well-swept walkways.

Twice, Ipis made them stop. Both times she uncovered and destroyed a cap while Elen held the lantern to give her light enough to see. Such young tendrils of Spore had not yet started releasing the scent Elen relied on to find them.

No one spoke as they went on. The path was easy to manage as they moved in and out of woodland cover. The lantern's aura gave just enough light, and they stopped twice to top it up with oil. A wind continued to tear apart the clouds, offering more light from the waxing moon.

Elen could not help but contrast the lofty, proud, unpleasant, and definitely unattractive way Gevulin held himself with the relaxed way the haunt had lived in the same body, and she wondered at it. She wondered that the bequeather had previously seemed chilly and unappealing to her, yet when the haunt ludicrously winked at her from that striking face and with those lambent eyes, her entire being lit up with stupid joy and a pleasing spasm of sexual desire. So inconvenient. So blessed.

He had come back for her.

At dawn, Jirvy shot a pair of rabbits. Xilsi tied them together and slung them over a shoulder for later. Kem began ranging along the line of march, scanning for edible plants. He spotted autumn savory and gathered a bunch, tying it into a bundle, which Xilsi took so he could continue looking. The prince kept his peace, settling back into the rearguard with Jirvy.

They reached the ridge and headed south along the chalky ridgeline path that ran just below the crest of the gentle slope. Elen let Ipis walk ahead.

When Simo came forward to walk alongside Elen, the haunt graciously gave way to walk a few paces behind.

The captain said, "I was surprised Ipis rooted out no Spore in the Moonrise Hills, for all the days we spent there."

"I've walked that route every month for ten years. I'm always sniffing it out as I go, so it's not as if Spore has months to fester and gain strength, as it does here. I've taught the villages on my route the best tricks to use with what they have. Anyway, as you know, the uplands aren't as infested with Spore as the lowlands. But Ipis is astoundingly good."

"It's why I brought her on this mission," he said, not that Elen had asked. "She's a little too good. It made some of the novices in her cohort envious."

"She's not Noble or August Manor?"

"She is, Vunnas Manor. In comparison, Jirvy and I are mere meritorious Manorborn, and from the provinces, at that. But although Vunnas Manor is one of the August Eight, Ipis comes from its most minor branch line. Her great-uncle was only granted a genius to build a Manor in the last years of the Lily Emperor, and that only because he brought in so much trade off the Tranquil Sea that the palace had to reward the man even though his own kinsmen recommended against it. Folk whispered the family were pirates and didn't deserve the honor, and the home Manor feared being tarred by such an unseemly brush."

"I used to think all the Manor-born were alike, but now I come to learn you have your own ladders and rungs." She paused, and decided to go straight to the heart of their predicament. "Did you suspect Luviara?"

Anger flashed in the set of his mouth, the twitch of his eyes. "I did not."

"How did the three of you come to travel together for so long?"

"By accident. Or so His Highness and I thought. We met the theurgist on the road, soon after His Highness first set out to travel the empire. She fell in with us one day. By a ruined Spires compound, now that I come to think of it. She and His Highness had a long conversation about the archives. He invited her to accompany us."

"She knows a lot, and she's entertaining. Having a theurgist as interlocutor seems useful."

"Now I understand it was no accident, but always by the Magnolia Emperor's design."

"I did not see that coming."

"Neither did I." He glanced back.

The haunt was watching them with an interested smile, but keeping just far enough back that it would have been awkward for him to join the conversation. In daylight, his face still bore the patchy remains of what looked like a sunburn, but she had a fair idea that by nightfall even that would be gone. A powerful magic, indeed.

"What did the prince mean?" Simo asked. "How is she not the bequeather?"

"Surely that question is the prince's to answer, not mine."

He shook his head, looking offended, and strode forward to join Ipis.

Kem came jogging up with a clump of radishes and stalks of leeks. "Look what I found! How soon to this Parlay Hill place? I'm hungry!"

Elen pointed south. "See that hump of ridge ahead? When we come around it, we'll be able to see the Spires. They're on a spur line, off the main ridge and a bit below it."

"Spires?" asked the haunt in a tone of sharpened interest. He closed the gap between them.

"I think so. I was just a child. I wouldn't have known then. But we'll soon find out."

"Well, then," said the haunt.

Kem fell in beside the haunt. "So, I just want to say, I'm keeping an eye on you."

"Kem!" For once in her life, Elen blushed.

Kem ignored her in favor of shooting an accusing glare at the haunt. "Don't think I haven't figured out that you're not the bequeather. You're the haunt, come back. Let me be clear. I learned a few tricks from my mother. You better mean well toward Aunt Elen. I'm not joking. I can give you the worst diarrhea you've ever experienced."

The haunt considered this statement in astounded silence for a few steps. "I find myself quite at a loss for words."

"You made her cry. I've never seen her cry before."

"Kem! This isn't your business."

"Of course it's my business. You took care of me and Mama. I take care of you."

"I know you do. But you're a warden now."

"All the more reason to make sure no one is taking advantage of you." He looked at the haunt who wore the bequeather's body. "But I guess you have to leave again, don't you?"

The haunt's amused expression vanished. "Nothing gives me more sorrow than this knowledge."

"I'm sorry, too, because you'll make her cry again," said Kem, scrunching up his face as if he needed to scratch his nose but couldn't because his hands were full of radish and leek.

About fifteen steps behind, Xilsi had kept an eye on the interaction, even if she probably couldn't quite hear what they were saying. "Hey, Kem," she called. "Come back here and we'll bundle that up."

He took the exit, dropping back to leave them alone together.

"I am well scolded for making you cry," said the haunt. "I do regret it."

"I'd regret it more if I'd never met you. If crying goes along with that, then I'll take it. But please don't feel you have to discuss me with my nephew!"

He laughed. It was incongruous to see the bequeather's features thaw in this way. "I wish you good fortune in putting a stop to his questions and comments. I was young once, too. I'm not so sure you ever were, though."

"What do you mean?"

"We all saw the child. That was you once, was it not?"

She shook her head, voice tight. "There is no point in dragging clean boots through the mud of a past I can't change."

"Ah. Let me say it another way. It seems to me that a child in such a situation must always be walking along the edge of life and death. Never any flying for the sake of flying. Constant danger wears a soul raw before its time. Yet, even so, after all of it, you see light, not darkness."

"I see the darkness, too. Oftentimes darkness saves us while light makes us vulnerable. Night can be a time of peace and joy as easily as day can. I do not judge them as opposites. I love them both for what they are."

With a smile, he took her hand. His fingers twined between hers, a warm contact that made her feel strangely cherished. Such an odd emotion to tremble in her heart amid the cold knot of the viper. She squeezed his hand. He squeezed back, a thousand promises made in that pressure.

She glanced before and behind and spoke in a low, hurried voice. "What did you find out, out there? Did you discover what the Pall is? Did you find other Shorn?"

"I found no other Shorn, but I found traces of their passage. I think there may be others abroad in the world. Or so I hope. As for the Pall, that is quite a mystery, indeed."

She waited.

After a few steps, he went on, carefully choosing his words. "It seems my first instinct was correct. The Pall is ashes. The ashes of sorcery."

She winced, a spike of dread like a harsh wind against her face. "Are you saying there are sorcerers at work in the world? Now? Somehow hidden from us?"

"No. I'm saying the Pall is ashes. The residue of sorcery, but not sorcery itself. If a deer dies—and is not gratefully eaten by a hungry, if not very particular young dragon—its corpse lies upon the ground and rots. That is the way of things. It does not crumble into dust all at once but by degrees. Leaves may cover its remains. Soil may build up and conceal it over the years. And then, a hundred or a thousand years later, a storm may wash away the leaves and the soil and tumble these fragments down to lower ground, where you and I might find the bones and wonder from whence they have arisen, as if overnight."

"When, really, it was just chance that they came to light. Are you saying the Pall arose by chance?"

"Maybe the noxious fumes and deadly residue of sorcery lay buried in the belly of the earth for untold generations, until it finally . . ."

"Burped? Farted?"

He laughed. "Never change, dear one."

"At Far Boundary Vigil, you said the Pall was alive. Now you're saying it's dead."

"I don't know. Like ashes, it still holds some of the substance of that which it burned. There is still power there, but I don't know how it could be used, or if it could be used. I'm no sorcerer to understand their secrets. When I swam through the Pall, I felt other souls alongside my own. Not spirits of air or metal or salt, such as theurgists bind, for they have a different taste to them, and sorcery cannot feed on them as it feeds on animals and plants. The souls I felt lacked the substance, the flesh and bone they should have been bound to, because they had been torn from physical bodies."

"Were they other Shorn, like you?"

"I think not. Had they been Shorn, they would have spoken to me. The currents that run through the Pall do not speak, nor do they have voices, yet . . . I cannot explain it. Water is alive but not alive in the same way. It harbors life, but only life that can survive within it. No, water is not a good comparison. I'm out of my depth."

The haunt walked in silence, gaze drawn inward. He rarely fell this serious, so she waited patiently as he combed through his thoughts. She hadn't yet grown accustomed to his expressions playing out atop the aivur's stark and inhuman beauty, so different from the prince's human ordinariness, however handsome the prince was. What had Sara'ala looked like when he had worn his own body? Had he been fearsome? Majestic? Elusive? Aloof? Intimidating? Glorious with his shine? Did it even matter?

He gave a little grunt of satisfaction. "What if that which survives in the Pall are the embers of the souls of those whose life force the sorcerers preyed upon? What if that *is* the Pall?"

"The Pall is dead, desiccated souls? That's creepy. And terrible."

"If true."

"But then, why does the Pall, and the Spore that creeps from it, devour and distort living things when they get their tendrils into them?"

"I don't know. Maybe these soul-embers have motive but not intelligence, and are acting on instinct to try to re-form themselves."

"Like a passage spell gone horribly wrong?"

"As good an explanation as any. But I don't know. I don't know how to know. That is the conundrum we face. Because there are no sorcerers left in the world—or so we hope—we can't know the truth of their wicked craft. Still, it is better to remain ignorant than to wish for sorcerers and their evil to arise again. Some things in this world are just wicked and wrong, and there is no making them good."

Ahead, rounding the rocky hump, Ipis called, "I see it! Simo, look!"

The haunt let go of Elen's hand as they quickened to follow. The trail ascended for about one hundred steps. Just at the hump, the lay of the land gave them a clear view back the way they had come.

Threads of smoke rose from the very distant South Ring. Its tower looked like a matchstick from this vantage. The prince got out his spyglass and studied the smoke.

"I believe there is a large troop of mounted soldiers heading south on the road. I can't make out the banner."

"We'd better get off this high trail then, lest we be spotted," said Simo.

"Is that where we're going?" Ipis asked. She shaded her eyes, looking east toward a valley on the other side of the ridgeline, out of sight of the holy road.

The towers could be seen in the distance, nestled at the valley's head, jammed up against the rising hills. The architecture of the two intact towers resembled those at Three Spires. The third tower, however, had a jagged edge, as if its top half had been broken off by the angry swat of a giant's hand. The haunt's tension was evident in the way he stared. His frown displayed more emotion than the bequeather had ever allowed herself.

"I don't see a way down to those towers, much less into that valley," Ipis said.

The area was overgrown, it was true, but Elen's feet knew these trails and paths and lanes even after so many years. Knowing them was how she and Ao had stayed alive.

Pointing, she said, "Behind that notch in the rock. Always look for yew."

They scraped past a growth of yew, its untrimmed branches

grown wildly in all directions. A steep trail half hewn out of the hillside descended through a tumble of boulders.

Xilsi caught up with her. "How does the bequeather know our warden signals? Why did I see her holding your hand? Why did the prince say that to her: 'You aren't the bequeather, are you?'"

Elen glanced at her. "Ask the prince."

"I'm asking you."

"Careful here. Loose rocks."

"Why are you avoiding the question?"

"The lady's court takes a longer route through the lowlands, so this path isn't used by anyone except messengers, soldiers, and outlaws."

Xilsi gave a curt laugh. "Very well. Don't think I'm letting this go. Yes, indeed, Deputy Courier, just as you say, this path *doesn't* look as if it's been used in years. Good news for us!"

The distance wasn't far—or at least not as a bird could fly—but it took them almost an hour of switchbacking and scrambling to reach an overlook directly above the towers. The compound was built to the same proportions as Three Spires. The compound wall and its towers stood on an oval terrace carved into the hillside, about one hundred ells above the valley floor. The valley itself extended east between two gentle ridges. In the distance, where the southern ridge dipped down, a thread of water glimmered, which had to be the Eelwise River.

At the head of the valley, below the terrace, lay a royal villa and village. Each set of buildings was surrounded by its own separate moat, and the whole complex was ringed by a yew hedge. Goats grazed outside the hedge in meadows where fat baby, split leaf, and nettles would flourish, come spring. Some in the Four Lands had claimed goats could eat and digest Spore without dying. It was true Elen had never seen a goat twisted into unrecognizable agony by Spore, although she'd seen every other type of animal taken by it.

Inside the hedge, eight retainers were pitchforking mown grass into a hay barn attached to a corral and livestock shed that sheltered a herd of horses. A carpenter was repairing one end of the villa's stable. Another man was reshingling a storehouse roof, the sort of work retainers undertook after the harvest was brought in and before snow made outdoor work impossible. Yet the air was more clement here, not as cold as up on the ridge.

The villa sat quietly, awaiting its masters' arrival come spring. In the kitchen yard, a retainer was tending a hearth and a large cauldron. In a courtyard, a pair of women were beating a rug. The thwacks of their stout staffs puffed little booms of sound into the quiet valley. No one looked up; they had eyes only for their work. It was a decent life, left alone most of the year to keep the villa in good working order. Yet any of these people or their children could be taken away at the masters' whim, never to return.

Elen experienced a strange sense of dislocation, a dim memory of herself and Ao—standing down on the terrace near the towers—looking over the valley in awe at a bird's-eye view they so rarely saw, two little girls with their eyes necessarily fixed on the ground. A raw surge of grief boiled up: How terribly she missed Ao. And how she would always miss her beloved sister, every day, every year, until she, too, was gone. It hurt so badly, but it was also sweet, in its way, that love will endure, that the years they spent together would always be part of her, just as she and Ao were woven into the bones and blood of Kem.

The prince said, "I see no movement among the towers."

Elen smiled sadly, letting the sorrow settle back into the half-obscured depths where it bided in her heart. "The locals don't come up here often, Your Highness. Or, they didn't used to. So we should be safe, for now."

The wardens descended through a stand of silver birch and reached the terrace without incident. The villa and village weren't directly visible from the terrace, although Elen supposed they could be seen from the top of the towers. She and Ao had never thought to climb the towers. The story of the child killed by being pushed down the stairs would have been enough to stop them, and anyway, the two girls were never allowed out on their own once they reached a villa. They were either locked in the atoners' pen or brought out for specific tasks like walking a field in front of a plow or accompanying the royal cook when she went a-gathering plants in the wood, or up on a protected terrace, like this one.

"What a pretty place," Ipis remarked.

The northern edge of the terrace's wide oval was taken up by the triangular Spires compound. In the central area, autumn-white peagrass and low-growing shrubs, like gentle-heart and sweet-blue, had been neatly trimmed, which meant sheep had been pastured here recently. The ground itself was so flat, Elen was sure it had been leveled long ago by its unknown builders to create a stable foundation for the mighty towers. She'd never noticed that as a child, never thought about what a massive construction project it would be or who might be able to manage it. She and Ao had only been brought up here once each visit because the head seamstress wanted the earliest starfall flower buds for blue dye. She hadn't wanted atoners handling her precious plants, so such expeditions had given the two girls a rare chance to wander at will throughout the terrace as long as they stayed in sight.

Thick stands of starfall shrubs still grew thickly along the southeast-facing side of the terrace, which got the most sun. There was also an old yew tree that Elen remembered well, so twisted and low to the ground that it was named Snake Mother. There was also a row of cypress.

Simo finished his study of the terrace and turned to her. "Why have we come here when we could have continued more easily along the ridge?"

"The ridge turns east, just south of here. We'd have to come down off it regardless."

"I think there's another answer," said the prince stiffly, "but perhaps only the bequeather can speak to what that might be."

"I didn't even know the towers were here," said the haunt sanguinely.

"The deputy courier knew," said the prince with an accusing glare. "I haven't forgotten how she warned me against entering the Spires by Orledder Halt. In retrospect, I suppose I should have listened. And yet . . ." He trailed off.

No one spoke. In truth, it was confounding to hear Gevulin muse in this way. Perhaps he'd never have done so before the passage spell and the haunt's temporary residence in his body. And she guessed he certainly wouldn't have done so in front of others, except maybe his blessed mother, and perhaps Lord Genia and Hemerlin.

He went on in a thoughtful tone. "Yet if I hadn't, I'd have taken Luviara's bait without having any retreat open to me. Which suggests that, strategically, I am alive now *because* I entered the Spires. A conundrum, is it not?"

"Your Highness, I hope you're not considering going inside any of that wall around the towers, not after you fainted last time," said Simo. "As well, there's no gate. I can't recommend any attempt to climb over the collapsed section of wall."

"Might I sit down for a bit?" Ipis asked. She was favoring her scraped leg, leaning on her walking staff.

Xilsi took a step forward. "Your Highness, I suggest we eat before we go on. A decent meal and an hour's rest would do everyone good. Cook the rabbits. Take a nap. No use getting too weak and exhausted to fight, should it come to that."

"Cook where?" said Jirvy. "The villagers will see our smoke and wonder. Lighting a fire inside the towers would be the only way to disguise smoke."

Everyone looked nervously at the tower compound and its wall, which had indeed collapsed into rubble in two places. Simo was right: It could be climbed over, but not easily. By their expressions, no one wanted to go inside. Likely, the memory of the prince's mysterious collapse still hit hard.

"I doubt anyone dares go inside," Simo said to the prince.

"I daresay at least one person does," said the haunt. "That person being me. There's no risk in daytime. But where are the Shorn who attend this place?"

"I don't think there's a gate here, not like at Three Spires," said Elen.

"There have to be Shorn," the haunt insisted.

"Shorn?" Simo asked. "Are you speaking of sheep? The grass shows signs of their having been here recently, but I see none here now."

The prince waved Simo to silence, his gaze on Elen and the haunt.

There was nowhere else to have the conversation with the haunt, so Elen simply went on. "Maybe there are no Shorn here. There's no approach avenue. No statues. The compound is set right up against the hillside."

"Then you and I will go inside and look." The haunt turned to the others. "There will be a pure-water spring inside. If access to it has survived, we can fill up our water pouches."

Elen said, "As for Jirvy's question about where we can safely cook, behind the cypress there should be a shelter and a hearth built up against the rock. It should be safe enough to light a fire there."

Xilsi looked at Jirvy, who waggled a hand in a signal the two of them clearly understood. Xilsi then said, "Kem, let's you and me and Ipis go find that hearth and shelter. Captain?"

"Yes, go ahead. Jirvy will stand watch. I'll sweep the terrace for Spore."

"I don't feel Spore," said Ipis, rubbing her knee.

"Nevertheless," said Simo, drawing his shrive-steel sword.

"I'll go with the deputy courier and the bequeather," said the prince.

"I'd rather you didn't," said the haunt in a tone that wasn't combative but so blunt, even if mild, that the wardens all gaped. One did not deny a prince.

Yet the bequeather was not an imperial official to be obliged to obey an imperial prince. In the wardens' eyes, they were dealing with a temporarily allied but potentially hostile aivur. Only Kem and the prince knew otherwise.

After a moment of awkward silence, the prince said, through a tight jaw, "I will do as I see fit."

Simo cleared his throat, his gaze coming to rest on Elen. "For my part, I remind you that I stand surety, day and night, for His Exalted Highness's safety. Do you understand me, Deputy Courier?"

"I do, Captain," she said, managing not to look at Kem.

The prince gestured toward the valley. "Captain, we'll need the horses. I'm tired of walking when we could ride."

Simo looked at Jirvy with a faint smile. It was so rare to see him showing any sign of amusement. "You're the expert here, Jirvy."

Jirvy chuckled. "I do know a bit about horse stealing, Your Highness. But under these circumstances, in broad daylight, I don't advise it. We'll be seen, or worse, we'll have to kill some of the locals, and I don't fancy killing menials. Besides the dishonor of it, the survivors will send word and our trail will be blown. Deputy Courier, is that a river out there? Flowing south?"

"That's Eelwise River. Yes, it flows south, into the Pall. I see what you're thinking."

"Boats are easier to steal and care for than horses, if we can get to the river without being seen."

"I know a way," she said.

The prince raised the hand of command. "We'll take two hours to eat and rest."

The haunt collected everyone's water pouches. Once he had them all, he scrambled up the collapsed section of wall. Elen gave Kem a nod of reassurance, then hurried after him.

31

ONE KISS

The upper half of the wall had fallen outward to mix in with the collapsed upper part of the third tower. The debris created a rugged spillway suitable for climbing. The texture of the remains struck her as odd. She'd thought the walls to be whitewashing over stone, but they were a single substance without seam or edge, not blocks of stone at all but rather seemingly something erected all at once, strong and mighty. When she reached the raggedy top she looked down to see the haunt waiting.

The interior courtyard looked very like the one in Three Spires. There was a circular pavement of holystone and a basin where a trickle of pure-water burbled softly before flowing away down a hole into the ground. The spring lacked a catchment trough. The hallow-wood trough at Three Spires had been installed by a previous courier. But as this was not the empire, no courier nor any other imperial official was inspecting or maintaining this courtyard.

The bare dirt surrounding the pavement was riddled with the detritus of years. The tower doors were shut. If there had once been a scaffolding linking the towers above, no sign of its destruction or debris littered the triangular courtyard. But there was an archway that, strangely, seemed to open directly into the hillside, as if into a tunnel. How bizarre.

The haunt patiently waited for her to examine the scene as thoroughly as she liked to do when encountering a new place. Since she was still up on the wall, she looked over her shoulder onto the terrace behind to check on the others. Simo was quartering the ground with his steel. Jirvy was nowhere in sight, having found himself a hidden spot to keep watch. Xilsi and the others had reached the cypress. Kem ducked through, in the lead, waving eagerly to the others as he spotted the hearth, which she couldn't see from here. He moved so naturally amid the others. The wardens were his future now. The thought gave her a pang. It also gave her ease, hoping he was in secure hands. As long as he wasn't executed for being part of the prince's treasonous plans.

From the middle of the sheep-mown pea-grass, the prince stared at her, tapping his whip against his leg. She was surprised he hadn't followed her up the wall, but on the other hand, he knew better than anyone here what the haunt's capabilities were. That was a protection she was glad for. It wasn't that she feared the prince as an individual, precisely, but rather the power a prince held. He could kill her or Kem and never be called to account for the deed. He might still do so, once the haunt departed, as the haunt must.

But not yet. Not today. Today was theirs.

She shifted her legs over and lowered her pack to the haunt, then lowered herself by her hands and dropped. He caught her before she struck the ground, softening the impact, and didn't let go. Instead, he held her with her back to his chest and rested his cheek against her hair. His breathing was as slow and measured as the inevitable procession of years. She might never need to move again, content to become stone as long as she could share the wait with him.

At length, he sighed, released her, and stepped back.

When she turned, she briefly expected the prince's face to be looking at her, so it was a bit of a shock to meet the bequeather's eyes. Yet it was the haunt, after all, who was awake and aware in the flesh he had borrowed. It was his presence, his emanation, his aura that attracted her. She couldn't look away from the shining glamor of his expression, which blended mischief and deadly power.

His lips quirked. "What? You have such a look that I question my very reason for existing in this world."

"The oddest thing is I can appreciate and even admire their physical beauty, but it doesn't attract me in either of them unless it's yours. Can you explain that?"

He pressed a finger to her lips. "Must I?"

His touch was so precious because it could be hers for so brief a time, a flower to bloom for scant days before its brilliance must pass. Not even to fade and to wither in the course of time, but to be plucked and thrown to the uncaring winds while still in its glory.

"El."

He withdrew his finger, and because she did not want the contact to end, she leaned after it, into his body. The bequeather was lean and tall, strong without being bulky. Her body had a womanly perfume, a scent like jasmine, if that was a woman's scent—and in the empire, it was said to be. Elen pressed against her, breasts warm against the bequeather's chest, whose breasts were small like her own, hips slender, shoulders broad. Nothing like her one-time lover Baima's generous body. But what did Elen know of aivur and how they were framed? None of it mattered. What passed between them was lightning, so bright that it lit the entire sky and yet could not be held in hand.

Well, maybe it could, because she dared to slide her hands around his back, to pull him close, to feel him embrace her in turn.

The sun drifted behind the clouds. A spatter of cold rain misted across them.

"One kiss, since it seems the bequeather kindly gave you permission for this one boon," she whispered.

He muttered darkly, "She and I bargained at length."

She smiled, charmed both by the prospect of him bargaining and by the mystery of wondering how he had managed it. She wondered what the bequeather had demanded in return.

"Well, then, Sara'ala. Why wait? Even as the High Heavens endure, the world we walk in will end soon enough, though we be not here to see it, our bones long fallen into dust."

His eyelids fluttered as at a rush of emotion too powerful to endure. "Only you, dear one, would speak of death as an endearment."

He bent his head. She rose to meet him.

It didn't matter what she might have imagined with her eyes closed at night. His lips touched hers as hers touched his, and all this was only a small part of all else they shared: arms clasped around each other, bodies trembling as if they might melt together in the heat of their desire, and even more, beyond that, the intangible pull that is two souls who yearn for what they become in and to each other. Warmth and trust. The sharp anticipation of desire and the heat of hands moving with such tender pleasure along the small of a back.

She kissed him, and he kissed her, and they were in no hurry about it. All she wished to say, she spoke into their embrace. As for him, if anything, he burned beneath her hands as if about to catch fire. Maybe it was what dragons did when they gave their hearts to another.

But a breath cannot last forever.

They had to part. Parting was sweet, and it was sharp, and it hurt, but Sara'ala smiled as if joy were also pain, and Elen had tears in her eyes, she who never cried. Tears of joy and of sorrow, of astonished wonder and anticipated pain and even of hope, whatever hope was.

For what was hope, if it was anything? What was love, if it was anything? Was it this? The weaving together of two chance-met souls? Even if the High Heavens had taken a hand in guiding her footsteps to Three Spires, where his shorn soul waited for what the ocean of destiny might wash up, the tide of chance was more powerful still. He was free, but he was not free. She was alive, that was true enough, but only because, years and years ago, a tiny girl cast into the sea to drown had instead been caught in a chance current and swept to shore, though maybe she had stubbornly swam. She would never know how she came to be alive and not dead, not that time, and not all the times after.

"I wish it were not so," he said in such a low voice that she barely heard him.

"I am glad that it is," she said firmly. "Better this than nothing. One slice of festival cake, even if that is all, is better than none."

"What is festival cake?"

"Quite delicious, I assure you," she said teasingly.

He studied her expression, for once not pouring his strongest emotions into a deflecting smile. "I love how you relish what you have."

"Just one kiss?"

He set his forehead against hers, eyes closed. "The bequeather said she'd have gone for more with Xilsi."

"Xilsi! What, I'm not pretty enough?"

"Whatever her objection may be is beyond me, I confess, for I can think of nothing but you. Are you offended?"

"No, no, I'm delighted on Xilsi's behalf, although apparently she would refuse any offer of pie. Still, it would help her get over Jirvy."

"Oh, no, I beg you, not more of that. Are they still at it?"

"Do you know, I think the journey has done them good? Even if they have somewhat farther to go on before they can find a measure of peace with each other. But what did you bargain with, my love?"

He pulled back, setting her at arm's length. "What did you call me?"

She smiled with a giddy sense of ebullience, floating on the sweetest breeze.

"Unfair to tease me with that smile, since I have already used up my one kiss." His features twisted into a bittersweet expression, resigned, mordant, and yet, like her also glad of even this span of time together.

The oddest thing was that although the prince and the bequeather looked nothing alike—he a human with black hair and willow-leaf eyes and she an aivur with shimmery skin and a lambent gaze—in each of them the haunt was entirely himself. She would know that mischievous, ironical expression anywhere. It struck her with a pang to know that, soon enough, he would give back this body too. Nor would she ever ask him to keep it, against all honor. Nor would he agree. That was part of what made him so beloved.

He sighed. "But you must have questions, dear one. We haven't much time."

"I do have questions. So many. Do you know the one that's been nagging at me most?"

"I do not! If I did, I would surely have answered it already, so you need suffer not a moment's distress."

"I should hope not." She laughed, then sobered. "Why didn't you tell Luviara about the dead griffin? Did you know?"

"I'm not sure what you're asking."

"Did you know that Luviara was an agent of the emperor all along? She betrayed the prince."

"Ah, I see. That explains why she's not with you. I didn't want to ask in front of the others, lest my ignorance betray me further."

"I think only the prince and Kem know about you. Instead of saying not to tell the other wardens, why did you specifically say not to tell *Luviara*?"

"There was something off about the tone of her."

"Tone?"

"The others rang true, each in their own way. They serve the prince or the order of wardens. Not that I care about the prince, but I appreciate honest loyalty, for as we say among my kind, 'Eyes for truth, wings for awakening to the width of the world, limbs for the loyalty that bears the weight of our kinship, and amid our bones we offer shelter to those who have nowhere else to run.' Which is a long way of saying that my whiskers tickle when they sense a lie. Why are you smiling?"

"Your whiskers. You have no whiskers."

"Not in this form, nor in that of the prince, although I suppose he could grow whiskers had he the desire to do so. But I think he is a vain fellow like me—"

"Not like you at all!"

"Closer than you might imagine! To finish my sadly interrupted thought, I suspect the prince feels whiskers would not enhance the pleasing symmetry of his handsome face." He turned his head a little from one side to the next to display both sides of the bequeather's striking profile: the broad cheekbones and sharp chin, the tufted ears, the spiky hair. "Yet this is a fine form, too, is it not? Strong and pleasurable. These soft mounds are breasts, I believe you call them! I like the feel of them! And such interesting nethers, quite different from the prince's!"

"More pie than sausage?"

He gave her a severe look. "What an astounding comparison!"

"There's a lot a person can do with nethers." Thinking about exactly what that might be made her a little hot. She instinctively pressed her hips harder against his thigh, then eased a step back as she remembered he hadn't gotten permission for anything beyond a single kiss.

He studied his hands, the metallic sheen of the aivur's skin healed of any trace of burns. "There's a great deal to be said with regard to the obvious beauty of this stunning complexion, which is not so much different from what I was once accustomed to delight in before I was shorn. Although, of course, I shone then with the gilded majesty of the golden sun. But enough about me! What do *you* think of this body?"

"I think I haven't had the chance to admire quite as much of this body as I did the other one. Although now that I think about it, I can't shake the bequeather's offputtingly cold stare from my memory. I'm not at all sure she'd be the sort of person willing to exhibit herself the way the prince so easily does."

He chuckled. "To parade around naked? No, indeed, I cannot argue with you in this regard, as she told me so herself."

"Did you actually ask her?" She shook with suppressed laughter.

"Shouldn't I have? I admit that sexual congress is but one small part of a larger life, but I have thought so longingly of you."

"Have you?" She wanted to put her arms around him again, but hesitated, not sure what the two of them had agreed to. Yet the bequeather wasn't an innocent, nor a passive participant. She'd agreed to a kiss and all that a kiss implied and, by the haunt's account, had bargained hard to get what she wanted in return.

"Enough! I have questions!" The voice struck like a blow hacked down between them.

They jolted apart as the prince dropped from the wall to land lithely on the ground, followed by a slap of his whip against stone to command their attention.

32

A Poetical Figure of Speech

The haunt spun to face the intruder, snapping into an aggressive posture. Smoky, intangible wings flared out around his form. A cold spatter of rain hissed where it fell on his face as if onto a sizzling-hot surface.

Prince Gevulin's expression flashed from arrogance into startled fear. He drew his sword.

"Put that away," hissed Sara'ala in a voice that rolled like distant thunder. "Unless you want me to snap you in half and eat you for my supper, although I confess it would be a sad waste of your handsome nethers. Is it possible that, after all that has passed, you have no idea what I am and what I can do? Is it possible you have the ignorant arrogance to believe I am but a vain and frivolous fellow which, even if true, is but a tiny part of the truth of me?"

For a breath, Elen thought the prince might succumb to pride and fight—because he certainly wasn't going to flee. But maybe he was smart enough or maybe he'd been humbled just enough by his recent defeat. He sheathed the sword but kept the whip in his hand.

"I thought you came in here to explore, but instead I discover you wasting precious time with sentimental playacting." He gestured dismissively. "I demand answers."

"Do you?" The haunt's smoky wings receded into a tight aura around him. "How do you mean to obtain them if I am not willing to speak?"

The prince ignored this statement. "What are you?"

The haunt lifted his brows in the haughty way he had that charmed Elen, especially when used against the prince. "I am as you see me. As I have always clearly and honestly stated, I am one of the Shorn."

The prince paced a few prudent steps away, to get out of biting and eating range, Elen supposed. But he wasn't cowering as any normal person would. Maybe cowering was trained out of a prince born into the Flower Court, or maybe only young princes who didn't cower were elevated to the Third Estate. After all, one couldn't hope to rule as emperor without an exaggerated sense of one's own importance, alongside a lofty belief that people would naturally bow to you because you were the single most consequential individual in all the world that existed below the High Heavens.

On the whole, it was more restful to be a deputy courier.

"Prince Sara'ala, I assume the deputy courier told you that I heard and saw all when you walked in my body."

"I am not a prince."

"But you are a dragon. Dragons are the royalty of beasts. Thus, you are a prince."

"Dragons are not beasts. We are intelligent beings in the same manner as aivur, gagast, swalters, fregir, and even humans, if humans can be said to have intelligence, which I often doubt. I must insist you cease such insulting language immediately. And I am not a prince. That is a human word. In my experience, only humans believe princes are different from ordinary folk."

The prince studied the haunt. Gevulin's utter confidence gave him a kind of power, but it also made him vulnerable. He couldn't fathom that the world might not bow to him because, for his entire life up to now, it had. But a prince's status was built upon the edifice of the palace. Where the palace's law did not reach, then he was just another man with a good-looking face, some useful skills, and a bad attitude. The haunt had something vaster than confidence. He didn't need the edifice of a palace. He had wings, however smoky and intangible they might be now that his soul had been shorn from his body. Yet he, too, was vulnerable. He had limitations as well. If the bequeather died right now—not that Elen wished any such doom upon her—what would become of the haunt?

Every soul was vulnerable. She'd staked her life on that understanding, never taking for granted any scrap of peace or happiness and cherishing all that flowed her way for the blessing it was.

The prince tapped the whip against his leg as he considered the haunt. It was clear he'd dismissed Elen as inconsequential and bent all his attention on the Shorn. "We can become allies, we two."

"Are you in need of allies? I thought the lady of this far land was your ally."

"She was, but she is overthrown. As are my carefully laid plans. The emperor has discovered too much. I cannot return to the palace until I can strike and win it in one blow. If you can come back, then why not the rest of your brethren, these Shorn?"

"How do you mean?"

"If I provide bodies for them, then they can use the passage spell. Is that not correct?"

"You would coerce your own people to give themselves up so the Shorn can inhabit their bodies in order to use their skills and magic to place you on the throne of the Tranquil Empire. Is that what you mean?"

"Why not?"

The words were spoken with exactly the blithe arrogance Elen expected from Gevulin.

"To start with," the haunt said acerbically, "because we Shorn are sworn to a different task. Not your petty ambition."

"That was my next question. Are there sorcerers at work in the world again? And if so, how may we find them?"

"You are exactly the sort of fool who believes he can enslave a sorcerer rather than becoming oil to a sorcerer's flame. But, so that we may never speak of such reckless idiocy again, I will tell you what I was about to explain to the deputy courier. Before you distracted us."

He glanced back to make sure of Elen. She nodded. No use in being annoyed with the prince, or no more than he generally deserved. Gevulin was desperate. It stood to reason that desperate people would act to save themselves. She knew the feeling well.

"Go on," ordered the prince.

"I am not sure you fully comprehend the circumstances of the ancient days of the sorcerer-kings, as you call them. Even Luviara had only a most fragmentary understanding. It seems the archives and chronicles of your empire lack a comprehensive account of the age of sorcerers. They rose in quiet fashion, one by one. Some were overly curious scholars, while others were greedy to engorge their hoards or hegemony. Many died, for they delved too deep into the lore and did not understand that sorcery gains its power through stealing the life force of living things. Therefore, sorcery is always evil."

"Not to the righteous."

"Especially to them, since they believe most fervently that they will not be corrupted. But sorcery corrupts all those it touches. Usually, it kills any who attempt it. But then some discovered they could leach what they needed from others, from animals first, and then from their enemies, and then even from their own allies. Power breeds lust for more power."

"A truism," said the prince scornfully. "The High Heavens must rule, else all would be chaos."

"So those who rule will claim. But let us not wander down this tedious philosophical path. My point is that, as sorcerers gained the skill to wield sorcery without killing themselves, they took more power, and more and more. Eventually, they made themselves rulers. As one may imagine, to be ruled by sorcerers is to be ruled by fear and death. This, the other dragons would not tolerate. For generations, a war raged between the sorcerer-kings and the gathered armies of the dragons who opposed them and their allies, among which were aivur, gagast, fregir, swalters, and even a few righteous humans, as you would say. The final conflagration produced a cataclysm that blasted coastlines, twisted and transformed the landscape, swallowed mighty rivers, collapsed the great swalter mines, and churned up storms of such severity that even dragons could not fly in them. In the end the alliance won, but at what cost I cannot tell you, for I did not witness the final battles. All I know is that the alliance sacrificed much to cast the last and strongest of the sorcerer-kings into the abyss."

"The abyss?" the prince asked sharply.

"It is meant as a poetical figure of speech. I do not mean some physical place out of which fools such as you, with great folly, would spring the cage doors and release long-chained evil onto an unsuspecting and unprepared world. The alliance killed and burned every single one of the sorcerers. So the world was changed, and most of the dragons were lost. The fregir vanished, refusing to say where they were bound. The gagast crept into hiding. The humans crouched in the ruins among rags and bones. The swalters fled their caverns for the forest. The aivur were scattered and their high halls and brilliant cities were broken."

"Is that what I saw from atop the Spires?" Elen asked, remembering the shadow city that she and Kem had seen at Three Spires on that long-ago full-moon night. "A vision of a lost past?"

"I do not know, dear one, for I have not seen what you have seen."

The prince gestured to the three towers. "Were these Spires raised by sorcerers? Are they vessels of sorcerous power?"

"By what power they were raised, I do not know. They were built to house the Shorn as guardians for the future. They have in them the power of holding and the power of listening and the power of releasing."

Elen began to see how the pieces fit together. "They hold the Shorn in stasis. Somehow the Shorn can listen for the signs of sorcery—the bells—and if they hear them, they can use a passage spell to release themselves, if there is a person willing to carry them in their body. The aivur must have retained some memory of the tradition, since the bequeather knew of the legacy of the Shorn and wished to learn more, so she could pass the knowledge on to the other clans. But in the empire, the Shorn have been forgotten, except for village stories about haunts. So what use is the guardianship of the Shorn against sorcerers if there is no one to go to the Spires to offer themselves up?"

"Memory is the weak link, is it not? I asked the theurgist about this, in a roundabout way. She investigated many Spires on her travels—"

"I saw them too!" interjected the prince, like a child who hasn't been given his piece of festival cake while others have already started eating at the public ceremony.

The haunt blinked. "Did you! Fascinating! As I was saying, she said that, in the empire, many statues were smashed or broken. People saw the statues as wicked and corrupted souls, not as honorable guardians. It grieves me, for these were my comrades, now lost to me. They were honorable and brave enough to give up the lives of our present in the hope of aiding a future they might never see. And will, now, indeed never see."

"What about here?" Elen asked. "Why does the archway here lead into the hillside instead of onto the terrace? As a child, I came here every spring. I never heard a single person mention statues of any kind, not hidden, not broken, not intact. Nothing. No one ever came inside these walls that I recall hearing about. Except, so people said, a child said to have died on the night of a full moon."

"So that is why you led us onto this route rather than taking the road," said the prince.

"Your Highness, it is true I wanted to give our companion a chance to explore this place because maybe it has answers that will be useful for him and for all of us. But it would have been foolhardy to take the main road regardless. You yourself saw a troop of riders headed south."

"You made a good decision, Deputy Courier."

She was so shocked by this praise that she offered him a bow.

Her deference was of little interest to him, though, not now that he'd got the scent of something he wanted. He raised his whip to point at the archway that led into darkness. "Let us go and see for ourselves."

33

Water Sisters

By the time she untied the lantern, filled its reservoir with oil, and lit it, the haunt and the prince had disappeared inside. She paused beneath the archway into the tunnel. The light swung her shadow into grotesque shapes on the wall. She caught sight of the two standing among a group of people faintly illuminated by rays of sunlight.

But they weren't people. They were statues.

The tunnel expanded into a small, domed cavern, with slits in its roof through which pale beams of light shone. The six statues were all dragons, at least they had once been, if the sleek dragon heads each clutched in an arm told the truth of how they had walked in the world before being shorn of their bodies and placed into human-headed statues.

The lantern light framed the haunt as he stood stock-still, a hand pressed to his chest as if he'd sustained a shock. He murmured, "My water sisters."

"Do you know them?"

One by one, he examined their sculpted features. First, the humanlike face, and then the dragon visage. Each time, he shook his head with resignation.

"I do not know any of them. They are my kinfolk nevertheless."

The prince watched intently. Avariciously. "Do they have powers like yours? With such a cohort, I could easily take the palace."

"Why do you want to overthrow the emperor, Your Highness?" Elen asked.

"Because she tried to kill me."

"You did rebel against her."

"No, she tried to kill me long before, when I was a child. That's why my blessed mother arranged for Hemerlin to protect me. Later, after yet another incident with the kitchen, Hemerlin brought in Fulmo."

"How can Hemerlin protect you? He's just one man."

The prince curled his lips disdainfully. "Because Hemerlin knows the palace better than anyone. But, of course, you cannot be expected to know that, a mere deputy courier, as you are. You grow too familiar. Address me with more respect."

"Yes, Your Highness."

"You needn't jump to his bark," said the haunt, a little snippily.

She gave him a gentle smile. "I will do so, and gladly, for I have to live on in the empire, as does Kem. But why are these statues here? Why are they not outside, as at Three Spires? Why go to so much effort—" She pointed at the slits in the roof. "—when they could just have been placed outside?"

The haunt cocked his head, listening. "What do you hear?"

A steady rush thrummed as a faint backdrop to the enclosed cavern, now and again amplified with a shriek, as of a whistle when the wind gusted outside.

"I hear the wind." A familiar scent tickled her nose. "I smell pure-water, although I'm surprised it carries all the way in here from the spring outside."

The haunt said, "Can you not hear it?"

"Hear what?" She shrugged.

The prince stirred, and he and the haunt exchanged a glance as if they had both come to the same conclusion.

"It's the sound of running water," said Gevulin. "But from whence does it come? Where is the water?"

The haunt nodded slowly as he thought over their surroundings. "We've got it turned around. It's not that the statues were placed in a cave instead of at the entrance. It's that the entrance to this compound isn't from the terrace. Whoever came here was expected to enter from deeper inside the earth."

"Well, then," said the prince, waving a hand toward the darkness.

Elen brought the lantern forward. They paced onward with caution. The floor remained smooth. The air was musty. The walls began to close in on each other. First, she could touch either wall with her arms outstretched, then with elbows, and then there was a mere hand's breadth between her shoulders and the solid stone. It was unnerving, as if the tunnel was deliberately tightening around them like a trap. Like an atoner's passage. But no, she was an atoner no more.

Ahead, the haunt spoke a warning and raised a hand. The tunnel ended at a big hole, like a well, that plunged into unknown depths. Steps carved out of the curving wall descended into black. Elen shivered. And yet she also wondered.

"Listen," said the haunt.

She listened to the soft rise and fall of their breathing, the hiss of the lantern's flame, and beyond all that a strange rustling rumbling sound she could make no sense of, for it reverberated in distorted ways, growing louder and then fading, before rising again.

The prince said, "Is there a river running down there? Underground?"

"So it would seem," said the haunt.

"How deep?"

"Hard to say," said the haunt. "Though I would swear to you, on the bones of my respected ancestors, that it is pure-water."

"Pure-water!" cried Elen. "That would explain how I can smell it. Could it be the source of the spring that rises inside the Spires?"

She held the lantern over the hole, peering down. The steps descended out of sight, down and down and down, with no visible bottom. What lay down there? Abruptly, she realized that she wanted to know.

"Descend, and tell me what you find," commanded the prince.

"I think not," said the haunt in a mocking tone. "I am not one of your wardens to command."

"I meant the deputy courier."

"No," said the haunt so quickly she guessed he sensed Elen's curiosity. "Perhaps your hearing is not as keen as mine, Your Highness. That is a longer way down than you seem to understand. Perhaps you cannot hear all the varied tones that water carries, but I can. This is no nearby trickle. It is a mighty flood. That we hear it so faintly means it is a very long way down."

"Hold on." El found a stone on the ground and, leaning out over the opening, dropped it, counting in her head at the steady pace she used when on her courier route.

She halted at twenty. She'd heard no splash.

"It's too far for us to hear such a tiny noise," said the haunt. "No one is going down such a distance, into darkness, on a narrow stair with no evident handholds. Not without a better idea of what may await them in the depths."

"It is time to test this passage spell you speak of," retorted the prince with a flash of anger. "Maybe statues abiding in darkness don't need moonlight to wake and cast their spell. I'll call Kem."

In a searing flash of anger, Elen began to protest, but the haunt cut her off.

"When I said no, I meant *no*." The words were calm, yet so threatening that the prince braced himself with a hand on his sword. Not that a sword would do him any good. The shadowy flare of intangible wings spread to fill the darkness around them, cutting ripples through the pale lantern light.

The haunt carried on in that same calm and intimidating tone. "You do not understand who the Shorn are. Even if you and I wait until the light of a full moon wakes these Shorn, even if you coerce Kem, or all of your wardens, to accept the soul of another to walk in their body, you do not command the Shorn. We are sworn to a purpose, not to your callow, selfish concerns."

"The stability and prosperity of the Tranquil Empire is not a callow, selfish concern!"

"Ambition makes fools of people. These water sisters will remain undisturbed because they are guardians of the world, not weapons to be wielded in service of your greedy desire for power. Unlike you, the bequeather had many questions for me because she wanted to understand the true nature and purpose of the Shorn, the better to aid them, if that was needed. I would have told her the whole without asking anything in return, although, as it happened, she had something I wanted."

He glanced at Elen with a softening of his gaze.

"Tell me what you told her!" demanded the prince.

"I think not," drawled the haunt.

Elen broke in before the prince threw a punch, and the haunt retaliated in a manner that could not be answered or forgiven. "In truth, I wish you would tell His Highness, so we needn't have this discussion again and again, as we otherwise will. His Highness already knows everything you told me when you were in his body."

"The deputy courier is correct," said the prince with a sneer.

"We need not give in to his demands," said the haunt a little peevishly.

The prince smiled, although not at all kindly, but more as if he'd just discerned the winning move in a game of Cock-and-Bull. "Need I remind you, Sara'ala, that for all your talk of honor and righteousness and the need to never coerce people into a passage spell, it could be said that you twisted your own words to me, back on that night when we first met, you and I. Is trickery not a form of coercion?"

The haunt sighed.

"I think you should tell him what you told the bequeather." Elen wrestled with how to say what needed to be said. "He's not wrong when he says he didn't fully understand the nature of the bargain he agreed to. You have said as much yourself, have you not?"

The haunt sighed again, wearily, much put upon, but she was right, and so was Prince Gevulin, even though it was a chore to admit it.

"Very well. I gave the good captain the responsibility to record and pass on—to bequeath—to the other bequeathers of the many clans this duty: that they must actively seek out and protect such Shorn who remain in the world, whether awake or still held within a statue. The aivur must remember, always, that in a day yet to come, some among their clans may be called upon to provide bodies for the Shorn. This duty was laid down long ago upon the descendants of those who defeated the sorcerer-kings. A few may need to sacrifice their lives so most can live in as much peace as can ever be found in the world. All this, she agreed to. If the world loses all its Shorn, then who will fight, should it come to that? Who will prevent another conflagration, should it come to that? Sorcerers must be tracked down and eaten before they become too powerful."

"Eaten?" murmured the prince, looking at the haunt with new suspicion. "Like the mouse at Grinder's Cut?"

"That is the only way to stop them," said the haunt without a trace of humor.

Yet Elen smiled, because possibly the moment the haunt had so blithely eaten that poor, doomed, Spore-ridden mouse had been the moment she'd truly fallen in love with him. It had been such a swift and decisive solution, if perhaps not so tasty.

"So after all that, what have you actually accomplished?" the prince went on inexorably. "You woke. You walked north in my body. And then you departed into the Pall. How did this expedition advance your purpose as one of the Shorn? Did you identify or . . . eat . . . any rogue sorcerers? Find any trace of them at all?"

The haunt shook his head regretfully. "I did not. I misjudged the bells, thinking them a sign of sorcery rising again. But probably I was simply too eager to cast myself back into the world. I found only the ashes of sorcery—the Pall—but no trace of living sorcerers, no active sorcery. Thus, my effort was wasted. A typically comic and pointless end to my noble sacrifice."

"So the Shorn are no longer needed, which means I can wake them and use them for my own purposes," said the prince.

"To the contrary. It means the Shorn remain more necessary than ever, as long as those who still survive in statues are not destroyed by ignorance. I suppose that means I have served some small purpose in warning the aivur," he added with a fresh lilt in his tone, never one to dwell for long on his own failings. He smiled slyly. "For that matter, I suspect it wasn't the bell of sorcery that called to me. I think I must have gotten distracted by the comings and goings of a certain deputy courier, which might seem months apart to her and yet to me but a blink of an eye."

"Yes, a song for the wineshops, I'm sure," said the prince sarcastically. "It would be a mercy if it finally pushed that honey-rotted melody about Xilsi Bakassar out of everyone's mouths, even after all these years."

"Why does everyone talk about the Xilsi song?" Elen asked.

"Did she not tell you, now she has befriended a deputy courier in her condescending way? She refused Astaylin's proposal to become her Elegant Consort."

"That's not surprising, since she doesn't like pie."

"Why would any Manor-born person eat pie? Pie is the food of menials. Anyway, what has food to do with anything? Such a match was a political triumph, but Xilsi turned her back on it and joined the wardens. The wineshops have been singing about it ever since."

"I knew they were singing about her, but I thought it was about her and Jirvy."

"Jirvy? What has Xilsi to do with Jirvy?"

"Can it be the observant prince has missed the entire drama?" murmured the haunt. "Fortunate man!"

Taking advantage of the brief span of privacy to ask a question she could not ask in front of the wardens, Elen grasped the haunt's hand. "If this is the end of your noble sacrifice, then what will become of you? Can't you go back to Three Spires?"

"How would I get there?"

"I would take you."

His wince was in his tone. "Ah! So you would, for it is exactly like you to offer, dear one. Yet that would be cruel, would it not? Always together, yet always apart. However, I was speaking the truth the first time you and I met. Because of the viper, the passage spell will not work on you. And anyway, even if it did, returning to Three Spires would serve no purpose. I do not know the spell by which a soul can be poured *into* a statue. I have no passage back into the shell I left. I was given only passage to get out."

"What about the Pall? You entered it and left it."

"It seems I can pass in and out of the Pall because the Pall has a similar substance to my own. That's what gave me the idea that the substance of the Pall is related to the substance of the souls of the Shorn, and thus, possibly, to souls in the general sense. All souls of living creatures, I mean."

Listening intently, Gevulin abruptly said, "You are no sorcerer, I'm sure of it. You've little enough ambition, that is for certain. Do you even know the means by which these ancient adepts wove or sealed their spells? How sorcery works? By what means this ancient alliance defeated them, despite their terrifying power?"

"I do not," said the haunt.

"You might be lying to mislead me," said the prince, "but after everything I have witnessed, I begin to think you are not. I think you actually do not know. A dragon you may have been, long ago, but I come to suspect that in wisdom and education, and in the discipline to improve yourself, you have more in common with the lowest rank of foot soldiers in the imperial infantry. You were given a simple task appropriate to your level of accomplishment and ambition in whatever sort of life you had back then."

Elen bridled at these insults, but the haunt chuckled. "I see we understand each other at last. Yet consider this, Gevulin. The most ill-educated and laziest dragon can still easily snap up the most highly accomplished and skilled prince. So, where does that leave us? I, for one, look forward to a bite to eat, even if it is spoilt by being cooked."

Elen snorted.

The prince, of course, had no such sense of humor. He took the lantern from Elen and walked past the shaft into the shadows at the back of the tunnel, poking around to see if there was another chamber or stairway. But it was a dead end.

When he returned, his expression had become intent and calculating, a promise of perilous demands to come. "What if this sound we hear truly is a river of pure-water? Rivers are marked on maps. Might not an underground river be a passageway that a mapmaker could know of and wish to record?"

Elen and the haunt exchanged a puzzled glance.

"What do you mean, Your Highness?" Elen asked.

The prince handed the first lantern back to Elen, set down his spyglass case, and unhooked his own travel lantern and tinder box. Elen didn't expect a prince to be so skilled at such a humble task, but he lit the travel lantern with one strike. Of course, this prince would never settle for anything less than mastery. Probably he could launder clothing and mend harnesses, too, if need be, better than any riverbank laundress or royal groom.

The wick took flame. The cavern brightened. Gevulin stuck his whip back into his belt and raised the lantern.

"I refuse to leave this mystery unexplored. We may never have another such chance."

With that, he started down the steps into the black pit.

34

The Brief Aura

The haunt pressed a hand against his eyes as if to shield himself against implacable folly.

"We have to go after him," Elen said.

His shoulders heaved. He did not lower his hand from his eyes. "Must we, dear one?"

"Yes, we must." Elen licked two fingers and pinched off the wick of her own lantern to save its oil, should it be needed later.

Without waiting for him to say anything more, she went to the shaft and set a foot on the top step. Here she paused, intimidated by the way the well-like opening went down and down and down, as if an impossibly giant spear had been driven deep into the ground with a single stab. The prince did not look back. Probably he expected them to follow, or perhaps he truly did not care whether they did. Maybe, just a little, she admired his determination. She no longer doubted that he was, through his own efforts and relentless practice, Adept of the Bow and the Spear, Conqueror of the Ten Peaks Race, Eloquent Grace of the Wind Dance, Artist of the Brush and Virtuoso of the Pen, Master of the Lyre and Preeminent Bard of the Twelve Cycles and the Three Hundred and Sixty Poems of the Glorious Founder, and doubtless more besides.

Enough of this woolgathering. The descent scared her, a truth she had to face. Either she was going, or she wasn't.

She exhaled, steadying herself by pressing her right hand against the curve of the wall. The haunt came up behind her.

"A fool's errand," he remarked. "Thus, I suppose, in the end it was inevitable I should feel obliged to go. Shall I precede you or follow? Is it the darkness or the depth that disturbs you so?"

"I don't know. I've never seen anything like this."

Below, the prince kept going. He wasn't in a hurry, but he wasn't dawdling either. His light—now the only light—slowly drew away, getting smaller as the darkness crept in around them.

She took another step down, then a third, then a fourth, each easier than the last as she became accustomed to the height and width of the steps. The best practice was to pay attention and not falter.

Don't get distracted or sloppy. Stick to the routine. Stay calm.

By keeping her right hand on the wall and her gaze fixed on her boots, she avoided the gulf of air to her left where her unlit lantern, held in her left hand, hung over the emptiness. The fall would kill. So, she wouldn't fall. The haunt's presence behind her steadied her nerves like the pressure of the sun on a fine, hot, summery day.

He had come back for her.

As they descended, the rumble below grew in volume, echoing weirdly and wildly around them. Even had they wished to converse, they soon could not have without shouting. The deeper they went, the stronger became the smell of pure-water, its blissful scent an embrace to shelter and bathe the traveler exhausted by the travails and troubles of an indifferently brutal world.

It was a long way down, farther than she would have thought possible. Who could create such a shaft to begin with, much less one that had remained stable for an unknown number of generations? Did the stonework resemble the swalter cavern, whose tunnels showed no sign of decay, no crumbling, just dust and abandonment? Here, too, she thought. Was this also a place swalters had once constructed and used, since abandoned or lost?

By now, the boom and rolling roar of flowing water had gotten so loud that it buzzed in her bones. All at once, the light ahead vanished as if flicked off.

She swore under her breath, drenched instantly in sweat from a spike of terror. What if they were trapped? What if she fell? What if a Pall had taken the prince, and his newly Spore-distended and monstrous form came surging out of the darkness to attack them?

A reassuring hand touched her back as if to say, *I'm here.*

So close to pure-water, there could be no Pall and no Spore. *Stay calm.*

The light reappeared, held steady. The prince had halted.

The steps ended at the base of the shaft. Gevulin stood in the mouth of a tunnel, grinning as triumphantly as a child who has just won his first competition against all expectation. The expression made the prince look younger and almost approachable. He mouthed words, shouting, but all she could make out were scraps of sound: *oo, ah, eee!*

He turned and led them into the tunnel. A short passage beneath rock opened onto a greater tunnel, a vast span whose roof and far bank she could not see in the darkness.

They stood on the embankment of a wide river. Its waters swirled and poured past like the floodwaters of spring. The boom and rumble changed tone and texture here, less clamorous and intense than it had sounded in the shaft.

The embankment ran about fifty paces to either side before it was cut off by rock. A stone jetty stuck out into the current to provide a sheltering barrier for a stone pier, marked with eight stone pillars where boats could be moored.

The prince knelt and stuck a hand into the waters, cupped his fingers, and tasted it. He shook his head in wonderment. "Pure-water!" he shouted. "Have you ever heard of such a thing?"

It was a question that required no answer. Elen walked to each of the pillars in turn, looking for any sign of mooring ropes or recent activity, but there was nothing. This embankment was surely as old as the Spires above, and possibly older, one of the lost secrets of the ancients. Either they had stripped away all signs of their presence here, or the span of generations had swallowed it, piece by piece, until no trace or memory was left.

The prince's lantern, set on the ground, sputtered and went out.

They were plunged into utter darkness. Elen could not see her hand in front of her face. The space around her was reduced to the river's relentless power, to the taste of its spray like hope on the tongue, to the ineffable sense that the water arose from an unknown source and flowed inexorably to an unknown outcome. Like souls who arise not knowing from whence and live out their lives inside the brief aura of a lit lamp, only to depart, not knowing to where. The world was great and terrible and wondrous and frightening. Each weak flame burned for as long as it could manage until it, too, was snuffed out.

But a deputy courier came prepared.

Kneeling, she set her lantern on the ground. It had enough lamp oil left to make the return ascent. By feel, she opened her tinder box, snapped, sparked, and lit the wick.

The lantern's flare wasn't so very great, but out of this darkness, its shine hit so harshly that she blinked several times until her eyes adjusted. The light caught the prince crouched in consternation at the embankment's edge, not knowing what to do with his light gone. She fought down the impulse to smile, but the haunt didn't. He seemed happy to mock as he scooped up the prince's lantern, which he offered to Gevulin with an exaggerated bow.

"Humble foot soldier I may be, but unlike you, I can see in the dark. And if I couldn't, I'd make sure I had enough oil for the return journey."

Elen did not wait, having little patience for this petty display of one-upmanship. She signaled to the prince with a wave of a hand and, without waiting for his command, headed back through the tunnel to the shaft. The haunt waited for the prince to follow her, and took up the rear. She assumed that, if Sara'ala slipped, he could unfurl his smoky wings to save himself. And could he really see in the dark? She'd have to ask him, should she ever have the chance.

As she ascended, she began to despair of ever having that chance for the most mundane of reasons: just getting there. Half of each month she walked the paths of the Moonrise Hills, so walking came as a second nature. But so many stairs were another thing entirely. At first, she climbed steadily, thinking it not much worse than a steeply sloping path in the hills. Then, starting to feel a burn in her legs, she counted, thinking to distract herself. Then, she halted to catch her breath, the prince waiting impatiently two steps below. Starting again, she made it another one hundred steps. Halted. Fifty steps. Halted, panting.

"We are almost at the top," shouted the prince. "Keep going!"

"Almost" had never seemed so far, but the sense of confinement and her fear of falling gave strength to her legs. At last, she staggered up and out, over the rim of the shaft. With an intense effort, she managed to set down her lantern neatly on the ground before collapsing next to it. Her legs ached, and her lungs burned.

The prince emerged looking barely winded. And why would he be if he were truly a Conqueror of the Ten Peaks Race?

He went to her pack and, without asking permission, unhooked her leather bottle of oil. The moment the haunt arrived and halted to kneel beside Elen, the prince took the empty travel lantern, filled it with her oil, and lit it again. He opened his spyglass case and slid out the spyglass. From the ground, watching him, Elen realized the instrument was wrapped in vellum. This he unrolled, anchoring the top edge with the spyglass and the bottom edge with the case.

It was the map they'd discovered in Mekvo's staff at Far Boundary Vigil.

Elen rolled up to sit and scooted closer. The haunt stood behind her.

"So, you see," said the prince, tapping a line on the map. "Here lies the watercourse we found below."

"Luviara said the map was a fake, drawn by the crown prince to expose you as a traitor against the emperor," objected Elen.

"She did say that. But explain this to me." Gevulin pointed to the first line of writing.

She read, as she had before, "Te veg ulbethot hal rad."

"Luviara does not know the language of the Four Lands," objected Gevulin.

"She says she does not know it. She might have been lying. It might have been a test."

"A test for whom? Not for you. Luviara had no reason to believe you had ever been in the Four Lands. Let me tell you a few things I learned about the theurgist in the three years she and I and Simo journeyed together. She is insatiably curious and loves to talk to people about any scrap of knowledge they might have that she doesn't know. She is always on the hunt for traces of old history and forgotten temples and lost lands. She has read a great deal in the archives. Yet she can read only two scripts, both of them standard practice in the palace academy. I picked up foreign languages more quickly than she did. I could understand the sailors' cant aboard ship when we sailed to Isle Tempest, while she was reliant on interpreters. As an interlocutor, she is useful only in the empire. Therefore, I believe she truly could not read what's written here. Why would anyone not show off their skill, if they had earned such mastery?"

Was he truly baffled that someone would not show off their skill? Maybe so, given his list of accomplishments and how he made sure everyone was reminded of it as often as possible.

"Your Exalted Highness." She chose her words carefully. "It seems likely that Theurgist Luviara was serving the emperor in a convoluted scheme to prove you had begun to take specific and measurable steps to claim the throne for yourself. She might have been playing the part of your loyal but somewhat hapless interlocutor the entire time she was traveling with you."

He pressed a hand to his forehead, then lowered it. "Like a theatrical performance, you are saying. Yet . . ." He shook his head. "Furthermore, how was my nephew, the crown prince, to have written this document, as she claimed he did? How can he have known the language of a land we have been so long cut off from?"

"I can think of a few ways," said Elen. "Luviara told you the crown prince wrote it. Maybe she meant he commanded it to be written, which, in the palace, may come to the same thing. Also, how do you know the emperor has never had any correspondence with any of the rulers of the north? The emperor must know things she's never told you. If the Four Lands was once Four Quarters Province, that means the palace deliberately suppressed the knowledge of its location and indeed its very existence."

"Four Quarters Province was recorded as having been swallowed by the Pall."

"Sure, and maybe most did and do think that. But I'm betting there are secret archives only an emperor has access to. Maybe not. I wouldn't know. What do you think happened, Your Highness?"

He frowned darkly. "I think Luviara knows this is a real map. But a map of something she doesn't understand. Something she wants to understand. Something she thought might be of value to the emperor. Something, most importantly, that she did not want Thelan to think was valuable, lest he take it from her. She spun a tale so he would dismiss it as trash he need take no interest in."

"I'm surprised she didn't get hold of it again when she had the chance."

"That's due to Xilsi's quick thinking." He lifted his chin in triumph. "Which means Luviara has no proof of my actions at the Vigil except her own testimony. The crown prince's scheme has failed. I can return to the palace with no one the wiser."

"But—"

"Enough! See here. Do you see?" The light cast a hazy glow across the crude map with its uneven shorelines and spiky letters collected into three clumps of text. He traced the lines that looked something like roads. "What if this is a map of underground rivers?"

"Rivers of pure-water," Elen breathed. "Which grants strength to the weary, and protects against Spore."

"Unnatural," said the haunt.

"Created by sorcery?" she asked.

"Or as a defense against sorcery. I wouldn't know. I am merely an eater of sorcerers, the most humble of tasks." Yet the haunt examined the map with interest as keen as hers or the prince's. "Gevulin, I think you are onto something. I daresay you are wasted as a purveyor of petty palace intrigue and a victim of a dreary appetite for political power. You should have been a warden, in truth."

"Or a surveyor," said Elen, breath hitching as she leaned closer to examine the crude outlines of what might represent the Four Lands, the Blasted Coast, and the Desolation, once a rich agricultural province and now an impassable wilderness stretching into the heartland of the empire. Exactly where surveyors got lost. This discovery was something indeed, something marvelous, something astounding, something incredible.

If it wasn't just a fake meant to indict an ambitious prince.

Yet what was that blurred, faded mark in the corner? She touched the scar on her neck, then traced the faded mark with a finger. It was a jagged line like a stylized lightning bolt. Hadn't the surveyor Berri worn a necklace with this symbol, belonging to his best friend and possible lover, the last surveyor known to have been lost in the Desolation? Rotho. Could it be Rotho's own map?

"Don't touch that!" The prince swept her hand off the map, fingers twitching as if trying to clutch a desired outcome beyond his reach. "*I should be emperor.* I am the deserving one."

"Pity," remarked the haunt sardonically.

"It is pitiful, indeed. The Magnolia Emperor is a hidebound, rigid bully who favors her snide, spoiled, vicious child simply because he was born of her womb, and she believes, therefore, that she can control him. Meanwhile, Astaylin simpers and pretends to virtue all the while she courts the minor Manors as if they are worthy allies."

"Wouldn't you want the minor Manors to support you, should you become emperor?" Elen asked.

"All the Manors are required to support the emperor if they wish to keep their geniuses."

"Why does that matter?" asked the haunt.

Elen said, "Without a genius, a Manor loses its status as a Manor and thus the rank, access, perquisites, and privileges that go with it."

"Ah."

The prince went on, still stewing over the unfairness of it all. "Everyone praises Astaylin, but she is six years older than I am and hasn't half my accomplishments."

"Not the Wind Dance? The Ten Peaks?"

"She is devoted to luxury and pleasure, not to hard work and discipline."

"Then how did she come to be a prince of the Third Estate?"

"She is said to be good company at parties," he said sourly.

"Ah," said Elen, and unfortunately, she glanced at the haunt. He had the bad manners to laugh outright.

The prince said, "Exactly so. No one ever judges an emperor's successful rule by how many guests they invite over and whether they are willing to sing the very wineshop song mocking them, but in a way that makes it seem they are wise and witty enough to enjoy the jest."

"Indeed, Your Highness," Elen said carefully, "I can see you would not tolerate such ludicrously entertaining goings-on. What about the map?"

"A prince succeeds by having weapons his rivals lack. You are one, Deputy Courier. This map may well be another."

He rolled the map up around the spyglass, carefully slid the two objects back into the tube, and rose briskly.

"These underground rivers are the key. That is what this map is trying to tell us. They might become a route to move soldiers and supplies beneath Pall-ridden land without detection. But as I have learned to my cost, a reckless move now will only put me in more danger. We have no leisure to survey their extent, not yet. Coming to the Four Lands almost resulted in disaster. I must move quickly."

"What is your plan, Your Highness?" Elen asked.

"It is not to be spoken of before the bequeather."

"The bequeather accepted the veil, and the temporary oblivion that goes with it," said the haunt. "She will remember nothing."

"But *you* will."

"I will be trapped in the Pall."

"Where you may find a new host, even this deputy courier, if I have not mistaken what she offered you earlier. I have seen what I needed to see. My path is clear. We go south, back to the empire."

"But Your Highness," Elen said, "the emperor knows you are a traitor who has made a pact with a foreign power to overthrow her."

"Were you not paying attention before? She suspects it but has no proof. Her lack of proof is what precipitated this entire sorry affair and her attempt to ensnare me. Luviara's testimony could condemn me, it's true. But Luviara must first travel north to the Highmost's cold capital, must wait for the sailing season in order to take a ship to an imperial port, and then must travel overland to reach the palace. That's if Thelan even allows her to leave, which he may not."

"She's a theurgist. He can scarcely stop her if she binds a powerful enough air spirit to carry her to a waiting ship in a harbor."

"Not if he locks her up in a cell. He's not a trustworthy man."

"Don't say it," muttered Elen, not looking at the haunt.

"Don't say what?" asked the prince.

"Don't say the haunt was right all along. It will make him insufferable."

"You mistake me for someone else of your acquaintance," said the haunt. "I am always sufferable."

The prince ignored this byplay, or perhaps he did not understand it. Maybe no one had ever affectionately joked with him. It would explain a lot.

Gevulin continued, "Once back in the empire, I will set wardens to watch for Luviara on the roads. She won't be expecting it. She'll never reach the palace. Yes, this will do nicely. The bequeather will grant us passage to Far Boundary Vigil, from whence we shall return south."

"Have you forgotten Lord Duenn and the Sublime Highness, last seen at the Vigil?"

"Not at all, Deputy Courier. Nor have I forgotten your viper. Kill the head, and the body dies."

"What do you mean?"

"You know exactly what I mean."

She did. He still intended for her to use her viper to murder the emperor. If he could get her within striking distance, she could manage it. That's what worried her. If the prince didn't die in the attempt, then once he became emperor, he'd either dispose of her or keep her chained to him by using Kem as a hostage. For all intents and purposes, she would become his atoner.

35

Though She Had Never Flown

The first thing Elen did after they'd stolen two boats from the banks of the Eelwise River was to roll up in a blanket and lie down to sleep on the floorboards.

When she woke, the short autumn afternoon had passed, and it was growing dark. Simo, at the oars, was guiding their boat under the overhang of a frostbitten willow. The other rowboat followed them in. The prince had placed the haunt and Kem in the other boat while keeping Elen close to himself. They all clambered off the boats to pee and stretch. Elen could have grabbed Kem and run, but she had no intention of getting trapped in her old homeland. Best to bide her time.

"Do we rest here for the night, Your Highness?" Simo asked.

"No, we push on," said the prince. "The clouds are moving off. We'll have enough light."

"Hush, I beg you, and get a fire started." The haunt had climbed out over the willow's angular, aboveground roots. Holding on to a sturdy branch and with his feet braced against the trunk, he dangled over the waters that ran deep and still where the bank had carved out a quiet pool against the old tree. He dipped a hand into the water and let it rest there as if it were just another bit of branch swaying in the current. The others stared as if he were an apparition, and in a way, he was.

Elen lucked onto a withered clump of summer dandelions and dug up their roots.

There came a splash, followed by startled laughter and the haunt demanding quiet.

She circled back, careful of the spongy ground with its layers of rotting vegetation that was a favorite breeding ground for Spore. Ipis was already out on patrol with a drawn sword, but her pace looked measured, not anxious.

Just as Elen ducked back under the willow's canopy, the shadowy figure at the river's edge twitched and, with a slap of his hand, catapulted a fish out of the water and onto the land. Kem pounced on it and killed the flopping fish with two smart blows from the hilt of his knife. While Elen had been out gathering, Kem, Jirvy, and Xilsi had found stones to make a hearth. They laid a fire with deadwood Jirvy had gathered. Elen lit it with her flint.

Kem gutted and cleaned the fish while she washed off the dandelion roots and boiled them in a pot with chance-met chives and a pinch of salt, for the autumn leavings were tough and bitter. With great relish, the company shared out five roasted fish, eating in silence while they traded off watch. Even the prince designed to eat the simple country fare.

Kem sat next to her on a log. "I'm glad I got to see it," he murmured.

"I've never seen anyone catch fish like that either. Hard to be that fast."

He snorted softly. "Never thought I'd see you like this."

"Like what?" she asked suspiciously.

He tipped his head toward the haunt who, having eaten with the others, had gone back to his fishing spot to see if he could catch a few fish for the next meal.

Her cheeks grew hot with a blush and she grinned with a ridiculous burst of joy. Fortunately, the night covered all.

Kem went on, but she could hear the smile in his tone. "I meant, this place. I feel I understand you and Mama better for seeing it."

"As long as we're not trapped here."

"So many things make sense now. I'll be digging them up for years. That child in the walls . . ." He grasped her hand tightly. "What an awful place."

"I'm sorry, Kem."

"Sorry you kept the truth from me?" He sighed. "I can't be angry after seeing that child. I wouldn't have wanted to talk about it either. And Mama certainly wasn't . . ." He wrapped his other hand around hers as though comforting her, little Kem, he whom she had comforted for so long. "I never understood how hard things were for her. Sometimes I guess I just thought she was weak and difficult."

"She wasn't weak, Kem, never think so. But she was difficult."

"There are so many things I wish I'd never said to her."

"But you didn't know. That's our fault."

"No, it isn't your fault!" he said stoutly. "If you force someone weaker than you into the jaws of a wolf, then you have become the wolf. You did your best. Anyway, how could I even have understood it, if you'd tried to explain? I didn't listen to Mama very well, did I?"

She shrugged.

"There's my answer," he said, half a sob.

"Don't blame yourself. We all do our best in a hard world. Hindsight is all very well, but that's all it is, hindsight. No one knows how they will act until the moment comes for action. No one can truly know what the best course of action is when every path looks overgrown and cruel with thorns. Learn what you can learn from what happened, then keep walking. Speaking of walking, how are your feet? Are those boots broken in yet?"

He chuckled. "I guess they are. No more blisters, anyway."

"So, after all, it takes time and patience."

He leaned his head against her shoulder, like old times. But he was growing up. He wasn't a boy. He was a young man now.

"I'm proud of you. Of how you've handled yourself. I didn't expect the wardens for you, but I think you've found a good situation."

"I like it with the wardens. But I hate leaving you."

She sighed. It was both bitter and sweet to see him come into his own.

He added, urgently, "Will you be okay?"

"I'm still a deputy courier at Orledder Halt. But listen, and don't react, it's likely the prince will keep me close now he knows about the viper."

He jolted up, about to protest out loud, but she tugged warningly on his hand. "Hush! Say nothing for now. We can't know what the future holds. I'm far less worried about my own situation than that you'll get caught up in the prince's treason."

He nodded. "Xilsi had a little chat with me and Ipis. Said she'll try to keep us free of any association with the prince's palace intrigues. But if anyone can slip out of his predicament, I'd say the prince can."

"Do you? Why?"

"Whatever we think of his qualities, he's smart, and determined, and ruthless. But what I meant by asking if you'll be okay is . . ." He gestured toward the haunt braced among the trees.

"I cried my tears. I made my peace."

"Do you wish you'd never met him at all?"

"Oh no. I'm glad I met him, even for this short time."

He squeezed her hand but had no other reply.

The river burbled on. Simo and the prince were conferring in low voices. Jirvy took watch while Xilsi and Ipis crept into the darkness to do their business, safety in numbers. The haunt hung out over the waters with a hand immersed, so still that he might have become a willow branch swaying ever so slightly in the night wind.

"Is he still fishing?" Kem whispered.

"Fishing or listening. I don't know."

Simo gave the bird-call whistle for *ready to go*. They converged on the boats and slung in their packs.

The haunt said, "Your Highness, for this leg of the journey, I intend to accompany the deputy courier."

"It does not please me to allow it," said the prince.

"Yet you escaped from the pit in which you were being held because I rescued you. I will be gone soon enough. I speak out of politeness. You, of all who are here, must most vividly be aware that should I choose to act, you can't stop me."

The others watched as the prince fumed, struggling to find a reply.

Finally, Xilsi said, "What is going on? This is all very strange. I don't understand it."

"It's a trifling request, one it would be foolish to refuse," added the haunt with a gentle blink of his mesmerizing eyes.

The prince huffed. "Very well. Novice Kem will attend me, Simo, and Jirvy. Xilsi, Ipis, the deputy courier in the other boat, with you."

Ipis had a look on her face as if she wanted to ask but knew better. She took the oars with the ease of a person who has grown up on the water. Xilsi sat at the prow, an unlit lantern beside her. The haunt settled himself at the stern, and Elen sat beside him. He twined his fingers through hers, the gesture hidden by the night. But Xilsi stared suspiciously at them from down the length of the rowboat, while Ipis flashed the oars and pulled them into the current.

"You don't act like the bequeather," Xilsi said. "Are you her twin, perchance? I have a pair of cousins who look more alike than peas in a pod. You aivur might have a similar trait."

"I am myself," said the haunt. "As I have always been."

"That's not an answer. Are you the bequeather we met before?"

From across the water, the prince hissed, "Silence!"

It was the correct command. Sound carried on night air, and it was a still night, the cold making the air seem likely to shatter if it were pressed too hard with shouts or laughter or even what Elen could imagine as Xilsi's exclamation of shock if she learned the truth this way.

Xilsi muttered, "Don't think I won't ask again later," before she stopped talking.

Elen was glad of the silence. She was content to sit beside the haunt, hand tucked in his. Part of her wished to know more and more and yet more about who he had been before he became Shorn. But it was enough to have this journey, to remain in his presence. He held her hand and sometimes made a funny humming noise so low she could barely distinguish it from the spill and burble of the swirling river currents, from the wind clacking and rustling in the trees and brush. Now and again, she secretly squeezed his hand, and he answered in like measure. The night flowed along as the river flowed. Elen was tired, but she did not want to sleep. She did not want to lose one moment next to him.

Eventually, in the other boat, Simo let Kem take the oars. Seeing the transfer, Ipis murmured, a bit sarcastically, "He was telling me all about how he and his great good friend Joef used to go out on the Sulwine Stream. Anyway, I'm tired. Who wants to row?"

"I don't know how," said Elen.

"I can," said Xilsi, "but I was at the oars all afternoon and I'm not that skilled at reading the water at night."

"I'll row," said the haunt.

The two wardens curled up at the stern to sleep while he took the bench. Wrapped tightly in her warm cloak, Elen took sentry at the prow. This meant she sat on her pack, looking ahead onto the glimmering river while keeping her back against his, feeling the strong shift of his muscles as he handled the oars, rocking her forward and back. It was so soothing, like the steady beat of wings, though she had never flown and could never fly.

In a whisper, he said, "They're asleep. Tell me about your favorite day."

She, too, kept her voice low, a murmur easily drowned out by the sound of the river and the slap of water against the boat. "A specific day?"

"No, I mean, what would a day be that would make it a fine day for you?"

She breathed as he breathed. In. Out. In. Out. "Being with the people I love. That's enough, to start with. That's everything, if you have nothing else. And then, to not be in fear for my life. To know my body is my own, that no one can choose for me what I would not choose for myself. Add to that the freedom to walk where I wish, as I wish."

"Isn't a deputy courier's route set by the intendant?"

"I have duties I must accomplish, but how I accomplish them is up to me, as long as they are fulfilled. I'm responsible for myself when I'm on my route. No one is treading at my heels, commanding me where to put my feet as I take each step."

"Is there more?"

"I'm not greedy. That's more than many people will ever know in their lives."

"But? Go on."

"Knowing I have a decent place to sleep at night, one that is safe and secure, or as secure as anything can be in this world. A place that is warm in the cold season and endurable when it is hot. And if I may be so bold, water to wash in, well-made clothing, and good boots. I really cherish good boots. To go with that, enough food that I need not go hungry more than one day out of ten, and, if it's a very fortunate day, a pleasingly sharp mug of cider."

"It shall be as fortunate a day as you please."

"Oh, and then, with all that on offer, a chance to raise my child in such peace as one can find. The chance for me, and for all those who can, to learn a skill like boot-making or surveying or herbalism, or even just to learn to sing or write or read or memorize the old poems, to do accounts or draw maps, all of that. It seems like a lot."

"It seems like so little to ask."

"What about you?"

"Me? Oh, to fly, I suppose." His tone was light but she sensed the heavy weight of what he had given up beneath it. "But that gift was shorn from me, so I never shall again."

She whispered, "What is it like to fly? You needn't answer if you prefer not to. I don't mean to bring any pain to you."

Something in the way his body shifted against her back made her think he was smiling. "The pain is not anything you have brought. It is there regardless, but as you say, I made the choice, so the choice was not made for me. I knew that in becoming one of the Shorn that I would lose that which I loved best. What I thought I would gain, I am not so sure. Glory? Praise? A sense of purpose? It was a long time ago. I have had a very long time to contemplate my folly."

"Did you . . ." She hesitated to ask, but he would be gone so soon.

"How did you endure the passing years? Were you awake and aware the entire time? How did you manage?"

"Not the whole time. The spell to place us in the shell is a complicated one, so I was given to understand. It is hedged about with all kinds of restrictions and limitations. Once we are contained in the statue, the presence of the bright moon—"

"The full moon?"

"Yes. The bright moon lifts us to the edge of awareness, so we can cast our senses into the world, to seek out any hint of sorcery. Then we doze again, as it were, a sort of slumber or stupor. So, I suppose each year would have seemed to pass as if it were but thirteen days, and even then as if a veil separated us from full waking life."

She winced, for it sounded frightful to her.

He said immediately, "It wasn't so awful, dear one. They warned us how it would be, though they could not have known the whole. We prepared, as well as we could. I memorized entire sagas so I might recite them to myself if I grew frantic or bored."

"Entire sagas? If only Luviara hadn't betrayed us, she would be second in line to hear them all."

"Who would be first?" he asked teasingly.

"Kem's friend, Joef." She angled her elbow to poke at his back. Even that gesture felt unbearably flirtatious, the first round of an evening's long foreplay toward a pleasing shared bed. How she wished . . . but what did wishing accomplish? It was not to be. "You didn't tell me about flying."

He said nothing for a bit, working the oars as the long night swept them on its inexorable currents. Her wool scarf, wrapped up to cover her face, had slipped, and her nose felt like an icicle. She tucked it up more tightly, her breath caught beneath and its warmth pooling against her chilled skin. The viper was quiet. Content. As she was content.

Ipis stirred, snorted, and sat up. "Where are we?"

"Still on the river," said the haunt.

"I can tell that! Don't you know, Elen? From your childhood?"

"I never boated down this river, but I am looking for a ford I remember, if it looks the same as twenty years ago."

"So it's true," said Xilsi. Who knew how long she'd been awake! "You really did come from here. I'd never have guessed. You have the Orledder accent, and a bit of an imperial lilt, too, I suppose from working in the Residence You'd have picked it up from the intendant's people."

From the other boat, not so far away, the prince hissed, "Silence!"

"Do you want me to take the oars?" Ipis whispered.

"No. I'm fine," the haunt replied.

The two wardens settled back to try to get more sleep.

Elen had a great deal of practice in the art of silence. For his part, the haunt seemed content to be close to her in this way as the shoreline glided past and the waxing moon rose amid stars crowded like carelessly flung jewels against the roof of the heavens.

Eventually Elen dozed off as he rowed on, seeming tireless.

Early she woke, shivering because her cloak had slipped to expose her legs. The first rosy glow brushed upward in the east, above a dense line of shrubs and trees grown along the river's edge. They came around a bend, following the wake of the lead boat.

"Look! The yew tunnel!" she said in surprise, for here the river split around a grassy sandbar. Ahead, the prince was now at the oars in the other boat, while Kem was asleep. Gevulin maneuvered into the main channel, but to the right, through rippling shallows, a trickle of backwater flowed beneath a row of ancient yew. Their majestic, curled branches made a kind of tunnel through which two hungry little girls might wade, on the hunt for lantern-berries.

A grievous weight pierced her heart. It had happened so long ago, and Ao was dead.

But they'd escaped. And, importantly, hadn't they passed by this very ford on that very last trek, their last day as atoners? She slid forward to kneel at the prow as she peered into the slowly lightening dawn.

"This is the path we took. Lady Eleawona's court came this way every year, in the summer. Usually, the advance party would pause here before crossing. Ao and I would have time to pick lantern-berries because they grow all through the yew, and no one else will gather them from here. They fear the berries are poisoned because they are wrapped so close to yew bark."

She turned to see Ipis and Xilsi awake and gazing at her with puzzled expressions.

"We're close," she added. "Not far now to the edge of the Pall. We'll have to hike west along its shoreline to reach the road. But I don't know how far the distance will be or what to expect."

In the boat ahead, Jirvy and Simo began readying their bows. Xilsi and Ipis got out theirs as well, stringing them, checking what arrows they had left. The haunt rowed, concentrating with such intentness that she guessed he was listening beyond what a human could hear.

She knelt in the prow, shading her eyes as they swept past the ford where the river widened and grew shallow enough for horses to cross, as long as the river wasn't full with flood rains. Because it was late autumn, no one was out. Folk stayed close to home, where there was heat and life. Nevertheless, she felt a prickling on her skin as if they were being watched. She spotted two crows perched on a branch overlooking the water.

They swept on, leaving the crows behind. The river's current grew faster, tumbling where it cut around the end of the ridge and descended from the higher ground to the lower shore along the White Sea. Elen wasn't used to boats. She gripped the gunwales as the boat rocked and yawed, sure she was about to pitch over the side, but the haunt handled the rapids with ease, as did the prince. Elen wondered if His Exalted Highness ever got tired of being good at things, or maybe his sour and harsh personality was the counterweight to all his skill and grace.

Abruptly, they emerged from the obscuring woodland. The Pall lay before them, about half a league away, past a blackthorn hedge, a yew hedge, and rocky ground studded here and there with withered grass that had managed to grow despite the salting of the White Sea's deadly shoreline.

"Thank the High Heavens!" cried Xilsi.

Wind gusted, rocking the boats.

A horn shrilled *ta-ra ta-ra*!

A troop of horsemen came galloping from the west, flying the banner of Lord Thelan's tree. They'd been spotted.

36

Like Sharpened Bones

One amid the ranks wore a circlet of gold hammered into his bright helm. Thelan had won his battle and, having anticipated their gambit, had come himself to reel them in. He was the sort of man who could not bear—ever—to lose face.

Jirvy knelt at the prow of the other boat, waiting for the enemy to come into range. Even so, with all his skill, they were trapped. If they put ashore on the eastern bank and ran for it, Thelan's troops could swim over and pursue them.

Across the gap between the two boats, the prince met her gaze. Though he said nothing, she knew what he wanted her to do. *Cut off the head and the body will die.* But they'd have to put her onto the western bank, even if they then fled to the east in the hope of her buying them time. She'd be cut down, and there was no guarantee the viper could even climb up a moving horse and reach its prey before it was itself killed. Even if the viper did succeed, there was no guarantee Thelan's troops wouldn't then kill the wardens in a vengeful rage. And the viper couldn't kill all the soldiers, not that quickly. She wasn't even sure if it had enough toxin in its system to kill more than one person at a time. Even if it could make it into the Pall to feed and gain more toxin, by the time it returned, she'd be dead ten times over.

She stared at the Pall as the current drew the boats inexorably toward the deadly white mist, which curved over the river but did not touch the water. The mist's arch formed a kind of low tunnel. She looked back to where the two wardens in her boat had braced themselves, arrows nocked.

"Xilsi! Is that story true?"

"What story?"

"The prince who sailed through the Pall and emerged alive."

"Oh. Oh! It's supposed to be true, but it could be one of those things. Are you suggesting . . . ?" She swayed, looking horrified, then sucked in a harsh breath. "Do you think it can work?"

"It's likely this river joins up with a bigger river, probably the one we crossed on that bridge in the middle of the Pall."

"Likely?" Xilsi shouted. "You think it's worth risking our lives with *likely* and *probably*?"

Jirvy loosed an arrow but, disturbed by the movement of the boat, his aim was off. The arrow skittered against the flank of a horse instead of burying itself in the chest of the rider. The horse was battle trained and kept coming. The soldiers howled in defiance as they charged. Their archers, in the back ranks, pulled up their horses and took aim toward the boats. The first volley fell like rain, most arrows splashing harmlessly into the water, but several striking the boats. One bounced erratically off the gunwale and caught in the prince's fly-whisk hair, a lucky shot. Lucky not to have killed him, that is. Gevulin didn't flinch, just kept rowing.

There was no time for discussion. Thelan's archers were good. They'd get their range in another volley or two. The boats were about thirty paces from the edge of the white mist. The choice to beach on the east bank and run for it, or to risk the Pall, was now or never.

Elen shouted, "Everyone down! Keep your heads down. We stay on the river."

To her absolute shock, the prince cried back, "We stay on the river!"

The boat he was rowing caught an eddy and turned halfway around just as Jirvy and Simo released arrows, which went flying into the Pall instead of at their enemy.

"Duck!" shouted Xilsi as she and Ipis shot. The haunt kept their boat steady as it swept toward the gauzy fog that shrouded the land ahead. Arrows whistled down upon them. Elen flung up her cloak like wings, the only thing she could think to do to protect them all, but the haunt was faster yet. His shadowy wings unfurled to create a great sheltering darkness. Every arrow that touched the shadow burst into flame and crumbled to ash before it reached the boat. But his wingspan couldn't protect the other rowboat. A shower of dreadful plunking noises hammered against water and wood as arrows struck the other boat.

A shout. "I'm hit!"

Hit!

Who was hit?

The white mist swirled toward them just as the boat she was in rammed into the stern of the prince's boat. Everyone jolted.

"Down! Down!" Elen shouted. She grabbed the stern of the other boat as they slid into a tunnel created by the archway of white fog. If she raised her arm she could run her hand through it, so she didn't raise her arm. The haunt was still sitting up, rowing, but the others flung themselves into the bottom of boat, gasping. Someone was grunting in pain, the sound a person makes when they are trying to choke down agonized screams. *Please let it not be Kem.* There wasn't time to ask. There wasn't time to know.

She said, "Keep rowing. I'm going to get us forward of this boat so we can tie our boat to theirs and steer from here."

"Yes," the haunt said with complete composure.

"Yes," said the prince from the other boat, equally composed. So, he wasn't the one wounded.

"Xilsi, keep your head down, but you've got to get rope secured in the back."

"Got it. Fuck me, I'll never criticize the blessed Willow Emperor again."

Arrows splashed into the water behind them, followed by an echoing wash of sound that might have been jeers or cheers or a roar of anger from their disappointed pursuers. What use was revenge if you couldn't wreak it with your own hands? What would Thelan do now?

No time to dwell on what might come. They had to survive this first. The boats heaved apart, bumped together, and gapped open again. Elen strained to hold the two close, thinking first that her arms would tear out of their sockets, then that her fingers would be crushed between the gunwales as they crashed together just beyond her gripping hands. The river slipped and slid between the jostling boats as she worked her way forward. Just when she thought she was about to lose her grip, two pairs of hands clamped down on the gunwales. Jirvy and Kem had figured out what was going on and shifted position to help her.

Kem was safe.

"Keep your heads down," she snapped, too relieved to modulate her tone.

She didn't have leisure to look into the other boat, but she heard the prince swear. He said, "Novice! Get my knife from my hilt and hand it to me. I can't take my hands off the wound or he'll bleed out. Cloth to bind with."

A pair of hands vanished.

Jirvy said, "Almost there. I've got rope secured to our prow."

"Good. Good."

The boats swung sideways until, between them, Jirvy and Xilsi got the two boats secured prow to stern. The haunt worked their boat forward, pulling first right, then left, until he got them centered in a strong current. Elen leaned forward over the prow, scanning the dim passage ahead, where sunlight filtered as through cheesecloth to make everything gray. The jostling current settled and smoothed. The boats rammed together with a loud, frightening thunk.

Simo moaned. Their captain was down.

"Give it more rope," said Ipis. "They're too close together. No, no, not yet. Let me get over there. Let me row the second boat. I know how to do this."

"Heads down! Heads down!" cried Elen as the ceiling of the Pall dipped. The mist was such an odd thing, not smoky but not solid, yet it had contours as land did. Everyone but her and the haunt flattened into the bottom of the boats, crammed together like sardines in a barrel. The mist brushed the top of her head. In its icy touch, like sharpened bones combing through her head, hissed the whispers of her worst thoughts: *kill them kill them steer them into our arms and we will reward you you and the dragon free to fly—*

The viper burned in her heart, hungering for the ashy voices, but she couldn't let it out with nowhere to go but the boat itself. The others would see it, and then what would they do? She couldn't risk it.

The current pulled them closer to the right bank of the river, a graveled shore where the Pall crept down to within an arm's length of the water's edge. Too dangerous to stop here.

"Keep to the center," she said.

The haunt pulled on the oars. Just ahead, the low ceiling of Pall began to rise another arm's length, for a little ways at least.

"Kem, Ipis, there's a bit of a gap up ahead. Get ready to switch. Be fast."

The prince grunted something. Kem said, "I'm staying here. I can help with the captain."

"Jirvy, then. On my mark. Wait. Wait. Ready . . ."

The Pall's icy touch receded.

"Go!"

The boats jostled wildly as Ipis and Jirvy switched places. Elen couldn't look because she had to keep watch on the Pall overhead.

"Fuck! That water's cold!" gasped Jirvy as he clambered over the stern and fell flat on his face. "Got my leg in it."

"Play out the rope!" called Ipis. "A little more. There! Tie it off."

They reached a long, level stretch where the river flowed easily between high banks. The Pall was high enough that she couldn't touch it even with arms outstretched.

Elen said, "Everyone, now's the time to pee over the side, whatever you need to do. Be quick. It'll lower again."

Jirvy knelt on the stern bench and loosened his trousers to urinate over the side. He glanced back to see Xilsi watching. "Really? It hasn't changed since the last time you saw it."

"I thought it might have fallen off. That, at least, would explain how things went."

The haunt looked over his shoulder toward Elen. "How long is this going to go on?"

"I don't know, but at least a day until we can hope to reach the causeway. Oh, did you mean their arguing? That's up to them, isn't it? Xilsi, come hold my hands so I can pee over the side. Then I'll help you."

The haunt made room for Xilsi to squeeze past, and the two women traded off relieving themselves. Jirvy made a great show of not watching. In the other boat, Kem and the prince huddled over Simo, speaking in the hushed voices of people who are helpless in the face of something terrible unfolding.

All at once, the prince sat back on his heels. Kem rubbed at his eyes with blood-streaked hands. At the oars, Ipis burst into sobs.

"He's dead," said the prince.

37

A Right to Know

Beneath the Pall, all lay hushed but for the rushing run of the water and the occasional splash of a fish. Beyond the Pall, the rest of the world might have ceased to exist, for all they knew. For all they knew, they might float through this tunnel of fog until they died.

Captain Simo was dead.

Grief fell as heavily as exhaustion, and they embraced it. The prince led the death prayers in a low voice, to which they uttered the proper responses. For a long time after that, the only movement in the boats was by Ipis and the haunt working the oars, punctuated by fresh outbreaks of crying from Ipis. The others wept silent tears or did not shed tears at all, yet they all mourned.

Eventually, the prince roused himself. He switched places with Ipis on the rower's bench. While he handled the boat, Ipis and Kem stripped the captain's body of his knife, sword, flint pouch, salt spirits, belt, and warden's badge.

"Shouldn't we let him keep his warden's badge?" Ipis asked.

The prince said, "No. Should his body wash up to shore one day, someone might steal it and use it unlawfully. It will be sent to his family, in memory of his service to the empire. The necklace, too. That was a gift from his mother and should be returned to his kin as well."

From the other boat Elen said, "Meaning no disrespect, but he won't need his cloak, his coat, winter tunic, and boots, not where he's going. His gloves, too. Ipis, his hands are large enough that you could pull them on over your own gloves. If it gets colder, we can't risk frostbite."

"That's horrible," said Ipis. "Wearing a dead man's gloves that were just on his hands."

Kem said, "She's right. No use us freezing, Ip. And if not us, then someone who doesn't have such quality gear."

"You're gross!" she snapped.

Xilsi called over, "No, Ip, he's right. Simo wouldn't begrudge you his gloves or anyone else his coat and cloak. It's what you do on the battlefield. Your dead comrade wants you to live, not to die because you thought it disrespectful to grab his spear out of his dead hands when the enemy is right on you."

In the end, though, Ipis couldn't do it. She wept, clawed at her own face, and, shaking, unclasped a plain wooden bracelet from her wrist and fastened it around the dead man's. Since stripping a corpse was beneath the dignity of a prince, Kem removed the outer clothing from the body while reciting the prayers for peace. With a final prayer for mercy bestowed by the High Heavens, he tipped Simo into the river. The splash hit like a thunderclap. Everyone winced. Xilsi rubbed her eyes. Jirvy crouched at the stern with a hand pressed to his chest, watching the body.

For a while—too long—the body bobbed and swirled in their wake, but at length, as the air left its lungs and water filled them, it sank. The last of Simo to be seen was his long black braid, trailing like a spirit-snake winding in the current. An eddy dragged him deeper, and then the braid, too, was gone.

Elen rubbed her face. Her limbs felt as heavy as if they were waterlogged.

Jirvy shifted restlessly. In a low voice, he said, "I remember that morning when he introduced you and me to each other for the first time."

Xilsi gave a soft chuff of a sound. Elen couldn't tell if it was grief or scoffing.

Jirvy went on, even more quietly, still with his back to her. "I did choose my obligation to my family over you. I'm sorry I was so much of a coward I couldn't tell you straight out. I didn't have the courage to lose you. Maybe I didn't have the courage to admit I chose my kin over you."

It was the longest speech Elen had ever heard him make.

Xilsi stared at his back, then at the river that had taken Simo's body. Finally, she sighed. "Peace, Jirvy. On the honor of the captain, let us have peace. You did what you had to do for your family. I can't even fault you for it. You are the only child of that line. It's not like you have twenty siblings and cousins to take up the slack of your branch of the lineage, like I do. But I'm still mad. We could have wept together. The wineshops would have made a song of our tragic love sundered by cruel fate and implacable law, and I'd still be in a rage forever and ever, but at least we would have done it together. Not this sneaking about while you were still fucking sleeping with me and pretending nothing had changed. That's what makes me so fucking mad."

By the twitch of his shoulders, the words hit home. He touched a hand to his eyes.

The haunt bent the oars to guide the boat back into the center of the current. "That wasn't a very peaceful or peace-making speech," he remarked. "Although one hopes it may mark the end of your quarreling."

Xilsi turned on him like a storm blasting in. "And who the fuck are you anyway? You sure as fuck aren't the bequeather! Even though you look exactly like her. And are wearing all the same gear she was wearing."

"Again, Warden Xilsi, I respectfully refer your question to the prince."

Kneeling beside Xilsi in the prow, Elen felt the warden tense as she drew in breath to shout. And shout she did.

"Your Exalted Fucking Highness, who the fuck is this person rowing the boat I'm stuck in? I fucking saw some kind of creepy shadow that burned up arrows. Meanwhile, our extraordinarily pragmatic deputy courier is acting sweet on someone—an aivur, at that!—she only recently met who, by the way, told her she was poison and wanted nothing to do with her, and yet now is acting just as sweet on her! So what the fuck aren't you telling me, Gevulin?" Yet her loud voice was muffled by the weight of the Pall around them, as if the fog absorbed all sounds of life in the same way it devoured the essence of life itself.

In the other boat, Kem and Ipis clutched each other, shocked by Xilsi's vehemence and astounding degree of disrespect.

The prince kept rowing and did not reply. Since he was seated with his back to them, Elen couldn't judge his expression, but Kem and Ipis glanced nervously at each other, like companions who'd just realized they were going to have to face down a charge of Blood Wolves mounted on monstrously large spiders.

Elen called, "The ceiling is lowering ahead. Get ready."

"But not you or the bequeather, Elen," Xilsi went on, still in high dudgeon. "Don't think I haven't noticed. Aivur are said to be immune to Spore, and the bequeather is aivur. But I don't get what's going on with *you*, because there's only one answer that makes any sense. Are you a human-passing aivur?"

"Heads down!" Elen called.

The Pall dropped low over the river as they all bent low, then lower still as the current churned on. The prince had to abandon the oars to lie down, leaving the haunt to manage the jerking and pulling of the two linked vessels as well as he could. The wardens lay flat. Even Elen crouched, folded over, rather than letting the Pall wash across her torso. She couldn't risk Spore crawling down her body, not that she'd ever had that happen to her, but a boat carrying vulnerable humans wasn't the place to find out if it could.

Yet the deadly fog pulled and tore around the haunt's body as clouds tear apart around a mountain's peak. He seemed unconcerned that deadly tendrils might use him as a foothold to get to the people who were in the boat with him. After all, like the viper, he could eat Spore and suffer no harmful effects. Maybe Spore was instinctively survivalist enough to avoid him.

For far too long, they rolled and pitched. Everyone stayed silent, lying low, holding on as they were violently jostled by the current. Elen was grateful for their silence, for the chance to collect her thoughts, come up with answers, but her mind was as agitated as the river.

The haunt rowed steadily onward, oars creaking in their locks. Now and again he missed a stroke as a fresh rattle of wave or wicked swirl caught the boat. After what seemed like a very long time, the water smoothed out somewhat, although the Pall remained low overhead.

From the stern, Jirvy finally spoke. "Xil's right. Elen, are you aivur?"

"I just don't get it," muttered Xilsi. "There's nothing about you that feels like the aivur do, all shiny and crackling. But we have a right to know."

"She's not aivur," said the haunt abruptly.

"I didn't ask you to speak for me!" said Elen, still caught in a raging current of disordered thoughts.

"I beg your pardon. I meant no offense. But it's the truth."

"Then what am I?" she demanded, taken off guard. "Why am I as I am?"

"Well I'll be fucked on the floor of the High Heavens," muttered Xilsi. "You don't know either, do you?"

"You believe me?"

"Of course I believe you. We're friends."

"I'm a good liar."

"Sure, but for once in my life, I'm wrong about something."

Despite the Pall drifting so perilously close above the gunwales, Jirvy snorted a laugh.

"Wrong about what?" Elen asked cautiously.

"That there's only one answer that makes sense."

"That sounds familiar," murmured Jirvy. Elen couldn't tell if he was amused or being sarcastic.

Xilsi went on as if he hadn't spoken. "It's far more likely there are many more answers that make sense than I have any notion of. What do any of us know, really? We wardens think we're the best-informed officials in the empire. Yet we had forgotten about an old imperial road that can't have been built by the empire, this very one we traversed that links Woodfall Province to a place we were told had vanished under the Pall. I'd never seen a swalter cavern before that one you guided us through. I thought they were a forest people. And the wardens didn't know about the rope bridge over Grinder's Cut, not that it would be on our route maps, but our central hall is supposed to have a copy of the most up-to-date surveyor maps. Or what about that bitch Astaylin lying to our all-seeing eye about the blocked road? If it was her, I mean. Maybe it was the crown prince all along! Maybe he was the one who told that prick Duenn to say it was Astaylin. And Luviara! I just thought she was a crazy old temple coot with some minor theurgy skills and an itching nose for knowledge, who could keep up with anyone. But she was scheming with the crown prince and the emperor the whole time! That's just to start with, from this fucked-up journey. The whole fucking world could be a lie."

"Don't go there," said Jirvy.

The haunt said, "Why not? I enjoy a good anguished roar."

"Fuck you, whatever you are," said Xilsi, without heat.

"Warden Xilsilin!" The prince's voice reached them like a whisper, but Elen thought he was shouting. "You are promoted to captain as of now."

"Fuck that! No! Make Jirvy captain."

"Like you'd ever take orders from me," Jirvy muttered to no one in particular.

"Captain, this is the command of your all-seeing eye. You will accept, or you will sever your relationship with the wardens and be discharged without honor."

Xilsi's hand found Elen's wrist and grasped it as if she needed to squeeze something or else scream.

"You'll be a good captain," said Elen encouragingly.

"The fuck I will. Simo was a good captain. I'm not him. I'll never be half the warden he was. Or that Mekvo was. Fuck this world." Softly, she began to cry.

Elen pressed a hand to her friend's back. Her mind might be in turmoil, but this small comfort she could offer.

The haunt sighed. "Anyone else need to roar? May we hope for some quiet hours? Yet no, it is not to be. I sense a disturbance ahead. A deeper voice. Stronger waters."

Elen said, "We must be reaching the confluence of this tributary with a larger river. Hopefully the river that runs all the way to the bridge we crossed."

So it proved. For a while longer, they had to remain pressed low. But eventually the Pall's ceiling rose again. The wardens sat up with a sigh of relief. Ahead, the waterway opened onto a wide river, which ran with the clamor of great force. Its steadily rumbling current reminded Elen of the underground pure-water river, a mystery, to be sure, as the real bequeather would have said.

In the other boat, Ipis took over the oars from the prince.

"I'll take the oars," said Jirvy to the haunt. "You deserve a short rest."

"I don't need rest in the way you do," said the haunt, "but with the deputy courier's permission, you might watch at the prow so the deputy courier can have a nap."

"I will accept with thanks," said Elen, and caught herself in a yawn.

With Ipis and the haunt at the oars, the boats managed the transition into the big river with ease. The Eelwise had been about thirty paces across, if Elen was any judge, and the new river was at least twice that, maybe three times that—a mighty stream flowing with boundless waters, although Elen did not know from what headwaters this river sprang. There were hills in eastern Woodfall, so maybe there. Perhaps it began within the Pall itself, or farther afield, for this river had the weight of waters rolling along and along for many leagues, as from a faraway country. She wondered if it could somehow be linked to the Desolation or the underground pure-water river.

The narrow span of open shoreline remained eerily empty of life, as it had since they slipped into the mist. The Pall's edge held steady at about an arm's length from the highest reach of the water. The best thing about the bigger river was that the Pall hung steadily far above them, giving breathing room. A pale disk glowed partway down the sky, its gleam made gauzy by the fog: the sun as it sank toward an early night.

"Let me sleep a while," Elen said. "Jirvy, do you remember the bridge we crossed when we were on the road through the Pall?"

"I do."

"That's what we're looking for. There's a spot by the piers that should be safe for us to put in and climb up to the road."

"Should be," he murmured.

"It's the chance we have to take. That bridge is part of the causeway across the Pall. Lord Thelan can't reach it without the help of the aivur. I'm betting the clan values their bequeather more than the lord."

The haunt said, "The Salt Spear Clan will honor the bargain to keep you all safe."

"There you go," said Elen. "Anyone have a better idea?"

No one did.

Elen curled up at the stern. To her surprise, Xilsi crept in beside her. "Mind if I sleep here? Sorry about my language. And what I said about you. I'm just really shaken. Two of the rare people I actually trusted are both dead now. It's hard to get my feet under me."

"Maybe you don't have to yet," said Elen. With the instinct that had saved her life more than once, she peeled back her glove. "I'm going to show you a secret that will get me burned if any imperial official ever discovers it."

"An official like me?"

"I reveal this to you as my friend."

Xilsi brightened, her smile swift yet tempered with sorrow. "You're a good one, Elen."

"Call me El. Now don't move. A viper is about to poke its head out of my arm."

Xilsi gasped, "What?" followed by a choking gurgle as the viper poked its head out of Elen's wrist, wriggled free, tasted the air with its tongue, and promptly slithered right back into Elen's flesh, evidently not liking either the boat or the river.

"It eats Spore, which means there's no Spore in this boat. It protects me, and those around me, by proximity. And no, I don't know where it came from and why it hatched in me when I was a child. It just exists. I've never had any reason to think of myself as anything but human, except for the viper."

Xilsi opened her mouth, shut it, shook her head, and said, "I'll be the High Heavens' latrine."

"You say that, but what does it mean? It seems terribly blasphemous and disrespectful."

"It references a poem written by the beloved Peony Emperor."

"I've never heard it."

"There's a reason you haven't. If that creature can eat Spore, and if it's a poisonous viper, and if you're not aivur, then why doesn't its presence in your flesh harm you?"

"That's a good question. I don't have an answer. But I believe that the viper is why the bequeather called me osge. Not that she ever saw the viper. She said she sensed it, and that the scar on my neck meant someone tried to mark me to warn others. So it means the aivur have seen it before and don't like it, that they consider people like me to be outcasts, to be shunned."

"Aha! So, by your own words, you admit it?"

"Admit what?"

"That whoever is at the oars isn't really the bequeather. Otherwise, why would Captain Raven, who so clearly avoided and distrusted you before, be canoodling you and holding your hand and throwing calf eyes at you like every lovesick youth in the throes of first love? This one here doesn't walk or even talk the way the bequeather did. If anything, it reminds me of how Gevulin was when we were tramping through the Moonrise Hills. He was rather pleasant to be around, which, I must say, has been the strangest thing of all about this entire fucked-up journey."

The haunt shifted his feet on the floorboards. They both glanced up. Elen was expecting to see him watching and listening to their conversation, but he was staring, head tilted back, at the Pall above. At a shadow swimming past, within the fog, like a gigantic eel . . . or a dragon made of molten ash.

"What is that?" Jirvy cried.

Everyone stared as the shadow flowed past, on and on, a more monstrous creature than Elen had ever imagined, larger than the biggest sarpa she'd ever seen.

Kem yelped, "Look out! Rocks! A spar!"

The rowers jolted into action, barely pulling the boats aside so they didn't slam into an islet of boulders thrust up along one side of the main current. In an earlier flood, a big mass of branches had lodged in the rocks. As the boats bumped back, the rope got tangled in the lowest branch.

The lead boat threatened to capsize as the rope pulled taut and jammed the vessel sideways, just before Ipis got the second boat pushed off of the grasping branch. It came free.

They floated onward again, panting in relief. Everyone was exhausted by the flight, by grief, by the knowledge that no one knew how this journey would end. No one but the haunt, and then only for himself, and not the end he sought but rather the inevitable outcome of the passage spell.

Elen met his gaze. He smiled wryly, affectionately, an unexpected expression to see on the bequeather's face, she who, in her own body, had walked with cold confidence and no displays of warm feeling.

Xilsi murmured. "I'm not letting this matter of the bequeather go. But I'll let you sleep first, because we all need to sleep. But mostly because I'm gracious."

"My thanks, Captain," Elen said with a teasing smile.

Xilsi grimaced and tapped Elen on the shoulder, exaggeratedly pulling a punch, but smiling as she did so.

Elen settled down and slept.

When she woke, it was dark. A sickly wan globe shone above, the pallid moon beyond the misty veil. Stars flashed off and on, which confused her until she realized the lights weren't stars but sparks adrift in the Pall. Were these the remnants of souls in truth, as Sara'ala had guessed? The embers of lives drained long ago by sorcery?

Oars cut in and out of the water in a steady rhythm.

The haunt said, "It's a lovely river. Shame about the Pall cutting it off from the many people and animals whose lives would be enriched by its presence."

"Jirvy, I can take watch," Elen said as she yawned. She was so tired, and not just in her body. Walking through the land of her childhood had drained her. Maybe reliving the past was a kind of sorcery, too.

Jirvy glanced back. "My thanks, but I'm wide awake. Too hungry to sleep. I get this way. Better you sleep more so you can take watch later when I collapse."

Xilsi was fast asleep and breathing evenly.

The haunt caught Elen's gaze and held it with a tender smile that was all the answer she needed.

"If I may?" She indicated the area at his feet.

"I wish you would," he murmured invitingly.

She positioned herself with the greatest selfishness, tucking her legs between the haunt's braced feet so that she might feel his touch as she slept. She lay with eyes closed, rocked by the water and embraced by his presence, while wishing with bittersweet pleasure of how it might be to have just one night to lie in his arms. But they would not be *his* arms, and so it must always remain only a dream.

She woke to daylight and Jirvy's voice.

"Eyes up! Is that a bridge ahead?"

38

At the Edge of the Pall

Elen scrambled forward to crouch next to Jirvy. Blocky piers and the low roadbed of a massive stone bridge cut over the river. The current had strengthened. They'd pass beneath and sail onward if they didn't make a decision right now.

"It looks like an imperial bridge," Jirvy added. "Do you recognize it?"

"From this angle I can't be sure, but it seems likely it is the one we crossed. What other road and bridge this size can there be?" She called over her shoulder. "We need to put in at the shore below the bridge. Ipis! Do you hear me?"

By now, Kem was working the oars of the second boat. He and Ipis had switched during the night. He heard her, and both boats began pulling toward the shoreline across the strong current.

A shout rose from the bridge. Figures hurried down the steep embankment to meet them. As the boats swirled in, tugging and shifting, the aivur threw ropes. Ipis caught one and looped it around her forearms, hanging on as her boat was dragged to the steep bank. Aivur wearing soldiers' garb helped the prince, Ipis, and Kem out of their boat. After Xilsi secured a rope, the aivur pulled the second boat in. One shouted a question to the bequeather. The haunt shipped the oars as he replied with a curtly spoken phrase in the same language. An aivur youth ran off, as if carrying whatever message the haunt had passed on.

Their stern bumped against the rocks. Xilsi got out unsteadily. Jirvy balanced deftly, his injuries mostly healed. The haunt tossed packs to waiting hands, then said, "Go ahead," to Elen.

When she rose from the rocking boat on unsteady legs and reached for help transferring to solid ground, the nearest aivur gave her a hard shove. She toppled backward and hit the water. The shock held her helpless for long enough that she swallowed cold river water and panicked. The current grabbed hold of her body and, with frightening speed, pulled her downstream. Her arms flailed uselessly as she tried to reach the surface.

An impact roiled the water next to her. Arms grabbed her. More than arms—claws pressed hard into her flesh. Wings enveloped her. She broke the surface, coughing. Her knees bumped hard against stone. People shouted, although she was too dazed to make out their words. The haunt hauled her out of the water and onto the side of the embankment. She sagged onto her knees and began retching while he slapped her on the back. A strange, doubled presence loomed above her: the bequeather's body and, above it, the shadowy wings of a larger, and more menacing, manifestation. When her heaves finally stopped, the pressure of that shadow retreated, as if wings furled, and the haunt stood.

He spoke to the aivur in their language, in a voice she had never heard from him before, deeper than mountains, stormier than the tempest-wracked sea, harsh and yet also golden, as the touch of molten gold that sears and melts.

A fresh spasm of coughing shook her. She couldn't get it all out. Couldn't catch her breath.

Xilsi knelt beside her, slapping her again on the back to force any last water up, but all Elen did was cough. "El? How'd you fall in? Did you lose your footing? That's not like you."

"She was *pushed in*," said the haunt in a grim tone that caused everyone to look at him.

He stalked up the embankment, the terrible shadow seething around the body he wore. It coalesced into the shape of a ghostly dragon with wings unfurling before they splintered into a thousand wings, spinning a whirlwind above his head. Yet there was no wind, no tempest, just the shadow.

Step by backward step, the fearsome aivur retreated to the top of the embankment. They brought out their weapons to make a bristling wall of swords and spears. The four wardens hastily stationed themselves in pairs on either side of Elen. Jirvy, Ipis, and Xilsi nocked arrows and drew, holding the strings taut. Kem secured the two boats in case they needed to flee.

Prince Gevulin scrambled up to the top of the embankment. He planted himself between the haunt and the aivur, with his arms extended as if to block any fight that might break out. "What means this assault on one of my officials! I demand recompense for this insult to my princely dignity. At once!"

The hostility between the two sides crackled like unseen lightning. Bit by bit, other aivur crowded up behind the line of spears and swords to see what was going on, reinforcing the armed barrier.

The seething haunt wearing the bequeather's body, the suspicious aivur, the proud prince: all held tense.

By now, Elen was starting to shiver as the cold seeped through her wet clothes. Kem draped his coat over her shoulders. The heavy wool helped a little, but as the confrontation dragged on—warden and aivur alike as still as statues awaiting a passage spell to release them—she wished desperately that something would happen, if only so she could get warm. The aivur were waiting, but for what?

A horn shrilled in the distance, answered by another, farther off, then a yet fainter one, a message passed down the line faster than a person could run. The wall of weapons remained poised, the silence uncanny. First, a few and then more and more of the aivur began glancing back down the road in expectation of seeing something. Or someone.

Jirvy touched his ear: *Listen.*

A clip-clop of horse's hooves carried to them, riders approaching.

Ipis whispered, "Do you think the clan sold us out to Lord Thelan, after all?"

Kem said, "I think we need to trust the, uh, the bequeather."

Ipis slanted a skeptical side-eye at him. "Back at the hall, Elen explained to the prince that the clan had accepted an offer of alliance from Lord Thelan. So why would we trust the bequeather?"

"Be patient, Ip. You'll see."

Xilsi nudged Kem rather more sharply than she needed to. "Whatever the secret is, you know it, too, don't you? You, Elen, and the prince, you all know. Don't think I'm not going to dig it out by one means or another."

"I love you, too, Xilsi," Kem said in that over-honeyed way he had that made people roll their eyes and smile.

"Don't think I won't kick your ass later, kid, when I put you through your training paces."

"I'm counting on it," he said brightly. "If that's what it takes to become a good warden."

Jirvy's rare smile quirked. Xilsi snorted, but Kem's charm assault had worked, or maybe Xilsi was too canny and experienced to push the question when they needed to concentrate on reaching the empire and not getting killed or taken prisoner in the process. Elen wasn't sure which would be worse. She was still shivering, teeth chattering, although the coat was helping a little.

Above them, the line of armed aivur took a step back in unison.

An unseen one of their number barked out a command. They lowered their spears and sheathed their swords. The crowd peeled away to either side to create an opening for the new arrivals.

A tall, iron-haired aivur appeared at the top of the embankment, escorted by two gagast. One was Fulmo—thank the High Heavens!—although he looked a little smaller than before, as if, on the journey from South Ring, he'd had to harden his skin against an attack and, afterward, crack his shell to move on. The other gagast was bigger, blockier, and startlingly aggressive in posture compared to Fulmo's gentle ministrations and passive demeanor.

This big gagast slammed open hands together, the sound like a crack of thunder.

In response, the massed crowd of aivur responded, "Hei! Va!" Their voices reverberated over the rolling river, almost as if the Pall, for once, reflected sound back instead of swallowing it.

Seeing the newcomers, the haunt climbed to stand beside the prince. He held up a hand in a two-fingered gesture clearly understood by the aivur, for they all dropped to one knee, except for the iron-haired person. The two gagast remained standing as well.

The haunt spoke through the bequeather's lips and in the bequeather's language as easily as the haunt spoke the imperial tongue. The iron-haired person answered in the same speech. Their exchange went on for some time and, at one point, became heated although neither moved. The rest of the aivur watched in ominous silence. After a particularly snappish exchange, the belligerent gagast raised their hands to clap again, but the iron-haired aivur gave them a sharp nod, and the gagast lowered their hands.

For once in his life, the prince made no further attempt to intervene. As his gaze flashed back and forth between the speakers, Elen remembered what he had said about picking up languages. Could he understand them? To her, the words were so much chaff in the wind, except twice, when she clearly heard the word "osge."

Abruptly, the discussion ceased. The haunt appeared disgruntled, the iron-haired aivur annoyed. Maybe that was a good sign, if neither were satisfied. Maybe.

The haunt turned back to address the wardens. First, he gave a nod to Elen in reassurance. Xilsi grunted softly, noticing it, but said nothing.

"Your Highness," the haunt said, "this individual is the lawgiver of the Salt Spear Clan's council. She has come on the council's behalf.

They will meet with you to discuss the situation in which we all now find ourselves."

"What do they intend to discuss? We are leaving the north. Fulmo is here, as I hoped he would be, so there is no reason for us to wait."

"I daresay their archers are better shots than Thelan's people. As well, Your Highness, this is not a request for a meeting. They *will* meet with you. Our arrival in the boats has complicated matters for them."

The prince surveyed the assembled aivur. More were arriving, lining the bridge to watch. Many carried bows. It would be impossible to cross over or even under the bridge against such a multitude, if the aivur did not want them to leave.

"Do they intend to turn us over to the Highmost?" Gevulin asked, echoing Elen's thoughts.

"No," said the haunt.

"No? You trust them?"

The haunt's sly smile flickered. "I trust the bargain I made with the bequeather."

Xilsi stiffened. She and Jirvy exchanged glances. Ipis scratched her head and gave Kem a look, as if trying to figure out why he wasn't puzzled by any of this.

"You've not spoken to me of the bargain you made," the prince pointed out. "Now would be the time. I cannot parlay with a council who means me ill."

"As I have reminded the lawgiver just now, the bequeather gave to me her oath that you and your party would receive safe passage from the Salt Spear Clan. *All* of your party," he added, nodding at Elen before shooting a dark gaze toward the lawgiver. Thus the repeated mention of osge, Elen supposed. "But in truth, Your Highness, you and your wardens are trapped until the council grants you leave to move on. I don't see what choice you have."

"We can get back on the boats."

"Yes, you can. To die under a rain of arrows. But let us say you did not die, or that they mercifully held back. Whence you will emerge from the Pall and how long it will take you to get there, I could not say, nor if you will survive the river journey, much less discover a path that will lead you home. As for me, my journey in this form ends here."

Elen winced. Beside her, Xilsi stirred but said nothing.

"That, too, was part of the bargain." The haunt sighed. He never feared to look at Elen, even when he grieved for what would come. Even the memory of shared sadness could be precious in a future that must be walked alone. He turned his gaze back on the prince. "Your Highness, it will be easier for all of us if you agree to speak with the council with no further argument. I will advocate on your behalf. You know what my interest is in the matter. I am a stubborn sort of soul when I can finally bestir myself to care, and in this case, I care very deeply, as you are aware."

Gevulin's frown had more consideration than displeasure in its crooked curve. "That alone is what inclines me to agree. Wardens, you will remain by the boats in case we must make a precipitous departure. I will meet with the council here, on the embankment. Nowhere else."

The haunt translated this to the lawgiver, who gave a sign.

The haunt said, "That is acceptable to the council. They are on their way regardless."

"Then it is agreed," said Gevulin. For people to come to the prince was, in imperial terms, a sign of his strength. Elen didn't know what it meant to the aivur.

Ipis murmured, "Xilsi, do you trust the aivur?"

She shrugged, her elbow giving Elen a nudge. "I don't know what to think about any of this. But as for trusting the word of an aivur, Mekky told me that, among aivur, oath breakers are executed. So, perhaps. But I don't see what choice we have. Be ready to move. Everyone. On my signal, if it's necessary."

Each signaled that they'd heard.

For a little while, nothing happened. People stood, watching and waiting. The aivur had the patience of trees. Meanwhile, unable to bear it, Elen took a few steps up the embankment, thinking to go talk to the haunt for what time remained to them. Why not use it to its fullest?

Every aivur stiffened. Spears and swords flashed out.

"*Osge,*" they murmured.

She halted, trembling. Their hostility hit like a blow. Maybe she was unaccustomed to being noticed; that was the way of the atoner, to stay small, to stay ignored. Or maybe it was fear for herself, for Kem, for the other wardens. For the haunt. Her shivering intensified.

Gevulin said, "Best remain where you are, Deputy Courier."

Across the space between them, the haunt met her gaze with a gentle smile that tore at her heart. She put on a brave face. He was caught between the two parties. They had to let it play out.

Behind her, Kem said, "Deputy Courier, why don't you come down here and change into dry clothing? You'll get sick if you don't get warm."

Bless the lad. She went back down to the boats and dug out her change of clothing from her blessedly dry pack. Kem and Xilsi held up blankets to create a changing space. Peeling out of the icy-cold, wet garments proved difficult and time-consuming. After tugging on dry socks, she toweled off as quickly as possible, the bitterly cold air painful against her naked skin. With dry clothes on and her sleeping cloak thrown around her shoulders, she finally began to warm up. Kem bundled up her wet things to be dried out later and tossed them in the bottom of the boat.

By then, they heard the rumble of approaching wagon wheels. The council had arrived.

"My thanks," she said to Kem.

Xilsi said, "Best you stand here next to me. The aivur sure don't like you. Or I guess it's that they sense the viper. Does 'osge' mean the viper, or you, the vessel that houses it? Funny to think of the dreaded aivur scared of you."

"Why is it funny?"

"I meant no offense," Xilsi said hastily. "Ironic, I should say. Useful, possibly. Unexpected, definitely."

"You're not scared of me?"

Xilsi gave her a long look. "No. You are who you seem to be. It almost all makes sense now. I'm waiting for the last ribbon to be woven into the wreath. But I know I'm not going to get an answer until after this meeting. Oh! Here they come."

She rested a hand on her sword hilt as she stared up to the top of the embankment. Aivur came forward, setting up a semicircle of seven stools at the edge of the road. Six aivur seated themselves on the stools.

Two appeared quite aged, to go by their wrinkled faces and brittle movements. Two looked so remarkably human in appearance that Elen wondered if the Salt Spear Clan included human members, here represented. Of the other two, one was the lawgiver and the other a man of similar appearance: upright, stern, unmistakably aivur at the height of his strength and wearing the armor and arms of a soldier. His hair had the color of copper, not iron.

The haunt said, "Your Highness, you are requested to take the other council seat, as their honored guest. I will act as translator."

The prince surveyed the tableaux and beckoned to Fulmo to stand behind him, as his honor guard. He sat on the stool, upright, hands in fists propped on his thighs with his elbows akimbo, taking up extra space.

The haunt threw a look back at Elen, waggling his eyebrows as if to suggest she should admire his coming performance. He turned back to the seven seated individuals and began with a speech in the aivur language, after which he addressed Gevulin in the imperial language.

"In the capacity of the bequeather, I have introduced you, Your Highness, with all of your many, impressive titles, none of which I would care to neglect."

Gevulin acknowledged the statement with a serious nod. The haunt's rascally humor slid right off him.

"In return, I shall relate to you the stations of the council." One by one, he indicated each of the six seated aivur with a nod. First, the two elders: "Healer. Logistician." Then, the two human-looking ones: "Navigator. Caretaker." Finally, the iron-haired lawgiver and the copper-haired warleader. "By these stations, and in service to all the clan, do these six serve as council. If you will be so gracious as to be patient, Your Highness, first the council would hear the report I promised."

"What manner of report?"

"All that I saw and observed."

"Ah. Spying." Gevulin nodded in approval. "And then we can address their alliance with the Highmost?"

"That will be the second order of business, Your Highness. I do not have the power to alter their ritual. Nor do you, I might add, however much it may chafe you to sit and wait."

The prince cast him a hard glance, nettled by words that must have sounded like a taunt. But the haunt was correct, and perhaps Gevulin was finally learning patience. Or, at the very least, he was smart enough to know this was not yet the time to kick.

As Elen waited with the wardens down by the boat, she was glad for her dry clothes. The report went on for some time, the council members asking questions, the haunt answering. She watched the flashing momentum of his quicksilver expressions and listened to the warm lilt of his voice, so different from the bequeather's chilly exterior and cool tone. How she wished to have the chance to watch and listen to his golden voice for hours. For days. For months and years. For a lifetime. She was unable to restrain a sigh, all her heart and regret in it.

Kem squeezed her hand briefly, but he needed both hands to be free should they have to move fast.

At length, the lawgiver gave an open-handed signal.

The big gagast clapped his hands.

"Hei! Va!" cried the assembly.

The haunt caught Elen's gaze. Always, he looked first at her. Only then did he address the prince.

"Your Highness, I will translate. The lawgiver of the Salt Spear Clan acknowledges that the bequeather of the Salt Spear Clan wove an oath in my presence that, in exchange for my testimony of the history of the Shorn, as well as my report of current conditions in the Four Lands, all persons in your party will receive safe passage to Far Boundary Vigil."

"You made such a bargain before you rescued us?" Gevulin demanded. "In my name?"

"In *my* name," said the haunt with a dangerous flicker like fire in his eyes. "It is my knowledge the bequeather wished to gain, not your personage nor your alliance. As for the other, if it is safe passage back to the empire you object to, then you may strike your own bargain, should you wish." His mouth quivered, halfway between laughter and scorn.

The prince stiffened with anger, but he controlled himself. "Go on. Can we trust this bargain?"

The lawgiver shifted on her stool but said nothing. Could she understand? Yet, how? Only the bequeather was a translator, surely. What need would aivur from the northern islands have to speak the imperial language? How would they have learned it?

"As for trust," said the haunt, "the aivur do not break their oaths, lest they be cast from the hand of grace, which lifts all their souls out of the White Death."

"I see."

"Yes, I think you do. A squad will escort you safely across the Pall, with the help of Fulmo and this other gagast, whose name I did not quite catch."

"Safely across and thus into the hands of Lord Duenn's soldiers?"

"Ah, well, Your Highness, that is not up to me, for I will not be with you."

"You will not?"

"This body is only a temporary housing, a borrowed shell, as you well know. The bequeather has been called urgently north to a parlay with the Highmost."

"With Lord Thelan?"

Xilsi cursed under her breath. Ipis said, "Oh no! He's looking for us."

"That is the complication I spoke of earlier," said the haunt. "The Highmost knows you escaped on the river. He can't know whether you are alive or taken by the Pall, but he will surely ask the aivur whether they have seen you. As well, he has his own alliance with them to finalize, arrangements to be made before he returns to his northern seat of power."

Gevulin tapped a foot as he thought. He met the gaze of each councilor in turn, assuring himself that they were willing to meet his gaze. But what did such a gesture—the meeting of eyes—mean to the aivur? Was it deemed a mark of honesty? Pride? Rudeness? Impatience? She didn't know, and Gevulin didn't inquire. After all, in the empire, a prince of the Third Estate may impose his gaze upon all whose status is below his—which meant everyone except the crown prince and the emperor. If such a gesture contented him, then Elen did not really care. All she could think about was that the haunt was going to leave her again. That she needed the wardens to reach safety, so Kem could be safe. For herself, she still thrashed as if submerged in the river, unmoored, no ground beneath her feet even as the embankment pressed solid beneath her good boots.

"Fear not," said the haunt. "The clan dismantled the northern portion of the temporary bridge. They do not wish the lord to learn about the middle causeway, this haven in the midst of the Pall, any more than we do. For this reason, the clan council wishes to hurry things along so the lord can never suspect they are not crowded helplessly onto the stub of the road, and that he might easily pick them off as they emerge. They still wish him to believe that most of the clan hides in the hills, where it is harder for him to track them down. Therefore, the bequeather must go at once to meet with him, for her clan's sake."

He broke off, shrugging with a smile that tore at Elen's heart. "Thus, must I also go, so that she may travel north and do her duty."

Elen understood the responsibility of Captain Raven to her people: the bequeather was tasked to protect their clan. In its way, protection had also always been Elen's task in life. Who was she now, with Ao gone and Kem leaving? She was still a deputy courier. Therefore, she would guide the prince and his wardens back through the Pall, to the empire.

Gevulin studied the haunt. Then, to Elen's utter surprise, he turned his head to scrutinize her, where she stood below. An emotion she could not interpret briefly twisted through his face, after which he nodded to himself, having made a decision.

"I am satisfied. Tell them so, and let us part in amity, for should we meet again, we may prove to be of help to each other."

These words, the haunt translated. The councilors stood.

The lawgiver gestured. The gagast clapped. The aivur shouted, "Hei! Va!"

It was done.

The younger council members helped the elders toward the unseen wagons, the warleader following, although the lawgiver remained behind. Gevulin descended the embankment, Fulmo right behind him. Jirvy said something in a low voice to Fulmo, who answered with a hand sign. Ipis said, "I was worried about you, Fulmo," and the gagast tapped her lightly on the shoulder.

"Gather your gear," said the prince. "We're going immediately, before someone figures out there's a better deal to be made."

The haunt hadn't moved. For a horrible instant, Elen thought he had already departed, that it was Captain Raven who looked at her. Then he extended a hand. His sad smile made her wary. More than that, it fell into her heart like a stone. She'd always known, but some part of her had hoped, wished, believed their journey together could stretch on for a little longer. Just a little. Just one more kiss. But it was not to be.

She took a step up the embankment. The aivur all took several steps back, even though she did not come near them. The haunt grasped her hand. His touch was firm but not tight or confining. The bequeather's skin, with its callused fingers and smooth palm, was not his, yet she would remember its heat and gentleness, which was his alone.

"We part here, dear one."

"You will return into the Pall?"

He said, even more softly, "What will you do, El?"

Powerful dragon he may once have been, but in that moment, he was simply a sorrowing person who wanted to know if someone he loved would be all right, because he had to leave. What she told him now was what he would live with forever after, or for as long as his soul subsisted in the Pall.

She put on her bravest face. "I'll see what my service with the prince brings me. He's interested in the map, and I'm curious about it, too, after what we saw in the deep earth. I'll work to convince him it's to his benefit to allow me to take the training to become a surveyor. If it's Pall and Spore that's been killing surveyors in the Desolation, then I have a good chance of surviving an exploration into that wilderness. Maybe I can find the trail of the lost surveyor I was told of, Rotho, the one who marked his maps with a lightning-bolt symbol. Maybe I can see if there is any trace of underground rivers. There's a lot yet to discover in this world. More than I ever knew to dream of as a child, that's certain."

"That will be just like you," he said. "Always finding a way."

It was hard to find words, but words were all she had. Hoarsely, she said, "I'll look for you in every Pall."

"I will search every nook and cranny, every inlet and sound."

Shorn of speech at last, Elen nodded to give him permission to let go, and they released each other's hand.

He blinked several times. Finally, getting a hold of himself, he nodded at each warden in turn, at Fulmo, and gave the prince a glance like a flash of fire. But he was going, and the prince's actions were out of his hands and out of his power. Sara'ala, too, had taken on a responsibility to protect, to become a guardian. His choices had led him to this time and this place and this leave-taking.

He picked his way to the outer wall of the embankment, not the part that ran down into the river water but rather the foundation built along the land, the one bordered by the Pall. No one, aivur or human, stirred. No one spoke. The river's complex blend of voices, high and deep, steady and erratic, was his only accompaniment.

He reached the base of the embankment and knelt at the edge of the Pall. One last time he looked at her, then pressed his hands into the mist. The darkness drained from his eyes. The bequeather's body collapsed.

Elen sucked in a sharp breath, staggered by it, but she did not cry, not this time. Not even when Xilsi put a hand on her shoulder, when Jirvy patted her arm.

The fog boiled, becoming a slender shadow that circled once and then twice. There was a flash as of wings, a crest of antlers, a spray of sparks. The presence coiled away, lost to the White Sea. Kem hugged her, holding her close as her legs trembled. She'd walked too far and could stand no longer. Yet still, she stood.

A pair of aivur soldiers pulled the bequeather's lax body back from the Pall. One breath. Five. Ten.

The bequeather stirred. A tremor ran right through her body. She rolled up to sit, shaking her head as if to clear it of cobwebs. With a grunt of effort, she got to her feet. When she looked around, she was clearly surprised to find herself at the river's edge, at the bridge, in the Pall, with an audience of curious aivur who looked delighted by the drama they'd watched unfold, laughing and chatting among themselves now that the matter was decided, the haunt was gone, and the osge standing as far as possible from them. It seemed the veil had worked, that she recalled nothing.

The iron-haired lawgiver spoke in a commanding tone. All the aivur stopped murmuring at once.

The bequeather tapped a fist to her chest in acknowledgment of whatever the lawgiver had said, and climbed the embankment. Already the crowd was dispersing. The show was over.

Reaching the top, the bequeather paused. Her gaze caught on Elen with a flash of revulsed curiosity, as if wondering what exactly it was the haunt had done and why he had bothered. She pressed the back of a hand to her mouth and rubbed, then spat.

Yet a different expression sharpened her brilliant face when she looked at Xilsi, who stiffened with a slight gasp. One nod the bequeather offered to Xilsi and the barest quirk of the lips that might almost have been the prelude to an actual smile. But that was all.

"Let it be known," proclaimed the bequeather in her cold, chilly voice, "that we of the Salt Spear Clan will undertake as our responsibility to search out and protect the ancient network of the Shorn. This bargain I made with Sara'ala, on behalf of our clan, our ancestors, and our descendants. I place it as an oath upon myself, our council, and our clan, forevermore."

She walked out of sight down the road, followed by the clatter of horses riding away.

Made reckless by sorrow, Elen turned to the prince. "Your Exalted Highness, what did you say at Three Spires that allowed him to work the passage spell on you?"

She thought the prince wouldn't answer. Simo would have called it an impertinent question.

Gevulin examined the Pall into which the haunt had departed, an odd expression fixed on his face. Was he amused at himself? At the situation? At the outcome?

Yet he did answer. "I said, 'I give you leave to try.'"

Elen laughed.

"Enough!" he barked, that glimpse into the secret heart of Gevulin shut back behind his usual arrogant expression. "We must hasten. I can't let the other princes get more of a jump on me than they already have."

39

ONE LAST RIVER OF PALL

So they headed out, weary and battered, toward the turtle-back rock. Once they reached it there would be only one last river of Pall between them and the empire. Far Boundary Vigil was, for Prince Gevulin, both the end of the secret scheming road he had been walking and the beginning of his path to open rebellion. He would win, or he would lose, but he had to move now because he had nowhere to retreat. If he didn't gain the throne, he would be dead.

Elen kept quiet on the last long day of the journey along the witch road through the Pall. She had little enough to do besides ride in the back of a wagon and eat when food was on offer, and she had even less to say. The others slept, exhausted by the journey and, most of all, by Simo's death. Even the prince was subdued, speaking little and demanding nothing. He had torn the expensive, undyed silk of a palace-woven undertunic into strips and tied the ragged ribbons into his fly-whisk braids. He'd offered ribbons from this exalted silk to the other members of the party. This outward sign of mourning surprised her most: that Gevulin could care about anyone or anything beyond his ambition. Maybe he just cared about doing things the proper way. Maybe it amounted to the same thing, to him.

She couldn't settle her mind enough to sleep, she who had long ago learned to sleep anywhere, any time. Thoughts churning in restless circles, she watched the Pall as the wagon rolled along the road.

Was that a shadow running in parallel to them through the fog? Were those spikes of mist antlers? Was that fluttering shadow the pulse of wings? Did a spray of sparks off in the distance mark his trail? An attempt to signal to her? Would she ever know? Would they ever meet again?

It would be easier to walk into the Pall. *Join us, become one of us, let go of your pain.*

But that was the Pall speaking into her heart. She knew better than to push away the heaviness. Let the sorrow dwell within her. Let it take root and become part of who she would grow into from this day forward: the bitter grief of knowing how briefly any one person walks in the world, how fleeting the touch of hands, yes.

Yet also the sweetness, enfolded in her memory, of how every spring, for a single hour, she would break her courier's route in a particular meadow high in the Moonrise Hills. Here, a lush carpet of wildflowers painted the hillside with glorious colors and vibrant life. She never passed it by, never failed to take a rest there amid the blooming splendor. In another month, the flowers would be gone and she would pass ordinary greens and yellows and browns for the rest of the year. But walking through the meadow in the other months would make her smile as she remembered what she had been blessed to experience. Her life with Ao, hand in hand. The beautiful child they'd raised together. The haunt, so fleetingly. One dead. One moving into his own life. One out of her reach. But they were her wildflowers, still and always.

At last, they approached the turtle-back rock. Since they had last crossed here, the aivur had rigged a temporary rope bridge from the broken end of the middle causeway and across to the turtle-back rock. The wardens reached the rock islet to discover an armed contingent of aivur waiting by the edge of the Pall, on the rock's north side and thus out of view of the tower.

Elen tugged on Xilsi's sleeve and drew her aside to whisper, "Does it strike you as odd the clan has created a sentry post here?"

"It's what I'd do," said Xilsi. "They can't hope to invade, but they could carry out any number of raid-and-runs before the empire can mount an effective response. This is a perfect raiders' base. So, yes, it's troubling. But on the other hand, we're alive because the clan chose to honor an oath. Which makes a person wonder, what's in it for them?" She gave Elen a sharp look. "As far as I can tell, they did this all because that . . . being who walked in the bequeather's body was a Shorn. Who are these Shorn, Elen?"

"Captain!" the prince called, then again when Xilsi did not react. "Captain Xilsilin! Attend me."

"Fuck, I keep trying to forget," muttered Xilsi. She waggled a hand at Elen, so Elen tagged along.

The prince stood at the top of the turtle-back rock, behind a ragged outcropping. A gap between the rocks allowed him to observe the Vigil tower as from behind a screen. He had his spyglass out and Fulmo beside him. The iron-haired lawgiver stood on his other side. She was accompanied by the other gagast and by a young man who gave first Xilsi, and then Elen, a cheeky smile and a wink. What a flirt! He looked as human as she did, though with an even darker complexion than her own, more like Jirvy's, and raven-black hair braided into a single plait.

The youth's long braid brought a memory crashing in: that last glimpse of Simo as his braid was sucked under the surface. The thought struck with more pain than she expected. She hadn't been close to the captain, but it was still a wound. They'd been comrades on a tough journey. That counted for something. He'd accepted Kem as a warden and given him the early guidance the boy needed. For that alone, she would mourn his passing.

The lawgiver gave each warden a nod to acknowledge their presence, something Elen would not have expected from a clan's leader; not in the empire, certainly, where a mere deputy courier would have stood invisible in the background. But what startled her most was when the lawgiver began to speak in Imperial.

"Your gagast can carry you and your people across easily enough, Prince Gevulin. Thus, the Salt Spear Clan has discharged any last obligation to you, as agreed between the bequeather and the Shorn."

Xilsi mouthed "the Shorn" and gave Elen a challenging look through narrowed eyes.

The prince said, "My enemies have placed a garrison in the tower. I don't know their numbers, but I have left to me four wardens, the honored Fulmo, and a deputy courier. Even with all their skills and my own taken together, and even if your aivur carry us over so we can attack in secret, at night, it is unlikely I can defeat an entire garrison."

"Are you offering me a deal?"

"How do you come to speak Imperial so well, Lawgiver?"

The lawgiver hadn't the bequeather's chilly reserve. She was a formidable person in both stature and presence, but there was a glint in her eyes that suggested she had a sense of humor and, maybe, a bit of a flirtatious streak, like that of the young man standing in her shadow.

"Why, because I was young once, too, Prince. Like my grandson here. He hopes to travel into the empire and learn your language and your ways so he may become a bequeather in time. I am able to speak to you because I was, in my more energetic time of life, such a one."

The prince gave the youth a startled look. The young man winked in answer, causing the prince to redden, although it was impossible to know if it was anger or attraction that caused the rush of blood to his fine, handsome face. "I thought he was human."

"Many of our youth appear so human that they can walk freely among your kind without your knowledge. We grow more into our metal spirit and our soul guardian as we age. So, you see, that is one of the reasons your Magnolia Emperor banished us from her empire."

"She doesn't trust your kind," he said.

"And you do?"

"I trust you can help me take the throne."

"Why should we?"

"I will rescind the banishment. Your people will be allowed to settle in the empire."

"Why would we want to do that when we have just made an agreement with the Highmost to settle in the south county of the Four Lands?"

"You and I both know he would murder you all in your beds if he had the opportunity. He made the pact with you solely to undercut Lady Eleawona. A treaty you may have with him, but it is like inviting a hungry predator into your house. Eventually, he will turn on you and kill or enslave you."

"It's true he has no love for my people. It was Lady Eleawona who approached us at first, and who had the courtesy to listen to us and get to know us. He merely followed in the path she'd laid down. What are your terms? If we wished to settle in the empire, would that offer be open only to my clan, or to all aivur?"

"Your clan, in return for your alliance. Other clans, once they can show title to the holdings that were stripped from them."

"Stripped from them?"

"The Magnolia Emperor does not trust the aivur for many and various reasons, too tedious to list, for they are all trivial enough. She's fussy, and not in a good way. But it is also common knowledge within the Flower Court that she inherited an empty treasury from our esteemed father, the Lily Emperor, now departed. She found it expeditious to fill her treasury from the impounded estates and vaults of the banished households and clans."

"You objected to this act?"

"I was six years old at the time so, no, I did not. I only survived the initial purge due to the eloquence, intelligence, and astute maneuvering of my blessed mother, to whom I owe my life."

The lawgiver cocked her head to one side, rather like a bird. "It's an attractive thought, that we, who have struggled to find a place in which to live in the peace we desire, may be offered settlement in a rich country. But one element of your plan eludes me. If you cannot even defeat a modest garrison, then how are you to overthrow a powerful emperor when you have no army?"

"I have a better weapon than an army to dispose of the emperor."

"Ah, the osge." The lawgiver glanced toward Elen.

The prince went on. "The palace does not yet have proof of my intentions, only suspicions. That's exactly why this entire charade was played out, to gain proof, which she still lacks. I need only travel swiftly enough to reach the palace before the theurgist, Luviara, arrives. This is easily done, since it will take months for her to travel from the Four Lands by sea and then overland, if Thelan even allows her to depart. Therefore, once the emperor and the crown prince are dead, neither event will be traceable to me. With Astaylin away, I will be the only prince of the Third Estate in residence at the palace. In such a time of crisis, I will take the imperial throne. Once I am seated there, in all my majesty, people will prefer to accept order rather than an outbreak of fighting."

"Prince Astaylin may not so easily submit, Your Highness," remarked Xilsi.

He shot a haughty look at her. "I will make her a good offer."

"What's that?"

"Maybe you."

She tensed, taken aback by this ambush.

His smile bloomed as a flag of triumph. "Indeed. Your cooperation with my plans assures you will remain in the wardens."

Since Elen could not envision Xilsi as a consort wafting about the Flower Court—if consorts indeed wafted as they were depicted doing in all the plays—it seemed like effective blackmail on the prince's part. Maybe part of being a prince was knowing how to manipulate those required to serve you. Like her and Kem.

Gevulin turned back to the aivur. "Lawgiver, do we have an agreement? Your soldiers will eliminate the garrison. Once I am safely across, I will make contact with Pelis Manor. Lord Genia will arrange a swift escort for me back to Orledder Halt, where I will take possession of my carriages and menials and return to the heartland. I will act immediately once I arrive at the palace. As soon as I am settled as emperor, I will rescind the decree of banishment. Your people may move into the uninhabited lands of Woodfall Province and farther west, along the Storm Coast. As soon as travel permits are arranged, you will install, in the palace, a garrison of your best soldiers."

"To protect you."

"To remind the palace officials and the Flower Court that I am not to be trifled with. That will give me the leverage needed to crush any opposition and unify the empire, so we may become tranquil and prosperous in truth." He touched the leather map tube, which he kept close. "There is a great deal we do not know and may yet discover, as long as we do not fear the answers to be uncovered, as the Magnolia Emperor does. In a way, Theurgist Luviara did me a favor when she betrayed me."

All this time, Jirvy, Ipis, and Kim had stood to one side, listening and prudently silent, while Xilsi fumed.

To Elen's surprise, Jirvy stirred at the prince's comment. "How may it be said she did you a favor, Your Highness?"

"I would have remained cautious, biding my time. But ambition cannot be cautious, lest it wither and die like an unwatered plant. I do not intend to wither or to die. Lawgiver?"

The aivur extended a hand. The prince stared at it with puzzlement.

"Among the aivur, we clasp hand to wrist as a seal of our agreement. Skin to skin. To break such a pledge is the greatest dishonor."

The prince was clearly reluctant to touch a person not of his exalted rank, and not one of his menials chosen to serve his bodily needs, as lesser to greater. For an imperial prince to engage in such a gesture of equality was unfathomable. Yet here he stood, facing the outstretched arm.

Xilsi snorted under her breath, amused at seeing him discomposed, but she remained on edge. As did Elen. As did the others—Jirvy mostly, while Ipis and Kem looked confused and wary. They kept glancing at the assembled company of aivur soldiers waiting in readiness in the lee of the huge rock, out of sight of the Vigil tower.

The lawgiver stood with the patience of a predator who knows how to stalk and wait—until the moment comes for a swift strike.

Gevulin pulled off his glove and extended his arm. They grasped hand to wrist, skin to skin. The alliance was made.

40

A Song for the Wineshops

Xilsi sucked in a breath, hissing with displeasure. But Gevulin was the all-seeing eye, her commander, as well as a prince. In the empire, the lesser obeyed the higher; the soldier, his captain, the deputy courier, her intendant. Where a person stood on that ladder was made clear to all.

"Not long to nightfall," said the prince.

"Yes," agreed the lawgiver. "I will send scouts at midnight. We'll strike in the belly-soft hour midway between midnight and dawn."

When most would be asleep. The garrison wasn't expecting an attack from the direction of the Pall because it was impossible. Or so they believed.

The prince said, "You can drag the bodies into the Pall and no one will be the wiser. The garrison will simply have disappeared."

The garrison was doubtless made up of Duenn Manor soldiers. Elen had no reason to love them, but she didn't hate them either.

She said, "Your Exalted Highness, surely no conflict is necessary. There are so few of us. Surely the two gagast can convey we six farther along the shore, and deposit us beyond the view of the tower. We can head south to Pelis Manor with no one the wiser that we've returned."

He scoffed. "Duenn Manor has insulted me and colluded with my enemies. Therefore, they are my enemy. This battle has been going on for longer than you can know and in ways you can know nothing about. Do not trouble me with these pointless apologetics again. Now, Lawgiver, I agree with the late-night strike. Think of it as a trial run."

"Yes. Our clan's fighters can test the mettle of imperial troops and fade back into the Pall, with no one the wiser. A good plan."

"Except for those of your soldiers who die," said Elen.

Xilsi grabbed her arm. "Just hush, you. This is not the time."

The lawgiver appeared not to hear Elen. Now that she and the prince had made their alliance, her attention was all for him. Her demeanor had an odd warmth, like a fire lit at the edge of an icy waste. "Prince Gevulin, let no poison twist your ears. If we do not sharpen our steel, then it will remain blunted and ineffectual."

"I understand. I will accompany you."

"That isn't necessary."

"My honor demands it."

"Ah, of course. Then so shall it be. I will fight beside you, as befits your status among your people. Now, we make ready."

She descended to speak to her soldiers as another cohort of aivur approached over the rope bridge.

The young flirt brought around a platter stacked with a cracker-like bread baked of rye flour and topped with sardines. Sara'ala would have adored the tiny, oily fish, so crunchy. The viper stirred as Elen ate, although she wasn't sure if it liked the flavor of the sardines or if it was growing restless because she had not let it out to slither into the Pall.

Not yet. Be patient.

The sun sank below the horizon. Kem and Ipis rolled up in their cloaks for a nap out of the wind. They would remain behind until the battle was over. Elen was too restless to sleep. At midnight, five scouts waded into the Pall like wraiths, headed for the tower marked by the ever-burning lamp on its top floor.

The prince readied his weapons alongside Jirvy. Xilsi knelt on the hard rock to check her sword and knife, to string her bow, to count her remaining arrows, and to uncap the sharp end of her walking staff. The warden worked methodically, in no hurry, since it would be a while before they left.

Looking up at Elen, she remarked, "Keeps my mind off what's coming later."

Elen crouched beside her. "Is he really going to fight? The prince, I mean. He won't just let the aivur do it?"

"It would be dishonorable if he did not fight. Especially since he is using foreign troops to attack our own soldiers."

"Do you approve of his intention to overthrow the Magnolia Emperor?"

Xilsi gave her a weary look. "My approval isn't needed or requested. I swore an oath to serve the wardens. I obey the will of the all-seeing eye. For now, he is my commander."

"What he's doing is treason."

"Yes, I am aware. You do know that his father, the Lily Emperor, became emperor by overthrowing his own uncle, don't you?"

"He did?"

"Yes. When the Hibiscus Emperor died, it was his youngest

brother who stepped up and named himself the Ailanthus Emperor. His reign lasted two years before his nephew—they were the same age—got tired of waiting for the throne. I guess they don't talk about it outside the Flower Court." With no change of tone, she went on the attack. "What is a *shorn*? Might it be a thing, a person, a spirit, a magic? A voice who says outrageous things through the mouths of people who would never speak those words, who laughs when he ought to glower, and who developed a bizarre habit of staring longingly at a humble deputy courier when he thought—or she thought—no one was looking. Just in case you're wondering if anyone noticed these oddities, and if I would even realize that the strange behavior of the prince earlier in our journey was a peculiar match to the strange behavior of the bequeather on this last, recent stretch."

"You have to ask the prince."

"Sure, and I did, and he refused to answer."

Here it was. Either she trusted Xilsi, or she didn't. And she'd already trusted her with the viper.

Elen said, "Let me ask first, what worries you most? Do you think His Exalted Highness will make a worse or a better emperor than the Magnolia Emperor?"

"He's more orderly, that's for sure, and less prone to favoritism because he has no friends."

"No friends?"

"He only trusts himself. And, to be fair, his mother. He's famously devoted to his mother."

"I suppose if an emperor is meant to rule impartially, then a man who has no friends might prove the most impartial of all."

Xilsi snorted. "He might, truly. But here's what you don't understand. If he succeeds, then fine. But if he dies, we will all die with him because we are accompanying him, whatever our own thoughts on his decision. My family might be able to extricate me, but Jirvy, Ipis, and Kem will be burned."

The thought struck Elen cold, and then hot. The viper stirred. "But they are obliged to follow him."

"Yes. And as their captain, I'll do my best to argue for them, but it won't matter. It's how things are. Luviara was right to try to extricate us four ordinary wardens back in the Four Lands, I'll give her that."

"Do you approve of what she did?"

"Eh, she was probably covering her own ass. Or she has her own ambitions, something we don't know about."

"Don't you have ambitions?"

"Yes! I have the ambition to live a quiet life of adventure, patrolling the imperial roads and indulging in friendly drinking bouts with the other wardens and maybe a few surveyors, they're not so bad. But let me tell you a story. My grandmother . . . I told you about her."

"The last and most beloved consort of the Hibiscus Emperor."

"That's right. She gave birth to five children by His Majestic and Most Beloved Highness, the Hibiscus Emperor. Only one survived to adulthood. The rest met with 'accidents,' as they call them. Food poisoning. Falling from a height. Drowned in a palace pond. Savaged by a boar on a hunt after an unexpected tumble from horseback."

Elen grimaced. The cold air seemed to freeze around them. "That's terrible."

"That's the palace. My mother survived because my grandmother found a much older scion of a cousin in the Bakas lineage willing to take a sixteen-year-old prince as his second wife. He was a widower twice over by then. He was more than fifty years older than my mother."

"Oh."

"Don't make that face."

"What face? That's an unusually wide age difference."

"My mother was fortunate to get out. He was the only one brave enough to defy the palace. He was old enough that death wasn't a threat he cared about. She bore five children in quick succession to cement her right to stay in Bakas Manor and not be hauled back to the Flower Court, as they might have done had he died and left her childless. Those five children are all princes of the Sixth Estate, which means they were born outside the Flower Court to a prince born in the Flower Court."

"Does that mean *you* are a prince of the Sixth Estate?"

"Yes, that's what it means."

"I don't know what to say," Elen said with a startled laugh.

"Anything but 'Your Highness' is fine." Xilsi sheathed her knife and sword, the blades hissing with a metal *shing* as they drove home into the scabbards. "My mother died when I was six years old. I don't really remember her, just my very old father standing beside the genius of Bakas Manor, shouting at a palace official that the official could go burn in his own pus-filled guts if he didn't get out of his hall. Then he went on to say that he, as a father, would deserve being used as the High Heavens' latrine if he allowed the emperor to haul his children off to the fucking Flower Court. Thanks to him, we were all raised in Bakas Manor, like good Bakassars are meant to be."

"So, you're saying you got your mouth from your father?"

Xilsi chuckled. "Maybe so. He wasn't scared of anything. He taught me my letters and how to tie knots. When he died—I was nine—my grandmother pulled one thread here and another thread there and got herself untangled from the Flower Court by claiming the High Heavens had called upon her to raise her orphaned grandchildren, those poor wee sprouts now bereft of living parents. That's why she took us out of the heartland to Arlewind Cross. She wanted us to grow up as far away from the palace as possible. She told me that even being the favored consort was never worth it, not for her. She said we must never involve ourselves in the palace in any way. That Bakas Manor could protect us only as long as we stayed outside the inner palace. Hold on."

Xilsi got to her feet. She walked over to the prince, exchanged a few words, and returned to Elen.

"No movement yet. How I hate waiting," she said. "Ask me another question, or tell me about the Shorn."

"What about your siblings? What happened to them?"

"They have lives as sage officials in the provinces. There are plenty of other Bakassars who serve as high officials inside the palace, so we didn't need to. But I wanted adventure, or at least, adventure without the glory of a generalship. Winning acclaim at war can also get you murdered, and I don't mean in battle."

Elen thought of the intendant's daughter's husband, who had died under mysterious circumstances in the east, fighting the Blood Wolves, and nodded.

Xilsi went on. "The wardens gave me the means to travel while keeping my head down and going unnoticed."

"I hate to tell you this, but you're pretty noticeable. As all the songs from the wineshops should have let you know by now."

"I did my best to keep my head down! But, in the end, the palace came for me."

Elen rested a companionable hand on Xilsi's shoulder.

The warden looked at her in surprise. "My thanks. I don't understand you, El, but I trust you."

Elen smiled. "That last question was just the roundabout way for me to tell you about the Shorn."

"Finally!"

"Ha! Well, as far as I know, very long ago, there was a devastating war in which some manner of alliance defeated wicked sorcerer-kings. The victors feared that the sorcerers would rise again. So, guardians were set in place to keep watch, like sentinels. These guardians were shorn from their physical bodies and each placed in a magical shell, like a statue."

"Like the statues at Three Spires, near Orledder Halt, where we stopped that first night because Gevulin wanted to go inside the wall."

"Yes. By means of a passage spell, on one of the nights of the fullest moon, the Shorn can transfer their essence, their soul, their consciousness, their breath—whatever you want to call it—into the body of a willing host for a temporary period of days."

"I'll be fucked," said Xilsi. "But Gevulin would never have agreed . . . Oh. Hold on. We thought he was just talking to himself."

"'I give you leave to try,' is what His Highness says he said."

Xilsi laughed. "That would be exactly like Gevulin."

Elen nodded. "More of a dare, double-dare situation, if you take my meaning, and have ever been young and stupid enough to jump out of the hayloft and break your arm."

"For some reason I have a hard time imagining you doing that."

"That's because it wasn't me," said Elen with a glance at Kem. He and Ipis were still huddled on the ground, cloaks wrapped tight for warmth. They weren't quite fully asleep, nodding off and then jerking up awake, too nervous to sleep and too exhausted to wake.

Xilsi grinned. "I didn't break my arm, but yes, young and stupid on a dare is how Mekky and I got to be friends, our first month in novice training. So the Spires. The statues. The way His Highness fainted. And everything afterward wasn't him. It was one of these Shorn guardians?"

"That's right. All the way up until we reached Far Boundary Vigil on our way north."

Xilsi grabbed Elen's wrist. "Oh, El. That's why he collapsed again. Why you sat there in shock. You hopeless fool. You fell in love with something that doesn't even exist, didn't you?"

Elen smiled wryly. "I fell in love with a person who sacrificed his physical life in order to guard an unknown future against the return of sorcery."

Xilsi put an arm around her. "Talk about a song for the wine-shops."

Elen gave a little laugh, leaning her head against the other woman's shoulder. Not since Ao's death had she shared a connection so profoundly based on trust and affection. Sisterly. Friends. Nothing more complicated. Yet what was more complicated and profound than friendship?

Abruptly, Xilsi stiffened. "I hope this doesn't mean sorcery has returned, somehow."

"Not as far as he could tell. The Pall seems to be the ashes of sorcery."

A whistle from the prince caused Xilsi to release Elen. "Time to go."

"Will you be fighting, too?" Elen asked nervously.

"A captain always accompanies the all-seeing eye."

"Should I come?"

"Can you fight? I mean, truly fight?"

"I trained in Duenn Manor's militia for a few years."

"Have you actually fought?"

"No. The rope bridge was the first time I've ever been in a real skirmish, with dead people and everything. I didn't like it." She grimaced.

"No one likes it. Well, no one you ever want to meet likes it, but you hope the ones who like it are on your side when the battle breaks out. You should stay with Kem and Ipis."

"Captain!" The prince strode up. "There's been a change of plans. There seem to be tides in these currents. The Pall is currently too high for the aivur to be able to carry us across. We must wait to cross until dawn, when we can be carried by the gagast. The aivur will attack without us."

Xilsi tapped a hand to her heart. "As you wish, Your Highness."

He frowned. "It is not my wish. It is a necessity. I would never choose to skirt the dangers of battle."

"Indeed, Your Highness, no one has ever accused you of being a coward."

He gave Xilsi an imperious look, as if wondering if she was tweaking his nose, but she gave him a respectful nod. He inclined his chin, just so slightly, and it was a marvel to see him respond in kind. Elen hadn't known he had it in him. But now that she thought about it, since Simo's death something subtle had altered in his demeanor, and she couldn't quite figure it out.

41

The Gift of Belonging

They ascended to the outcropping and stood, watching and listening. A company of about sixty aivur waded into the Pall and vanished in the darkness.

The prince said, "Better to have them on our side, now they know how to reach us where we are vulnerable."

"What if they're just using you?" Xilsi asked.

"Of course they are just using me. As I'm using them. It's a mutual arrangement that, for now, benefits us both. The empire balances on a perilous edge. The war in the east goes poorly. Although we haven't lost, we also haven't won. The Blood Wolves are a fearsome enemy, and they count many aivur among their hordes. Should the Sea Wolves find common ground with their Blood and Forest brethren, where does that put the empire? That's what the emperor doesn't see. All she sees are people she doesn't trust only because they are shaped somewhat differently from us."

"Infused with spirits of metal and the souls of animals, as well as their own High Heavens–granted souls," said Xilsi, "if what the lawgiver said is true."

"If we understood what she meant, which we may not. But the aivur are also flesh and blood and bone. They can die, just as we can. The empire's best path forward is to secure as many allies as possible. To make treaties and truces where we can. The Salt Spear Clan lost its place in their homeland, so they need a home. It's a good bargain for them and for me, and thus for the empire. But enough. Listen."

Listen they did, peering across the mist toward the holystone tower and its steady light. A wind danced across the turtle-back rock, cold and heavy. Clouds covered most of the sky. No sound of battle erupted across the distance. Not yet.

Elen studied the Pall for signs of movement. Sparks winked in the distance, then closer, then off in another direction, no rhyme or reason to it. The cloud cover parted to reveal stars. The moon appeared, casting odd shadows over the gently seething Pall.

Was he there? How did magic peel a body away from its soul? For

Elen had always thought of herself as one thing entire, woven together, inextricable. What got left behind when a person was shorn from their body? There were also people like Kem, who couldn't live restfully in the body they were born in until they came to understand who they really were.

Who was she? Had she been different before the viper hatched? She did not think so. She touched the scar burned into the side of her neck. The egg had rested inside her already. Someone had left a warning on her skin, but they hadn't killed her outright. Nor had that person told her, or if they had, she had been too young to understand.

In life, maybe the best a person could do was discover who they were at their deepest core, the place they were most true to themselves, whatever else might come to them in the course of their years. That was why she felt so unmoored. Ao dead and Kem leaving. Who was she now? She had to live not to protect them but to uncover her own being, the unhatched egg of her that she'd never allowed to crack open because she had spent all her energy and all her love on them.

"Is anything happening?" Xilsi whispered. "It's been so long."

As if on a stage cue, a shout of warning rang out across the distance. A flurry of clashing steel. A scattershot of drumming, like hail. Silence.

The prince shifted from foot to foot. "I hate this."

"Yet when you become emperor, Your Highness," said Xilsi, "to stand behind the lines and watch will be your fate. Not to excel at the front of the crowd, as you have striven all your life to do."

"I had no choice but to excel, so no one could say I had not earned my way."

"I am merely remarking, Your Highness, that you are said to be a man who cannot bear to come in second in any race, and that you will train to exhaustion in order to win."

"Thus did my blessed mother teach me, that it didn't matter if people liked me, only that they respected what I had accomplished."

"Can you bear, then, to stand behind the lines and watch? Because if you can't, then you will not last long as emperor. You will chew yourself to pieces."

He scoffed with a light, sarcastic laugh. "The arrow is already loosed, Captain."

"Is it? As you said yourself, no one knows. I can return with the other wardens to Warden Hall and tell them you were lost in the north. When Luviara returns, if she does, I will inform her that Lord

Thelan released us and kept you, or that you met some other grim fate. You can shave off your beautiful hair, grow a beard, and take a new name. You handled the rowboat well, Your Highness. Trade ships are always looking for hands on the southern sea, if that's to your liking. Or you might become a carriage driver. The empire is large. There are many backwaters off the imperial roads. You can make a new life."

He regarded Xilsi for a long while, seeming more thoughtful than angry. At last, he said, "Are you giving me an exit, Captain?"

"I am."

"This is unexpected, I confess." He gave Xilsi an odd look.

That was the change, Elen thought. Gevulin had learned to listen harder to what lay between the words people were saying.

Xilsi smiled wryly. "Your Highness, I don't like you, nor do you need me to like you. I respect your skills and that you don't play favorites. I'm not interested in the palace, or I would be living in the Flower Court now. You have served fairly as all-seeing eye. Simo respected you. For all that, I make this oath, that I will look the other way if you choose to walk away now. Because once we reach Pelis Manor North and Lord Genia, there is no going back."

"There was never any going back. I will never dishonor my blessed mother. I will become emperor. I will teach myself to stand behind the lines and watch others act where I no longer can."

Xilsi shrugged and glanced, with an eyebrow lift, at Elen, as if to say *I tried*. Elen gave her a nod, as friends did. She'd have been shocked had the prince entertained the suggestion for even one breath, even though it was a plausible solution.

The sky lightened in the east. The two gagast stirred, trembling first, then blinking, then tilting their heads down and looking creakily around as the night stupor wore off.

All at once, from the Vigil, a great shout split the quiet. "Hei! Va!"

The prince nodded, acknowledging the victory. His first step toward taking the throne.

"Fulmo, we cross now."

"I pray you, Your Highness," said Xilsi, "let Warden Jirvy and myself go first to clear the way."

A faint smile played about his lips. For a heartbeat, Elen thought she caught a glimpse of the haunt in his sardonic expression, but the prince's expression was fully human, that of a man who had, for perhaps the first time in his life, learned how to laugh at himself.

"I'm not emperor yet, Captain. The deputy courier and I will go first. You'll follow with Jirvy. Ipis and Kem, last."

Elen said, "I can walk across on my own, Your Highness. Then you might take over another on the first wave."

He glanced over at Kem, who was awake and sharing a platter of sardine crackers with Ipis. "Yes, I suppose you won't make a dash for it."

Xilsi followed his gaze, then glanced at Elen, puzzled because she had not quite yet figured out the relationship between Kem and Elen. Would it matter if she did? Kem was Duenn Manor on his sire's side, and apparently he was seed of an old Four Lands royal line on his mother's side, even if bastard born, because in the empire there was a princely estate for that, too, where every person was accounted for and acknowledged. By imperial measure, Kem was more than eligible to be a warden, however he had been conceived and raised.

"I beg leave for a moment's solitude, Your Highness," Elen said quickly, "because I need to pee."

As she clambered down to a slightly concealed hollow, she gestured to Kem, who made his excuses and followed her down.

She did her business squatting, cheeks to the wind, and buttoned up her trousers afterward as she stood. "Kem, I can only say this once. When we get across, we will have a chance to run."

He tied up his trousers. "He's going to have you kill the emperor with the viper, isn't he?"

"You're in danger as long as you're with him. You'll be executed."

"If he loses, Ipis says we can claim sanctuary at Warden Hall. Say we were under orders."

"Xilsi doesn't think that will work."

"Xilsi doesn't know everything she thinks she does, does she? She kept sleeping with Jirvy for five years after he'd gotten married."

Elen blinked. "That's a long time."

"Like I said, she doesn't know everything. I like being a warden. I want to train. It's you I'm worried about."

"Me?"

"They'll burn you."

"Only if they figure it out. Why would they? No one knows except you, the intendant, and the prince. And Xilsi."

"And the entire aivur clan! Not to mention Lord Thelan. Ipis has it half figured out, and I wouldn't take any bets about Jirvy. He's really observant, and he keeps his mouth shut." He rolled his eyes.

"Speaking of which, why did you tell Xilsi? She's got charm, I'll give her that. Bad idea, though."

"I trust her."

He shrugged. "She's a snob. But I get it. I catch you looking for Mama still, sometimes, when you forget."

She rested a hand on his arm and, for once, had no answer.

"Anyway," he went on, oblivious to the thick grief caught in her throat, "I'll run if *you* have to. But I don't want to run all my life. I like having a place to belong, with the wardens. I'm willing to take the risk."

There it was. She and Ao had given Kem the gift of belonging, yet that gift had an edge: He could not turn his back as easily as they had. They'd had nothing to lose and no expectations for how their lives could be, but he did. He and Joef had been reckless in the way youth are reckless children who know they are loved and safe, taking the right kind of chances, not the terrible ones. He couldn't see the possibility of death, only a chance for a life he wanted.

She tightened her hand on his, wishing all her affection to pour into him. "I love you. And your mother loved you."

He wiped an eye, squeezing her hand in response.

"Deputy courier!" The prince was annoyed at being kept waiting.

Elen gave Kem a swift hug, and let him go.

At last, they set out across the gap with the prince perched awkwardly on Fulmo's shoulders and Jirvy riding atop the other gagast, his bow ready. Elen followed them into the Pall, its icy touch prickling against her legs. *Soon. Soon,* the mist whispered. *Soon all will be ours. Help us, spread our seeds beyond this binding, and it can be yours too.*

She knelt to release the viper, and the whispers faded. The viper slithered at her feet, swimming in and out of her sight as threads of mist thickened and thinned. Twice, the Pall rose almost to her chest. She'd never have been able to carry Ao across, had it washed so high back on that day. Was it indeed tidal? Yet, when she considered the river-like inlet she'd seen pressing south within view of Pelis Manor North, she had to wonder if the inlet of creeping fog was being pushed by the pressure of rising Pall. And what might that presage?

"Sara'ala, I'm here," she whispered to the White Sea.

But although she looked for his shadow and listened for the rush of wings and the flash of antlers, no presence touched hers. He was gone.

42

The Wind Dance

She reached the pier, climbed onto the rocks, and knelt to let the viper crawl up her body. It tasted no Spore on her extremities and sped home to her heart to rest.

The prince and Jirvy had unsheathed their shrive-steel swords and were busy skewering a few stray Spore that had caught on the legs of the two gagast. They checked each other, as well, and only then turned to her. Jirvy pressed the flat of his blade against Elen's back, a pain she tolerated, although the shrive-steel's buzzing sting made her eyes water.

The lawgiver strode out from the tower, two aivur at her back. They looked calm and collected, not even bloodied.

"We took them by surprise and killed most of them while they were still asleep. Thirty-three bodies, so you may take an accounting. None escaped."

"Was there a sentry at the entry gate?"

"He was the first one killed. We lost one of our own, and seven are wounded. It wasn't much of a fight. Disappointing, really. My people are complaining it wasn't a challenge."

"Ill-trained militia are no match for soldiers," agreed the prince. Elen wondered if his words were meant as a warning not to underestimate the imperial army. He beckoned to Fulmo and said, "You will run ahead to Pelis Manor North. We will catch up with you by nightfall. Our goal is to push through to Lord Genia at speed. You will also act as scout in case there is trouble on the road. You know the drill."

Fulmo gave a hand sign of assent. There followed a flurry of hand signs and gestures between the two gagast, after which Fulmo departed.

On the shoreline, aivur dragged corpses into the Pall. Some aivur stood guard out at the entry gate, while the rest cleaned up the compound, scrubbing blood from floors and walls, bundling up and burning stained bedding, neatly going through chests and cupboards and then tidily putting things back except for the objects they wanted as reward for their victory. An iron skillet. Balls of yarn in a splendid rainbow of colors. A sewing kit with extra needles stuck in a scrap of wool. All the kitchen knives. Horse blankets and harnesses. Perfumed latrine paper, of all things. Imperial coins, stacked in neat rows according to denomination. Maps.

As soon as Xilsi arrived, the prince set her to catalog and approve the loot while he went through the maps. He set aside one of Woodfall Province, dated to the reign of the Willow Emperor, whose surveyors had completed the first re-mapping after the rising of the Pall.

The prince gave this map to the lawgiver. "Here is a map of this province as surety for our agreement. Anything further, we can discuss after I am become emperor."

She studied it, then looked up at him. "There was another map. The bequeather spoke of it, said you had it in your possession. She said, by its style and content, it is almost certainly a map drawn by or copied from a mapmaker of one of our clans. I'd like it back, as surety for our agreement."

"It was lost in South Ring," he lied without blinking.

If Elen hadn't known the truth, she'd never have guessed he was lying. Maybe he would make a good emperor, if emperors needed skill at lying to rule, and she supposed they did. How else could you tell your own sibling that he was appointed as all-seeing eye, a position of great respect and trust, and meanwhile, behind his back, approve a scheme to bring about his downfall?

The lawgiver looked at Gevulin, then at Elen. "This osge will be the death of you, mark my words. When she was a child, the moment an egg was seen in her heart, she should have been thrown into the ocean to drown instead of just a warning cut into her skin."

Into the ocean to drown. As she had been!

At the Heart Temple, where she and Sara'ala had stood in front of a pure-water mirror—where she had seen the shadow of his true form for the first time—she had told him of her earliest memory, of being a tiny child and looking at her reflection in a pure-water pool, and seeing the egg like a seed nestled inside her.

She laid a hand against her neck, over the scar. Had the unknown person who had thrown her into the water been trying to drown her, or to save her from those who intended to kill her?

Most likely she would never know.

"The deputy courier will serve me," said the prince. "But I thank you for your advice."

The lawgiver tapped her own left shoulder, and called out to her followers. "Then we will depart, and perhaps, in time, Prince Gevulin, you and I will speak again."

The aivur returned across the Pall with their dead and wounded and their loot. The prince combed through the map room and the Vigil captain's office one last time, searching for any useful information while Elen rolled up the maps for transport. Below, the wardens gathered supplies, saddled what horses the Duenn Manor soldiers had been riding, but left the bull elks behind.

They were ready to depart by midday, gathering in the courtyard between the tower, the stables, and the barracks.

Before they could mount, the prince raised a hand. "In honor of his loyal service, he who was captain in the Imperial Order of Wardens, Simo Yarmissar. Xilsilin, will you sing the melody?"

Xilsi was holding Mekvo's walking staff like a badge of her new captaincy. "I can, Your Highness. It would be an honor to distinguish my comrade Simo with 'The Long Whisper of the Ceaseless Voice.' May I ask that Mekvo and the others be so honored as well?"

"Yes," he said, holding up a piece of paper. "I collected the roster from Captain Mekvo's desk."

"I can clap the rhythm," said Ipis. "If I may be so honored."

"You may," said the prince.

"I'll keep watch." Jirvy indicated the stairs up to the inner wall's walk, where he could look over the rest of the compound, the outer fields, and south along the road.

"Yes," said the prince.

Elen gave Kem a questioning look. She had no idea what they were talking about.

Kem said, "Your Highness, if you mean the mourning dance observed in the palace, then I know how to recite the descant of names."

"How can you know the descant?" Ipis demanded. "I don't even know it."

"Joef found a notation penned by an exiled palace musician—"

"Of course, the great good friend Joef did," said Ipis, but she shook her head with a resigned grin, as if she'd finally accepted this was how it was always going to be.

"Just two cycles of the Wind Dance," said the prince, handing Kem the roster. "Then we depart."

The Wind Dance! Elen had thought it a boastful display of endurance and fast footwork, not a memorial. As Ipis began to clap out a steady and rather plain rhythm, the prince took a position with his arms outstretched and his palms open to the sky. He met Xilsi's eyes. She began to sing, not with words but in a mournful melody that flowed up and down like a searching wind across a wide and empty land, seeking a soul that no longer walked in the world. Her singing voice was light, higher than Elen expected from all her tough talk, but her tones rang true.

Even that didn't matter once the prince began to dance, for he spoke with his precise gestures and graceful movements. *The wind is a ceaseless voice, here a whisper and there a howl. So does grief accompany our lives as the wind blows in the land, never quite gone even when it is still.* His gestures were gentle but the unfolding of the dance was implacable. *We lose those we love, or we are lost to those we love. The world fades, or memory fades. Death comes to all things.*

Elen's heart ached for Ao, for Sara'ala, for the intendant's wife and older daughter and for the younger daughter's lost husband, for Simo, and for the garrison killed by a sarpa's acid who she'd never known but who surely had kin and friends who would mourn them. For all those she had known and cared for, who had passed from this world as all must do in the fullness of time.

The prince's elegant dancing wound the burden of mourning through the air, speaking for all.

At the appropriate place, Kem sang the descant, a recitation of the names of those being honored. Surely it was the highest honor to receive an elegy from a prince. According to the implacable hierarchy of the empire, all their lives were his to burn on the fire of his ambition. Yet had he never traveled north, they'd almost certainly still be alive. Perhaps this was Gevulin's way of acknowledging that they had died because they'd become inadvertently involved in his deadly duel for the throne.

After the recitation of names, the prince turned a slow circle, and with a dip of his knees and a sweep of his arm, gestured for Xilsi to begin again. The second cycle.

Jirvy's warning whistle broke into the melody. Xilsi fell silent. Ipis stopped clapping. The prince spun to grab his weapons, laid on the ramp of the entrance into the tower. Elen ran to the gate and climbed up beside Jirvy.

He pointed south at the sky, at a strange, squiggly line that writhed and wriggled against the pale blue of a sky streaked with clouds. Elen pulled out her spyglass and set it to her eye, fearing what she would see. It sprang into view through the lens, a winged snake that, from this distance, might have been no larger than her viper. But it was large enough to hold a rider's platform on its back.

"Sarpa," said Jirvy.

43

SARPA

Elen lost the breath to speak for the fear of seeing death approaching, as if called by the prince's wind dance. All she could do was hold out the spyglass to Jirvy, but he was already climbing down.

"Your Highness, a sarpa and its rider. There's no reason for one to be on patrol here."

"They're hunting for me." The prince sheathed his sword and picked up his bow and quiver. "How long?"

"Half of an hour, if we are fortunate."

Xilsi said, "Kem, Ipis, put the horses in the stables. In stalls, but don't tie them up. Keep them saddled."

The two youths hurried into the stables.

"Only the tower's holystone will protect us," said the prince as he scanned the courtyard and surrounding doorways. "The sarpa's acid can burn through the shutters, even if we close them."

"Our arrows can't pierce its hide," said Jirvy. "A shot to its eye may madden it, which could work in our favor."

"The rider is the key," said the prince. "Simo told me the Blood Wolves would target the riders, not the sarpa, since aivur have no weapon that can damage a sarpa except poison, and that only if they can get poison down the sarpa's gullet."

The viper stirred in Elen's heart, waking to opportunity.

"And that meant sending a person wreathed in poison vials running into the sarpa's mouth. One death in exchange for saving many lives." He tapped his fingers against his sword hilt, a fine weapon rendered useless against this foe. "Even if the Salt Spear Clan still watch from the rock and have not retreated to the road, we cannot cross back to the rock with only one gagast to carry us. Not in time. We'll shelter in the tower and hope to escape notice. The rider will move on if they don't realize we are here. If not, we kill the rider."

"Your Highness, you could surrender," Elen said.

Xilsi snorted. Jirvy sighed.

"How little you understand this conflict. A sarpa killed this Vigil's entire warden garrison, most likely this very sarpa and its rider. They will not spare anyone who is found with me. I suppose there might arise a situation where I would nobly cast my life upon the coals, so its heat would carry my blessed mother through cold danger and back into life. Though she'd scold me for it. But my death will not save any of you. Yet, I suppose you are not so concerned about yourself, are you, Deputy Courier? You're worried about the boy. And about the wardens, too, I imagine. You have that tiresome way about you, like Astaylin, always asking after other people. But in your case, for some unfathomable reason, I believe you honestly care."

"I prefer to live a peaceful and harmonious life, Your Highness. So I must imagine others do, too."

"Enough! This tiresome conversation solves nothing."

Jirvy said, "Your Highness, we could hide in the tunnel below."

"Trapped like animals? We could easily be walled in and starved out. I think not."

Kem and Ipis hustled out of the stables, closing the doors. The prince led them up the ramp into the tower. Floor by floor, they closed all the shutters, leaving open only one north-facing window on the sixth floor, looking over the Pall, and a south-facing window on the third floor, high enough to see over the walls to the entry gate. The prince and Jirvy stationed themselves at the third-floor window, leaving Xilsi above to watch the Pall, and Kem and Ipis on the lowest floor, by the locked gate, with orders to hide in the tunnel if need be.

Elen watched beside the prince. The sarpa sped toward them with a lashing of its featherless wings. By now, they could see the rider braced on a cramped, chariot-like platform fixed back from the monstrous head, wire reins attached to the sarpa's nostril slits. The rider's uniform was made of treated sarpa skin, immune to acid and difficult to puncture with arrow or blade. Their only vulnerability was an open-faced helmet with glass goggles.

Swiftly, the beast closed the gap. Like griffins, sarpa would not fly over a Pall. It banked awkwardly and cut close to the tower as the rider balanced on the platform. It was magnificent—until the sarpa spat acid toward the open window.

They all jerked away as droplets spattered across a pair of couches. The fabric sizzled, melting. The floor hissed as the carpet darkened.

"Fuck," swore Jirvy, shaking his arm. "I'm all right. Just a drop."

"The rider knows we're here," said the prince.

"It must have seen Fulmo," said Jirvy.

Blessed Heavens. Fulmo. Out in the open, on the road.

"It's swinging back around," said Jirvy, pressed to one side, keeping his body hidden as he peered out. "No, no, wait."

When the prince made to approach, he waved him back.

"Is it leaving?" the prince asked.

Jirvy made a grim sound through gritted teeth. "Ah, no, I see what the rider intends."

Elen and the prince crowded up to get a look. The sarpa landed at the compound's outer gate. The rider twitched the wire reins. All Elen could think was that it had to be painful for the sarpa. Nostrils were sensitive.

With a burst of power, the sarpa battered the dome of its huge head against the closed and barred gate.

Boom. The sound crashed over them like thunder. And again, *boom.*

"What's it doing?" said Elen. "The rider can't fight us alone. Can it?"

"It's small for a sarpa," said the prince. "Small enough to come up the stairway like a rat snake hunting into a hole."

Wood gave way with a splintering crack. The sarpa slithered through the outer compound, down the abandoned street, its muscled body rippling in the most horrific way. What its acid did not kill, its body would crush. Its lashing tail ripped part of a roof from a nearby building.

Xilsi appeared in the stairway arch. "What's happening?"

Boom. The sarpa had reached the inner gate. Elen stared, too shocked to move, and yet her mind raced furiously as she gaped at the monstrous creature, who was no monster to itself.

"It's too big to land in the courtyard," said Jirvy, sounding remarkably calm, "so it's battering its way in."

"Holy fuck," said Xilsi.

Another impact shuddered through the ground, so hard they felt it through the soles of their feet. One of the gates buckled, torn half off its hinges, but there wasn't quite enough room for the sarpa to slither through. Not yet.

"We can't fight it on the stairway," said Jirvy. "Its head will fill the space. Maybe once it pokes its head into the courtyard in front of the tower, I can get a shot at the rider from up here."

"You'll just get the top of his helmet," said Xilsi.

"If I yell, he might look up."

"That's exactly what I would do, if I was an idiot."

"You have a better idea?" Jirvy said, on a laugh. With his sassily knotted kerchief and his cool, collected demeanor, Elen suddenly and incongruously saw why a temperamental and snobbish Bakassar heir might have fallen in love with him.

"I have a better idea," said Elen as her thoughts lurched to a halt on one specific point. "If it's true what Simo said about poison."

"Simo wasn't a liar or an exaggerator," snapped Xilsi.

"Nor did I say I thought he was. Your Highness, what do you think?"

"The army has indeed lost sarpa to enemies who run up their gullets," said the prince. "But your viper is surely too small."

"A foul-cap mushroom, no bigger than the tip of my finger, can kill a grown man. We ourselves saw a griffin that had been felled by three poisons working in concert, through the flesh, not even ingested. I'm thinking we have two chances. Jirvy gets one shot, and if that doesn't work, then I try."

"Three chances," said the prince. "I will distract the rider from up here. He may yet back down, if commanded by me."

Boom. The gate cracked again. The sarpa's snout nosed through, but was now impeded by shattered spars. Elen ran for the stairs and pounded down them, passing Kem and Ipis with a "Get up to Xilsi and the prince. *Now.*"

At the door to the ramp, she heaved off the crossbar as Jirvy climbed up to a narrow platform, built under the arrow slit and above the door, that would give him a clear shot down the ramp.

With a crash and a loud tearing, crunching burst, the gate shattered fully. Elen tugged the door open and stuck her head out. At the gate, the lipless snout nosed into view. Big enough to open and close over her body in one gulp. The sight shocked her into immobility. Her limbs went nerveless as the big head emerged. Huge eyes gleamed as if filled with hot embers. Their glowing warmth reminded her of the bequeather. Maybe the bequeather's cold demeanor had stemmed from a very different source than a raven. *And I kissed her,* thought Elen at utter random, thoughts skittering as the sarpa's muscles bunched and moved, the wall shuddering as it shoved its way through. The rider crouched low to avoid his riding platform being scraped off. As soon as the beast's head and neck came clear, the rider leaped to his feet to balance on the platform. Scanning the tower, his gaze halted on a sight Elen couldn't see from where she waited.

From above, the prince shouted, "Stand down, Imperial Rider, by my order."

"Who are you?" shouted the man.

"I am His Exalted Highness, Prince Gevulin, Prince-General and All-Seeing Eye of the Imperial Order of the Wardens—"

Was he going to recite his entire list of accomplishments?

The rider raised his crossbow and loosed a bolt toward the window. That shut up the prince, who had to duck out of the way.

From inside the stables, panicked horses and bull elks kicked at their stalls. They could smell the beast, and so could she, a pungent reek that made her eyes water.

The sarpa muscled forward across the courtyard, a short distance for a creature of that size. Its snout would reach the ramp with its tail still under the breached gate. No wonder it had come through the gate. It couldn't have landed in such tight quarters.

Arrows shot by the prince and Xilsi rained down on sarpa and rider alike but could not pierce either its thick hide or the rider's sarpa-skin armor and bulbous helmet, both doubly protected by the sarpa flaring out a fibrous wing to deflect the arrows. The sarpa's head reached the stone ramp that led up to the entry door. The ramp was barely wide enough to accommodate the monster, whose snake-like body was wider across than Elen's outstretched arms. Its massive tongue flicked the air, scenting prey.

"Now," said Jirvy.

Elen released the viper. It slipped free, such a small and delicate thing, more like a thread than a snake, a fragile tendril with which to confront the sarpa's massive force. She knew she ought to close the door all the way, for the sarpa might spit acid at any moment, but she refused to leave the viper with no escape route. It slithered unconcernedly for a few ells down the ramp before finally pausing and lifting its head, as if with interest or with a sharpening desire to hunt.

The sarpa raised its head, too. A boulder might have swayed so, held suspended, ready to drop. Its tongue flicked out and in, tasting the air. A shiver of uneasiness rippled all the way down its monstrous length, all the way back to the gate and the tip of its scaly tail.

The rider cursed. "Up, up! Damned beast. What's ailing you?"

He hadn't seen the tiny viper, white against the white holystone, so he looked up at the door, trying to spot the threat.

Jirvy took his shot.

The arrow shattered the rider's left goggle and pierced the man's eye. Gargling, spasming, the man toppled sideways, hanging halfway down the sarpa's great body, twisting as he tried to claw the arrow from his face.

The viper lifted its head and hissed as softly as a whisper of love passed between an illicit pair of lovers who dare not be overheard by their jealous spouses.

The sarpa coiled back, wings beating angrily, tail thrashing with such strength that it battered down the remaining stone around the gate. It curled sideways, filling the courtyard with its body. At first it was trapped, hemmed in. In a panic, it recoiled clumsily back through the gate. The movement scraped the wounded rider off its side.

Once it reached the lane beyond, the sarpa roused its mighty wings and battered the air as if to kill the wind itself. Rose, fell, rose, fell, and at last it rose above the buildings. With a lumbering lift, like bellows flapping and blowing, it swung a long curve around and flew west, parallel to the Pall.

By this time, Jirvy had jumped down from the arrow slit, pushed past a shocked and staring Elen, leaped comically high over the motionless viper, and run down to press a knee into the chest of the limp rider as he extracted his arrow with a tug.

He called cheerfully over his shoulder. "Already dead! Your Highness, can I claim this armor?"

The viper returned to Elen and burned back into her flesh.

The prince and Xilsi came running past, followed by Kem and Ipis, all exclaiming. Elen caught her breath, rubbing her eyes. On shaky legs, she followed them to Jirvy.

The prince knelt beside the dead man. The goggles had been torn off the rider's face. He had the weathered skin of a middle-aged man who has spent most of his life out of doors, in the wind and sun. The skin around his eyes was paler and smoother than that of his cheeks and forehead, where the goggles had protected it.

With the tip of an arrow, Gevulin fished out two necklace chains from beneath the man's leather armor. From one dangled a whistle carved from bone. The other chain bore a stylized, five-petaled oleander flower. A bloom so pretty to look at, and poisonous in all its parts.

"This is the badge of His Sublime Highness. It does indeed appear this elaborately planned attack on me has had nothing to do with Astaylin at all."

"Much as it pains me to say so," remarked Xilsi, "but it never has felt like her style."

The prince flashed her an accusatory gaze as he rose, but instead of replying to her, he addressed Jirvy. "Bring the whistle, but leave the armor on the rider."

Jirvy grimaced as if this was not the answer he had wanted, not at all. He briefly pressed the back of a hand to his forehead, but he made no protest, nor did he ask a second time. All at once, Elen wondered if this had been his very reaction when his Manor had ordered him to marry a woman of their choosing, for an alliance that benefited them: a superb warden, scout, and archer, but not one to kick even when he might have wished to.

"We move out at once." The prince gestured to Ipis and Kem. "You two, get the horses. The deputy courier and I will toss him into the Pall. Let them wonder."

He grabbed the shoulders and Elen took the ankles. The dead man had a stocky, muscular build, and the impenetrable armor added weight. They lugged him under the tower—the road a familiar sting—and to the end of the pier. With a heave and a ho they flung the body outward. It thumped into the Pall, out of sight beneath the white fog. Elen peered toward the turtle-back rock but saw no sign of aivur. Turning to go back to the courtyard, she halted, because the prince hadn't yet moved. He was examining her as he might a sword given as a gift, wondering if it is as fine a weapon as promised.

"Deputy Courier, I am not a patient man. You are disrespectful and impertinent, lacking graceful deportment and proper humility. So we will have this out now. This is what we are up against. I doubt you comprehend it fully, or ever will. I am ambitious, it is true. But I will make a better emperor than my nephew, who is cruel, impulsive, and, worst of all, believes himself superior to others although he has excelled at none of the skills and study we princes are set to. He thinks his position as sole child of the Magnolia Emperor gives him the blessing of the High Heavens, but he has done nothing to deserve it except be born."

"The same could be said of you, Your Highness."

His expression grew hard and dangerous. "You will not insult my blessed mother."

"I meant no insult to her, Your Highness. Nor to you, if it comes to that. Captain Xilsi says you earned your accolades through hard work and endurance, not because anyone handed them to you."

"Did she say that?" He cocked his head to one side, a peculiar vulnerability on his face.

"She did. Nevertheless, you were born a prince, and in the empire that is what gives you the right to contest for the throne." She paused.

He gritted his teeth, his hand twitching as he gripped the handle of his sheathed whip. "What is it you wish to say? My restraint wears thin."

"Here's the bargain I will make with you."

She thought he would draw his whip and slash her across the face, but the journey had tempered him. After a moment, he released the whip's handle and raised his hand to indicate she could keep talking.

"I will kill the emperor and the crown prince if you will swear to me, by the High Heavens and on your mother's honor, that you will let Kem continue to train as a warden and not use him in any of your schemes. Ever."

His beautiful willow-leaf eyes narrowed. He did not know about Ao's ancestry, but in time he might figure it out. It would be easy to decide that the brilliant-haired Kem was more useful as a puppet ruler in a northern province, able to claim Four Lands status because, in the empire, at least, his "illegitimacy" was not a barrier.

"Go on."

"Let him serve as a warden for life. In return, I'll do as you ask."

"Ah, so you weren't necessarily going to do it, once we reached the palace."

"We haven't reached the palace yet. A lot can change in a short time."

"I should have expected nothing less from you. Very well, on my mother's honor and by the High Heavens, I will allow the youth, Kem Duennol, to serve as a warden and not involve him in any further schemes, as you so poetically state it."

She took off her glove and pulled back her sleeve, the way she did to allow the viper to emerge. He tensed, although he did not take a step back.

"Skin to skin, like the aivur," she said.

He met her gaze, neither surprised nor fearful. Perhaps, for once in his life, he was curious. "You could kill me right now."

"I could, but the others would know I'd done it, and I don't believe they'd take it well. Furthermore, I'd become a fugitive, an outlaw, and it turns out that I don't want that life. In the long run, if you become emperor, as you hope to do, I would best serve you as a surveyor. Let me take the training and I can go into the Desolation and figure out whether that map is fake or real. Where that underground river goes. What it means for the empire."

"An interesting proposition."

"Yes," she said, and then pointedly added, "Your Exalted Highness."

In that moment, they shared a flash of understanding, of how far each was ready to go to get what they wanted. The prince took off his own glove and clasped hand to wrist, skin to skin.

The bargain was struck.

So be it, she thought. She could go forward from here with a clear heart, knowing she had done what she could to secure Kem's future, and to some extent her own, even if no one knew what disaster—or triumph—the coming days would bring.

Together, they returned to the courtyard.

Elen said quietly to Jirvy, "How long have you known, and why didn't you say anything before?"

He shrugged. "I follow the prince's lead. Beyond that, it's none of my business."

Everyone mounted. They guided the nervous horses through the wreckage of the gate, past scraped-off scales and the dry, hot smell of the departed sarpa. A cloud covered the sun. Beneath a cold autumn sky, they rode grimly south.

44

A Five-Petaled Oleander Flower

In late afternoon, with Sheep Bladder Halt's tower visible in the distance, they found Fulmo.

The gagast was standing at the edge of the road, unmoving although it was daylight. He'd hardened his skin, but even so was horribly pitted and marred by acid. The sarpa must have spat repeatedly to do so much damage. Which meant the rider had known who was in the prince's party and had been ordered to kill them all on sight.

"Is he dead?" Elen asked as they dismounted beside the statue.

"How can anyone survive a close acid attack?" Ipis pressed hands to cheeks, her voice thin and trembling. "I keep thinking of the garrison. Their bones. How it must have burned right through their flesh. They must have been screaming the whole time."

Kem winced, pressing a hand to his eyes, and excused himself by marching down to the road to stand watch on one of the raised distance mounds that marked each league.

The prince rested a bare hand against the gagast's thick arm. "He must have been forced to twice create his shell."

"Do you wish to halt here for the night, Your Highness?" Xilsi asked. "While we wait for Fulmo's emergence?"

"No, once he emerges we will keep going."

"Leaving Fulmo behind again at nightfall? What if there is another sarpa?"

"If there is another sarpa, it will catch us on the road. In that eventuality, we need not worry about Fulmo because we'll be dead. But it matters not. Since he was twice forced to protect himself with a shell, he will be small enough once he emerges that we will be able to tie him onto a horse and carry him as cargo. Unfortunately for him."

"Why is that unfortunate?" Elen asked.

He had a lofty way of raising an eyebrow. "I suppose the care and keeping of an exiled delinquent lies outside the purview of a deputy courier."

"Delinquent?"

"Why else would a gagast serve the palace? Among the gagast, the punishment for delinquency is to be remanded into a term of service to outsiders. It's considered a death sentence."

"Slavery always is a death sentence," said Elen. "For the soul, if not the body, although usually the body too."

"I am speaking of a specific physical phenomenon. For the gagast, size determines life. You saw yourself that when they break the shell of their armored skin, they become smaller. When they become smaller, they become weaker. When they become too weak and too small, they expire. That's why the gagast are a peaceful, philosophical, and artistic people, on the whole. Why their worst punishment is exile."

A crackling sound interrupted him. Lines like the splintering of ice raced outward across the pitted, blackened shell of Fulmo's acid-burned skin. With a loud crack, the shell burst into fragments and clattered to the ground. Beneath was a second shell, less horribly marred but still damaged. After not too long, while Ipis and Kem cared for the horses, this shell splintered in its turn and shed into yet more shards that fell into heaps that reminded Elen of roof tiles spilled to the ground after a storm.

After this doubled shedding, Fulmo stood no taller than the prince, although he had once towered a head and a half above the others. The gagast blinked, popped a bead from his mouth, and offered the bead to Gevulin. To Elen's surprise, the prince accepted it without any sign of disgust, although he did not string it back into his braids. By now, the sun was setting. Elen hated the way they bundled Fulmo onto the back of one of the remounts, secured like a sack of potatoes and concealed beneath canvas. Needs must, Fulmo made no protest, and the prince was determined to ride through the night. He needed to reach the safety of Pelis Manor North and Lord Genia's militia.

Ride they did, and hard, with breaks only to switch mounts, water and feed, and to relieve themselves. Under cover of darkness they passed Sheep Bladder Halt, hushed villages, isolated farmsteads with a single lit lamp to mark their presence alongside the road, as was required by imperial law. Elen was glad she'd had time to sleep in the rowboat and the wagon, for there was no rest to be had now.

The next morning dawned as cold as ever and unusually clear. Soon enough, they met travelers on the road and folk about their work on farms. Captain Xilsi demanded reports on the condition of the road and if they'd seen any unusual activity or signs of Spore or Pall. No one questioned why wardens on patrol on the imperial road wanted such information. But it was the presence of a deputy courier and Elen's more gently probing questions that got the locals to open up.

A saucy farm lass insisted she'd seen two sarpa flying together, ten or twelve days before, writhing in the sky in the far distance. Her elders scoffed and said it was just branches in the wind over by the woodland known locally as Lovers' Forest. "Oh, Lovers' Forest, I'm sure it was nothing to do with that, but we could go look," said the girl, with a flirtatious wink for Kem. He blushed. Ipis scowled.

A weather-beaten merchant hauling sacks of barley complained that he and his wagon had been overtaken by a company of militia marching north, a week or more earlier, wasn't it? The rude fellows had requisitioned the best-quality wheat he'd been taking to Sheep Bladder Halt to sell at the last autumn market. Their captain hadn't paid but a cheap coin, and that with a mean laugh, while a pair of highborn lords watched in sneering silence. He didn't recognize what Manor their banner belonged to, only it wasn't Pelis Manor North, nor one of the Noble Six, like that one from the wineshop song "Bakas Manor Beauty," wasn't it? Nor was it any intendant's sentinels, of course not, for the local intendant paid the prices set by the emperor, or he'd be clapped into irons, wouldn't he? Thank the High Heavens for that! But they were riding bull elks, not horses, that's for sure! Belligerent beasts!

A closed-mouthed young peddler, pushing a cart piled with baskets of carefully polished old spoons and refurbished clock movements, was less eager to share his story, although he was quick to flash the imperial license that granted him leave to ply Woodland Province under the gracious umbrella of the emperor's peace. Elen judged it a forgery, but she merely gave him a hard look, after which he became more forthcoming.

He had been settling in at a farmstead before sunset, just four nights before, when a company of armed men had marched south, singing ill-mannered soldier ditties. He even named a few of the more lurid songs, which made Elen wonder if he'd been a militiaman in his youth, though with that accent, not from Woodland Province. He had a few heartland tells in his speech that he wasn't quite adept enough at covering up.

Yet his story was intriguing: He and the farmers had watched apprehensively, hoping the militia would not stop over, since one never knew what demands they would make, did one? They had elk riders among them, though that wasn't so uncommon in the northwestern provinces. Surely the emperor did not approve of big parties of armed men clomping about as they wished with no imperial oversight! Perhaps the good wardens might take a report to the Order of Sentinels or a local intendant.

Of course they would, Elen assured him, wondering if he was a shadow warden spy sent to observe the provinces. If so, he gave no sign of recognizing Prince Gevulin. By now, the prince's clothing was so battered and dirty, his fly-whisk hair so greasy from lack of washing, and days-old stubble giving him a disreputable profile, that it was possible for him to act as if he were just another warden. He just had to keep his mouth shut and not speak, because his palace accent would give him away.

Midmorning, they stopped at Norvest Halt. The prince might have demanded favors or approbation, but again, he remained in the background. Xilsi acquisitioned supplies and paid the mandated imperial price. The wardens and their incognito prince took a meal in the wardens' hall and grabbed an hour's sleep. As fresh horses were saddled, Elen chatted amiably in the stables with the local grooms. Yes, a company of elk riders had come through. Their elks were so noisy and had kicked one of the lads, and never an apology! The local intendant had been chastised by the lord—Duenn Manor, that was it! His lordship had been as ill-mannered as the elk! He'd criticized the lack of luxury in the intendancy's modest imperial wing.

"Why would a Manor lord complain of that?" Elen inquired of the talkative stablehands. "Manor-born have no license to use an imperial suite that I've ever heard or seen. Did someone in his party stay there? Was he traveling with an imperial official?"

A sarpa rider, they told her. A slight young man wearing a palace harness and an unusual necklace of a five-petaled oleander flower. He'd flown off on his sarpa at dawn, before the militia marched out.

"Going north?" she asked, although the description didn't match the rider who had died at Far Boundary Vigil.

No. He'd flown south, and taken a bag of provisions as for a long journey. Four days ago, it was. They'd not seen a second sarpa.

Midafternoon, the wardens reached the rim of the long southeast-sloping valley in which lay Pelis Manor North and its fields and orchards. The layout of the valley's rises and dips hid the Manor itself, although a corner of its sarpa pen was visible within a greater ring of hallow-wood. The watchtower flew the striped "all is well" flag. From up here, she thought she could see, beyond the watchtower, a tiny thread of white fog snaking through the lower valley reaches. Was it the inlet of Pall that Surveyor Berri had mentioned, the one she'd seen for herself from the top of the tower, or was it just the angle of the afternoon light falling on autumn-whitened grass? The road ramped in gentle switchbacks down into the valley. Smoke rose peaceably from outlying farmsteads. All looked quiet. No one else was on the road.

"Your Highness, if may," said Elen.

"When did that stop you?" he muttered to himself.

Ipis gave the prince a startled glance. Jirvy looked away, hiding his mouth behind a hand. Kem smirked.

Xilsi said, "Oh, just go on, El!"

"You have my permission," remarked Gevulin in a sardonic voice edged by princely peevishness.

"My thanks, Your Highness." She could play this game forever, but meanwhile they needed to survive. More than anything, she had to make sure Kem could never fall into Lord Duenn's hands again. "It seems to me we should proceed cautiously. If there were two sarpa riders, as we suspect, then the other might still be at large and scouting this area. The Duenn militia *might* have turned south for home, but they might also be guests at Pelis Manor."

"Aunt Genia will not have tolerated Duenn's crass presence or his ill-advised and insulting attempt to marry his son to Worvua. She'll have sent him on his way."

"What about the sarpa rider?"

Gevulin ran a finger along his patchy beard. The unshaven look altered the unwelcoming cast of his perfectly sculpted jawline, making him seem more approachable, until he turned his imperious gaze on his lessers. "It doesn't make sense that there were two sarpa riders. That girl must have been mistaken. Sarpa riders travel alone."

Kem shaded his eyes to examine the valley's rumpled folds. "Your Highness, could the Sublime Highness have been the second sarpa rider? The deputy courier's report about the conversation she overheard at Far Boundary Vigil suggests that the person who was addressed as 'Sublime Highness' knew the garrison was killed by a sarpa. Might he even have been the one to . . . do it?"

The prince gave a huff of annoyance. "You don't know the palace. You should not presume to know."

"I beg your pardon, Your Highness." Kem ducked his chin.

Xilsi said hastily, "Kem, princes born into the Flower Court don't join the Sarpa or Griffin Corps. They're too valuable for such dangerous work."

Gevulin raised a hand. Xilsi stopped speaking.

"But!" said the prince, to everyone's surprise. "Novice Kem is correct in wondering if these particular sarpa—if there were indeed two—might have been working under the auspices of Min-lo. Prince Minaylin, I mean. If anyone could wheedle a pair of sarpa riders out of the emperor for their own selfish uses, it would be him. His household sigil is the oleander flower. Everyone supposes it will become his reign name, in due time."

"A poisonous flower?" Ipis asked.

"Perhaps more poisonous than anyone has guessed," said Gevulin, then added, "Or at least, than I ever contemplated. I think it prudent for you to ride ahead to the Manor, Captain. Ascertain whether it is safe for us."

"Very good, Your Highness. Let's find a place for you to wait in more comfort than this cold, windswept height. If I don't return by dawn, then . . ."

She trailed off with a glance toward Jirvy, who wasn't looking at her but rather studying the sky, bow in hand. Not that an arrow would stop a sarpa.

"Then we will know Pelis Manor is compromised," finished Gevulin.

Descending into the valley, they met no one on the road. Travelers would not be leaving whatever hostelry the Manor's roadside Heart Temple offered, not this late in the day. There wouldn't be much gleaning or woodsman work in the upper valley during the cold months either. At a river crossing, a small stone shelter had been set up off the roadway and over a hallow-wood bridge onto a stony little island barely large enough to hold a party of seven and their horses.

Xilsi rode on. Fulmo busied himself preparing a meal at the outdoor hearth while Jirvy set himself as sentry in the crook of an old oak tree overlooking the road. Kem and Ipis watered and fed the horses, then lay down to nap, curled up back-to-back on a raised stone slab inside the shelter. A strong scent of urine permeated the enclosed space, but nothing worse than many other places Elen had taken shelter. She sat on a wooden bench, resting her head in her hands as she surreptitiously watched the prince walk along the island's shore, a frown on his face. If only he was the haunt, slyly smiling. But he wasn't, and he wouldn't be. He had his own life to live, as it had to be. With a sigh, she curled up on the bench and dozed off.

When she woke, the two youths were still asleep, Kem snoring softly, the way he did when his nose got clogged.

She got up and went outside. The prince sat on a bench, rubbing his forehead as if it hurt. That vulnerability, more than anything, made it obvious he was not the haunt but rather a young man of the greatest privilege who has finally run into a problem he cannot surmount merely by training harder than everyone else.

"Your Highness." She broke off, not sure why she had spoken.

He did not look up. "Ah, Deputy Courier, what words of wisdom have you to share with me? Some insight into the workings of the inner palace, something gleaned from the copious reading of Kem's great good friend Joef, who I must meet someday? Perhaps a comment about the slipup in accent by that peddler we encountered?"

"You noticed that?"

He straightened, offended. "Do you think I am unable to discern such things?"

"I confess, Your Highness, I did not think at all about whether you might have noticed."

Almost, he smiled, the strangest look to cross his face in all the time she'd known him. He observed her startled expression with a prim pinch of his mouth, reverting to his usual disdain. "So am I wounded in this bout of wits."

"Your Highness!"

"Yes, this once. It won't happen again." He examined her keenly. "Your fate, and that of the boy, is tied to mine."

"So you have informed me more than once. Be assured I have not forgotten. Odd as it may seem to you, Your Exalted Highness, after my one brief and chance encounter with His Sublime Highness—if it indeed was the most sublime and honored crown prince—I should favor you over him to become the next emperor."

He blinked. "Should you?"

"My viper didn't like him."

He leaned forward. "Does your viper like me?"

She laughed. "Your Highness, the viper is indifferent to you, alas. But the viper liked the haunt."

"Of course it did," he said drily, sitting back with a look of disgust. "Like to like. Monster to monster. You may go. Ah! At last!" His expression brightened, although not at her.

She looked around. Fulmo approached with a pleasingly arranged platter of bread, cheese, candied turnips, the last of the spicy cabbage, and a single, and thus precious, sweet rice cake leftover from the meal they'd taken at Norvest Halt.

She went to the hearth, brought food to Jirvy in his tree sentry post, and tucked herself in beside him to watch the road as they ate. The candied turnips made a lovely contrasting flavor and texture to the salty, soft cheese and chewy, nutty bread.

Jirvy said, "Do you reckon there were two sarpa?"

"I don't know. One thing I've learned in my years as a deputy courier is that people often give poor testimony even when they mean to be truthful. Especially when they mean to be truthful. Sometimes they tell you what they think you want to hear, or try to impress someone, like that lass was flirting with Kem. Sometimes they just don't see a thing that was right in front of their eyes. Or they think they see something else because it's what they expected to see."

"A sarpa did overnight at Norvest Halt."

"So said the stablehands. Maybe they were bribed to say so by Lord Duenn's people."

"Nah." He shook his head. "I took a quick look round."

"When?"

"When everyone else was sleeping. There was fresh dung, a few days old."

"Wouldn't it have been cleaned up already?"

"No. It's excellent fertilizer. Reserved for the palace gardens."

"The palace gardens! What? Does the palace send out special couriers to gather up sarpa droppings?" She grinned. "I can't believe no one has written a play about the spritely travels of the dung-gatherers. The drama, the misunderstandings, the dangers in the east, the time the wagon hit a pothole and a full barrel fell out and broke in the field of an impoverished tiller whose beautiful daughter then attracts the eye of the noble official."

Jirvy stiffened as if she'd said something offensive.

Her lips parted to apologize, not wanting to offend him, he who had shown her and Kem much kindness through his actions. Then she heard the grind of carriage wheels and the rumble of horses' hooves.

A fine carriage swept into view, pulled by panthers and driven by a magnificent woman dressed in a silk gown overlaid with a splendidly embroidered long wool jacket. With deft hands, she halted the carriage at the stone post that marked the side path to the shelter. Menials hurried around from the back to offer her their assistance in dismounting from the driver's bench. She swept them away with a dismissive wave of a hand. Her graceful jump down to the road was accomplished with a swish of skirts as entrancing as any theatrical entrance. She looked right at the oak, as if she'd once wedged herself into that very crook to keep an eye on this same stretch of road.

"You must be Warden Jirvy," she called. "No, no, stay at your post, as you should. Don't come down for my sake."

"By the fiery pit," swore Jirvy.

"Who is that?" Elen whispered, yet surely there was only one person it could be.

Footsteps sounded on the path. Gevulin appeared below the tree, thunder in his expression and his hands clenched as if restraining an urge to punch something. Anything.

"There you are, Beloved Little Brother!" the woman called gaily. "Exactly as my dear Xilsilin said you would be. And yet! That frown! I always say you'd be twice as handsome should you only smile once a day."

He gave a curt bow, just respectful enough. "Honored Elder Sister. What brings you into the north, Astaylin?"

45

A Fragile Twig

What brings me to the benighted north? There's a fine story! Yet, by the High Heavens, it is far too cold out here for me to relate the tale. Let us gather about a warm fire with hot mulled wine, pleasant company, and a few spicy tidbits to nibble on. Speaking of which! Here is our darling Xilsilin. I outpaced her, as ever." She laughed gaily. If Astaylin resented the woman who had turned her down, Elen could see no sign of it. But, of course, an outward mask might hide any shadow.

Xilsi rode a fresh horse and was accompanied by a squad of mounted sentinels wearing immaculate palace uniforms, along with a squad of Pelis Manor militia who escorted none other than Lady Worvua. The young Pelis Manor scion's flushed cheeks gave her an especially attractive appearance, windblown and eager.

"Do not dismount, for we shan't tarry here for long!" commanded Astaylin in a cheery voice, before turning back to Gevulin. "This is a new look for you, Little Brother! I would never have recognized you! For you look rather like a disreputable bandit in one of the old tales. It had never occurred to me that you might become accomplished as a master of disguise. After all, you are the consummate prince, are you not? Proficient in all things princely, as we have all been reminded, time and again. Not that I have not always felt the deep bond proper between imperial siblings, but I swear to you by the Five Pools of the Ancients, seeing you this way makes me like you rather better. It delights me to know you can exist for an hour as something other than perfect."

He sighed with a heave of his muscular shoulders. Elen wondered if his older sister often made him lose his composure. To speak to him in this manner—in front of an audience!—was certainly her right as the elder sibling, but it seemed deliberate and possibly mean.

"I'll collect my people," he said in a chilly tone.

"Indeed, and do ride whatever horse you came in on, for I shan't allow you to stain my carriage cushions with all your dirt. Gracious!" She slapped him companionably on the shoulder, then blew imagined dirt off her glove. The light in her eyes didn't seem hostile, but Elen wasn't sure what else to call it. "I am glad to see you, even if you doubt it. I came north to find you, if you must know."

"You did?" She'd startled him.

"Of course I did. We might be rivals at times, but we are not enemies, or so I hope. Yet, enough. This cold is brutal. Let's go back."

He gave way, as he must, being the younger sibling.

A shivering Astaylin got into the carriage. Worvua cast a measuring gaze at the disheveled Gevulin and abandoned him to follow Astaylin into the interior. Elen found herself shunted toward the end of the procession, in front of the menials and behind the imperial honor guard of sentinels.

As they proceeded toward the Manor, Xilsi dropped back to ride beside Elen. "Imagine my surprise to discover her here."

"Are you concerned at meeting her?"

"Concerned? No, I'm delighted. Ever since Asti and I resolved our dispute about the matter of consorts, and took a few years away from each other, we get along famously."

"Truly?"

"No need to be skeptical! She is a lot, it is true. Too much at times. But she's one of the few people who isn't intimidated by me."

Elen gave a snort of laughter.

Xilsi's grin popped out. "Yes, besides you. And poor Mekky. One or two others." Her expression darkened as she studied Jirvy, who rode alongside the prince. "I thought him, too, but it turns out I was wrong."

"Wrong, or unaware?"

"Ah, El, always the sting at the tip of your tail. Or should I say, your venomous bite. Yes, I didn't think about what my noble status meant for him. I should have."

"I hope you two can finally have a long and *private* conversation about your troubles, but meanwhile—"

"That's told me!" If there was an edge of annoyance in Xilsi's voice, she covered it with a lopsided smile.

"Given everything we've dealt with, I have an urgent question. Do you think Her Exalted Highness's arrival has anything to do with Lord Duenn or the Sublime Highness?"

"There hasn't been time to ask. I can already see Worvua's angling for a consortship, though."

"With Prince Gevulin?"

"No, with Astaylin."

"I don't understand this dance at all. Is Worvua high-ranking enough for such an honor?"

"Captain! Attend me!" Gevulin called brusquely from his place beside the carriage, where Jirvy, Kem, and Ipis rode in attendance on him.

Xilsi made a face. "Captain Xilsi is summoned. Keep your eyes open. If Astaylin has come all this way, that means the palace's attention has shifted in this direction. No one should ever want the palace's gaze to alight upon them. I don't envy you your situation, El."

"What are you imagining is my situation?"

"A fragile twig tossed into a rushing cataract."

"I'm not fragile."

"No, you aren't, are you? But the palace has the sharpest knives and the roughest waters. Know you can count on me, should such a day come."

The words kindled a strange warmth in Elen's heart. The viper stirred with a flicker of satisfaction. She met Xilsi's guileless gaze. "My thanks, Xil. The same to you, such as a deputy courier has to offer. But I have to ask. Did you really keep sleeping with Jirvy for five years after he'd gotten married?"

She flushed. "Oh. *That*. Ip must have told Kem the warden gossip. You're wondering if I just refused to see what was parading right in front of my face. Or simply couldn't imagine anyone choosing another over me. Honestly, I don't know. At this point, I'm not sure I need to know. Let the past flow like water downstream. Let it go. That's wisdom, isn't it?"

Elen smiled. So Sara'ala would certainly have hoped, never to hear their carping out loud again.

"Xilsi!" Gevulin's voice cracked like a whip.

The two women shared a nod. Xilsi rode forward to her commander.

Elen enjoyed an hour of peace and quiet in the autumn afternoon as the procession made its way to the bridge over the outer moat and through the gate onto the estate. It was a relief to be able to let down her guard at last, for this short ride at least. They ambled along the long lane through straw-strewn fields, past orchards wrapped and mulched against the coming winter, and amid the tidy outbuildings that marked a well-managed holding. Folk came to line the road and bow, dazzled by the unprecedented presence of two Exalted Highnesses. A tale to be passed down to their children's grandchildren!

The procession reached the fortress-like walls of the Manor, where the great gates stood invitingly open. Both Astaylin and Worvua climbed down at the threshold. Worvua clapped her hands and called out the name of the genius.

A wind rose, spinning into an agitated funnel cloud. The genius's ashy voice emerged. "What newcomers seek entry?"

The prince rode to the threshold. "I am Prince Gevulin, Prince of the Third Estate, All-Seeing Eye of the Imperial Order of Wardens, and much else besides, but my party is weary and much abused, those who have survived our journey. Ervis, allow me through so I may greet my blessed elder, Lord Genia."

"Let through His Exalted Highness!" a woman called from the other side of the gate.

Beyond lay the paved entry courtyard and a sweep of wide stone stairs leading up to the main portico and doors. Here stood Lord Genia, flanked by what, to Elen, seemed like a large village's worth of householders, kin, officials, soldiers, and menials standing in honor formation.

Gevulin dismounted and handed off his horse to a groom, then proceeded beside Astaylin and Worvua to the stairs. Genia greeted him warmly, tears in her eyes, and with but a slight flinch, after which she touched a scented handkerchief delicately to her nose.

In the tone of an aged aunt who may act in the most familiar manner even with an Exalted Highness, the woman clucked her tongue. "A bath first, Gevulin. Much desired, I am sure."

He placed a hand to his heart, perhaps too overcome to speak, or perhaps embarrassed at his filthy condition.

She went on so brightly that Elen could see she was fighting back a sob of relief. "Then we shall gather for a welcoming feast. I swear to you, youngling, I was quite overset when the appalling Lord Duenn told me you were dead."

"Ah. As expected, unfortunately."

Astaylin gave him a close look. "The news does not surprise you. Which part? Your supposed death? Or that news of it was delivered to Lord Genia some days ago by Lord Duenn himself?"

"What do you know of Lord Duenn?" he demanded. "He walked in your procession, under your wing, at the Feast of Lost Couplets. Is he one of yours?"

"One of my what?" she retorted with a sharpness she'd not shown before. "Don't play this dangerous game, Gevulin. You're not as good at it as you believe yourself to be."

Lord Genia opened her hands, palms up. "Your Exalted Highnesses, I pray you, from my seat of ancient wisdom, let us allow the travelers to be settled before we contest these unexpected questions. Gevulin." She used the name with gentle admonition, as might a noble nursemaid who has helped a little child take his first steps. "Clean hair, clean clothing, and a fine meal of food and drink will go a long way toward soothing the agitated spirit. We have much to speak of."

"Starting with the visit of Lord Duenn and the unexpected arrival of my honored sister!"

"Indeed. Let us continue this discussion in a way that honors our imperial manners."

He gave way, having been reminded of palace courtesy in front of the entire assembly.

Seeing Kem safe beside the other wardens, Elen had hoped to be dismissed and given leave to make her way to the barracks, among the other servants. Gevulin had other ideas. Astaylin had brought his entire original cavalcade with her, all three carriages, the beasts, and his entourage—including Hemerlin—who fell to their knees and wept to see him, having been told he was dead. The two concubines threw themselves at the prince's feet to lay their perfumed and perfectly coiffed heads against his grimy boots. Gevulin blinked as if ill at ease. He began to speak, stopped, fell silent. Had he remembered he was supposed to have an interlocutor? An awkward pause began to draw out.

With tears still streaking his cheeks, Hemerlin took charge. He lashed the menials with his fly whisk, saying, "Up! Up! To your duties!"

The concubines and body servants swept the prince off into the bathing rooms of the imperial wing. The four wardens were escorted off to the bathing chambers they'd used the first time they'd stopped over here. Prince Astaylin and the Manor-born went inside to wait in more comfort. The household dispersed.

Elen was left standing on the steps with no one to direct her where to go, wondering if she would be allowed to wash at all. While on the road, she could endure the dirt, since there was nothing for it but to live with it, but now every crawling itch and pimple of rash and budding sore prickled with urgency. Still, if there was no one to direct her where to go, that meant there was also no one to stop her from going to the barracks and seeing what accommodation they might have for a deputy courier. Warm water in a tub for washing. Somewhere to launder her clothing and hang it to dry. Hot soup, and a hunk of fresh bread, and a chance to pick up the local gossip. A bunk to sleep on. Such modest comforts would be glorious.

A voice snapped into her reverie. "Deputy Courier! Do not dilly-dally around. You are to attend the prince, by his order. Come at once!"

Hemerlin glowered in front of her.

"Chief Menial," she said politely.

He looked her up and down with a glare she could not interpret. "He sent *me* to fetch you," he added, in a tone that suggested his presence on this mundane task was so extraordinary that it baffled even him.

"Yes, Chief Menial."

When she picked up her pack, he clapped his hands twice. The youth, Snip, hurried forward, intending to carry the pack for her.

She halted Snip with a gesture. "My thanks, but I carry my own pack. Perchance, Chief Menial, might I be allowed to bathe?"

He gave a sniff, and grimaced. "You are *required* to bathe! I am to attend you, to make sure you do not run away, although why you would think to do so lies beyond my comprehension."

She followed him around the exterior to a side entrance that reminded her of the servants' entrance at the winter palace in South Ring, only this was better kept, with a bustling forecourt of its own surrounded by the many household services and workshops that kept a Manor running day to day. Even in the forecourt, blessed warmth poured out of every open doorway. A fire burned on an outdoor hearth, so people might not shiver too much as they crossed the pavement, going about their work. Inside, stoves radiated so much heat that she soon started sweating.

A small bathing room had been set aside for her use. Hemerlin himself collected a basket of soap and scrub brushes and followed her into where a wooden tub had been filled with hot water, with full rinse buckets set beside it. He shut the door so the two of them stood alone in the stone and hallow-wood-walled chamber.

Through the drain holes in the floor, Elen could hear water running from other bathing chambers, maybe those being used by the wardens. Maybe the prince, in the adjoining wing, if all drains ran to the same cistern, used for watering the gardens. That is, if bathwater that had touched the precious corpus of a prince was allowed to mingle with the wastewater of lesser folk. But no, this wasn't the Four Lands. The emperor might stand apart, but even an emperor was bound by the extensive network of law and procedure needed for tranquility to reign across the land.

She turned to face Hemerlin. "Chief Menial, if you please, I prefer to bathe myself, with no assistance."

"Is it true?" he demanded.

"Yes. I am not accustomed to having a bath attendant—"

"That you saved His Exalted Highness's life? That you will become the means of elevating him to the position he deserves? That you are more valuable to him than any regiment of loyal soldiers? So he told me."

"If he told you, then who am I to argue?" Sighing, she rubbed her forearm.

He watched the movement before lifting his gaze to her face. "I am to be personally responsible for your safety. I am commanded to treat your well-being as if it is directly tied to his security and, indeed, to his very life."

"Is that so?" She set her pack on the changing bench and dug out her one set of "indoor" clothing, wrinkled and redolent with a whiff of dampness from being crushed at the bottom for so many days. "In that case, might you see that these garments are shaken out and pressed and brought back, so I may look presentable in this noble Manor?"

Hemerlin stared at her as if she'd just sprouted a white viper. "These garments will not do, but I will take them so they can be measured for appropriate garb. Then they can be disposed of, or given to the indigent."

"I would like them cleaned and returned, if you please. Also my courier's gear."

"You are impertinent, Deputy Courier."

"So I have been told. Now, I would like to bathe."

When Hemerlin did not move, she sighed and tried again.

"Chief Menial, His Exalted Highness once informed me that you are his most valuable weapon. Not that I doubt his word, for who would ever doubt the word of an Exalted Highness? Not that I doubt your utility and importance to the prince's household, but it seemed to me, at the time, that he meant something specific. Might you enlighten me? If you and I are to work together to bring to the prince all he deserves, we must cooperate, must we not? I sense there may be more to you than people guess. They see an aging menial. I see a man whose experience and intelligence have protected a vulnerable prince for all his life within a hostile court."

Something hardened in Hemerlin's expression. She was treading on slippery ground. When they had first met, he had tried more than once to strike her with his fly whisk, which he considered his right. She'd do better to be mild and obedient, but instead a reckless urge overtook her. She was hungry and dirty and stuck, and that made her want to push.

"Shall I guess? You are no gagast, not like Fulmo. Not a swalter, obviously. Not an aivur, for you'd have come into your metal spirit by now, given your age, if what the aivur told us is true of their kind. What a fregir is, I do not know, nor if dragons walk among us unseen, as the playwrights would have it. A theurgist, perhaps, though it seems to me unlikely the Heart Temple would have allowed it. A sorcerer? No, surely not, for he'd have known—"

She broke off. She would not say Sara'ala's name, not here.

"Who'd have known?" Hemerlin demanded.

"If what I've learned is true, sorcery gains its power by leaching life out of living things, and you leave no sign of dust and ashes in your wake. Not that I saw. I suppose you might be that rare thing, a truly loyal servant. Precious, of course. But is it enough? So, what else might you be? I can only think of one other thing."

Again, she paused.

"Are you finished?" he said, fly whisk twitching in his left hand as if he itched to whack her but had been expressly forbidden to do so by the prince.

"Are you one of the Shorn?"

He touched his hair. As a palace menial of distinction, his long hair was pulled back into a knot at the back of his head and adorned with a trio of beaded ribbons. "Do you mean to insult me? Is this a test to see how far you can press your brazen cheek, now that His Exalted Highness has shown you such undeserved favor?"

Belatedly, it occurred to her that Snip, the servant boy, had shorn-short hair. She had no idea if short hair signified something in the palace hierarchy or was a temporary measure against lice. But of course, in the Four Lands, a shorn head was one of the visible signs of an atoner. Sara'ala had atoned for not joining the fight against the sorcerer-kings by becoming one of the Shorn. Were the customs related, far down some crooked path that led from ancient days to this day?

"I beg your pardon, Chief Menial. I meant something different by the word 'shorn.'" She didn't mind admitting it. His distress made her wonder if his childhood had left him with as many troubled memories and concealed scars as hers had. "If through my ignorance I have offended you, I apologize. If I am to join the prince's household, then I hope I may ask for your tutelage in such matters. I know nothing about the palace, while you know everything."

His grimace of distaste was not conciliatory. "We must hope you are able to learn, for you surely are ill-mannered and uncultivated. His Exalted Highness has let me know he will explain the whole later, when there is time. But don't believe you can bamboozle me with lies and flattery. There's nothing in the palace I haven't seen and don't know how to deal with! Here! Give me those ill-suited garments!"

He grabbed her spare clothes and slammed out of the room.

What a wild shot! But she saw a path to creating an alliance with him, if it came to that. People loved to impart their wisdom to others, and asking him to help her learn might soften him toward her. What if there really was nothing in the palace he hadn't seen, in his long life of service? Maybe all Gevulin had meant about the old man being his best weapon was that Hemerlin knew all the grubby corners and shades of intrigue necessary to keep a young prince safe in a hostile court. Knowledge was its own weapon.

She undressed, folded the dirty clothes she'd been wearing, and settled into the tub for a thorough wash and rinse. After drying off and wrapping a towel around her body, it took her some time to untangle all the snarls in her hair. She never minded the trouble, since it was her choice to keep it long.

The chamber was warm. The water copious. The soap scented. The towel soft. Would life in the palace be so bad?

But of course it would. She would be trapped in a cage.

No. Let go of that which cannot be solved today. For this day, she was clean and had a hope of getting a decent meal and an uninterrupted night's sleep. Kem was safe. Tomorrow would arrive regardless of her fretting.

With no warning, the door was opened from the outside. Hemerlin strode in carrying fresh garb: good-quality undergarments, trousers, tunic and indoor jacket suitable for Manor wear, and her boots, which had been cleaned and polished with expert skill.

"These will fit," he informed her. "Other garments appropriate to your new position in the prince's household are being requisitioned. Do you embroider?"

"Not with any skill. I'm a great mender, though. Why?"

"The prince's household must be dressed in a manner appropriate to his exalted status. Someone else will have to embroider your clothing for you, if you are not capable."

His tone implied "not capable" as being next door to "uncultured and unwashed." Although now she was washed, a fact that made her feel infinitely more cheerful.

He turned his back, making it clear he did not intend to leave while she dressed. She didn't like his refusal to go, but she wasn't self-conscious about her body, so she dropped the towel and dressed. He kept his back to her with stolid patience, a courtesy that allowed her to grant him a grudging scrap of approval.

The garments did indeed fit well. Someone had measured her other clothing. Even the sleeves on the jacket fit correctly, with neat, fresh stitches that suggested they'd been let down and resewn to be longer while she'd been washing. The undergarments had a fine, smooth slip against her skin. The trousers and underjacket paraded embroidery trim on their hems: festive fruit and jolly bats. A pair of elaborately beaded indoor shoes, more like slippers, completed the ensemble.

"My thanks for these tidy garments," she said. "They fit well."

He turned around to look her up and down, approving the fit with a sour nod. "Slovenly dress in a prince's entourage reflects poorly on the prince."

"Nevertheless, I appreciate it. Will I get my own clothing back?"

"Why would you want the garments returned, when you can have better?"

"Because they are mine, gotten through my own efforts."

"Very well," he said with a faint sneer. He gestured to the clothing she'd taken off before her bath. "These garments can be laundered and returned also, if you are so insistent."

"My thanks," she said drily.

"Do not presume, Deputy Courier. I am Chief Menial for His Exalted Highness. You are but a deputy courier."

She smiled graciously, hoping it would annoy him. "So I am, and

I am proud of my loyal service to the empire. How old were you when you came into the prince's service?"

His lips twitched. "Old enough."

"What was your position before that? How did the Exalted Highness's blessed mother find you and come to trust you enough to assign you to become her son's most loyal servant and guardian?"

"You ask too many questions."

"So I have been told." She gave him her best sunny beam of a guileless expression. "Yet how I am to learn what I need to know to make my way if I do not ask questions?"

By the way his hand gripped the fly whisk, she could tell he wanted to hit her but dared not. She bit down on a smile. Best not to get overconfident. She closed the flap of her pack and tied her boots to a loop on its side. Because she could be petty when she really wanted to, she handed the dirty clothing directly to Hemerlin rather than waiting for Snip to enter and take it.

His nose wrinkled up at the smell. He hastily opened the door to reveal Snip standing silently behind, head bowed. The youth took in the situation in an instant. Gathering the clothes, he hustled off.

"Come along," said Hemerlin brusquely. "It will not do to be late."

46

My Entire Storehouse of Wit

Hemerlin preceded Elen through the work wing and along a servant's walkway that ran the length of the massive ceremonial hall. Here, the entire household and countryside could gather for an august event or a seasonally ordained feast, with its gift-giving and formal readings of imperial proclamations. Now, however, the hall lay dark and exceedingly cold.

Past the hall, the walkway opened into the residential wing for the Manor-born. The balmier temperature in these rooms marked the change. Even in her light indoor clothing, she felt perfectly warm. Stoves and fireplaces glowed everywhere, fires crackling, youths stationed in every room to keep an eye out for dangerous sparks. Like treason, Elen supposed, where an unquenched ember might ignite a fire that burned down the entire edifice.

The chief menial led her into a spacious formal dining chamber adorned with huge tapestries depicting famous gardens in the imperial heartland. Elen counted nineteen people in total, seated at three different tables. The two Exalted Highnesses were seated at the round head table with Lord Genia to Gevulin's left and Worvua to Astaylin's right. Xilsi sat beside Worvua. She wore a pristine warden's uniform and had cleaned up startlingly well, scarcely a trace of their arduous adventures on her sweet bloom of a face. The last place at the table was taken by an older man Elen did not recognize; she hadn't seen him on their previous visit. The man's fly-whisk hair was almost as impressive as the prince's newly washed, braided, and beaded hair. Perhaps he was a lesser prince, like Xilsi.

Fulmo stood behind Gevulin. Astaylin had no gagast, just as she had not, Elen belatedly realized, spoken through an interlocutor earlier. Only the Pelis Manor interlocutor was present.

Three lesser scions sat at a second round table with three high-ranking officials. The three remaining wardens had been seated at a third table, along with an imperial historian, an elderly Heart Temple theurgist, and two people wearing the tabards of the Imperial Order of Engineers.

Hemerlin showed Elen to a seat between Kem and the historian.

She hesitated. It seemed perilous to join such a feast, in the sight of so many, like announcing you meant to join the race. She'd far rather have eaten among the deputy officials and other congenial folk in the barracks. At the head table, Prince Gevulin looked her way and gave an impatient nod of command. Even so, she paused with a hand on the back of her chair. It was only when Kem gave her a beseeching look that she sat.

Kem bent close, squeezing her hand too hard. "I didn't know where you'd gone."

"Ouch. A less exalted bathing chamber."

He released her hand. "Those are nice clothes. I got a new warden's uniform. It needs alteration, but it'll do for now."

She rubbed her fingers along the fine wool of his sleeve. "This is really good quality."

"Mama would have been beside herself!" He preened, proud of his new clothing. Ipis cast him an amused look.

Jirvy nodded to greet Elen. He had foresworn his jaunty kerchief for the staid heartland custom for Manor-born men, his hair pulled tightly back into a bun and wrapped by a ribbon.

A bell rang. Everyone fell silent as Lord Genia rose with a glass of wine in hand.

"Blessed are those who the High Heavens allow to share their bounty with unexpected guests. As it is said, 'Let the heart shelter any who seek its haven.'"

The interlocutor spoke a prayer, and then it was time to eat. A stream of servers came and went, delivering platters of food. Fulmo tasted none of the food, a mark of Gevulin's trust in Lord Genia. For the first stage of the feast, people ate with close attention to the various dishes: Pan-fried meat-and-ginger dumplings. Slices of chicken marinated in sesame oil and dressed with scallions. Noodles with smoked duck. Pickled bamboo shoots. Steamed perch. Mutton-stuffed bread. Poppyseed buns. Sliced fruit soaked in batter and then fried. The only conversation was a commentary on the flavors, textures, and variety of the food.

At length, the onslaught of dishes ceased. Soothing after-dinner drinks were brought in and poured. At a nod from Lord Genia's chief menial, the servers left the room, leaving only the twenty seated people, the three chief menials, the gagast, and the interlocutor. This represented some manner of trusted inner council, Elen guessed. The wardens, Hemerlin, and Fulmo served Gevulin, of course, but of the other officials present, she wasn't sure who had come with Astaylin and who was part of Pelis Manor.

Genia rapped her spoon against her glass. "Now then, Gevulin, I have many questions that will not wait." She addressed Astaylin. "With your permission, Your Exalted Highness."

"I, too, have questions for my little brother. Pray relate your story, Gevulin. We are all ears."

As the younger sibling, he had to obey. He took a moment to compose his thoughts, sipping at his wine, before setting down the glass and clearing his throat as a prelude to speaking.

"As you wish, Honored Sister. I came north in answer to a message from the warden captain of Far Boundary Vigil. Beyond Orledder Intendancy, I discovered the road through Grinder's Cut was blocked by a pair of landslides. More troublingly, I discovered the road had been blocked for almost two years because the Imperial Order of Engineers have not yet managed to clear it."

Astaylin showed no sign of taking offense, despite the implication that the order under her personal oversight had failed in their duty. "Yes, I'll have something to say about that. Go on."

"I was in a hurry, fearing for the life of my Vigil captain. I was right to be concerned."

"Captain Mekvo is dead?" exclaimed Worvua. "We knew him!"

Across the gap between the tables, Xilsi glanced at Jirvy, who gave her a sympathetic nod. She replied with a sad smile of shared grief.

"I will get to the Vigil in a moment," Gevulin went on. "When I returned to Orledder Halt, I thought I would have to take a detour stretching into many weeks of traveling through the western provinces in order to eventually turn northeast and cross into Woodfall Province. However, the Orledder intendant offered me the services of his deputy courier. She knew of a way to cross Grinder's Cut with a delay of some ten days. This we accomplished, although it was clear someone working in association with the palace tried to stop us. Lord Duenn, for one, whom I encountered at Orledder Halt. Know you anything of his business, Honored Sister?"

Her gaiety had vanished as his tale unfolded. "I do not, but I'm getting an inkling of an idea that I do not much care for. I shall speak of that later. Go on."

"We met trouble at Pisgia Moat, where we found a dead griffin and its rider."

Astaylin shut her eyes in a spasm of grief. "I feared this," she murmured, then opened her eyes again. "Go on."

"We crossed the canyonlands. We spent a night in comfort here at Pelis Manor North."

"It is always a pleasure to host you, Your Highness," Lord Genia replied, "and especially this past visit, when you entertained us with such congenial and amusing conversation. As a boy, you were never one to venture jesting remarks, so I was surprised by how your sly wit has grown during your years in the palace."

"Were you?" Gevulin's jaw twitched. Elen could feel the intensity of his spiking anger.

"Humor sits well with you, Your Highness."

"Jesting remarks and congenial conversation! From Gevulin!" Astaylin chuckled. "Will wonders never cease?"

Gevulin's hand tightened on his glass and, reflexively, he raised it toward his mouth before lowering it without taking a sip. He swallowed something, not wine, that was for sure; probably he caught back an aggrieved response. Yet a moment later, remarkably, a smile flickered on his lips as if he could finally glimpse a scrap of humor in the situation. He looked at the two women in turn and spoke in a dry tone.

"As it happens, I have used up my entire storehouse of wit, so you should expect nothing further."

Astaylin laughed delightedly. Genia smiled. Worvua exchanged a startled glance with the older man at the high table, the one with the princely fly-whisk braids. By their reactions, a fish might as well have walked into the room and asked permission to sing "The Ballad of the Lost Trousers."

"Let me return to the matter at hand. During our stay here, I heard from Lord Genia that Duenn had made an impertinent offer of marriage between one of his sons and Lady Worvua."

"Which we briskly refused," put in Lord Genia. "The nerve of him!"

"Indeed," Gevulin agreed. "After that, we went on. We reached Far Boundary Vigil, only to discover the garrison dead. Killed by sarpa acid."

"Sarpa acid!" exclaimed Astaylin. A grim tension gripped the people in the chamber. "What do you think of that, Nwelin!" She addressed the older man with princely familiarity.

Nwelin replied gravely, "It would be an appalling misuse of the sarpa to attack our own people."

"Indeed, so I concluded myself," said Gevulin. "Yet there was no chance to consider the matter further. Lord Duenn made a most untimely arrival at Far Boundary Vigil. Because he had with him a substantial company of militia, I felt obliged first to hide, and then to flee, to my shame. I lost my good captain, Simo."

How deftly he glided over the entire journey into the Four Lands!

"No shame, Little Brother. Just prudence. This is troubling news."

"More troubling still, at Far Boundary Vigil, Duenn was in company with a hooded person whom he addressed as 'Your Sublime Highness.'"

"What do you mean?" asked Astaylin sharply. "Someone must have misheard."

"I said what I meant."

"It's not possible. Minaylin never leaves the palace."

"I stand by it. He was there. Min-lo is involved."

She leaned forward. A tall woman, she had bulk on him; he was leaner and more lightly built. In a wrestling match, Elen would have put her money on Astaylin. But for a dance up and down the Ten Peaks or a strenuous overland journey, she'd absolutely bet on Gevulin. Perhaps Astaylin meant her looming to intimidate her little brother. He regarded her with an impatient disdain that Elen admired for its haughty superciliousness, even as she remembered how the haunt could have defused the same tense moment with a sardonic joke. Seeing that Gevulin was quite serious and so cocksure as to be impossible to argue with, Astaylin sat back. She looked at Xilsi for support.

Xilsi shook a scolding finger at her. "You should believe your brother."

Jirvy watched the exchange with a slight flinch, the sting of a long-awaited blow. He could never sit at the head table, but Xilsi would always be able to, and it bothered him as it did not bother Elen.

Astaylin raised a hand in the manner of a poet ready to declaim in a battle of rhymes. "Let me interpolate my tale here, to help make sense of yours. As prince-general of the Imperial Order of Engineers, I received word at the time of the avalanches about the blocked imperial road across Five Bridges at Grinder's Cut. I sent my best engineers and supplies to deal with the matter. I received interim reports and, eventually, a message that repairs were well on their way and would be completed soon. This was months ago. Yet one month ago, I received a private communique, from a source I cannot name, that the road was still closed, and that a prince had been barred from going north because of it. You will understand why this became an urgent matter for me to look into."

"Yes." Gevulin's tone wasn't gloating, rather calm and analytical. "It made you look bad to the palace, as if you aren't competent enough to manage the engineers."

Astaylin's anger, Elen saw at last, was not directed at Gevulin.

"That's right. Someone deliberately deceived me in order to undercut my reputation. What made the entire affair even stranger, Little Brother, is that when I came through with my carriages a few days ago, the road was open. That's how I was able to bring your carriages with me as well."

"How could the road have been opened so quickly, when it was so thoroughly blocked when I saw it?" Gevulin shook his head.

Astaylin gave a distracted tug on her fly-whisk braids as she considered. "Perhaps the road had been repaired and a scheme put in place to temporarily block you."

"That's a great deal of work to go to," he objected.

"It does seem so, but let me return to your earlier question. Duenn Manor did walk under my awning in the Lost Couplets procession. Yet that courtesy toward Duenn came about in a strange manner. Our benevolent and most majestic and imperial sister the Magnolia Emperor personally asked me to grant a small show of favor to the Duenn people because of our pressing need for more hallow-wood at a better price."

"Ah, yes, the imperial treasury runs low." Gevulin nodded.

"So it does. Yet here I arrive at Pelis Manor North to discover they have been expanding their hallow-wood reserves for years, with a view toward increasing the supply for imperial needs without demanding grasping prices for the lumber." She raised her glass toward Lord Genia. "Thus we return to your encounters with Duenn Manor, Esteemed Genia."

The old woman took up the story. "So we have, as Gevulin mentioned. Lord Duenn proposed a marriage between his son Rienn and Worvua. Duenn Manor is a mere provincial Manor. We might consider one of our minor cousin branches as a partner for Rienn, perhaps, but not a sar of the line like Worvua! My own granddaughter! I confess I was shocked by Duenn's brazen offer, for it was couched more as demand than humble request. We sent him on his way, I assure you."

Worvua leaned in excitedly. "Papa and I thought that was the end of it, yet not three days ago Duenn returned here with a yet larger force. That's when he said you were dead, Your Highness."

Elen stiffened. Hearing Duenn's hateful voice at the Vigil had made her feel sick. Kem nudged her, looking concerned but not worried for himself. He had no violent memories of Duenn to burden him. She ventured a wan smile to reassure Kem as Worvua went on.

"Duenn again proposed the alliance, only this time he had his son with him. A sorrier creature I have never met. Poor temperament, poor manners, and atrocious fashion sense. Besides that, the Duenn people are grasping and rude and rough."

"We are sure they are behind the attacks on our hallow-wood plantations," said Genia, "but we haven't been able to prove it is them and not local troublemakers."

Astaylin nodded. "Duenn wishes to control the bulk of Woodfall Province's hallow-wood supply. A lucrative prospect. What happened on his second visit?"

"He threatened me," said Genia through gritted teeth.

Worvua added, "That boorish son of his tried to kiss me without my permission! I kneed him in his winesack. Disgusting creature."

"Like to his crude father, then," said Gevulin.

Kem shifted restlessly next to her, and Elen rested a hand on his knee, while Jirvy offered him a reassuring nod as if to say *You belong to us now, not to him.*

Gevulin added tartly, "Having met the man, I am only surprised you did not have your genius whip him out of the Manor."

"When is it you met Duenn, again?" Astaylin asked.

"At Orledder Halt. He tried to take one of my wardens from me, claiming he had more right to the youth than I did."

"By the High Heavens' latrine, that's a shocking breach of propriety and rank!" breathed Astaylin.

Gevulin turned back to Genia. "After you refused Duenn's proposal the second time, did he leave, as he ought?"

"Oh no! He refused to depart, not even when the Illustrious Nwelin informed him that his presence was no longer acceptable in our Manor."

Nwelin nodded. "It was disturbing, I will confess. Duenn seemed convinced I could not require him to leave. I! And him a mere provincial, not what I would call Manor-born."

"He did have many more soldiers than we do," explained Lord Genia. "He posted them all about the Manor in a most threatening way. I feared we would have to hustle Worvua out by cover of night, on the back path and past the sarpa pen and the Pall inlet all the way through Thunderbolt Hollow. Fortunately, it didn't come to that."

"I arrived here at the Manor on my fact-finding mission in a most timely, if unexpected manner," said Astaylin. "Duenn did not expect to see me, that is certain. I chased him and his people off. He could scarcely refuse once I gave him the order, after all."

"He refused Nwelin," Gevulin pointed out. "That's shocking enough."

"Little Brother, you and I are not like the other princes, are we?"

Gevulin acknowledged her with a nod. Neither needed to say aloud that they two were in line for the throne, should such an eventuality occur. "When was this, again? Two days ago?"

"Yes."

"Have any of you seen sarpa in that time?"

"Sarpa!" Astaylin exclaimed. "What have sarpa to do with this?"

Gevulin pulled the bone whistle from around his neck and set it on the table.

Nwelin gestured, and Worvua pushed the whistle across to him. He examined it intently. Elen leaned forward, caught in the tension of the moment. Why did he not look surprised?

After a moment, Nwelin looked up. "As it happens, two nights ago my attendants spotted a riderless sarpa laboring in the sky, flying south. We lured it down. I settled it in the sarpa pen, where it continues to lie in a cold stupor."

"Riderless, but it had been ridden?" Gevulin asked eagerly.

"Yes, the harness was intact, but the rider's cage missing, broken off by an unknown force. No rider to be seen. I deduce this is the rider's whistle."

"It is. The rider is dead." How careful Gevulin was to give no hint of how the sarpa rider had died!

"I see," said Nwelin. "There were no other identifying marks on the sarpa, but there were dried smears on the harness that might have been the rider's blood. Quite a mystery, you may imagine."

"The harness held a corps badge, surely?" Astaylin asked. "Which unit did it belong to?"

"No military badge or unit designation at all," said Nwelin. "But the sarpa's harness has brass buckles incised with a stylized five-petaled oleander flower."

"Minaylin's device." Astaylin's tone was harsh.

All Elen could think of was that slight, hooded figure at the Vigil, with his whispery, malicious voice.

47

Enough of This Sad Poetry

Astaylin called an abrupt end to the feast. Basins were brought for washing, after which the Exalted Highnesses rose. Everyone agreed they must visit the sarpa pen immediately, although it only mattered that Astaylin and Gevulin wanted to go.

"This way," said Lord Genia graciously. As host and guide, she took the lead.

Elen walked at the back of the procession, with a pair of imperial sentinels pacing at the rear. Her years of courier duty—*keep your eyes open*—overrode her apprehension about Duenn's whereabouts, so as they walked through the main wing she examined the surroundings. The grand foyer ran past a formal receiving room with a plush chair set upon a dais overlooking ranks of stone benches, followed by three richly appointed salons where special guests would be entertained, each more expensively furnished than the last, according to some ladder of status whose rules Elen did not know. The gilded decorations of the public rooms gave way to a mural-lined hallway that opened onto luxurious offices and parlors for meetings among intimates and sitting rooms that had a more lived-in look.

A child peeped out from behind a partly open door and said in a piping voice, "He's very handsome! He must be a prince! And look at her! So beautiful! Like from the song, *a flower caught my eye and now I dream of its sweet bloom!* No, not the taller one in front, that's Prince Astaylin, I know that! The one there, after Uncle Nwelin and Cousin Worvua."

A sharp voice hushed the child. The door abruptly shut.

Genia said, "My pardon, Your Exalted Highness."

"No, no, say nothing more. Truth spoken by infants, as they say." Astaylin smiled as she glanced back at Xilsi, who walked behind Astaylin, Gevulin, and Nwelin. Xilsi wore an impassive expression, pretending she hadn't heard. But Elen abruptly wondered if the order of march indicated status, which suggested Nwelin was indeed a prince of some kind, as his hairstyle suggested. Whatever "Illustrious" indicated about his estate. Worvua walked a pace behind Xilsi. How odd.

A soft click caught Elen's ear. She glanced back in time to see the door crack open again and the same small face peek out. She would have waved in friendly amity, but deputy couriers didn't do that sort of thing in the grand corridors of one of the Noble Six Manors.

Still, the poem the child had quoted made Elen think of Sara'ala, who would have winked flirtatiously at the child and offered an answering couplet, something so dry and witty that everyone would have laughed. Maybe even Gevulin would have chuckled, even though he had the most reason to hate the haunt. But how could anyone hate Sara'ala? Such a prospect seemed unfathomable, not once you got to know his smooth talking, his ability to not take himself seriously, and the veins of honor and regret and pride that ran through him like seams of precious ore. Just as knowing him had been precious, for however short a time.

A painted door let onto a main service hallway. Servants stood with their backs against the walls and their hands pressed together, heads bowed, as the Exalted Highnesses passed.

The passage let onto the eastern courtyard, where rose the Manor's Heart Temple. A Manor had as large a population as a prosperous village, and thus its own custodian and healer. They processed past the temple's four-arched entrance and reached an outer gate set into the Manor's encircling wall, which was also the limit of the genius. A swirl of ash spun overhead as they crossed under the threshold and into the garden beyond, the genius on watch over the Manor's comings and goings.

Fulmo halted just outside the gate. Dusk had taken hold. By lamplight, the group continued walking along a raised hallow-wood boardwalk. Elen felt odd wearing indoor shoes while outdoors, but the walkway was as polished and well swept as any interior floor.

She eased up beside Hemerlin. "My pardon, Chief Menial. I can't help but notice that Worvua seems on close terms with the older man, the Illustrious Nwelin. And that he walks ahead of Xilsi. He is a prince, I take it?"

"At least you have discerned that much," he groused sourly. "He is a prince of the Fourth Estate. He married Lord Genia's daughter, who is deceased. An excellent match for Pelis Manor, reward for Lord Genia's long friendship with the Elegant Consort. A lesser match for Nwelin, of course, as Genia's daughter could claim no palace lineage on either side, but the marriage allowed Nwelin to leave the palace and live in greater freedom here in the north."

"Worvua is his daughter?"

"Yes."

That explained a great deal! "So that is why Xilsi walks behind Prince Nwelin, because she is a prince of the Sixth Estate."

Hemerlin gave her a penetrating glare. "Her Highness Xilsilin does not speak of her lineage nor bandy it about. How did you figure that out?"

"Oh, she and I have become great friends," said Elen gaily, enjoying his expression of bafflement as it was slowly succeeded by outrage. Hemerlin was too easy to bait. She knew better, yet she could not resist testing how far her worth to the prince extended. "But, Chief Menial, might that not mean you are therefore also of princely lineage? Hemer-*lin*? I never thought about it before."

"Of course you did not think," he observed tartly. "A mere deputy courier, and a provincial at that. I daresay you have never even set foot in the heartland, much less the palace."

"I have not," agreed Elen with her sunniest smile. "Apparently, under your esteemed guidance and protection, I shall soon do so."

"Hush your unseemly chatter!"

They crossed a bridge over the holystone moat and entered the outer precincts of the Manor. Here lay more extensive gardens, orchards, moat-ringed stables for valuable horses, and kennels of hunting dogs who barked excitedly as they walked past on the raised walkway. Both the hallow-wood planking and the gap between their exalted feet and the mundane earth separated the highborn from the risk of encountering Spore. It was remarkable how status and wealth protected a person against the dangers that tillers and carters and gleaners and other small folk faced every day, they who walked about their lives on ordinary paths and slept behind unprotected walls.

A cold wind sheared through their ranks. Branches rustled. Evergreens swayed. A bird called *ee-voo ee-voo lar-loo ee-voo*. Elen relaxed a little. Noisy birds signaled safety at dusk and dawn. Birds had a sense for Spore and would fly away if disturbed by its rising presence.

The highborn walked ahead, the rigid indoor order of march sliding into a set of less hierarchical pairs. Most of the conversation flowed between the amiable Astaylin and the voluble Worvua, who Elen would have said was trying too hard. In comparison, Gevulin said very little, responding only to questions put to him directly by

Nwelin. The wardens and sentinels remained quiet, as they must be while the highborn spoke among themselves.

Their group crossed a second moat and passed through an ironbound gate onto a gravel-strewn field plucked clean of weeds and sprouts. In the middle of this bare expanse rose a rectangular barn-like structure with a faintly gleaming roof: the sarpa pen. Chimneys lined one side of the outer wall, but no smoke emerged. The fires weren't lit.

A pair of servants wearing Manor badges hurried out to greet Prince Nwelin, accompanied by a youth with shorn-short hair, who carried a lantern to light their way indoors. Realizing they had neglected to recognize the princes of the Third Estate, the two servants knelt before the Exalted Highnesses, covering their faces with their hands.

"The fault is ours."

"Nay, nay, it is dark and you could not have known we were coming, good people," said Astaylin in a kind voice. "That you do your duty faithfully and well is all the observance we need."

Astaylin was good at being the compassionate, well-loved prince, Elen reflected as she watched the servants' grateful expressions. But was Astaylin too good? Was it a part of her game? Or was it real?

Gevulin said, "We don't have time for this. Show us the sarpa."

"Let us go to the viewing deck." Nwelin gestured for Astaylin and Gevulin to precede him, although the youth with the lamp led the way.

The lamp was a sealed glass sphere. Its light held the blue-white brightness of a fire spirit, the most difficult of spirits to bind with theurgy because of fire's volatile nature. Because a fire spirit inside a glass sphere gave off much less heat than oil, wood, or coal, it was a form of light crucial for a sarpa pen, that had to stay cold.

Inside lay a suite of rooms with an office, a barracks corridor where several servants were asleep beneath heaps of blankets, a harness room, a cache of barrels, an entry into a cellar where ice would be stored during the summer, and a large shed brimful of cut wood and boxes of coal. Only the office and the workshop were lightly heated with braziers. The other spaces were all bitterly cold. Encased in only the flimsy indoor slippers, Elen's toes began to feel stiff.

A new, musty scent tickled her nose. The viper stirred.

They took a stairway up to a balcony that ran all the way around the interior of the sarpa pen. The entire building was a single pen, sarpa being aggressively solitary creatures. Four spherical lamps illuminated the large space, one midway along each wall. Even with four such fire-spirit lights, the vault-like interior was dim, and the single sarpa little more than a murky bulk curled up on a bed of sand. Stoves lined the long sides of the pen, although none were lit. Barrels stood against the lower walls, marked with the word "ice." For now, the cold weather was enough to keep the sarpa in a safe stupor until its handlers needed to wake it up.

Gevulin stood at the railing to examine the sarpa, his frown deepening. "Jirvy, what do you think? Is that the one that attacked us?"

Jirvy studied the beast, then said, "I'll need a closer look at the kit it was wearing. Hard to see features in this light, but that pale streak above its left eye might be a scar from the damage it took smashing through the gate. Is there something stuck in its tail?"

"You went into no detail about the sarpa's attack," said Astaylin. "I sense there is a great deal you left out of your account. Do assuage my curiosity, Little Brother."

"Not standing here, in this cold," said Gevulin. "To be honest, Honored Sister, I would be grateful for a comfortable bed before we consider the whole of our situation."

"*Our* situation?"

"Do you not see it so? We both have been herded into compromising situations by someone in the palace who has the means and the desire to do so."

"Perilous talk."

"So it is." He drew a hand over his eyes, took in a weary breath, then recalled where and with who he was and straightened resolutely. "So it must be, given what we now know."

"Yes," she agreed. "But you have ridden a long way in exhausting and harsh circumstances, I can see that. The rest of our discussion will wait until morning."

Lord Genia set a hand on Gevulin's arm. "If you will, Your Highness, your suite will be ready by now. Chief Menial?"

Hemerlin gave his fly whisk a swish that sent Ipis skipping back out of its way. "Your Highness, you will benefit from a good night's rest."

"We wouldn't want our dear Gevulin to lose his looks, would we?" said Astaylin. She threw a wink at Xilsi, who had so far maintained a silence appropriate to a warden captain. "Few are so fortunate as you, my love, unworn and undiminished."

"Enough of this sad poetry," said Xilsi, goaded into breaking her silence. "You lot go ahead, Your Exalted Highnesses." Her exaggerated palace drawl gave the honorific a sardonic lilt. "The wardens and I would like to look over the harness. I'd also like to keep the deputy courier for the length of our investigation, with your permission, Your Exalted Highness."

Gevulin hesitated, mouth pinched as he considered. "Very well. Hemerlin, you will remain with the wardens and bring the deputy courier back when they are finished. Kem will attend me."

Astaylin's gaze darted from Xilsi, to Gevulin, to Hemerlin, to Kem, measuring the odd interaction. She skipped right over Elen. A deputy courier was too far below her exalted limit of vision. What a relief. Maybe a humble deputy courier could survive the palace, if no one in the higher ranks deigned to see her. Gevulin hadn't been able to see her when they'd first met. He'd only learned to see her because he'd been forced to witness what Sara'ala saw, and what Sara'ala cared about. No wonder his princely perspective had shifted. Some things in life could not be unseen once they became visible for the first time. The world must look different to him now.

Elen caught Kem's eye as he left. He gave her a nod. They were back in tune, after the days of his anger and hurt. She could let him go without worrying too much. At least he'd be warm.

Nwelin remained behind. Once the two Exalted Highnesses, Genia, and Worvua had departed, the older prince settled into a more relaxed manner.

"I'll take you down, if you wish," he said to Xilsi, adding a nod for Jirvy. "You can inspect the sarpa yourself to see if you recognize any further identifying marks."

"Isn't that dangerous?" Ipis whispered.

Nwelin lifted the wall-sphere in its wire basket and, holding it out in front, led them to an interior stairway that descended behind the wall and down into the enclosure. "Less dangerous than Spore, young warden. What is your name?"

"Oh, uh, Your Highness, I am Ipis Vunnussar."

"Wave-lashed Vunnus, on the shore of the southern sea. I've hunted sarpa there." He drew a hand along the curve of his neck, where pale scars striped the skin like rope burns.

"You have? In the Snarling Lagoons?"

"Quite right. And more desolate areas as well. The Golden Sands, do you know it?"

"No, Your Highness. Not to have gone there, but isn't it southeast of the Venom Shoals?"

"Exactly so, young warden. Well done. You've paid attention to your lessons."

Ipis beamed.

"Anyway, my point is that Spore can only be eradicated, so we use blunt methods to destroy it. But sarpa can be controlled, and thus to hunt and train sarpa is an art. For example, cold keeps the sarpa in a stupor. Autumn and winter are an easy time for sarpa riders since they can use heat to control their sarpa. It's summer when most accidents happen. Aspiring riders train in the winter. Newly badged riders patrol in the cooler months. Only experienced riders patrol in the heat. So it may be that the rider on this sarpa was a trainee."

"He was a middle-aged man," said Xilsi. "Sarpa riders start young, so surely he'd been riding sarpa for a few years at least."

"Perhaps he trained and served outside the corps," Nwelin mused.

"Is that possible, Your Highness?" Jirvy asked. "For a sarpa rider to not be a member of the Sarpa Corps? I thought all sarpa came under control of the palace."

"The two are not mutually exclusive," said Nwelin.

"If the crown prince is involved," said Xilsi, "he is of the palace, is he not?"

"Exactly. His Sublime Highness is in and of the palace. Thus, he has access to sarpa."

48

A Testimonial

The steps ended in a metal-sheeted doorway, which opened onto a landing set on stilts on the floor of the pen. Nwelin halted as they took in the sight of the sarpa's massive shape. It seemed much larger from this angle, and more so now that it was still, even with its long body and tail curled up. Its musky smell permeated the air, accompanied by a scent as of burned flowers. Down here, on the floor of the pen, the air had a weighty quality as if the sarpa's slow respiration was sucking up the light.

The prince spoke softly. "As a youth, I wished to become a sarpa rider, but it was not allowed. Thus, I chose a more scholarly pursuit of my obsession. I have spent my life studying sarpa. This sarpa pen, for example, includes a few innovations I and my hostlers have designed. Most specifically, better control of heating and cooling, so fewer physical restraints are needed." Well launched, Nwelin kept speaking with the eagerness of a person who loves what they do. "Five years ago, I sent a testimonial to the palace containing my observations. I included detailed suggestions for new methods of training for riders, meant to reduce mishaps and injuries. An official course of apprenticeship for hostlers. A plan to expand the breeding program by adding provincial hostelries in the north, where the winter would allow for longer gentling periods for young sarpa."

"What happened then?" Xilsi asked.

"I was sent the compulsory receipt from the Inner Secretariat to show my testimonial had been received. But I never heard anything more. Nor did I receive a reply from the Magnolia Emperor, as I had expected. What would you make of that, Hemerlin?"

His question startled Elen. Up to now, Nwelin had ignored the chief menial, but if you looked closely, the two men might be said to bear a family resemblance. Although maybe it was just the dim surroundings that made Elen think so.

"One cannot know," said Hemerlin primly, "but given the circumstances and recent events, it suggests the testimonial came to the desk of the emperor and was removed from it by one of the four people who would have had an opportunity to pluck it from her desk."

"Yes, my thought as well."

"Who would those be?" Elen said in an undertone to Xilsi.

She said, "The head secretary. The emperor's chief menial. The Dowager Consort, who is the emperor's birth mother. And, of course, the crown prince."

"Exactly so," Nwelin said. "I heard a rumor through the loose network of sarpa scholars and hostlers that the crown prince has developed an interest in sarpa. I dismissed it at the time as youthful hijinks or reckless stubbornness. His benevolent and majestic mother would surely forbid such activity. Yet perhaps the other rumors are true after all, that she forbids him nothing, and therefore, he gets everything he wants."

Hemerlin pressed his hands together. "Your Highness, do you think Gevulin is in danger?"

Nwelin fixed his gaze on the motionless sarpa. "I should say the Exalted Gevulin is in exactly the same degree of danger as the Exalted Astaylin. The only two living princes who stand in the Third Estate. The only current potential heirs to the crown prince's position."

Silence met his statement. The answer was obvious now that the question had been asked.

"That is why we are here." Nwelin gestured toward the massive beast lying somnolent on the sand. "Who wishes to inspect the sarpa up close?"

"I do," said Jirvy at once.

"I did not catch your name, Warden."

"Jirvy Ayannol, Your Highness."

"Ah. A meritorious Manor." Nwelin's interest in Jirvy immediately took a precipitous plunge. Jirvy's jaw tightened but he gave no other sign he'd noticed as Prince Nwelin turned to the others. "Anyone else to enter the pen?"

Xilsi waved a hand in the negative. Ipis shook her head very, very hard. Hemerlin took a step back to shelter in the open door.

"I'll go, if I may," said Elen softly.

Nwelin's keen gaze fixed on her. "Deputy Courier, is it?"

"Yes, Your Highness. Out of Orledder Halt."

He did not ask her name. "Sarpa are sensitive to heat and cold, as we have discussed. They are also sensitive to pain around their nostrils. And to tones from their rider's whistle, each one of which is crafted out of a hatchling sarpa rib. By these methods, their riders control them. Sarpa are also sensitive to vibrations. For that reason, there are stepping stones set into the sand. Follow my steps on the stones. Don't walk on the sand. Once we set out, do not speak. Save your questions for afterward, or ask them now."

When neither Jirvy nor Elen said anything, he set out across the stepping stones, holding the sphere in its wire basket to light their way. The stones were flat and wide, close enough together that they created an easy path while still allowing the level of sand between them to rise and fall for reasons Elen supposed had to do with sarpa management. The basket of light enfolded them, rippling through the darkness as they moved steadily forward, Nwelin in the lead, Jirvy behind him, and Elen at the trailing edge of the sphere's pale aura.

The viper stirred, coming awake with a sting as if its tongue had licked her heart. It nosed within her chest. It wanted to make its way down her arm. To confront the sarpa.

It hissed, the sound like a buzz inside her. None of the others heard, but around them, the sand trembled, shifted, spilled to create new crests and hollows, then quieted.

Nwelin halted, peering intently toward the sarpa. When there was no further movement, he went on.

The stone path split, allowing them to move around—out of range of the head with its deadly acid—to the sarpa's shoulder, where the wings met the body. In rest, the wings were folded upright like a tall crest. Its skin had abrasions. Some looked like the wear marks of an ill-fitting harness. Others were consistent with scrapes and welts from stone and splintered pieces of wood, as it would have received at the Vigil gates. Jirvy crouched, the better to study the length of the sarpa's shoulder, the peak of its leathery wings, the long neck, the feathery brows, and the marks above its eyes.

The resting beast loomed like a spiraling mound of cruel death. Its girth was greater than a tall man's height. Stretched out, it would span the entire length of the building, some forty strides. Elen's breath steamed in the cold air.

The sarpa's eyes moved beneath closed lids. Ripples coursed through its coiled body. The prince froze, gestured at them to move no closer. But the cold weighed it down, too heavy a force to lift. Its tongue flickered as its huge mouth parted slightly, tasting the air. It sensed the restless viper.

Elen had to get away before the presence of the viper jolted the beast out of its cold-induced stupor. She tapped Jirvy on the shoulder. When he looked back at her, she tapped her chest twice and her forearm once. He grasped the situation immediately and gestured toward the landing.

Nwelin had caught the exchange, but he said nothing. Beneath the sphere's steady light, he led them back by a route that took them past the beast's crooked tail. A ragged sliver of wood, about a forearm's length, had gotten stuck between two segments of the tail. The fragment was hallow-wood. So was the Vigil gate. After taking a moment to observe this injury, they crossed back to the landing and, with the other three, ascended the stairs to the balcony.

Once they were on the other side of the door, Xilsi said to Nwelin, "Do you have a copy of the testimonial you sent? And the official sealed receipt?"

"In the office."

Nwelin replaced the sphere in its holder. They made their careful way back through the darkness until they reached the living quarters of the hostlers. The office seemed balmy compared to the frigid enclosure. Nwelin lit several oil lamps and placed them on the table. The on-duty hostler took herself off to the workshop to give the highborn privacy for their consultation.

The prince went to a cabinet and brought out two documents. "This is my own copy of the testimonial. The original was sent for the emperor's eyes only, since one would not wish to have such information fall into the hands of an enemy who might think to trap and breed and train their own sarpa corps. This is the receipt."

Xilsi sat and began to read the testimonial.

"Your Highness, may I examine the receipt you received from the palace?" Hemerlin asked. "Do you have a magnifying glass with which I may examine the seal?"

"I do have a glass," said Nwelin with a surprised laugh. "I confess, it never occurred to me to examine the seal closely. But of course it would occur to you, would it not, uncle?"

Jirvy gave Elen a look that suggested he was as confused as she was by what this address—uncle?—suggested about convoluted palace relationships. In a village, elders were generally addressed as "aunt" or "uncle" regardless of kinship ties, but it seemed unlikely such casual usage was commonplace in the rigid palace hierarchy.

The Nameless Land

Hemerlin brought the receipt with its wax seal to a lamp and proceeded to make an intensely close examination.

"Your Highness," said Jirvy, "if I may, might I request something to write on in order to record my observations of the sarpa?"

"In that cabinet." Nwelin sniffed with a disdain that reminded Elen of Gevulin, only Gevulin always treated Jirvy with respect. Nwelin then pointedly engaged Ipis in small talk, asking about her Vunnus relations and the south coast. He seemed unconcerned by, or ignorant of, the rumors of piracy that had evidently caused the novices in Ipis's cohort to shun her. Elen got the impression from the conversation that the south coast Vunnus people knew all the currents, shoals, and backwaters where sarpa could be found, as pirates might well need to do, so maybe Nwelin simply didn't care how they enriched themselves as long as he found sarpa to study. He spoke not another word to Jirvy, while Elen was a deputy courier and thus beneath his notice.

Despite this snub, or perhaps because of it, a pleasing quiet descended. Xilsi read. Hemerlin studied. Jirvy wrote up a report. Ipis chattered about her childhood on the sea, warmed by the prince's attention. Elen stood next to the brazier in blessed silence as her toes slowly warmed up. She yawned, blinked as she swayed on her feet, and shook her head to get back her focus.

The office had the kind of expensive furnishings that weren't flashy but made to be useful and long-lasting. A cabinet for correspondence and testimonials. A cabinet for unguents and lotions needed for sarpa care and riders' and hostlers' injuries. A miniature stove suitable for heating drinks, a luxury that hostlers settling in for a cold night of watch would appreciate. The table legs were carved to depict sarpa heads and wings. The chairs had padded seats and backs of fine wool dyed the iron gray and sky blue of the Sarpa Corps. The rider who had attacked them at the Vigil had not been wearing either color.

Elen went over to the stove and poured tea, serving the highborn first, setting a cup next to Hemerlin, and bringing Jirvy and herself a cup last of all. Jirvy saluted her with a chin lift and a wry smile as he took the cup. She sipped at the hot brew with its smoky flavor. The stimulant acted quickly, kicking her out of the drowsy haze she'd been slipping into. But she still had to wait.

At length, Hemerlin tapped a specific spot on the hardened wax.

"As I expected. This is not the emperor's seal. It looks exactly like hers, except for a single detail on this lower magnolia petal. This impression was stamped from a seal she carved with her own hands. She made it for the crown prince. Three years ago, it was."

Xilsi looked up with an expression of shock on her face. "Why would she do that? Make a copy of her imperial seal?"

"I did not ask." Another might have spoken the words with sardonic amusement. Hemerlin simply stated the fact.

Nwelin came over to look. "So, the emperor may never have seen my testimonial at all."

"That cannot be known, Your Highness," said Hemerlin. "By the evidence of this seal, however, it is certain the crown prince saw it. He wears the seal on a chain around his neck. It never leaves his person."

Xilsi looked up from the testimonial's precise calligraphy. "This is a thorough report. An ambitious person with access to the treasury and an isolated estate near to the summer palace might use it to set up their own sarpa training corps, in defiance of imperial law. If they were reckless enough, they might even attempt to ride a sarpa themselves."

"The Sublime Highness is already crown prince," objected Jirvy. "What has he to gain by acting against imperial law, and with such recklessness?"

Xilsi extended a hand to Hemerlin, who gave her the receipt. She looked it over with a frown before setting it down on the table. "Sometimes a conniving prince seeks to move up in the world and fails. Sometimes, princes of lesser estate back the wrong horse and are executed. Or, if they are young and were misled, are castrated and remanded to the lowest rank of menial in the palace."

She held Hemerlin's gaze with her own. He looked away, as he must, his cheeks pink with emotion. Anger? Shame?

Jirvy whistled under his breath. Ipis scratched her head, looking confused.

But the words shifted the ground beneath Elen's feet, like sand slipping. Hemerlin's youth could be glimpsed in his aged face. It must have happened at the time of the ascension of the Lily Emperor, rumored to have overthrown his brother by underhanded means. How naïve had the young Hemerlin been, a prince of lesser estate and yet a prince all the same? Maybe he hadn't been naïve at all. Maybe he had loyally supported the overthrown Ailanthus

Emperor and been punished for his faithfulness, made an object lesson to any who thought to contest the new ruler.

What had such a young, disgraced prince endured among the lowest of the palace menials? Joef had once shown Kem and Elen an archival list of the duties of the lowest rank of menials in the palace: emptying and cleaning latrines, hauling water, washing paths and walls, and taking out refuse. If she understood the hints she'd heard, Genia had eventually plucked Hemerlin out of this labor and given him to the Elegant Consort, so he could devote his life to her son, young Gevulin.

Maybe he had loved the boy for himself. Maybe simply as a means to escape his cruel punishment. Maybe he saw it as a path to revenge.

She could not unsee the past Xilsi had hinted at. Hemerlin had become a new person to her, if just as annoying and overbearing. Not that he would care what a mere deputy courier thought of him.

"It could also happen," Xilsi went on, "that a crown prince loses the favor of the Noble and August Manors and the high palace officials, perhaps for good reason. A more competent prince may arise out of the Third Estate to take the place of a distrusted crown prince, if they were to strike at the right time and with the right backing. Some say the Lily Emperor came into power in much this way, do they not, Nwelin?"

"So they do," he agreed with a glance at the silent Hemerlin. "Which is why I have spent my life as far from the palace as I could manage. Not unlike you, I perceive, Xilsilin."

"I would never have been in line for a throne I did not want anyway. Although I have no inclination to seek it even if I were, High Heavens forfend! But I must suppose a cunning and unlikable young crown prince might perceive himself as under threat because of the elevation to the Third Estate of two capable princes with a praiseworthy raft of accomplishments to their names. Both are his elders and more proven than he is. Such a crown prince might seek to eliminate his rivals."

"These are speculations," said Nwelin as he examined the receipt with a severe eye. "Dangerous speculations, should any word of our conversation leave this room."

"I'll never tell!" cried Ipis stoutly. "I swear on the honor of the all-seeing eye, and by my oath as a warden, and before the genius of my Manor!"

"What of these two?" Nwelin asked Xilsi, indicating Jirvy and Elen.

"I trust them."

He nodded. Xilsi's word was good enough for him.

Xilsi studied the testimonial with an expression of misgiving. "I am more troubled by what we may have uncovered, here and elsewhere. Like you, I left the palace and all it represents. My loyalty lies with the Imperial Order of Wardens and thus to the all-seeing eye. If we say or do nothing, then what ill may we be complicit in unleashing upon the empire?"

An outer door banged open, people entering in haste. Xilsi quickly rolled up the testimonial. Nwelin locked scroll and receipt into a cabinet drawer just as the inner door was flung open.

A Pelis militia captain rushed into the room. Blood stained his tabard. He dropped to one knee, barely able to cough out the words. "Your Illustrious Highness! We are under attack!"

49

A Ghost of Warmth

Xilsi was already on her feet. "Are you wounded, Captain?"

"Nothing. That. Matters." The man panted out the words with a hand pressed to his side.

"Slow down. Take a breath," ordered Xilsi.

He attempted a bow in Nwelin's direction, grimacing. "Your Illustrious Highness, you are safe! Is the area secure?"

"Secure?" said Nwelin. "How do you mean?"

"Is there another way in?" Xilsi asked impatiently, releasing her sword from its sheath.

"Only the big pen doors," said Nwelin. "We'd have heard drawbells if anyone tried to shift the crossbar. We and the hostlers are the only ones here, Captain."

The militia captain called back through the open door, "Secure!"

Then he toppled forward. Elen caught him before he crashed facedown onto the floor, easing him to his side. But her gaze stayed on the door. What had happened to the others, who had returned to the Manor? Where was Kem?

Jirvy had already slipped his bow out of its case and strung it, and he came up with an arrow nocked to the string just as Prince Gevulin strode aggressively into the room with sword drawn.

"Your Highness!" cried Xilsi. "What means this?"

Jirvy shifted his bow's aim past the prince, to the open door.

Gevulin took in each individual in the office. His tense shoulders dropped. He set his sword on the table, grabbed the cup Elen had set down for Hemerlin, and downed it in one gulp. The snap of the cup back down on the tabletop made everyone jump.

"Duenn Manor has attacked," Gevulin said.

Elen scrambled to her feet, craning her neck. Was Kem waiting outside?

"Lord Duenn came and went two days ago," objected Nwelin.

"He may have left the Manor, but clearly he and his people did not leave the area. I must suppose they retreated to a safe distance and made ready their attack. Easy enough to hide in the forest, as long as Spore doesn't get you. Had Simo been with us, the air spirit bound to him would have spotted them. But we had no theurgist to bind a spirit to Xilsi once she was elevated to captain."

Xilsi winced but quickly wiped the expression of distaste off her face. This was not the time. She said, "Nwelin, did no one at the Manor suspect Lord Duenn of further treachery?"

Nwelin pressed a hand to his forehead, blinking in a hazed confusion. "How would he dare? He is merely a provincial lord with delusions."

Gevulin said, "Unless all along he has been serving Min-lo. Then his delusions make sense."

"Yes, I see," said Xilsi. "Control of the hallow-wood supply and a prestigious marriage, in exchange for ridding His Sublime Highness of *you*."

Hemerlin gave a trembling moan. "Your Highness," he gasped, "the fault is mine."

"How so?" Gevulin demanded, his irritation plain.

"I should have known. I should have seen. That is the whole of my duty!"

"Stop it! The blame is not yours, Hemerlin. I did not suspect Min-lo either. Perhaps Astaylin did, but she and I have not had time to compare notes, and I certainly did not trust her before. Be that as it may, Duenn's militia far outnumbers the armed servants in Pelis Manor. Three or four times more, I should think. A veritable flood of soldiers poured out of the night. So many that the genius could not see, and thus not protect, all the places they breached the wall with ladders and ropes."

"Where is Kem?" Elen demanded, by now beside herself with terror for the boy. "Did you hand him over to Lord Duenn in exchange for safe passage out of the Manor?"

"How dare you!" Hemerlin struggled to his feet, raising his fly whisk.

"Sit down!" Gevulin snapped.

Hemerlin sat, bristling with indignation.

"The deputy courier should know me better by now," said the prince angrily. "I will never surrender one of my wardens or household to the likes of that grasping ignoramus. I escaped because I was upstairs, making ready for bed. My people were warned by the genius. We got out by a servants' passage through the cellars. Even so, we ran into trouble coming through the gardens, as you can see. I got separated from my people in the skirmish."

"*Where is Kem?*" Elen was too furious and frightened to be prudent.

"I don't know. He and Qari had taken the rear guard." His tone was hard, but not in response to her questioning him. Gevulin was a man who hated to lose anything he felt belonged to him, whether it be rank, contests, or people.

Elen swayed as a hot flood of fear rushed through her. What if Duenn had captured Kem already?

Xilsi's hand steadied her. "Come now, El. We don't know what's happened yet. Was His Sublime Highness among the attackers?"

"I don't know. Though I doubt it." A sneer trembled on Gevulin's lips. In the palace, a prince of the Third Estate must be cautious with his words, but not here. "Little Min-lo is the sort who would never put himself in any real danger. He sends others to take the risk for him."

"Yet he might have been riding a sarpa," said Xilsi. "That's danger enough, surely."

Gevulin gave her a sharp look. "Know you nothing about Sarpa Corps training?"

"No, I don't. I don't know a single sarpa rider. Nor have I ever asked about their training. Why would I? For that matter, why would you?"

"It's my business to know as much about the workings of the empire as there is to know. Trainees get their start on older male sarpa, whose acid ducts have been sewn shut. The basics are not much more dangerous than learning to ride a horse, if rather higher off the ground. But you raise a good point. We need information in order to decide how to proceed."

"Once again, do you think Astaylin is involved?" Xilsi asked, looking so weary.

"Not in Min-lo's plans," he replied curtly. "For all I know, she's been taken prisoner with the household."

With Kem, Elen thought with dread gripping her throat and weighting down her tongue.

"The question," Gevulin said, "is what we do now. Do we retreat, much as it pains me to be forced to that cowardly prudence again? Or is there a way we can fight back?"

"I'll scout," said Jirvy. "If a local can accompany me, I can take a look and return."

Xilsi's jaw went tight, but she made no protest. "Ipis, stay with me and His Exalted Highness, and Prince Nwelin."

Elen said, "I'll go with Jirvy."

The prince's gaze was cold and implacable, nothing soft in it, yet there was a new awareness in his eyes that the Gevulin she'd first met in Orledder Halt had lacked. "No. You will remain here with me."

She opened her lips to protest, and he drew his whip.

"No!" he snapped. "Whatever it is, I don't need to hear it. You stay here."

Jirvy said kindly, "This is my skill, Elen. Let me go. I'll keep an eye out for your lad."

Nwelin said desperately, "You must discover what has become of my Worvua!"

"Of course Jirvy will," said Gevulin. "Esteemed Nwelin, sit down. You look ready to faint."

The older man sat, clasping his hands together on the tabletop and twisting his fingers together and apart with anxious restlessness. Elen paced, feet a mirror to his hands.

Jirvy left. The militiamen remained outside, guarding the approaches. The sarpa pen was a long way from the main house, but eventually the invaders would come this way, unless Pelis Manor's militia had fought off the attack.

"Hemerlin, find a first aid box." As the chief menial scurried off to a shelf, Gevulin knelt beside the fallen captain. "I will look at your wound."

"Your Highness," gasped the man. "You honor me."

"I do my duty as a prince." He got out a knife and cut away cloth in the manner of someone who knows what he is doing. Because of course he did. He'd trained as a healer and certainly had been the best student.

Xilsi caught up with Elen's pacing and touched her arm. "Here, now, Deputy Courier. You and I shall go investigate the harness in the workshop. See if it matches the harness we saw at the Vigil."

Though phrased as an order, Elen knew Xilsi meant to be kind, to keep her busy until Jirvy returned with his report. If he returned.

"Kem's not alone," whispered Xilsi, voice tight. "Qari is there now, too. You don't know him. He's the one who tells fart jokes. I'm sorry we had to leave him behind at Orledder Halt. You'd have liked him. And he's fast on his feet and knows how to make quick decisions."

"I hope Qari is fine," she said tightly. "But I'm specifically worried about Kem being captured by Lord Duenn."

"Yes, I can understand that after I saw Duenn make that absurd claim about the lad at Orledder Halt. Worry isn't a plan, though. And we need to rescue Astaylin, too."

"You don't think she's in league with Duenn?"

"Duenn is clearly Minaylin's puppet, so no, she's not involved in this. I don't think Duenn will have permission to kill her." Xilsi glanced impatiently toward the door. "But we need a scouting report. I suppose I'm even a little worried about Jirvy. What if he's caught?"

"I doubt that," said Elen. "So do you."

"After everything we've been through, I can't be sure of anything any longer. Now let's go examine the harness. That's a plan."

Ipis said anxiously, "I'll come too. I need something to do."

"Ipis, you stay with the all-seeing eye. He must never be without one of his wardens beside him. Come get me if I'm needed." When Ipis nodded, Xilsi turned to the older man. "Nwelin, have you any other correspondence with the palace regarding sarpa? Can you compare their wax seals with the recent one?"

"Ah, I see. Yes. Yes! It may be possible to deduce how long ago the crown prince began intercepting my sarpa research." With a look of relief at having something useful to do, he turned to the cabinet.

Xilsi then turned to address Gevulin. "Your Exalted Highness, with your permission, I would like to take the deputy courier with me to examine the harness from the sarpa to see what we can discover. We will not leave the building. We will be just down the corridor."

He glanced at Xilsi, then at Elen, then nodded. "That is acceptable."

"All is ready, Your Highness," said Hemerlin, who had laid out instruments and unguents.

With the chief menial's assistance, Gevulin began to carefully peel away fabric and bits of thread from the gruesomely long gash across the militia captain's torso. The man gritted his teeth and suffered the pain in little choked grunts.

Xilsi grabbed a lamp and led Elen down the corridor to the workshop.

Elen said, "What use is a genius if it can't stop an attack?"

"Geniuses represent prestige more than anything. They can move swiftly anywhere within the Manor, although they are, like us, a single creature with but one set of eyes and ears. Still, it is a puzzle how the attack could have taken Lord Genia by surprise."

"You're sure Prince Astaylin wasn't involved?"

"One never knows, but I don't see it. There's no benefit to Astaylin. The crown prince surely wishes her as dead as he wishes Gevulin, but he has no hooks for her yet. Even he needs some semblance of an excuse, some accusation of treason. I have to suppose this plot against Gevulin was concocted months ago and set in motion weeks ago."

"Gevulin *is* plotting treason."

Xilsi halted in front of the closed door to the workshop and turned right around to stare Elen in the eye. The warden was a little shorter, but not by much, and she had a griffin's fearlessness. "Never say that out loud again, anywhere, any time."

"I'm sorry."

"I'm not mad. It's just that you don't yet comprehend how dangerous and slippery the palace is."

"I'm starting to."

Xilsi opened the door and they entered the workshop. A single brazier breathed a ghost of warmth into the workshop with its table, hooks and rings on the wall, and shelves stocked with harness in various stages of repair and polishing.

As Xilsi looked around, she said, "But as for your question about the genius, the Duenn militia must have hidden in the woods. Or stationed a conspirator inside the Manor."

"A theurgist, perhaps? There was a theurgist at my table at the feast. He never said a word. I thought he was part of the Manor."

Xilsi frowned. "That's an interesting point. Manors don't keep theurgists in residence. Only the palace and the Heart Temples do. He might have introduced himself as an itinerant, like Luviara, about some fact-finding Temple mission."

The warden set the lamp on the table, which was covered by an unfolded harness whose sarpa leather was crisscrossed by scrapes and gouges. She began examining the harness in slow stages.

Without looking up she said, "Tell me more about the Shorn. Did he have a name?"

Elen found her tongue turned to stone. Too many emotions crashed inside her all at once. He was gone.

Xilsi's hands paused in their work. She looked up. "Or not, if speaking of it troubles you. If you need something to do, start at the other end."

To think of Kem—cut down, dying, dead—froze her blood,

made her sluggish. She had to wait, and waiting crushed her, fearing for the boy. After the avalanche, she had been forced to wait for days to hear of Ao's fate. Would it be that way with Kem, too?

Sara'ala would have reminded her to not cling to her fears. He would have said, the future cannot be known. Only now, this moment. A chance look. The touch of hands. A sweet kiss. Precious words delivered in that sly, smooth tone that had warmed her viper's heart.

She found a sliver of a voice, barely more than a whisper. "He went by the name Sara'ala. You mustn't laugh, Xilsi. But before he became one of the Shorn, he was a dragon."

Xilsi laughed.

Elen laughed, too, because it was absurd. "You don't believe me, do you?"

"Not at all, El. It's exactly the kind of thing I can believe, but only because it happened to you. All that time, you never let on the prince wasn't the prince, or at least, you didn't mean to let on, although you did in little ways. I understand his odd behavior now. It wasn't him! It was a dragon in a human body! A dragon! I thought all dragons died in the great wars of ancient times, slain by wicked sorcery, since it is legendarily difficult to physically kill them. Or if there were straggling survivors, then they fled to the ends of the earth, where to this day they brood in dark caverns and slumber beneath the waters of hidden lakes. Go on. Tell me more. Tell me everything. I'm famished with curiosity."

The story came more readily than Elen had expected. Memories shared give life to those left behind. For the most part, Xilsi kept silent, her eyes on the harness, which made it easier for Elen to talk. Now and again she asked a question, and occasionally offered a cutting comment that made Elen laugh and, once, wipe a tear from her eyes.

"Kem knew all along?" Xilsi said at length.

"Of course Kem knew."

"Why 'of course'? See, that's puzzled me for a while now, once I finally started to notice how strangely you and Kem act together. He's Manor-born. Raised in the Halt. You're a minor official who was accused of being a thief and a murderer. Don't think I forgot that bit. At the time, I thought Lord Duenn was creating obstacles by any means possible. But you and Kem act as if you are kin. First, he was mad at you, and then you made up, the way family does. And let's not forget the mystery of the Four Lands. You knew too much about South Ring, as they call it, though it was just a run-down Halt. And then it turned out that you knew the language. You'd been there before. And something was going on with him in the Four Lands, too, with that hair. I daresay Kem has some lineage relationship to both the Four Lands and Duenn Manor."

"Didn't I already tell you this?"

"I'm happy to hear a more extensive explanation. There are a lot of missing pieces."

Yet Elen hesitated.

Xilsi gave her a keen look. "On my honor and my Manor's honor, El, whatever you tell me now, I will keep Kem in the wardens. If that's what you fear."

"It is what I fear. He loves the wardens. It's what he always wanted, it turns out, although I didn't know it before since we never thought he would qualify. His mother and I escaped from the Four Lands as children. We were . . ." The word stuck in her throat, but she found the courage to go on. "We were atoners."

Xilsi's eyes widened with horror. "Like that poor child in the walls? May the High Heavens bless us with peace!"

"We got away and reached Woodfall Province, though we didn't know where we were or even that there was an empire, only that Duenn Manor opened its gates to the likes of two girls not more than twelve or thirteen years old. After a year or two, I became a militia apprentice and Kem's mother one of Duenn's concubines, not by her choice."

"So young." Xilsi nodded grimly.

"She wasn't even fifteen when she gave birth to him. Two years later, when Duenn handed her over to the barracks, we ran away, with him."

Xilsi winced, face pinched with sympathy. "I'm glad you all escaped. But it means you stole Duenn's child, to whom he has a legal right that outweighs anyone else's. Except imperial service."

"Yes. We washed up in Orledder Halt. I saved the intendant's life during a Spore outbreak, so he let us stay. We built a life there. We kept Kem's lineage a secret. Ao died in the avalanche that blocked the road, in the village below where we found the remains of the dead griffin. Kem truly is Duenn's child. But it was only on returning to the Four Lands with the prince that we learned that his mother, Aoving, was the bastard-born sister of Eleawona, of all people. It was Lord Thelan who told me."

"What is this word? 'Bastard'?"

"A child born of an illicit relationship. In the Four Lands, such a baby is not recognized as a worthy child of the line."

"How odd. A prince's child is a prince. It doesn't matter the status of the other person in the relationship. Only in what rank the child stands from birth. If I'm understanding what you're telling me, your sister, Aoving, wasn't your blood sister but your chosen sister."

"That's right."

"Then by imperial measure, she would be a prince. Of a lower rank than Eleawona because Eleawona was clearly born of the ruler, in their equivalent of the palace. So Fifth Estate, I'd say."

"Does that make Kem a prince?"

Xilsi smiled wryly. "Would you consider that good news, or ill news?"

"I honestly don't know. I'm sick with worry." She pressed a hand to her belly, her entire body a churn of anxiety.

"What of your own lineage?" Xilsi asked as tentatively as if poking a nest of sleeping vipers with a too-short stick.

"I know nothing of where I came from. That's the bare truth."

"There's no answer to that! What seems strangest to me is how unpleasant the northerners were. Everything stank and was so dirty and glum and drab. I'm glad we got out of there. I only wish Simo had made it."

"That was an ill-fortuned shot. He was a good man."

"No captain better." Xilsi sighed.

Elen gave Xilsi's grief a gap of silence. But questions did rise to the top, even in such extremity.

"What do you know about Simo's air spirit?"

Xilsi shuddered. "Now you see why I never wanted to be a captain. Besides the extra duties, it's required that a warden captain have an air spirit bound to them. I find it creepy. Don't you? Crawling around inside you?"

Elen laughed.

Xilsi cracked a grin. "Oh. Yes. I suppose you wouldn't find that so strange. But back to Kem! Now it all makes sense. He considers himself to be your nephew because you acted in all ways as his aunt. Did he know he was Lord Duenn's child?"

"Not before the day you and I and the others all met."

"Oho! That explains his grouchy demeanor for the first days of our journey, eh? Discovered you and his mother had been keeping secrets from him, did he?"

"Just so," said Elen with an affectionate smile for his sour behavior and the slow process of healing. "He and I worked it out."

Yet even as she said the words, a rush of fear swept down on her with such staggering power that she had to squeeze her eyes shut and grip the table edge to stay upright.

"Here, now." Xilsi put an arm around her. "Take a breath. That's right. Slow in. Slow out. Now another. Slow in—"

She broke off as footfalls approached. The door opened, and the two women turned to see Ipis, staring at them with a wide, worried gaze. Elen couldn't move, numb with terror as she saw the distraught look on Ipis's face.

"Jirvy's back. You must come hear. It's bad."

50

The Glint of a Slithering Scythe

In the office, Gevulin was wrapping the groaning captain's torso with strips of cloth. He glanced up as Elen and Xilsi entered. His gaze flickered with a twitch of anger, as if for some unfathomable reason he thought they were judging him for the man's agony.

"I do not have intangible magical powers to ease pain as some do," he remarked snidely, "but I did study field medicine in the palace temple. It will have to suffice."

"Your Highness, how could anyone doubt that you excel at the art of healing," said Elen, relieving her anxiety with a petty rejoinder.

Gevulin's lips twitched, anger transmuted into something more nuanced. "Of course I do," he retorted without heat, almost as if he got the joke.

But joking could not calm her, nor could any intangible spell. The old sick dread clutched at her throat. Duenn would find Kem. *Had* found Kem. *"Is Kem alive?"*

Hemerlin twitched. "Deputy Courier, this rude—"

"Enough." Gevulin raised a hand to compel silence. "Kem! Come inside."

Jirvy, standing in the doorway, stepped aside. Kem appeared, looking unharmed, although as grimy as if he'd been crawling on the ground.

Elen swayed, so dizzy she could scarcely think. For an instant, she thought her soul had departed her flesh to leave her dead with relief.

Xilsi steadied her with a hand to her back. "There, there," she soothed.

"I'm all right, Captain Xilsi," said Kem, keeping up the pretense, even though he was speaking to Elen. "The other warden shoved me under a hedge and made a big noise of getting himself captured with the rest of the retinue. That was to cover His Exalted Highness Gevulin's escape. Afterward, a Pelis servant helped me crawl out through the sewer gate. *That* was aromatic. I suggested we head to the sarpa pen. On the way, we met up with Jirvy." He coughed, rubbed his mouth with the back of his sleeve, and blinked as if holding back tears of shock and concern. "I hope he's all right, that warden. Qari. That's his name, right?"

"It is," said Xilsi. "What a Qari thing to do."

"Yes, this is all very affecting, I am sure," said the prince, "but we haven't time. Jirvy, give your report succinctly."

"Your Highness." Jirvy took a moment to gather his thoughts. "We spoke to multiple servants who got out and hid in the orchards. I compared their testimonies and consider them reliable. A militiaman named Torges had the most complete account."

"I remember him," said Elen. "He showed me the watchtower. Is he here?"

"Yes, outside with the others who escaped. About twenty in all. The Duenn militia has taken over the Manor. A palace theurgist constrained the Manor genius using his own spirits. The theurgist arrived in the party of Prince Astaylin—"

"So she was part of it?" Elen asked, with an accusatory glance at Xilsi.

"Silence!" said Gevulin. "Jirvy, go on."

"It seems unlikely Her Exalted Highness was part of it," said Jirvy, "since she was taken prisoner along with all the Pelis highborn. According to an eyewitness, Her Exalted Highness was as shocked as everyone else. If she was involved, then she is acting a part."

"She's many things, some of them unpleasant, but she's not false," said Xilsi. "The theurgist must have been Minaylin's agent, placed in Astaylin's retinue as Luviara was in yours, Your Highness. You know how she loves her Heart Temple prayers the way you love your maps and roads. Jirvy, was there any sign of the crown prince in company with Lord Duenn?"

"No."

"Min-lo doesn't like to get his hands dirty," said Gevulin. "If there's any chance he'll lose, he'll stay out of it and let others win or cheat on his behalf. He'll have fled home to his mother's skirts, on a sarpa, which doubtless has sewn-shut acid ducts."

Xilsi whistled. "Your Highness, I've never heard you speak so cuttingly."

"Now that my back is against the wall, I am freed from stale convention. However, I agree with you about Astaylin. She has as much to lose as I do. While she would gain from my dishonor and death, my absence in the palace sets her up to become Min-lo's chief rival. I've been a useful foil, drawing attention off her as she builds alliances on the side with her congenial demeanor. Jirvy, go on."

"There was initial fighting. Lord Genia ordered her people to stand down once she realized her genius was trapped and her people so badly outnumbered that they could not win. Lord Duenn had ordered his men to kill anyone who resisted. And their bull elk are aggressive."

Jirvy paused to take a drink, then went on. "Based on witness accounts and visual surveys from a distance, we estimate Duenn has about three hundred soldiers. The entire complement of Pelis Manor militia is one hundred and forty-eight. The surviving Pelis militia, as well as Prince Astaylin's squad of sentinels, has been locked into an underground storeroom beneath the barracks. The main force of Duenn militia is in place around the Manor and within the building. They are searching the grounds for stragglers. For you in particular, Your Highness. Eventually, the search will make its way here. We don't have long in which to make a decision. But there was one other notable thing I saw. The ceremonial hall has been opened, and its lamps lit and hearths stoked."

Nwelin gripped the back of a chair, white-knuckled. "If I had but a knife and the chance, I would kill him myself. Him and his foul son."

"How appalling," said Xilsi. "Esteemed Nwelin, I'm so sorry."

Elen said, "I don't understand."

When Xilsi saw that Nwelin could not bring himself to answer, she spoke. "The marriage of Duenn's son to Worvua will happen tonight, in the ceremonial hall, according to the immutable dictates of imperial law. Any theurgist can gather the necessary implements and recite the ceremonial honors. They'll need to write up a contract first. That will take a while because it has to be done just right, no word out of place, and in a case like this, they'll need a spirit to seal the bargain. Worse, Duenn doesn't have to negotiate. He can make whatever terms he wants and force Genia to sign them. Astaylin will no doubt be kept locked in a room until it's over."

"We have to stop it," said Gevulin.

"How can we stop it?" Nwelin clutched his belly, bent in pain, tears on his cheeks. "The beast will insist on bedding her this night as well. My precious child, to be so abused!"

The sphere that contained the fire spirit gleamed with the cold implacability of a clever scheme relentlessly pursued on the part of the crown prince.

Although, perhaps not. Elen saw a different sight in her mind's eye. A memory burned into her life. She saw a ragged outlaw in the trees, flinging two small, sealed ceramic jars onto a forest path. One jar cracks, and the world around El sharpens. Her instincts flare, a whisper in her heart.

Heat.

Gevulin looked at her, sensing a shift in her posture and a change in her expression. "Speak, Deputy Courier. You have the means to kill Duenn."

She said to him, "If Duenn dies, he alone amid the Duenn people, then his son Rienn becomes lord of Duenn Manor, immediately, by right of succession. He was about twenty when Ao and I fled Duenn Manor fifteen years ago. Even then, he was as ruthless and crude as his father. So Duenn's death changes nothing except to get me killed for my trouble, and you, too, depending on how such a scenario plays out. But there's another way, if you are desperate enough."

"What is it?" demanded Nwelin.

"Go on," said Gevulin.

She addressed Nwelin. "Your Illustrious Highness, you said sarpa are attracted to heat. If all the fires and lamps between here and the Manor are extinguished, the sarpa will crawl or fly to the heat. It's likely its acid could kill many of the Duenn militia, although it's not a death I'd wish on most of them."

"They'll have fucking earned it," muttered Xilsi.

"What of my Worvua?" demanded Nwelin. "Sarpa acid can kill her as easily as them."

Gevulin raised a hand eagerly. He'd caught on. "You will return to the hall first, Nwelin. No one will question why you would rush back to be with your daughter. Then you can quietly warn the others to get out of the way when the sarpa arrives. The Duenn people won't know. They'll be stuck in the hall or outside. It's a gamble, but the disruption will allow us to free the imprisoned militia while the sarpa is busy elsewhere. Does anyone have a better idea?"

"We can retreat, Your Highness," said Xilsi. "I'm not saying I think it's a better idea. Just that it is the alternative. If Duenn's people capture you, you'll be killed, and your corpse pickled in brine and sent to His Sublime Highness as a trophy."

"Exactly so," said Gevulin. "Any objections?"

Ipis muttered something under her breath.

He said, "Ipis? Have you an objection?"

"No, Your Highness, of course not."

"Will we need keys for the cellar storerooms?"

"Yes." Nwelin reached into a sleeve pocket and handed over a set of long chatelaine's keys, pulling one free of the others. "This one will open all the cellar doors. The others will work elsewhere in the Manor. No door is closed to me."

"Excellent. Nwelin, leave me one hostler and the soldier called Torges to guide us. Take everyone else. Let the soldiers spread out to warn anyone still on the grounds to douse their fires and hide indoors. You go to the Manor."

Nwelin shook his head. "A fine idea, but one proposed by a person who doesn't know sarpa. It will take hours to build up fires in the stove to heat the pen enough that the sarpa will wake. Even then, it will take some doing to get the beast out of the pen and into the cold air, and no rider to coax it along. By the time all that happens, it will be too late."

Elen exchanged a look with Gevulin.

"Leave that to us, Nwelin," he said. "The sarpa *will* wake and it *will* leave the pen quickly."

Nwelin studied Prince Gevulin. The prince looked back at him with the composure of a man who can honestly boast of having earned, through his own efforts, the accolades of Adept of the Bow and the Spear, Conqueror of the Ten Peaks Race, Eloquent Grace of the Wind Dance, Artist of the Brush and Virtuoso of the Pen, Master of the Lyre and Preeminent Bard of the Twelve Cycles and the Three Hundred and Sixty Poems of the Glorious Founder.

Reluctantly, Nwelin gave a gesture of agreement. "To retreat will condemn my girl. If there is even the slightest chance this will work, then I will do it. If I die with her, so be it. I will die knowing I have done my utmost to protect my child's honor." He pulled on gloves, threw a cloak over his shoulders, then paused. "Allow me to take the whistle. You can't wake the sarpa with the whistle, but it should respond to the proper signals once out of its stupor. Should I need to, I can call it off the attack, pipe the tones that will send it flying back to its home pen."

"I can do that!" Gevulin objected.

"Have you memorized the signals? Absolutely, under any circumstances?"

Gevulin twitched as if aghast at the realization that someone might have practiced more than he had at a specific skill. Then he recovered and took off the necklace with the whistle, holding it out.

After taking the whistle, Nwelin left.

Most of the gathered people departed with him. Soldiers raced off into the night to spread the warning. Kem sidled over, and Elen grasped his hand, squeezing once before releasing him.

Torges stuck his head in. He looked much the worse for wear, including a scrape on his cheek and a cut on his arm. "Deputy Courier! Fare you well?"

"I'm glad to see you got out of there, Torges."

He bobbed his head, casting a sidelong glance at the frowning prince. "Best I get back to sentry duty, eh?" The door closed behind him as he went back outside.

"Deputy Courier, how much time will you need?" Gevulin asked.

"Hard to say."

Jirvy said, "Based on the intensity of that tremor when you and I were walking out on the sands, not long. We'll give Prince Nwelin enough time to walk the distance. Once that sarpa is awake, it will move fast."

"What if it flies?" Xilsi asked.

"Fly or slither, we must trust it will head to the place that's warmest," said Gevulin. "Like most animals, sarpa are sensitive to the tiniest fluctuations of air, wind, fire, and earth, and the spirits formed of those elements. It will sense the hall's heat. Once the sarpa is released, we need only follow the path it clears for us."

"It's a gamble," said Xilsi.

"When has anything in the palace not been a gamble? Even your choices, Prince Xilsilin."

To this, no one had a reply, especially not Xilsi.

Gevulin washed his hands in a bronze basin and, afterward, browsed through the drawer of sarpa correspondence alongside Hemerlin, comparing seals. The hostler went out with Xilsi to unchain the pen doors. Jirvy helped the servant move the wounded captain to a barracks bed. Kem went outside to keep watch with Torges. Elen sat in a chair and drank so much hot tea that she had to use the latrine. When she returned, Jirvy was back, having left the servant to watch over the injured captain.

"They should have had enough time to walk there," said Jirvy. "If we're going to attempt this, now is the time, before it is too late."

"I'll do my part alone," said Elen.

Gevulin gave her a nod. Of command? Of approval? "As for you, Hemerlin, remain here with the wounded man."

"But Your Highness—" The old man trembled, clearly loath to be separated yet again from the prince he'd protected and served for so many years.

"That was an order. A battle is no place for you."

Hemerlin wiped tears from his cheeks. Jirvy looked away as if he was intruding on an intimate moment he ought not to witness.

"As you wish, Your Highness." Hemerlin went down the corridor to the barracks, as he had been commanded.

With Torges leading the way and Gevulin holding the basket with its glowing sphere, they retraced the passages past the workshop and storerooms. Elen turned aside at the stairs while the four wardens followed the prince and Torges toward the far end.

In silence and darkness, she descended to the landing over the quiet sands. Her viper stirred, woken by her intense emotion and by the sarpa's scent, but she held it in check, although it writhed in her heart. The sarpa lay in its unmoving stupor upon the sand. There was just enough light for her to see the far end of the pen with its vague outline of double doors as high and broad as a city gate. Nothing stirred inside the pen. She had to wait until they were opened from the safety of the outside.

She shifted her weight from foot to foot on the landing. The sarpa's body contracted and relaxed in slow waves as it breathed. The cold that held the beast in its stupor bled through her clothing as well. Her hands felt numb, or maybe the numbness was fear as she considered what she was about to attempt.

Sarpa acid had turned the bodies of the Far Boundary Vigil garrison into sludge. She was not so afraid for herself, but what if they lost and Duenn captured Kem in the wake of their failure? Yet once Duenn had Pelis Manor, once Duenn secured a place in the crown prince's honored entourage and His Sublime Highness destroyed Gevulin and took control of the wardens, Duenn would take Kem anyway, as part of his reward, and that would kill the boy in spirit if not in body.

Wait, she told herself. *Wait,* she whispered to the viper.

With a grinding and clanking the doors swung back. A gust of even colder air swept through. One of the wardens whistled the go-ahead signal. The sarpa slumbered on.

Elen pulled open a gap between her sleeve and her glove. The viper burned down her arm and emerged, tongue tasting the air with excitement. It writhed off the landing, plopped the short distance down onto the sand, and wound across the sand at such speed that it flashed in and out of shadow like the glint of a slithering scythe.

She leaned over the edge of the planks and pressed a hand against the cold granules of the sand. So attuned was she to the viper that she could feel the feathery vibration of its passage. Farther from her, and closer to the slumbering sarpa.

The sand trembled as if shaken by a passing wind. The sarpa had sensed the viper.

She jumped up and retreated to the door that opened onto the stairs. Just as she stepped back beneath its threshold, a wild, keening moan, like wind through haunted eaves, shook the beams and pillars of the big building. The sand exploded in a spray that peppered the walls. The sarpa spasmed awake and spun in a great lashing curl. She leaped back just in time as its tail whipped past so hard and fast she felt the cut of its weight and speed through the air. Its wings snapped out, then furled as it shuddered, turning once around all the way again. This time, the sarpa's heavy tail hammered into a wall, cracking thick wood.

Suddenly, the creature went still.

Silence settled.

Elen huddled in the threshold, peering out cautiously. The viper's hiss drifted in the air, so soft that it might have been drowned out by an exhalation. Out on the dark sands, a white thread of movement swayed as the viper lifted its tiny head and hissed again.

The sarpa keened so loudly this time that the sound hurt Elen's bones, hammered in her blood like a nightmare. Sand erupted to either side as the beast lurched toward the safety of the open doors and the open sky. It poured outward, breaching the pen, and, with a scraping and rustling and shuddering weight upon the earth, struck off across the ground and into the night.

51

Their Bright, Bloody Hearts

They ran: the prince, the four wardens, and the soldier. The deputy courier waited only long enough for her viper to return to her body before she ran, too. The hostler remained at the pen gates in case the sarpa returned.

The viper shivered restlessly against Elen's heart, agitated by the encounter. Had it wanted to strike the sarpa but held back? Had it been afraid? Excited? Curious? Angry?

What was the viper, after all? She wasn't sure she would ever know, or that anyone knew, not even the Sea Wolves who called her osge and considered her poison for what she carried inside herself. Not even the unknown person who had cut a scar into her neck, like a warning.

Did it even matter, when measured against Kem's life or Ao's happiness or Sara'ala's sly smile? The viper existed, as did she and all those she ran with and all those they sought to rescue and all those they would battle today and all those she had served as deputy courier and all those she would never encounter.

Torges ran in the lead, guiding them along narrow trails with the ease of a person who has grown up amid a landscape and knows it well. Pale moonlight gave the paths a chalky gleam, for it seemed the menials had used an old smugglers' trick of sprinkling reflective shavings onto obscure trails meant to be used at night. Even so, Ipis tripped twice, and the prince stubbed his exalted toes and spat out a crude word Elen was surprised he knew.

Once, they crouched behind a hedge as an enemy squad thrashed their way through an orchard, too clumsy to notice anyone was nearby. They soon came to a half-hidden tree ladder that led up to a narrow platform, built amid the branches of a stately spruce, with a view overlooking the watchtower and its lamp. A children's hideout, Elen thought as she crouched on the platform among the others, out of sight.

As a rising wind rattled the trees around them, they watched a pair of Duenn soldiers who were arguing at the tower's base. One of the men was worried about the distant inlet of Pall that could be seen from the top of the watchtower, certain it was oozing closer. Just as the other man was telling him that he was an ignorant fool, droplets of acid spattered across them from above. Their shocked shrieks pierced the night as they crumpled to the ground, clutching their bodies and writhing. A vast shadow undulated in a circle overhead, drawn by their lit lamp, then changed course as it caught a breath of warm wind off the Manor. It was so dark everywhere else that the Manor glowed like the most alluring of baubles, with the promise of light and heat and warmth and all that is good and safe in the world, for surely even a monstrous sarpa wishes for a warm and secure nest.

Elen whispered to the High Heavens, she who never prayed a single word for herself. *Please, by all that is just and right in the world, let my darling boy be safe at the end of all this.*

Torges leaped down the ladder and raced to the watchtower. By the time the others reached its base, he had killed the two Duenn soldiers and was dragging them into bushes to hide them. Elen scrambled up the ladder to get a better look. A dark shape poured across the sky and dropped toward the Manor. A burst of sound erupted as those below spotted the sarpa: ragged shouts, a clamor of frightened dogs, and the high-pitched warning bark of elk.

"Come on!" cried Xilsi. "We're going!"

Elen jumped down and raced along at the rear. They quickly reached the outer fence of the gardens, where a trio of Pelis soldiers awaited them. Beside the back gate lay four dead Duenn soldiers, bloodied, not acid-burned. By now, the noise coming from the Manor had crescendoed into terrified screams and a rumble of hooves as the elk broke and ran. The great beast circled overhead. Arrows hissed in sheets as desperate archers took frantic shots, even knowing they could not pierce its thick skin, yet trying anything with the hope of driving it away.

There was no time to halt, to think, to stare. They had to keep moving.

Instead of going into the rear courtyard of the Manor and past the Heart Temple, Torges led them down a back alley suitable for servants and handcarts. At the rear of the barracks block, they encountered a squad of Duenn militia coming up out of a cellar door, trying to figure out what the commotion was all about. The clash hit hard, the Duenn soldiers confused and taken by surprise, the Pelis militia enraged, and the prince and his wardens brutal and effective. Elen stayed back beside Kem, blade drawn, hoping the skirmish wouldn't reach them. She wasn't afraid, precisely, but she knew better than to think that two inexperienced fighters would help matters by wading in.

The murky chaos of the half-seen skirmish cleared, all quiet.

Xilsi appeared out of the darkness, panting, unharmed but for a scrape. "You two all right?"

"Yes," said Elen.

"I need to learn how to fight," said Kem impatiently, angry he'd had to stand back.

"If we survive this, you will, my lad. Now! Pay attention! We're going down to release the prisoners. His Highness says you two are to stay up here by the doors. Keep them clear for Pelis militia to come up. If Duenn people arrive, come down to warn us. Don't fight if you don't have to. Once we've released the prisoners, we'll meet back up here."

"Understood," Kem said in a grumbling tone.

"Yes," said Elen curtly, nudging him with a foot. But once the others descended into the darkness, Elen said to Kem, "You stay up here. I'm just taking a quick look."

Out of long habit, he obeyed. She descended part of the way down to get the lay of the land. The cellar had been dug deep into the earth and had, for extra protection, been lined with holystone and hallow-wood, although it still smelled damp with a hint of mildew. The others reached the bottom of the stairs and disappeared out of her sight. All she heard were whispers, then a clink and a clank. Footsteps raced toward her. Beyond, a sudden outbreak of raised voices exploded into a clash and clamor of steel.

She hurried up the steps, followed by a line of Pelis militia released from below. They pushed past her and headed back down the alley, toward the Manor's rear courtyard. She wasn't sure what they intended to do. All at once, she realized she'd lost track of Kem. Had he gone down into the cellar after her? Had he followed the militia, eager to get into it?

Nearby, a great weight thumped onto the ground, sending vibrations through the dirt, the buildings, even her bones. The sarpa had landed. The viper twisted eagerly, wanting to get out.

The clamor from the forecourt spiked into noises of wordless terror.

What if Kem had gone to see? What if the sarpa was even, this instant, turning its feral glare on the boy?

She ran down the alley and found herself at the corner of the barracks. Hidden by the corner, she peeked around onto the forecourt, with its paved plaza, the wide stairs into the main building, and the portico surrounding the ceremonial hall. The sarpa had indeed returned to earth. It sprayed its acid around, felling soldiers who, by now, were simply trying to scramble away. The stench of acid and seared flesh was appalling, the moans and strangled cries a nightmare of pain. Duenn militiamen sprinted toward the outer gate. One turned his head and saw her, but what did he care? He kept running after the others. All that mattered now was getting away.

The sarpa spat after them with a harsh cough. Elen gritted her teeth as droplets sprayed the backs of the soldiers. Some stumbled and fell, frozen in fear, while others staggered on in utter panic. An intense smell rose off the beast, like inhaling air radiating off hot sands, pungent and eye-watering when combined with the charry stench of acid-burned flesh.

Where was Kem?

The sarpa surged forward to batter at the closed double doors of the ceremonial hall. The doors cracked but did not open. It could not get inside to the heat it craved. The sarpa's tail lashed against a carved wooden pillar on the portico. With a splintering snap, the pillar toppled. The portico's roof tipped. A second swipe of the sarpa's tail sent tiles spilling to the ground in a tumultuous rattle.

Again, the sarpa battered at the door with its blunt head. Another crack, yet the door held. It recoiled, muscles bunching, and slammed again. Its power was staggering. The hall's roof shuddered, yet more roof tiles clattering to the ground. At last, the right-hand door broke, but although the sarpa nosed at the opening, it could not get inside.

It was furious, frustrated, and determined as it gathered its wits and strength. The long body filled half the courtyard. Each of its twisting, curling movements unthinkingly rolled across the fragile human bodies littering the ground. Perhaps being crushed was a merciful death for those still dying. If there was mercy in the world, and if a swift death was truly a mercy.

The sarpa bunched back again, making ready for another assault on the hall.

Where was Kem? She shook herself out of her stupor.

"Ervis," she called, but the genius did not come to her, and why would it? She was nothing and no one, just a deputy courier, and not even an inhabitant of the Manor. Her hands were sweating. Her heart was cold, and the viper felt sharp and hot inside her. All at once, a crowd of people moved up, pressing her into the wall, trapping her with their bodies. With her arm pinned, she was helpless to defend herself.

But it was the prince. Xilsi. Jirvy. Ipis.

And Kem.

By the High Heavens, Kem had found them. He'd joined up with the wardens, not foolishly run to see the terrible carnage, as she had. He knew where he had to be, her dear boy.

From inside the hall, a sharp whistle blew. Its shrillness ground into her body. Mercifully, the sound stopped, only to be followed by four short pipes, and yet one more high tone so long and harsh she thought the force of it would crumble her bones to dust.

The whistle ceased. Everything in the courtyard went still, as if wrapped in a fog of Pall.

Responding to the command in the whistle, the sarpa unfurled its wings. Their leathery span hid the hall from her sight. It heaved toward the front gate, rolling right over anything in its path: a crawling man, an unmoving elk, a stone bench that toppled sideways to reveal two militiamen cowering behind it. But all this was as chaff to the sarpa now.

It lurched forward, gathered its wings, huffed as it tried to rise. A puff of sooty ash burst above its left eye—the genius was herding it toward the front gate. The sarpa plowed forward, shattering the lintel as it burst out onto the open ground. There, it launched with a staggering gust of its wings. Trees bent down. Leaves rattled. The sarpa rose into the sky, accompanied by hysterical laughter, bitter moans, agonized weeping, the pounding of elks running beyond the wall, and so many voices rising in a thunderous blur of unrecognizable words.

Strewn across the courtyard lay the wreckage of the sarpa's passage.

Elen took in a breath, thinking she'd have a moment to take stock, to check in with Kem.

Gevulin said, "Forward, with me."

His wardens around him and Elen three steps behind, he strode out recklessly. Maybe he had to prove to himself that he hadn't fled Far Boundary Vigil as a coward.

Prince Nwelin appeared in the broken doorway of the ceremonial hall, waving frantically. Warningly.

Too late.

A flood of armed men emerged from the main building and onto the stairs. All wore the Duenn tabard, and their faces had the lighter coloring of Woodfall natives. Thirty or more, easily enough to slaughter the prince and his tiny retinue.

"We meet again, Your Exalted Highness, and for the last time, as I give my oath," cried a booming voice from the stairs.

"Oh, the hells," said Kem.

Elen stared, hands clenched, heart in her throat.

Lord Duenn tromped down the steps, laughing cruelly. He wore the lord's circlet and keyring sash that belonged to Pelis Manor North, last seen on Lord Genia.

The prince strode directly toward the stairs and Lord Duenn, his upright carriage and sneering glower impossible to look away from. "Where is Lord Genia?"

"His Sublime Highness gave me the consequential task of arresting her for treason against the throne. You shall be next!"

The prince did not halt or retreat. All attention remained fixed on him as he approached the lord. "You have not the authority to arrest me."

Duenn gloated as he tightened the noose. "As an intimate advisor honored by the trust of His Sublime Highness, I have been granted the authority to detain anyone known to have been in recent contact with the former lord of Pelis Manor North and her allies. Therefore, I am required to insist you disarm and surrender to me, Your Exalted Highness. By the order of the Most Sublime Highness Minaylin, Prince of the Second Estate."

Gevulin reached the foot of the wide entry stairs and halted, waiting for Duenn to descend to him. As the lord clomped down the steps, Duenn's soldiers swarmed out to either side.

Astoundingly, the prince drew his sword from its scabbard and held it out, not to fight but to surrender it to Duenn, as ordered. What was he thinking?

A Duenn captain took the blade as one might a precious implement and, with a courtly bow, offered it to Lord Duenn. The lord smiled mightily as he took the sword. Another might relish triumph in silence, but he couldn't shut up. He was always a man who had to hear himself talk and talk and talk.

"As a reward for Duenn Manor's faithful service, His Sublime Highness most generously and expeditiously named me as lord of Pelis Manor North, incorporating its territories into my own. My favored son Rienn is in residence as well, come to celebrate a most joyous occasion, as he marries the most fortunate Worvua. In truth, the marriage ceremonials were interrupted by your appalling and misguided attempt to attack. Yet, I understand your frustration. I hear the most fortunate Worvua was under consideration to become your consort, Your Exalted Highness. It is not to be. Rienn will have the plowing of that field."

The prince stared at Lord Duenn as if he had opened a treasure chest to find it filled with manure. "A fine display of the ill-mannered breeding of the provinces, I see," he remarked in his most acidic tone, worthy of a sarpa.

Lord Duenn's expression clouded stormily. "You are not in a position to insult me, Your Exalted Highness."

"I am always in a position to insult you, Lord Duenn, although I would merely call it telling the truth. Whatever happens to me, I will always be a prince whose unparalleled accomplishments were witnessed by all, and you never more than a donkey dressed up in Manor clothing, who can do nothing but bray like an ass."

Duenn went red. He raised a hand to strike. The prince drew his whip. And there came the meat of it: not even Duenn could bring himself to directly assault a prince of the Third Estate.

Flayed by the prince's contemptuous stare, Duenn sputtered. "You will be placed in chains and hauled to the palace, where you will be executed. You can be sure that before your execution, I shall be delighted to inflict upon you a lash for each of my men who has died here today. That will content me."

"The correct address is 'Your Exalted Highness,'" said Xilsi in chilling tones.

"Who are you, a mere warden, to speak to a Manor lord with such disrespect?" barked Duenn. Then, and only then, did he really look at the others: Xilsi with her hair in a tangle and her face smeared with dust, Jirvy with his utter cool calm, Ipis with the shock-faced determination of a frightened person who refuses to break and run.

And then—

"Kema!" Duenn's shout rose in triumph as he found the boy, standing half-concealed behind the others. "My lost daughter! My prayers to the High Heavens, answered at last! I shall waste no time. You will marry alongside your brother this very night! I'll bestow you on my cousin Marloen, who rode out with us for the hope of getting in a bit of slaughter. He'll whip this rebellion out of you, with my blessing. What a joyous celebration awaits us tonight!"

All her life Elen had prided herself on keeping a level head, unlike Ao, whose storms of emotion swept through like gales. Stay calm.

The fury and fear that lashed through her blinded her. All she could see was rage.

No.

Never. Not Kem.

Cut off the head.

She tugged off her glove. The movement caught Duenn's attention. His gaze lit upon her, where she stood in the prince's shadow.

"And you have brought me the thief and murderer as well! Why, we have a burning ground right here. How convenient!" He clapped his hands. "Lay a fire. We shall celebrate the two blessed marriages with a bright burning. I shall relish the entire performance. Two children married, and justice served, at last!"

Elen dropped to her knees and pressed her hand against the ground.

Seeing this, Kem lunged toward Lord Duenn, shouting, "I won't! You can't make me!"

All eyes flew to Kem. Duenn slapped him hard across the face.

The viper burned out of her arm.

Xilsi stamped a foot like a bull threatening to charge, the noise calling attention to herself now, and thus away from Elen. "You have laid a hand on an imperial official, a sworn warden. That is a criminal offense! I arrest you, in the name of the Magnolia Emperor and by my seal as a captain in the Imperial Order of Wardens."

The prince struck with his whip, the tip slashing across Duenn's cheek hard enough to draw a welt. The lord howled.

Jirvy leaped forward to take onto his own body the powerful backhand Duenn leveled at the prince. The blow slammed Jirvy backward and spun him into the Duenn captain with an impact that tumbled both to the ground and knocked the prince's sword out of the captain's hand.

For good measure, Ipis screamed.

The viper reached Lord Duenn's foot and curled up his boot, still unnoticed. No one was looking at the ground, except Elen. The performance was all at eye level, deadly theater at its best. Joef would have been proud.

Elen slipped free the small knife she kept tucked in her boot, ready to stab.

Lord Duenn twitched and yelped. He sucked in a seizing breath and gave a sound like a strangled scream, so harsh and agonized that every person in the courtyard froze in their tracks with the instinct of people who have feared Spore all their lives.

Did Spore track movement? Many said it did. It could eat plants, and did when it had to, to stay alive, but Spore craved animals and their mobility and the pulsing energy of their bright, bloody hearts.

Not even his own people moved to help him as Lord Duenn took a stiff, jerky step, as he choked out a mangled word. He took a second, spasming step. A shudder racked his body. He moaned as if hot nails had exploded in his belly.

Everyone near him, including his own militia, retreated in a scramble. All except the prince, who stared down his imperious nose straight into Lord Duenn's terrified gaze, as if to make clear he feared no inferior provincial. The viper slithered, unremarked, past the prince's boots and back to Elen's waiting arm.

With a strangled "Gah!" Duenn stumbled a step closer to the prince. He toppled to one knee, grasped at the air while trying to stand, as if standing would save him. No one moved or spoke, but his own militiamen continued to back away from him. Terror was the greatest silencer of all.

Duenn clawed at his throat, mouth working open and shut, but no sound emerged, just a hollow, throttled whistle. So had Captain Roel died all those years ago, body poisoned from within by the viper's swift-acting venom. Elen grabbed Kem's arm and hauled him backward.

Duenn saw her. Saw his child beside her.

"For Ao," she spat.

With a last burst of energy, a final gasp to wield the power of life and death, Duenn fumblingly drew his sword. He swung with all that remained of his strength, his rigid arm reaching farther than anyone had imagined it could. He was reaching for her, that she knew by the fixed malevolence of his gaze.

Instead, the blade cut with raw strength deep across Prince Gevulin's abdomen.

52

In an Instant, the World Changes

Lord Duenn collapsed with a whistling sigh. He twitched once, twice, before going limp. A white, foamy substance bubbled out of his nostrils and leaked, hissing, from his eyes and ears.

The prince looked down at his belly as blood bloomed in a gush, inundating his tabard.

Ipis screamed, "Murder! Lord Duenn murdered the prince!"

Worvua's voice rang out from above. "Pelis! To arms!"

The young sar appeared at the top of the steps, incongruously dressed in wedding finery, her hair piled atop her head in an architecture of dazzling beads. She wrenched a sword out of the hand of one of the stunned Duenn militiamen and plunged it into the man's gut.

The Pelis militia who'd been released from the barracks cellar raced out from behind her. They leaped down the steps to attack the Duenn soldiers from the rear. They'd come in through the back of the building while Gevulin held Duenn's attention at the front. That had been the plan all along, Elen realized.

More people flooded into the forecourt, spilling out of hiding. With a roar of righteous anger, the people of Pelis Manor waded in with shovels and pitchforks brought from the stables, knives and cleavers from the kitchen, and swords and spears grabbed off fallen militia. Caught between the Pelis defenders behind them and the enraged servants in front, with their lord fallen and their comrades burned and crushed in front of their eyes, the Duenn militiamen lost heart. They bolted for the gate, so desperate to escape they stampeded past the prince and his wardens without a second glance. They wanted to survive, as Spore wanted to survive. That's why it had to keep moving.

The prince was still standing, a hand pressed to his abdomen, his fingers stained red as blood oozed down his skin to fall drop by spattering drop onto the ground.

"Your Highness, let me just help you." Xilsi slid an arm around his back.

"I am struck," he said in an oddly measured tone.

"Your Highness, I pray you—"

He swayed, eyes shutting. His jaw clenched.

"Kem, Ipis, help me hold up His Highness. Ah, now is the time we need Fulmo! That will have to wait. Elen, get the prince's sword. Jirvy, clear us a path through. We need to get him to the Heart Temple."

Shouting broke out inside the ceremonial hall as a new flank opened up in the battle. Worvua hadn't shifted from the portico that led into the interior, directing people toward the hall as they rushed out of the main building. "Hurry! My blessed father is inside! Find him! I want the enemy rooted out!"

Xilsi, Ipis, and Kem got the prince hoisted between them and started toward the main doors with Jirvy in the lead. Xilsi cast a glance back and pointed with a chin at Duenn's body. "Elen! Take the keys off that motherfucker. Those are the Pelis Manor keys, they unlock everything. Get them to Worvua. Then follow us with the prince's sword. Move!"

Lord Duenn's corpse lay like a felled elk rimed with spume. No one dared to come near, so no one troubled Elen as she unclipped a ring of keys from the Pelis lord's ceremonial sash. No sense of victory infused her. *Ao, you are avenged,* she thought coldly, calmly. But all she could see in her mind's eye was the blood on the prince's tabard. When she thought of his face, it was the haunt's gaze she felt, as if he had been murdered too.

A press of Duenn militia charged out of the ceremonial hall in a disciplined formation surrounding Rienn, now their lord. They fought their way toward the gate, calling other survivors to form up on them. The genius's seething ash cloud boiled out to obscure their vision, causing a few to stumble or run into the encircling wall, so dazed they couldn't see the shovels and hatchets aimed at their heads. But even with all their casualties, Duenn Manor still had enough people to clear a path, to get past the gate, to run after their fleeing elks. A few Pelis archers shot at their backs, but there came another flurry of fighting from the direction of the barracks, and the melee swirled into a new direction.

Elen grabbed the prince's sword and ran for the stairs, her walking staff in her other hand, in case she needed to block any blows. The battle had blown apart into clumps of desperate fighting. She dodged past people grappling and hacking, and raced up the stairs toward a knot of fierce-looking folk who surrounded their young sar.

Worvua called, "Let the deputy courier through!"

Pressing through their ranks, Elen handed her the keys.

Worvua gave one of the keys to a burly menial. "Unlock Prince Astaylin and my grandmother from the gaol." The man hoisted a stout iron fire-poker and ran into the Manor.

"The prince is wounded," said Elen.

"Bitter tidings. Where is Chief Menial Hemerlin?"

"At the sarpa pen."

Worvua beckoned over a youth wearing Pelis garb. "Take horses and lamps and armed guards. Get Chief Menial Hemerlin here as fast as you can."

The youth ran off.

Worvua examined the swirl of movement in the courtyard, the dead and dying strewn like twigs after a storm has blown through. The Pelis militia continued to press Duenn stragglers toward the outer gate. Behind, Pelis servants methodically stalked from fallen body to fallen body and, with their knives and scythes, cut the throats of any Duenn soldier who still breathed.

"Nothing to do about the gagast until dawn, although it would be good if he were here to assist with the prince," she remarked as if the scene of death and slaughter did not trouble her one whit. Perhaps it did not. This was not the Four Lands, yet Worvua was still a master, and servants and soldiers died so that masters might retain their lives and possessions and privileges. So it went.

"Sar Worvua, if I may: Captain Xilsi asked me to bring the prince's sword to him." Elen spoke with numb inevitability. She already knew how this would end. She had seen too much injury and death not to know. What if she was too late? Yet, too late for what? The stricken face she saw in her mind's eye was not the prince, for he wasn't the person she had come to know best inside that body. He wasn't the haunt, now trapped in the ashes of ancient sorcery. Sara'ala, whom she loved.

Worvua beckoned to one of her attendants. "Escort the deputy courier to the healers' annex."

The attendant hurried inside, Elen following, half ready to leap out of her skin with adrenaline and half in a blundering daze. They ran through the extravagantly decorated public corridors, and were twice blocked by a file of Pelis militiamen racing past. All was chaos as a room-to-room search thundered through the building. Finally, they crossed the threshold into the residential passages and worked their way past knots of weeping people until, at last, they reached the back courtyard.

Beyond the Heart Temple's four-arched entrance stood a humble gate into the healers' annex. The youth led her to a waiting area, where the pavement was smeared with streaks of blood and other fluids. A few acid-burned people lay on cots, still clinging to life, all wearing Pelis Manor tabards. No Duenn-folk had been brought here for aid. One woman's shoulder was so badly burned away that the bone was exposed, though the woman was mercifully unconscious. A man cradled his own badly hacked arm with his other arm, white around the mouth as he panted to get through the pain.

Ipis was throwing up into a basin, while Kem stood beside her speaking in a soothing tone, even as he wore a queasy grimace. When he saw Elen, an expression of relief cleared his face. A moment later, he lost control of his own stomach and began heaving.

She hustled past as nausea curdled in her own belly and followed the sound of murmured voices into a surgery room. Inside, Jirvy stood to one side with a kerchief covering his nose and mouth. Xilsi had tied one of his spare kerchiefs over her own face. She glanced up to note Elen's entrance with a grim shake of her head.

The prince was laid on his back on a table. A young man in healer's garb stood nervously beside him.

Somehow, Prince Astaylin had arrived before Elen. She wore the same clothing she'd had on for the expedition to the sarpa pen, not a pin out of place from wherever and however she'd been locked up. With an expression of detached interest, she examined her brother. "Yes, cut away his garments."

The young healer's gaze darted toward the door. "But I am waiting for—"

"Do it!"

"Of course, Your Exalted Highness."

The healer ever so carefully cut away layers of cloth to reveal the wound in all its wicked, horrific splendor. Duenn was a strong and angry man, even in the throes of death. The blade had cut through the prince's coat, tabard, undergarments, skin, and muscle, to lay bare his intestines. The stink of blood and feces was foul. Astaylin did not even flinch as she studied the appalling damage.

Without fanfare, an old woman walked into the room as she tied on a stained surgery apron over a splendidly beaded gown. It took Elen several blinks to recognize the lord of Pelis Manor North, washing her hands in a copper basin like any other temple healer. While drying her hands, she came to the table to examine the patient. Lord Genia showed no sign of disgust at the stench as she examined the moist curls of gut bulging from the jagged cut.

"What do you make of it?" Astaylin asked.

Genia spoke without emotion, although emotion weighed heavily in her weary gaze. "As you know, I spent some years as a battlefield healer. This is a mortal wound."

"There is no possibility he can survive?"

"None, Your Exalted Highness. Even if I stitch it up, it will suppurate due to the feces that have been released into the cavity. I cannot clean out all this putrid mess. I have tried in the past, with injuries not so deep as this one is. Always, my efforts have failed. He will die. Perhaps not tonight, because he's strong. Maybe not even tomorrow, but within two days, at most. In drawn-out and unspeakable agony, I fear."

"I see. Poor Gev. Such a wasteful, unpoetical death." Astaylin's cold expression did not alter. "Well. This earthquake will rock the Flower Court. He was a useful foil, though naïve. At least I now know better what I am up against. I must leave now, Esteemed Genia. I must reach the palace before the emperor and that wretched Minaylin receive the news of this event. I must prepare a new strategy with my advisors."

She took a step toward the door, halted, and looked back at Xilsi. "Dearest, you and the wardens can return with me in the comfort of the palace carriages. I give you surety that no harm will come to any of you, nor will any fault accrue to you as wardens under Gevulin's command."

Xilsi met the other woman's gaze with such a freight of emotion that Elen finally grasped how deep their history together ran. "We wardens will remain with our all-seeing eye, Your Exalted Highness."

"So am I put in my place." Astaylin's mouth twisted with more regret than she had shown when gazing upon her dying brother. "So be it."

She swept out. From the waiting area, someone said, "Your Exalted Highness, what shall we do with the wounded Duenn militiamen?"

"Kill them."

Her footsteps receded. She was gone, leaving the moans and whimpers of the wounded in her wake. Was this not the measure of the palace? A fresh new strategy to be laid atop the blood and agony of the old one.

Voice trembling, Xilsi said, "Is there truly nothing you can do, Esteemed Genia?"

"Alas." The old woman shifted her grieving gaze from Gevulin's grotesque wound to his handsome face. Incredibly, he was awake, aware, and watching her. She put both her hands over her face, briefly, then lowered them. "Prince Gevulin, the fault is mine. I did not post scouts to follow Lord Duenn when he left in such anger after Prince Astaylin's arrival. I should have been more suspicious. He made no mention of the favor shown him by the Sublime Highness. Nor did I see any sign of the Sublime Highness in his company. I assumed Duenn would ride south to his Manor with his tail between his legs like a beaten cur. It simply never occurred to me he would bide his time and attack later. Not such as he! A jumped-up mongrel groveling for scraps of fine food his like has never deserved!"

Gevulin's mouth moved but no sound came out.

She nodded, as if she understood what he meant to ask. "You will die in agony. The best I can do is offer you poppy juice to dull the pain, and heart-bane to kill you quickly, should you request this mercy."

His tongue flicked over his lips; his throat convulsed. He tried again. He could manage only a whisper, scarcely louder than his labored breathing.

"My blessed mother . . . Xilsi . . ."

"Yes, Your Exalted Highness, I am here." Xilsi moved so he could see her without shifting his head. "What it is you wish to say?"

"She must . . . not suffer . . . for my . . ." His eyes closed. His throat worked again. His expression spasmed as he gathered the will to speak. "Min-lo will go after her as soon as . . . Luviara returns with proof of my rebellion. Perhaps sooner. When it is known I am dead. He will ruin her. Imprison her. Kill her."

Xilsi pressed a hand over her eyes to hide her expression.

Genia said, "Your Exalted Highness, what is it you are asking? Those of us who walk outside the Flower Court cannot interfere with what goes on within the Flower Court."

Blood pulsed from the prince's wound, though not as much as there ought to have been, as if it were pooling internally instead. Gevulin set his jaw. He grunted softly, swallowing the pain. Licked his lips again.

Xilsi said, "Can we give him water?"

"No," said Genia. "There is nothing to do but drug him into a stupor. I wish it were otherwise."

Running footsteps thudded outside. A youth wearing a Pelis badge appeared at the door.

"Lord Genia, Sar Worvua sent me to tell you that our militia has driven the intruders out of the Manor. They and Honored Ervis are searching the building for stragglers room by room. Be on the alert. Sar Worvua will come as soon as she can. There are many wounded who will need your attention."

Genia nodded, and dismissed the youth before turning back to the prince.

"Help me bind this up," Genia said to the young healer. She spotted the whip. Its braided leather cord was exactly the right size to fit between the prince's teeth. "Gevulin, bite down on this. Prepare yourself."

Deftly, swiftly, she and the young healer bound clean linen around Gevulin's abdomen. He made not a single sound through his clenched jaw, although the young healer himself was sweating, so overcome by emotion that Elen was amazed he didn't faint. It was done as swiftly as a battlefield surgeon could manage, faster than Elen thought possible.

The old woman and the young healer washed their stained hands in the copper basin as Genia gave further orders to the young man. "Now, child, go set up as many examination tables as you can. Bring in tables from the kitchens if need be. If we need more room, put tables in the temple."

"What of the Duenn wounded?" the young healer asked.

"You heard Prince Astaylin."

Was it right to kill menials for obeying orders, Elen wondered. As if guessing her thoughts, Xilsi caught her gaze and made a throat-cutting gesture to silence her. And Elen knew better. Any words she spoke would change nothing. By killing Lord Duenn, she'd killed his people, too, those who had been left behind.

The young healer tapped fist to chest and went out with the messenger.

Genia set the whip aside. She met the prince's pain-filled eyes with a resigned and compassionate gaze. "My dear Gevulin, this you know, for I myself taught you field medicine. It is the task of battlefield healers to determine who might be saved and who must be left in peace to die. You have wardens to attend you, so I must attend to those who may be saved."

Xilsi broke in. "Esteemed Genia, can someone fetch Hemerlin from the sarpa pen?"

"Sar Worvua already dispatched riders to bring him here," said Elen.

Genia nodded, still speaking to the prince. "It is what Hemerlin himself would wish. I will send poppy juice and heart-bane, should you choose to have Hemerlin administer either or both. He knows the correct doses. In the meantime, Captain Xilsilin, my recommendation is for you to burn oil of lavender to soothe him and ease the smell for the rest of you."

"My thanks, Esteemed Genia," said Xilsi. She turned away, overcome with emotion. Jirvy rested a comforting hand on her upper arm and, this time, she did not shake it off.

Genia sighed and took hold of Gevulin's hand. "My dear child, I did not think I would ever have this conversation with you. I regret that it is so. But part of a healer's duty is to assist those who leave this world. Many dying people find a recitation of 'The Slow Descent of the Water's Last Fall' to aid them in their passage. I know you have it perfectly memorized, and I hope your wardens can speak it for you when the time comes. For now, I leave you under the mercy of the High Heavens. May your journey lift you into the grace of the glorious heart of all. You were always a good boy, if a bit too serious, but we are as the High Heavens decree. I'm glad you learned to laugh a little, in the end. You will remain the best of princes, respectful to your elders, and a loyal son to your esteemed mother."

She wiped the tears from her eyes, bowed to the prince, kissed his hand, and left the room. As she went out, she said to someone outside, "Let no one enter. He deserves to die in peace."

From outside could be heard the squeaking grind of tables being shoved into place, a voice calling out orders, people running, and the groaning cries of the wounded as they were carried in. No one else entered this room, or even looked in, but beyond the door, they could hear Ipis's sobs broken by bouts of retching, and Kem saying, "It's all right. It's all right."

The prince's whisper broke the stunned silence. "I require the deputy courier."

53

Let Your Heart Live in the World

Elen approached the table. Gevulin's hand moved as if grabbing at phantoms spinning in the air. She realized he could not see her, although his eyes were open. She grasped his hand, an action which made both Xilsi and Jirvy inhale sharply, for it was never suitable for a humble deputy courier to touch a prince.

"I am here, Your Exalted Highness," Elen said.

"Captain, take the wardens and leave us. The deputy courier and Fulmo will remain."

Elen caught her breath, as a strange feeling lodged in her chest.

"Your Highness, our duty is to remain with you," Xilsi objected, with a startled glance for Elen.

"Take the wardens and return to Warden Hall. Claim refuge there. That is my last command to you as all-seeing eye. Take my seal ring as proof of my death. Say I was . . ."

He grimaced as an unfathomable wave of pain tore through his ravaged abdomen. No cry escaped his lips, but he panted heavily to calm himself.

Xilsi bent her head. "Your Highness, I will take the seal ring and inform the palace that you are dead. I will tell them you were murdered by Lord Duenn when you tried to stop him from usurping the rightful rule of Lord Genia—"

"No. Do not take sides, Captain. The wardens do not take sides. Let Astaylin fight that battle. When you give your report, say only that I was killed and my body burned for fear of Spore. This is my command."

"But Your Highness—"

"Leave now. Make haste. You will live, all of you."

He was a prince of the Third Estate and their all-seeing eye. They had to obey.

Jirvy clasped Elen's arm. Xilsi gave her a hug. Ipis was still gagging outside, unable to enter, but Kem came in and embraced her.

"Be well, my beloved boy," she said in a low voice. "Send a message to me as soon as you can, so I know where to find you."

"Will you be safe?"

"I'm a survivor, Kem. Surely you have figured that out by now. You have your own journey to make. It's time for you to go your own path, without me. I'll send word, I promise."

He wiped his eyes, but he nodded agreement because he was a brave lad, and because he wanted to go.

Xilsi took the seal ring. They bowed to the prince as courtiers might in the palace, Kem giving a creditable imitation. But for the stench and the dying man, it might have been any ordinary formal leave-taking when people think they may see each other again if the High Heavens gift such a fortunate event upon them. Elen did not cry as Kem went out last of all, giving her a final parting look. He had found trustworthy comrades and work that he wanted to do. And he had good boots. She could not have asked for anything better.

The door clicked shut behind them. She took in a breath, let it out, and turned back to the prince.

"Your Exalted Highness, what do you wish?"

She had to bend close to hear his whisper. "We wait for Fulmo."

For once, she was fully obedient, without question. She stood in the silent room, as an attendant would. A brazier crackled, its charcoal glowing red. A lamp set on the side table hissed. The prince's eyes remained open, but he tracked nothing. He breathed in short huffs. Another would have succumbed from the pain, but he was determined to wait for a reason she could not fathom. Yet if anyone's determination would carry them through this long night, it would be his.

A noise scratched at the door. The latch clicked down. Had Lord Genia returned with poppy juice and heart-bane?

The door opened. Hemerlin halted in the doorway as he saw the prince. His face contorted with terrible pain. His lips parted and—for an instant, for an eternity—Elen expected a howl of grief to escape him. No sound came out. He shut his mouth and swallowed all of it. With a supreme effort, he smoothed his habitual scowl over his face. He came into the room carrying a tray with vials, a bowl, a pitcher, a cup, and folded linen.

"I thought you departed with the wardens," she said.

He shot a look at her. "You may address me as Chief Menial."

Elen welcomed the arrival of the old supercilious Hemerlin. It gave her something familiar to hold on to.

He bustled in as if to any palace chamber, speaking in a low voice as he set out the items he'd brought onto the side table. "Your Highness, I have poppy juice and heart-bane. The poppy will dull the pain. The heart-bane will stop your heart, should you ask for such a mercy."

"No," whispered the prince. "Wait for Fulmo."

Hemerlin stopped stock-still, breath coming fast as he worked through another deluge of anguish. At length, he sighed. After this, he moistened a cloth in water and set about gently cleaning the prince's face, his hands, his feet, all the while complaining in a low, steady voice about the inferior chamber in which the Exalted Highness had been left to languish, and that he ought to be moved into the imperial suite in the Manor, as would be fitting to his consequence.

The prince's lips quirked up slightly. "Ever the defender of my consequence. No moving. Wait for Fulmo."

Hemerlin cast a loathing glance at Elen, as if she were to blame for this inexplicable request, and she was. Duenn had been trying to kill her, not Gevulin.

The prince said, "I am dying. Sing the proper descent . . . the way you taught me. Not the short version. I hate that. People should have more . . . discipline and learn it all."

The old man's chin trembled. "As you wish, Your Highness."

He brought a freshly moistened cloth and dabbed its cool wetness against the prince's dry lips. In a tender voice, he began to recite "The Slow Descent of the Water's Last Fall."

Elen had often heard the short version, trimmed down to span only six hours. Most people hadn't the time to memorize the entirety of the great poems and ceremonial prayers. Or they hadn't Gevulin's discipline. She had heard the full version only twice. The first time, when the intendant knelt beside the moat beyond which lay Wormwood Moat, the village where his elder daughter had died, eaten by Spore and therefore unreachable. After three days, the Spore consumed all that lived inside the moat and, without further life to devour, collapsed upon itself into wispy threads and tiny mushroom caps that could be rooted out, burned, and destroyed by wardens, surveyors, and deputy couriers.

The second time, for all those, including Ao, who had died in the avalanche.

In the quiet chamber, Elen had nothing to do except listen and wait. The chief menial's voice was often fragile, perhaps because he was choking down his grief, but his tone held true. She stoked up the brazier with fresh fuel when needed and refilled the lamp when its oil ran low. No one looked in on them. It was never prudent to pay too much attention when a prince fell so precipitously from power. Pelis Manor North had to move on in order to survive, seek new connections and lines of influence in the palace. Would Worvua marry Astaylin? After some contemplation, Elen realized she honestly did not care.

As for herself, she could rest easy knowing Kem was in as secure a place as might be hoped, whatever service in the wardens brought him. Beyond that, she was free of the prince, free to return to Orledder Halt. But past the Halt's welcoming sentries and the door of her cottage, her thoughts would not cohere. She floated, unmoored.

Autumn nights ran longer in the north. Because the chamber had no windows, she knew morning had come only when the door opened and Fulmo walked in carrying a tray of food and drink. The gagast set the tray on the side table and tasted a spoonful of each dish in his customary fashion. When he finished, he gestured to show it was safe to eat.

Hemerlin wound a verse to a point where he could pause. He took a drink, that was all, but said to Elen, with prim distaste, "Deputy Courier, you may take some of this meal, lest you weaken while the prince needs you."

"My thanks, Chief Menial."

The fare was simple but well flavored: warm porridge, warm bread, warm spiced milk, and a cold slice of chicken she suspected was left over from the wedding feast that was never to be.

All at once, the prince startled, blinking as if coming out of a stupor. "Deputy Courier."

Hemerlin's lips pulled back in a snarl, angry to hear her addressed by his beloved prince, the man he had served. He hastened to the prince's side. "Your Exalted Highness, what do you wish?"

"Where is . . . the deputy courier?"

"I am here, and Fulmo is here," Elen said, then added hastily, "along with Chief Menial Hemerlin, Your Highness."

"It was no lie . . . what he claimed. He was a dragon."

Hemerlin smoothed back the prince's fly-whisk hair as if by making him tidy, he could make him live. "Nay, Your Highness, be not afraid. You are falling into a delirium."

"Was he not?" the prince persisted.

"Yes, Your Highness. He was. He is, in so far as he still exists."

Gevulin's voice was rougher and harder to hear, so faint was it becoming. "Fiery salamanders regrow their limbs. So is it said . . ." He trailed off.

"So is it said of dragons, that they have been known to regrow their limbs, which makes them hard to kill." A thick, syrupy weight left her immobile, scarcely able to think or breathe.

"Luviara's handbook."

"What speaks he of?" demanded Hemerlin. "What has Theurgist Luviara to do with dragons?"

"Hush!" snapped Elen. "Your Highness, what are you saying?"

"Heal me."

"He can't heal you. He didn't heal Jirvy. He cast a calming spell on him that allowed him to keep moving without pain until his body healed itself."

"Heal this body. You were not at the rim of Grinder's Cut when he fought there. You but saw the shadow from below. He was one, they were many. I saw all . . . and felt all. He was wounded. Three times. Three cuts. Of those wounds, there remain but faint scars."

It was worse to be given a cruel glimpse of hope all the while knowing that which she longed for was impossible.

"Even if it were true that dragons can regenerate themselves in the manner of fire-marked creatures, it's days back to the Far Boundary Pall. You'll not survive the journey." She doubted he would survive until sunset. "The Shorn can only enter a living body. Even in a carriage we can't get there . . ."

She broke off.

No. That wasn't correct. It wasn't days back to a Pall. She'd mentioned the inlet to the haunt. She'd told him she would walk to the inlet when they reached Pelis Manor North, although she had no idea if Sara'ala had heard or understood her from within the shadow that was all that was left of him.

"What are you thinking, Deputy Courier?" Gevulin's eyes tracked the air above him as if he couldn't figure out why he couldn't see.

"If we took you to the inlet of Pall that lies near here, I could call him. But he might not hear us. He might not come. And if he did come, then what?"

"I give him leave to pass into my body."

"But he can't—"

"He can't heal me. I understand. I am dying. My gamble . . . failed." His harsh breathing filled the room, but at length he could speak again in that whispery, halting voice. "So be it. Prince Gevulin is dead. But my mother . . . must live. This, I owe her. You and the haunt will help me save her."

The words struck like a hammer smashing into Elen's already exhausted frame. Her legs gave way. She sank to her knees, clutching the edge of the table.

Hemerlin was weeping soundlessly, tears running down his lined face. "Now I understand why he felt as a stranger to me after Three Spires, when he dismissed me and the others. It wasn't him at all, was it?"

"It was not," she said.

The prince grunted as a dying animal will as it fights to stay alive for one more hour, one more breath. "Ah. Ah! It must be this way. Deputy Courier. All I ask . . ."

His eyes fluttered and closed.

He exhaled, and did not inhale.

Elen leaped to her feet. How could this be the end?

Hemerlin wailed and grasped the prince's hand. His touch somehow yanked Gevulin back.

The prince spoke in whispered bursts. "Pledge to me, Hemerlin. Deputy Courier. If this happens, if it can be, then with the aid of the dragon you will get my blessed mother out of the Flower Court alive. Her, I will save. Promise me."

"This I promise," Elen said, "for I am selfish enough to hope you may die that he may live."

The prince's hand twitched, maybe from his lifelong habit of whipping people who spoke to him with disrespect. "Take the greenfinch ring as the imprint of my will."

His glove was already off because Xilsi had removed it in order to take the seal ring. The greenfinch ring was a knotted band on his little finger, a trifling bit of jewelry for a prince. Elen worked it off and slid it onto her own forefinger, then pulled her glove back on.

"I have the ring," she said, not sure if he could feel his extremities any longer. "Your mother's honor I will hold as my own, though I cannot say how I will manage such a rescue. As you have so often reminded me, I am but a humble deputy courier, who knows less than nothing about the palace."

"I can manage a rescue," said Hemerlin, with a sniff of disdain. "No one knows the palace better than I do."

"Yes. Get there. Quickly." Gevulin's voice was ragged and desperate. "Don't you hear them coming?"

She heard nothing but the muffled sounds of the injured crying in pain, a child wailing for its parent, weary voices barking out requests and orders. Wasn't that one of verses of "The Slow Descent of the Water's Last Fall," that *death descends upon manifold wings*? If he died, he could not grant Sara'ala the passage spell. So, it had come to this after all, that she carried the burden of life or death. Even just physically, for she wasn't sure she and Hemerlin could carry the prince all the way to the inlet.

"Fulmo will carry me." He panted, each word an effort. "His sentence is bound to my life, or to his death."

The world around El sharpened. Her instincts flared as a tightening in her heart. They had to move now. Before he died.

Worvua had said to let no one disturb the prince without her express order. "How are we to smuggle him out? What if Lord Genia or her people try to stop us?"

Hemerlin acted with remarkable swiftness, as if he had practice smuggling people in and out of tight spots where they weren't meant to go. He unfolded a linen shroud and covered the prince head to toe, as though he were already a corpse. Cracking the door open, he peered into the corridor, then beckoned to Elen. Another body, covered by a shroud, had been shoved up against a wall. No one was in the corridor, busy in rooms, or out in the annex's courtyard, because there were injured to be dealt with, supplies to move, blood to be mopped up. She and Hemerlin grabbed the unattended body by its shoulders and ankles and dragged it into the chamber. They got it up and arranged on the other half of the table.

"I will remain here to sing the descent," said Hemerlin. "My beloved prince is dead, by his own proclamation. You and Fulmo will go, in obedience to his dying wish. I doubt you will honor your pledge, Deputy Courier, but should you possess enough honor to do so, then come to the palace and send in the ring to gain my attention."

"I might surprise you," said Elen.

"I doubt it." The shrouded body wore a Pelis Manor menial's cap. Hemerlin tugged it off and handed it to Fulmo. "Put on this cap. Go, while it is still early. As long as I am singing, they will not disturb me and will not become suspicious."

Elen hadn't any idea how much weaker the gagast might be in his smaller size, but Fulmo got his arms under the prince and lifted him as gently and easily as one would carry a sleeping child. The prince's limbs dangled so loosely that she grabbed a wrist and felt for a pulse. Was he dead already?

A faint pulse brushed at her skin. He'd lost consciousness. She didn't know how much longer it would take him to die.

"Follow me and don't look at anyone," she said to Fulmo. "Just keep walking."

She tugged her own thistle-green knit cap over her head and pulled it down to her eyebrows and the nape of her neck, stuffing all her hair under it. Slung her pack over her back. Her coat was an ordinary winter coat, not embroidered with Orledder's badge. Her pack likewise displayed no imperial insignia. Deputy couriers had to provide their own winter coat and journey pack; like boots, neither were part of the gear issued to them.

She and Fulmo walked down the corridor, past rooms crammed with injured people. Once a person called after them, but Elen kept walking and so Fulmo kept walking. They walked out through the annex gate, through the temple courtyard, and out a secondary gate into the gardens behind the Manor. It was easy enough to pass the outer walls and make their way back along the path their group had taken last night, up the hill to the watchtower.

If the prince died, would Fulmo set down the body wherever he was on the path and walk away? Was that how it worked? If the prince died before they reached the Pall, it would all be for naught, regardless. Best not to think about it. Best to walk like an atoner, one step at a time, mind fixed on what was right around her and not on a past she could not change or a future that might not come.

The watchtower was empty, the bodies gone. There remained only scorched patches of ground where acid had scalded vegetation, and no guard in sight. Probably they were out pursuing the enemy. She was glad of it because there was no one to see them go. Hemerlin would know all the devious tricks to cover for them back in the Manor. She found the trail Torges had indicated so many days ago, in what seemed now a simpler time. An hour to go down, around, and over the next ridgeline, he had told her. An hour for the prince to hold on, if he could.

Each step was an eternity of hope and of dread. Elen set her boots on the well-kept trail and walked and walked and walked. Fulmo kept pace behind her. She didn't stop to check if the prince lived. It was a pointless exercise. Either he would hold on or he would die.

At length, they trudged down into a gully. Here, the path had been paved with holystone, and the vegetation cut back, trees felled and replaced with hallow-wood saplings growing in military lines like soldiers set on guard. Past the saplings, where a half-frozen stream trickled, lay the dense inlet of Pall. It was more robust than she'd expected, not a fraying thread like the stream of Pall that flowed along the floor of Grinder's Cut but a dense, ropy mass about ten paces across. If anything, it reminded her of the sarpa, massive and threatening as it pressed its deadly nose south toward what destination she could not know. The surveyors were tracking it.

A line of holystone stretched along either side of the Pall, fencing it in, the work of many hands over many months. Elen halted at the edge. The Pall had a powerful buzz, as of swarming bees, if bees could be ghosts. The viper stirred restlessly in response. She pulled off her glove and set her bare hand to the ground. The viper stung down her arm and burned out of her skin, tongue flicking. It slithered eagerly into the Pall, far more eagerly than it had attacked Duenn at her order.

She then pulled the blanket away from Gevulin, tossing it onto the ground. The prince's face looked drained of blood, but, remarkably, he was still breathing. There was still time.

She set one foot in the Pall and knelt to press a hand down beside it, both foot and hand hidden by the dense white mist. An icy chill nibbled at her like minnows.

She said, "Sara'ala, can you hear me? I'm here. Come to me, I pray you."

Her voice was a plaintive note lost in the still air of a cloudless day. The sunlight seemed pallid, as if with the clutch of despair. It wasn't enough. She needed another way to capture the haunt's attention.

"Fulmo, carry His Exalted Highness into the Pall and set him down gently."

The gagast waded halfway across. Where the Pall rose to his midsection, he knelt and settled the prince on the ground. The body vanished beneath the fog. Even from five paces away, Elen could see no sign of Gevulin.

Fulmo paused there. Had the Pall forced him to protect himself by building an outer shell? Was he frozen? Trapped there? But no, he made a sign, the meaning of which she did not know and could not guess. A benediction? A curse? A farewell?

He backed out and planted his feet on the holystone. Spore wriggled off of him like little, twisting worms. With a fastidious and remarkably agile grasp, he caught each one and squished it between his fingers as one would pop a maggot.

Above the spot where he had laid the prince, the Pall began to shudder, and then to boil. Spore, grasping at life. What a fool she had been. It seemed obvious now. Once Gevulin went into the Pall, there was no coming back.

"Sara'ala," she called, but her voice faded into the air. The prince would be consumed by Spore long before the haunt could arrive, especially if the haunt never heard and didn't know.

She took in a sharp breath for courage, then laid herself flat on the ground and, like a viper, crawled headfirst into the Pall.

The mist crept icy fingers over her skin, caressing her face with malice and glee. *Liar. Thief. Murderer.* It was all true.

If she opened her mouth, the Pall would crawl inside her. So, she opened her mouth and she said, clearly, boldly, desperately, "Sara'ala. I'm here. Come to me, I pray you. The prince awaits you. He gives you leave to pass into his body. Sara'ala."

Her throat went numb with the cold, frozen into silence. The Pall closed its power around her head and torso like the crushing of a great hand, like the cage of a terrible spell. The ashes of sorcery melted onto her tongue. They tasted of misery and fear and malevolence and the wicked joy of souls who can find no pleasure except in forcing others to suffer. *Let us in,* they whispered. *Let us out of this prison.*

She had one foot still touching the world outside the Pall. One knee that, when she twitched, scraped against an edge of holystone pavement. The pain snapped her mind away from the brink. The voices were old ghosts, not living people. Shoving, she scrambled back, as if pulling against chains weighted with all the souls of those killed by another's power.

When her head came free, she flung herself backward, onto her behind, and sat there panting as if her lungs had been scoured in a race no one could win. How much time had passed, she did not know, but she was stunned to discover the sun now stood high in the sky. Hours had gone by.

If Gevulin was dead and Sara'ala beyond reach, she still had to wait for the viper to return. All she could do was wait, hope fading as the sun descended span by span into the west.

At length, at last, alas, twilight settled its drowsy cloak over the world. Fulmo stood frozen, head tilted back as he inhaled the starlight. The bubbling Pall softened, stilled, sank as if into a stupor. Had the prince died? The viper did not return.

She wrapped the prince's bloodied shroud around her and sat on the edge of the Pall as the night made its slow journey toward the hope of another day. The bright moon rose, staring down upon her as if surprised to discover she lingered still, when she might better have given up and walked away. Yet on a cloudless night, there was beauty to lift the spirit, the moon and the stars, the High Heavens in all their glory, which the living can never touch. So it is said in the temple: Let your heart live in the world.

Ao was dead. Kem had left, as he must. She had lived for so long for them that it was hard to imagine who she might be, for herself. A sister, always. An aunt, however far she and Kem would walk apart henceforth. A deputy courier, of course. A surveyor in training, perhaps. A sort of niece to a lonely, grieving, kindly old man. A friend to a snob. A comrade to those she met and worked with. And just plain El, who had walked, and lived, and loved, and who was still here.

Whatever happened here, now, to be El was enough.

The night passed, and the viper did not return. The Pall lay like the cold grave it was. The moon sank into the west. In the east, the sky lightened to a hazy gray touched with a pale-gold kiss of promise.

Fulmo tipped back his head, sighed, and stirred. He raised his hands toward the Pall, stamped three times, and, without a word to her, stumped away south, following the inlet along the gulley. Free of his obligation.

The prince was dead.

The haunt was lost to her.

Elen pressed a hand to her chest. It hurt. It would keep hurting in the days and weeks and months to come. Yet her heart was still beating. She was still alive. The world would go on as it always did. She could—and she *would*—get up and keep walking.

But where was her viper?

Something stirred beneath the Pall. The fog churned as if an eddy was spinning out its last gasp of energy.

A head appeared, popping up so abruptly out of the mist that she cried out in alarm, and then lost her voice. For there the prince stood. He coughed heavily, clearing his lungs, before wading out of the Pall.

She was too stunned to rise. Her body lost all volition.

He stepped over the first line of holystone and onto the bare ground. Extending his arms, he turned his hands palms up and then palms down, examining them as if counting all his fingers. He probed at the mess of sticky, blood-soaked fabric hanging around his torso, for the tabard hadn't been fully cut off his shoulders, just cut away. His lean, muscled torso was visible past the strips of fabric, his skin smeared with blood but otherwise unmarked except for a faint white scar that ran from hipbone to hipbone. The scar was particularly visible because several of the prince's trouser buttons had been sliced off by the killing blow, so the tops of the trousers just barely caught at the hips, looking ready to fall. He hitched them up with a frown, but the tabard and undertunic were beyond saving.

A tendril of white twined down his arm and plopped to the ground in a tangle. It was her viper. It raised its head to look her way with a satisfied air.

He said, "I hope something can be done about these sadly mutilated garments because I am rather a shy fellow, and while I admit I have, at times, admired this body in all its glory, if I am to walk in the world, I should rather not do so naked. Unless that is what you would prefer, dear one."

Elen staggered to her feet, swaying as if she were drunk.

"It's you," she said.

"Alas, it is me. By the stricken expression on your dear face, I come to fear you were hoping for someone else."

"You heard me call for you."

He gave her a puzzled look. "I heard nothing. The viper found me and led me back to the prince. When you are ready, I hope you will tell me the whole, for I was quite shocked to find his body so mauled. Where are the others? Where is Kem? I hope they were not harmed." His shadow flared in distress.

"No, no, they're all fine. They had to return to Warden Hall. I stayed behind because the prince knew he was dying. He asked me to take him to you, if I could find you."

"Yes, he was waiting for me. Or his soul was, anyway. It departed as I entered, which I suppose was him dying. It took me some time to repair the damage, even for one such as me. I must assume he was killed as a result of this tedious quarreling for power these princely folk do love to indulge in—"

She flung her arms around him and pressed her face to his chest, holding so tight he stopped speaking.

"I thought I lost you," she murmured.

He blazed with an unnatural warmth against the bitterly cold dawn. When he cautiously placed his arms around her, she sighed and nuzzled closer. They stood that way for a long time, breathing together. His heart beat like any ordinary heart. His breath stirred her hair as he rested his cheek against the side of her head, as a lover would.

"Not that I ever really had you," she added, pushing back to gaze up at him.

His face was still the prince's face, yet also changed, a little leaner, the chin a little more pointed. The willow-leaf eyes were just as beautiful as they had always been, but where the prince's had been a deep and mellow brown, Sara'ala's were touched with flecks of gleaming gold. A dragon's eyes.

His rascal smile flashed. "It seems you are stuck with me now, dear one. Unless I mistake this welcome for something else."

"You don't." She caught his face between her hands, drew him closer, and kissed him. The bliss of it overwhelmed her. They embraced. The sweetness of his lips and the way he held her, one hand creeping down her back as if the hand had developed a life of its own. She leaned closer for another kiss.

A sharp snout poked an icy blade against her calf.

"Ouch!"

Sara'ala stepped back with a look of alarm. "Are you hurt?"

She laughed, kneeling, and set her hand on the ground so the viper could crawl back in. When it settled into its nest around her heart, she sighed. Perhaps, after all this time, she finally understood it wasn't separate from her but part of who she had been and would always be.

"No, indeed, I have scarcely felt more well. But even you can't safely stay out in this cold without proper gear. Take off the tabard and undertunic."

He smiled coyly as he pulled off the shreds of the tabard and the bloody, cut-up undertunics, one wool and one silk. His torso was, as ever, an appealing sight: sturdy shoulders, trim arms, a sculpted chest worthy of admiration. Gevulin had trained hard.

Raising a hand to his hair, Sara'ala scratched, then frowned. "This is somewhat cleaner now, but I well recall how it became a rat's nest, and it is rather too oily, and I become concerned that creatures may be living in it. Not Spore, I mean. *Lice.* How lowering. Infested with bugs like a common animal. Not even any sun-heated sand to roll in."

"We'll have to think about how to go on. If you shave your head and grow a beard—"

"A beard?"

"Whiskers."

"Yes! I look quite handsome with whiskers, if I must say so myself!" But he rubbed his bare arms, shivering. Even he could not pretend he wasn't cold. Any human body could freeze to death in such conditions.

Elen dug into her pack and found her spare outer tunic, loose on her and tight on him when he pulled it on. She gave him her cloak to throw over it. In digging out the tunic, she found, tucked against the inside of the pack, a slender tube of waxed leather, the kind in which a person could carry a single rolled-up vellum map.

The prince had left her the map.

"I'll be cursed as the High Heavens' latrine," she murmured.

Sara'ala didn't hear because he had gotten distracted by flapping up the cloak and letting it float down, something in the manner of wings.

She rose as she slung the pack onto her back. "We need to get moving, my love."

He let the cloak settle. "Where are we going?"

She pressed a hand to her chest, over her heart. "We're going home."

"Home! I like the sound of that. What is home?"

"Orledder Halt. I hope. We do have a task to complete." She thought of Hemerlin. Was he still singing the descent to an unknown corpse? Or did he somehow already know, and had slipped away? They could not return to Pelis Manor North regardless, so she had to gamble Hemerlin would make it all work, as he apparently had for many years.

"And then?"

"Well, then . . ." It was difficult to know how to respond when life renewed in this astonishing fashion.

He took her hand. His skin was humanly warm, and his touch

was humanly gentle, but the shadow of his shorn body cast an aura around him, and the truth of what he was gleamed in his golden eyes. "These exciting pauses are exceptionally endearing! Well, then, what?"

"First, the task I mentioned. After that, I'm going to train as a surveyor. I'll convince the intendant to train you as a surveyor too. We'll have to be cautious. We can trust the intendant. He needs to know about the Shorn and Three Spires regardless. But no one else can suspect what you are or that your body once belonged to the prince. It's for the same reason I have to be cautious about the viper. If the legal mechanisms of the empire find out, we will both be condemned to death by burning. Are you willing to risk that?"

He raised her hand to his lips as if she were a great prince of the land, and he smiled at her over her knuckles so flirtatiously that she thought she might swoon.

"Then we shall burn together," he said, as if he were inviting her to his bed.

She laughed and thought of kissing him again, but it was too cold not to get moving. They needed to find a warm place to spend the next night, one well away from Pelis Manor North and all the intrigues and fighting it represented. They would find a nice, warm, narrow bunk where two people might feel obliged to snuggle together.

Sara'ala smiled, seeing her thoughts in her face.

"And how are we getting there, dear one?" he asked.

Elen looked around at the pale blue morning sky, the silent Pall, the holystone path and the hallow-wood saplings, the stolid ridgeline, and a pair of curious goats come to stare at these strangers.

She grinned. "We each have two good feet, and good boots. And I'm grateful for them."

ACKNOWLEDGMENTS

First, I thank my generous Patreon supporters. They got the initial glimpses of the earliest iteration of the Witch Roads universe, and even voted on several world elements, which I then incorporated into the setting. Your patronage literally made it possible for me to write this duology.

Shout-out to my writing group, Cheri Ebisu, Emma Candon, Nick Candon, and Krystle Yanagihara, who were so incredibly encouraging as they read the rough draft. To the nest, Aliette de Bodard, Vida Cruz-Borja, Zen Cho, Victor Fernando R. Ocampo, and Rochita Loenen-Ruiz. To my children and their partners, who always have my back. And to my many writing friends and acquaintances and the community that holds us up as we move forward during complex and often difficult times. I could not do this without you all.

As always, a special thank-you to my brilliant editor Lee Harris, his doughty assistant (and assistant editor) Matt Rusin, publisher Devi Pillai, editorial directors Claire Eddy and Will Hinton, copyeditor Christina MacDonald, proofreader Norma Hoffman, jacket artist Raja Nandepu, jacket designer Jess Kiley, production editor Sam Dauer, managing editor Rafal Gibek, production manager Steven Bucsok, designer Heather Saunders, publicists Jocelyn Bright and Saraciea Fennell, marketers Emily Honer and Becky Yeager, and social media marketer Sam Friedlander. Your professionalism shines.

ABOUT THE AUTHOR

April Quintanilla

KATE ELLIOTT has been publishing fiction for more than thirty years, with a particular focus on immersive world-building and epic stories of adventure and transformative cultural change. She's written fantasy; science fiction; space opera based on the life of Alexander the Great (*Unconquerable Sun*); young adult fantasy; the seven-volume (complete!) Crown of Stars epic fantasy series set in a landscape reminiscent of early medieval Europe; the Afro-Celtic post-Roman alternate-history fantasy with lawyer dinosaurs, *Cold Magic;* and two novellas set in the Magic: The Gathering multiverse. Her work has been nominated for the Nebula, World Fantasy, Andre Norton, and Locus Awards. Her novel *Black Wolves* won the 2015 RT Award for Best Epic Fantasy Novel. She lives in Hawaii, paddles outrigger canoes, and spoils her Schnauzer.